A Long Time Dead

When fighting a killer becomes a battle for revenge

Andrew Barrett

The Ink Foundry

© Copyright 2009

The rights of Andrew Barrett to be identified as the author of this work have been asserted in accordance with sections 77 and 78 of the Copyright, Designs and Patents Act 1988. No part of this publication may be reproduced, stored in a retrieval system or transmitted in any form or by any means electronic, mechanical, photocopying, recording or otherwise without the prior permission of the copyright holder.

Published in the United Kingdom by The Ink Foundry.

For rights and copyright enquiries, please contact:

permissions@andrew.barrett.co.uk

This book is a work of fiction. Any names, characters, companies, organizations, places, events, locales, and incidents are fictional or are used in a fictitious manner. Any resemblance to actual persons, living or dead, or actual events is purely coincidental.

Praise for A Long Time Dead

I've never read a more authentic and detailed crime thriller.
I enjoy Andrew Barrett's writing style, touches of humour, meticulous attention to detail, and well-drawn characters.
I couldn't put it down, finished it in 2 hours.
Your fingers burn the pages to digest the story lines and characters.
It's a long time since I read a book as exciting as this one.
Very few books keep you wrapped up in such a way.
A very detailed and spell binding thriller about corruption within the police and forensic investigations at murders. Brilliantly and scientifically described and researched.
Strong characters and good atmospheric descriptions.
Brilliantly written, characters that actually feel real you care about them.
Love the author's style of writing and the tale he told.
Although the murder scenes are gruesome, the technical details of the forensic examinations are really quite gripping.
Lots of convincing technical detail that doesn't overwhelm the story.
It was exciting right to the last chapter and what a last chapter, superb.

Dedication

This book is dedicated to Les Barrett – my dad, my mentor, and my hero.

Chapter 1

Friday 15th January 1999

Someone banged on the front door.

It boomed in the naked hall.

In the lounge, Sally's tired eyes opened and struggled to focus. She peered at the clock on the chimneybreast. She wasn't expecting anyone.

Whoever it was, banged again.

She climbed from the sofa, kicked empty lager cans under the chair, and nudged aside plates of dried bread crusts and greasy old chicken bones.

They banged the door again.

"Okay! Christ's sake." With dirty, shaking hands, she concealed syringes and empty foil wraps behind cushions, and stuffed burnt spoons and Rizlas in there too. If it was the coppers, there was no sense making their job easy; because if they banged her up for possession, Richie would put her in hospital. Again.

She glanced around at the lounge. Pinned across the chimneybreast was a single twisted length of red tinsel. And on the mantelpiece, two Christmas cards and her dull, leather-covered diary.

The hallway was dark and uninviting. Freezing cold, dank. Goosepimples erupted across her flesh. Her nose was running and she swiped an arm across it.

They banged again, hurried this time, annoyed this time. She flinched.

Sally inched the door open, looking past the rusted chain and out into the oppressive greyness of Turner Avenue where the visitor stood with his arms folded, foot tapping the step. A cold breeze stung her eyes.

"I haven't got all day."

The chain rattled and she stood aside. "Sorry," she muttered. "Plenty of arseholes out there. Idiots too."

The stranger brushed past Sally, and she shivered as his bulk settled in the hall, making it feel cramped, claustrophobic, an invasion of her space.

"Do I look like an idiot?" His voice was smooth yet gravelly.

She swallowed, brushed a hand through her hair and looked at the floor as he stared at her. "No," she said. "You don't look like an *idiot* at all."

He eyed her, came really close. "How many other sluts work in Kirk Steeple? Ten? Fifty? Hundred?"

"Look, I'm sorry." That was her second apology. She smiled up at him, a little nervously, but it was still a smile, a welcoming smile. A don't-beat-the-shit-out-of-me, smile. For an instant, she felt almost brave.

She closed the door and shut out the breeze, and she looked at him glaring back at her with deep-set eyes; dark and piercing. His nose was bracketed by indentations as though he wore glasses.

"Stinks toxic in here," he said. "You live like a bloody tramp."

Sally deftly sidestepped the confrontation but knew this punter was different; this was a power man, a man who fucked hard before using his fists. But if he did, he wouldn't get back in here again. Richie didn't like her beaten to a pulp by punters, bad for business. Except when he was doing the beating. She sank into the role, "Listen, my bedroom's upstairs... Here, let me take your coat."

He wriggled out of it, handed it to her, all the while absorbing his surroundings as though listening for something, as though contemplating something. She hung the coat on a broken hook, and slid the chain back on. "How 'bout a nice massage before we get going?"

The man squinted at her.

"It'll do you the world of good; get rid of your tiredness."

"Will it take away the smell?"

"I'm good at it too. Had recommendations, I have," she said proudly. "Bet you come back for more," she hoped like hell that he wouldn't. The claustrophobia eventually got the better of her and she squeezed past him and back into the sanctum of the lounge. "I got some new oils. It's only an extra tenner—"

"Are we alone?"

"Yes," she said. "Why?"

"Where's the toilet?"

"Upstairs. On the left."

Without another word, he strode through the lounge and disappeared from view.

"I'll bring the oils up," she called after him. "Just go straight into the bedroom." He offered no reply. "Okay?"

Still he didn't answer.

Sally moved to the window and peered through the nicotine-stains, dirty fingers fidgeting. Her mouth was dry.

His footfalls grew quieter as he ascended the bare wooden stairs. The eighth stair creaked as it always did. Sally raced back into the hallway and began searching the overcoat, glancing over her shoulder as her hand found a wallet-sized lump.

Then she heard the toilet flush.

Quickly she fumbled for the pockets, hands working faster. The coat could have doubled as a marquee, and no matter how she turned it, mounds of fabric blocked her path. "Fuck," she hissed. It was *there*, she could *feel* it. But she could not find a way in.

She heard the first footfall on the top step. He was supposed to stay—

Her breath came rapidly.

Her shaking hand found an opening in the silk, reached in and grabbed the wallet. Permitting another glance over her shoulder, Sally scanned its contents, flicking through it like the pages of a book. "Christ," she whispered. It was full of credit cards and cash. The eighth stair creaked. Sally randomly snatched a note, mimed *quick, quick, quick!*

The footfalls grew louder. She heard a rustling sound.

Come on, come on! She slapped the wallet shut, thrust it back into the silky opening and in her haste, almost fell into the lounge. She heard the grit beneath his shoes grinding on the bare wooden steps. Echoes crashed around the walls.

Sally's dry mouth clacked and she looked down at the note – a *fifty*-pound note – in her hand, as she tripped through the lounge floor litter. Christ, if he catches me—

"You got the oils?" he shouted from the stairway.

She almost cried out.

She grabbed her diary, stuffed the booty inside and threw it on top of the wall unit. It skidded and smacked a photo frame. Dust plumed.

Her new client peered around the doorframe and watched her. "What was that?"

"I...It was...I was just—"

He stared.

Sally took down the picture frame. "It was this," she whispered, "my son." Turning it over, she showed him the photograph of a baby boy. "Robin," she tried to smile, "I like to remember him." Her hands shook.

He ignored the picture. Stared at her. Unfeeling. Grey light fell on him as he walked into the room. The thin glass from the photograph shattered across the floor and she backed away, throat closed up tight, hands curled into fists across her chest.

He wore a green plastic smock. It rustled. The latex gloves he wore were tight against his skin, knuckles protruding. And the knife was in his right hand.

Sally collided with the settee and almost fell, jerking breaths, unable to turn away as he advanced. His feet crunched glass.

"You want the money?" she yelled. "Take it! It's yours, just—"

"Don't want anything from you," he said. "This... It's nothing personal." The blade flashed. "I just need the practice."

Chapter 2

Saturday 16th January 1999

— One —

"Hope this hurts."

The dart punctured Inspector Weston's drooping left eye with a thud. The second one pierced the left nostril in his bent nose, and the final one caught him smack in the middle of his brow. Roger stepped up to the dartboard. "Prick." He spat the word at the tattered photograph.

Behind him, in the kitchen, the toaster beeped.

"Breakfast's ready," he called.

No response.

"Yvonne," he called louder. "Your toast is—"

"I heard you, dammit." She moaned as she negotiated the last few steps into the lounge.

He buttered the toast, listening to her. "You okay?" Sucking melted butter from his fingers, he entered the lounge.

She didn't even look up. "Just leave me alone."

"Knees?"

"Yes, knees. Always bloody knees."

"Where're your tablets?"

She glared at him.

"I only—"

"Well don't. I'm not your personal cripple."

"And I'm not your personal punch bag—"

"You should go to work. That's what you should do."
"Bollocks to them."
"Wrong attitude for someone wanting promotion."
"Right attitude for someone…"

Yvonne looked up, eyes already made up with mascara. "You'll never make a martyr, Rog."

He stood silently cleaning his glasses on his waistcoat, before returning to the kitchen. "Want me to run a bath before I go?" He poured away her cold tea and made a fresh cup.

No reply again.

"It's a simple question. Bath or not?" He grabbed the toast and tea, and marched back into the lounge.

"Leave me the *hell* alone."

Roger stopped dead. The toast slid off the plate, landed butter side down.

"Just go!"

— Two —

Roger parked in one of the designated Scenes of Crime Officer bays, ignored the sneers from two passing police officers and almost felt like apologising for having the bay, while they had to park at the far side of the compound. Instead, he winked at them.

He climbed out, locked the car and shuddered at the endless winter's drizzle. It was 7.30am, the sky was a turbulent lake, steadily decanting its load over Wakefield, and in particular, it seemed to Roger, over Wood Street Police Station. Floodlights caught the rain as it patted his shoulders. His feet trudged through slushy leaves engraved with tyre tracks, and the sounds of a busy morning in a city centre assaulted his ears.

Across Wood Street, next to the County Hall and Museum, shop windows shone on bedraggled commuters hurrying along beneath drab umbrellas, avoiding puddles and islands of sodden rubbish. In a few hours, the streets would heave with Wakefield Trinity fans on their regular encounter with humiliation, this time at the hands of local rivals Leeds.

For once Roger was glad to be working on a Saturday.

Near the ever-open barrier, an arm suddenly waved, followed by, "Mr Conniston. Sir!"

Hobnail, Wood Street's ever-present beggar, stood in the car park entrance with an expectant grin on his face.

Roger looked at him through the rain, sighed and changed course. "Run out of people to piss off already?" He handed over a fiver. "Treat yourself to a scotch and a pint chaser, you old bugger," he smiled. "And get out of this weather; fucking freezing."

Hobnail's face had already cracked open into a nicotine-stained grin, deepening the furrows around his eyes. His blackened nails pincered the fiver, pocketed it as quick as a magician. "Saw you in town again, couple of nights ago," he said. "You do keep some strange hours."

Roger stiffened. "Pull your neck in, Hobnail. Subject closed, okay."

"Sorry, Mr Conniston; I was only pulling your—"

A black BMW hurtled past into the car park, splashing water, brake lights a red mist fast disappearing.

Hobnail stared after the car. "Prick. Does he work 'ere, or has he come to a pay a speeding fine?"

"Inspector Weston. Ask *him* for money and he'll pull your eyelids off."

"He'll kill somebody one of these days, Mr Conniston."

Roger pondered Hobnail's words as he walked towards the back entrance.

The dingy corridor leading to the Scenes of Crime Office was cold enough to cloud his breath. Roger strode along not thinking of Hobnail or even Weston. He thought of Yvonne and wondered why she, a woman who would not be going anywhere today, just as she didn't go anywhere yesterday, and who wouldn't be going anywhere tomorrow, had make-up on.

— Three —

The room was utterly black but still warm, humid, wisps of steam curling and it smelled of burnt rubber and nylon; so noxious it made their eyes water, suffocating like a pillow.

Roger feathered the torch around the scene, and as the fogged beam moved along the damp, sooty walls of what until recently was someone's lounge, his eyes hovered for an instant on Paul, making sure he was okay. "This your first arson?"

"Yeah. It's fucking…"

"Awesome?"

"Seriously awesome." Paul smiled.

They'd arrived on scene at 9.10, and five hours had already vanished into a steamy black blur. "Learn anything?"

"Learned to carry on working even while my stomach's shouting at me."

"Could be worse," he whispered, "could be your wife shouting at you."

"Not married."

"Ah, wise beyond your years. But I mean are you okay with excavating the seat of a fire?" Roger crunched over the charred remains of a foam-filled sofa, felt its brittle frame crumble beneath his steel-soled boots. He stood in a puddle of water and heard glass crack.

"I know what they mean by pool burning, at least," Paul pointed his own torch to the piece of carpet now in a clear nylon bag but shielded from view by a film of condensation. They found it beneath the skeleton of an armchair. A small pool of burning petrol or kerosene had charred the carpet, and as the fuel burned away, it left a wavy melted edge as distinctive as a tidemark in sand. "And I'll try to get down through the layers of burnt material quickly, to the floorboards, or to the carpet, keeping my nose open for accelerants," he said, paraphrasing.

"Don't forget scorch patterns on bare brick or spalled plaster, how the blackened 'V' of rising flames usually points to the seat. Don't forget how things look completely different when burned – think laterally," his torch picked out the remains of the TV. Curtains of molten black plastic draped over the exposed tube. "Find out if a door was open or closed by seeing if its edges are scorched. Look at broken window glass; wavy cracks indicate heat damage, but sharp, orderly cracks are from something more physical. That's when you should be suspicious, that's when you ask the fire brigade if they broke it while putting out the blaze."

"And if they didn't?"

"Heck boy," Roger clapped Paul on the back, "then you fingerprint the glass and seize the milk bottle."

Paul smiled, unsure. "The milk bottle?"

Roger nodded to the centre of the room. Farther back than the armchair, near the neat edges of carpet from where they sliced the pool-burnt sample, was a broken milk bottle. Spalled plaster partially covered it. "That's your incendiary device. Your Molotov Cocktail."

"Shit, yeah!"

"What you going to do with it?" Roger folded his arms.

"Same as all the other exhibits: nylon bag it."

"Not forgetting to—"

"Swan-neck it." After photographing the bottle, Paul dropped the broken pieces into a nylon bag which crackled loudly, too noisy to talk over. "Stinks of unleaded," he shouted. Then he twisted the neck of the bag, folded it over to provide a seal and tied it off with string.

Roger adjusted his hard hat. "You wouldn't have found it if you'd followed the burn patterns."

Paul shrugged.

"Use your intuition. Picture how things happen, why they happen. Don't stick rigidly to first impressions, and once you've read the rule book, throw it away. Better still, burn the bastard."

"But that's how Chris always—"

"I know." Roger removed his glasses; they were fogged up again. "He swallowed a book on forensic procedures, and that's how he works. He gets good results, too. But there's more to it than that, much more than procedure; *feel* the scene, absorb what it has to tell you."

Later, after six hours of fire-scene examination, Roger Conniston trudged into the archaic Scenes of Crime Office at Wood Street Police Station and closed the door with a heel. Soot smeared his glasses, aluminium powder coated his nostrils and more streaked his forehead in a silver smudge. Paul was upstairs in CID, showing his fingerprint lifts and the sample of pool-burned carpet to some DC.

Through the rotten window frame, an icy breeze whistled accompaniment to a length of broken plastic gutter that tapped against the rippled glass. From across Wood Street, the Town Hall and the Crown Court buildings stared in sympathy.

Roger tossed a handful of exhibits onto his desk, and an envelope containing fingerprint lifts into the wire tray marked 'Assorted Crap'. The tray below it declared 'Lord Lucan Files'. He took off his waxed jacket and then noticed her. "Helen? Everything okay?"

Helen too was a Scenes of Crime Officer, though she had problems peeling her arse from the office chair. She sat hunched over her desk, sweater sleeves pulled way past her fingers and her greasy hair falling forward to obscure all but her chin. She ignored him. But it was nothing personal. She ignored everyone equally.

Sighing, he threw his CID6 report book on his desk. "How're things with—"

"Don't mention his name, Roger. I don't want my aura polluting."

"Your what?"

"Just leave it; I feel delicate right now."

Roger rubbed his glasses on his waistcoat. "Delicate. Right."

He perched on the chair next to her, replaced his glasses. "You know, Helen, if you need to talk. I know a really good brick wall…"

For a while, she said nothing, and it was a long enough while for him to feel awkward. Then she whispered, "Roger?"

"I'm here."

She didn't speak for a long time. Then, "Never mind."

He came closer. "Can I ask you something?" He didn't wait for an answer. "Why would a woman put make-up on if she wasn't going out?"

"Maybe she's expecting a visitor."

"But…" Annoyingly, it made sense. "Any other reason?"

"Why, what's all—"

"Just wondering, nothing to fret about."

"Is this woman married?"

He shrugged. "It's just a hypothetical question."

"Is this hypothetical woman married?" Helen didn't move. The words could have been coming from a loud speaker wired up near her desk.

"Could be. Yes."

"How come men are so thick?"

"Beg your pardon," Roger said.

"Why do *you* think she puts make-up on, Roger?"

"She never used to—"

Paul barged into the office.

The privacy shattered, Roger blew an exasperated sigh. "It's okay, Paul, we have spare doors."

"Just enthusiastic, that's all." Paul hung his coat up.

"Yeah, well stop it; you're annoying those of us who don't give a shit." Roger returned his attention to the tip of Helen's chin. "You okay?"

She looked up. It was the first time today that he'd seen her face. She flicked her sweater-covered hand in his direction.

"Don't fool me," Paul said. "I know you give a shit." He straightened his purple tie. "Hey, if you get this promotion, will you still come to scenes with me?"

Roger laughed, "Nope."

"Won't you miss it, being a Scenes of Crime Officer?" Paul asked. "You've had a month of acting-up, of pretending to be a boss. Which do you prefer?"

Roger rubbed the scars that ran across the bulbs of his left fingers, licked his lips, and said, "Retirement."

Paul pulled at his tie again. "Chris's turn now."

"I wish him well."

Jon Benedict, another SOCO, as much a stranger to work as Helen, appeared in the doorway. He stared at Roger.

"What now?"

Jon came closer and whispered, "Heard the Bulldog on the phone just now."

"Saying what?"

"Dunno, exactly. All I caught was 'meeting', and 'half an hour'."

"Meeting?"

"Don't know what about though," Jon shrugged.

"That it?"

"He's just left his office. Looked very suspicious to me."

"Your mother looks suspicious to you."

"The info's there, mate, if you choose to use it."

Roger thought for a second or two, then grabbed his coat and left the office, hurrying down the corridor, already searching in his pocket for the van keys.

— Four —

Inspector Colin Weston sat at his desk watching the slivers of cold sunlight glint through the blue lights of patrol cars parked in the back yard at Wood Street. It turned them a curious liver colour. Another forty minutes and the sun would be kissing the Wakefield horizon. He spat a chewed nail across the room then drummed his fingers.

The phone startled him.

"Weston." He recognised the caller's voice, listened intently to the caller's words. "When's he due for release?" He listened, nodded. "Where? Right, I want a meeting. Half an hour." He stood and leaned against his desk, was about to hang up when he paused. "You still there? Good," he said. "Don't ever call me on this fucking line again."

— Five —

The floodlights buzzed, blinked into life and then glowed almost humbly across the car park, slowly growing in intensity as Roger sat in his van and watched Weston's BMW reverse out of its allotted space and snake towards the gate.

Roger started the van's still warm engine and followed.

Weston nosed the BMW out of the junction and broke into the line of traffic.

A moment later, Roger tried to follow but Weston had already vanished. "Bastard!" He thumped the steering wheel and abandoned any thought of trying to find him now. He decided to wait for a better opportunity to arise. Where was he heading, Roger wondered, and who was he going to meet?

Across the busy street, silhouetted against the window of Mum's Pantry, an old man ambled by, leaning forward as though walking into a private gale, the streetlamps glinting on his balding head. "Be careful out there, Hobnail."

— Six —

Inspector Weston could have walked. But he chose to go by car because there was less chance of Conniston following. He parked the car in a narrow street behind the Theatre Royal and Opera House, and punched a hole through crowds of shoppers and rugby supporters. Any other day, the short journey on foot would have taken ten minutes; today it took twenty, and elicited countless profanities through Weston's clenched teeth.

During the walk, he removed the epaulets from his white shirt and tucked them away in his coat pocket, followed by the clip tie. He slackened his top button. Weston was off-duty now. Head down, shoulders forward, he moved past the blackened façades of Victorian buildings and cobbled alleyways that shrieked in the wind, barging aside inattentive people.

Redundant Christmas lights stretched across Westgate and looked cheerless like pendant skeletons. And then he walked the periphery of the Bull Ring, a two-hundred-yard wide pedestrianised circle of banks, travel agents, pharmacies and beauty shops, glistening jewellers' windows; filled with the smells and noises of cafes and delis, of newspaper vendors, *Big Issue* sellers. Busy introspective people.

A greying statue of Queen Victoria overlooked all this. Plastic benches surrounded her, and fake gas lanterns glowed in the twilight. The Town Hall clock spat four bells as Weston stepped onto Northgate. The Joker, his favourite town centre pub, loomed up on his left, its caricature sign creaked back and forth in a northerly breeze. He checked the Cartier that dangled next to a thick gold chain on his wrist and quickened his already rapid stride, hurling himself at the bland crowds.

The Joker was a proper pub, not one of these new-fangled theme pubs. The beams in here were real, take them away and the ceiling would fall down. Behind the bar, Mac pulled ale from real pumps. The shine on the carpet was genuine one-hundred-percent blood, beer and puke. It added to the ambience – and kept the wine-drinking 'elite' away in their droves.

Weston strode for the far left corner, which afforded a good view of the only entrance, a place away from the public phone and the toilets, a place where he had met this man before. A double whisky waited for him. He removed his glasses, stared through heavy smoke and swallowed the scotch, revelled as it burned his throat.

"You're late."

A wooden chair creaked under Weston's weight. "Tell me about this kid."

The man's hand reached out of the seclusion, placed a pint glass on the table and flicked cigar ash onto the floor. "He's fresh. Wants to play in my gang."

"I want it doing right. I don't want no kid having a go just to impress you."

"Everybody's got to learn—"

"Not on my job. Break him in on a fucking ram raid or something."

"This is where I break him in. My man, Colin, my rules."

"I want someone else."

"Take it or leave it."

Pub noise blared. "What makes you think he can do it?"

"Because he's desperate. Jess told me all about him."

"Jess? If *he* was so fucking clever, he wouldn't be in the clink."

"Like I said, take it or leave it."

Weston's jowls wobbled above his shirt collar. "Better not let me down."

"This Conniston, family man. Going for promotion you said."

"You lost your best source because of him," Weston said.

He nodded thoughtfully, "He's the one grassed you up, eh?"

"Straight to my DCI." His eyes narrowed, "I had to threaten him with the magic words 'compensation' and 'publicity'."

"But you've traded with me since—"

"No smoke without fire… One-offs, here and there. I've had to pull my neck right in!" He looked around at the crowd. No one paid him any attention.

"Just be careful—"

"I'm trapped. Every time I leave work to do business, he's there following me around like a fart in a space-suit."

The contact drained his beer, snapped his fingers at Mac. "He sounds like a pleb, Colin. Threaten him. Usually works with his sort."

Weston drained his whisky, then peeled a cigar from his breast pocket, lit it and added to the smoke. "I caught him following me once; said if he ever came near me again outside work I'd pull his innards out through his arsehole." He flicked ash every couple of seconds, hands always moving, fingers feeling the sticky grain of the table.

"It wouldn't look good for his promotion if you complained he was harassing you."

Weston shook his head. "It would draw more attention to me."

The man stubbed out his cigar. "So you need to use action."

"At last, the penny drops. I'm losing business because of him." And then he growled, "I'm losing *money*."

"Shouldn't live so rich, Colin. It gives the game away—"

"My money, my lifestyle."

The man tipped his empty glass. "Touché."

"I want him out of the way; if he ever gets proof, I'm finished. And just because I bluffed 'em once, don't mean they'll never investigate again."

Mac coughed, placed two pints on the table.

"Seems you have another problem, then," the contact said.

"Only one?"

"You'll have to supply the metal and meet with the kid yourself. I'm in Manchester for the next ten days or so. Leaving tomorrow."

"Marvellous. Some help you are."

The man shrugged, watching Weston fidget. "Listen, I've got you a man, you provide the metal and the target. Job's a good 'un." He sank back into the shadows. "Anyway, it's good that you see the business from the sharp end for once. You barely get your stubby little fingers dirty these days."

Through a defeated sigh, Weston said, "Gimme details."

"Beaver. Thursday. Noon. Don't be late."

"Where?"

"Final RV, stable."

Weston nodded.

Chapter 3

— One —

WEST YORKSHIRE POLICE HEADQUARTERS on Laburnum Road displayed a classical decorum lacking anywhere else in the Force. It was a huge brick-built monolith that boasted private gardens and silver service in its own restaurant; a place where visitors were shown the hub of police management. This was where the Senior Officers made the big decisions and this was where Chris Hutchinson now found himself. Like Roger before him, he was under scrutiny again by his Head of Department, Denis Bell, as part of a four-week promotional trial initiated by the death of Charles 'Lanky' Richardshaw of heart failure five months ago.

Chris was Roger's colleague at Wood Street. They shared the same office and had developed a close friendship. Thanks to Lanky, things were about to change.

In co-operation with Bell, the Personnel Department had put eight prospective candidates for Lanky's job through a series of role-playing scenarios that lasted a full day. Four of those scored high enough to qualify for an interview. Out of those four, only two made it through to the final stage. Chris and Roger.

Already friends, they were now rivals. And while each had congratulated the other and said *May the best man win*, Chris had said it with his fingers crossed. In another two weeks,

Bell would decide which of the friends gave the orders and which acted on them.

On this particular Saturday afternoon, Chris was one of nine sitting around a polished mahogany table in the Old Library, listening to Bell ramble. The others were Supervisors within the Scenes of Crime Department, in charge of up to fifteen SOCOs, and responsible for providing forensic cover within their own Divisions, their own particular segment of the West Yorkshire County.

Chris twisted the gold wedding ring on his finger, then rested his chin on his fist.

All significance leaked out of Bell's voice as it sank into a monotonous drone like listening to a conversation through a brick wall. The audience's attention drifted; in particular, Chris's mind wandered back to the promotion race, the promotion *fight*, and his impending victory.

"...refresher course at Durham, Chris?" Bell waited. Bell coughed.

Chris's chin fell off his fist. "Sorry, Denis."

"I trust you will take more notice of me in future Supervisors' meetings. Should you be lucky enough to have any future meetings."

"Sorry, Denis."

"Mr Bell, to you, Chris. Mr Bell."

Chris sat up straight. "Right. Mr Bell."

"I want a list of those who qualify for a refresher course."

Chris nodded.

The meeting, the *lecture* as Chris now thought it, lingered for a further ten minutes before Bell thankfully wrapped it up. "Okay, ladies and gentlemen, any other business before we leave?" He loitered only briefly. "Wonderful. Well, thank you for your attendance and don't forget if there's anything I can do for you, my door is always open, blah blah."

Everyone stood to leave.

"Chris, a word, please," Bell muttered.

"I'm really sorry about—"

Bell hushed him with a stare and moved towards the door.

Silently, Chris followed him along a series of corridors, absorbed by Bell's short legs jabbing each stride as though stretching them any further would release whatever was clamped between his arse cheeks. He smiled at the image.

Bell unlocked his office door, admitted Chris and closed it behind him.

"Sit down."

Spotlights illuminated a bookcase containing manuals of *Forensic Science Case Studies*, *Post-mortem-* and *Scene Examination Best Practices*, *ACPO DNA Recommendations* and several management manuals, all of which appeared unread. The office smelled of old men in green corduroy trousers; warm and dank.

Bell sank into his leather chair. He had cholesterol-ringed eyes and dark yellow teeth. "Paul settling in okay?"

Chris sat opposite on a cheap fabric chair, and prepared himself for the game – 'the mind-fuck game' as he called it, a delving session where the Old Man would prod his brain and assess his suitability for the post. He looked past Bell's counterfeit smile and saw the contempt in his eyes.

"He's doing fine. I think experience will—"

"What are you going to do to convince me to promote you instead of Conniston?"

Chris's mind was blank. "Well, Roger's a good man, Denis—"

"You're supposed to be scoring points for yourself not the opposition."

"Well—"

"And it's Mr Bell, Chris. You're not there yet. Don't forget it."

The barriers in Chris's mind rose quickly.

Bell continued, "I have to say that you're bordering on the Fail-to-Impress side of my desk. I've heard good things about you over the years and it's why you're here now, but you have to move up a level, a *distinct* level, in order to fulfil the role of Supervisor. And daydreaming in a meeting is not a quality I admire."

Chris struggled with a vision of himself flying across the desk and wrapping his hands around Bell's neck, squeezing until his fingers met his thumbs. He looked away, gathered himself.

"How would you feel if you got the job and Conniston had to take your instructions?"

Chris flushed with anticipation. "It would be an honour. And Roger? I wouldn't treat him differently to anyone else on my staff. I think that's important."

"I think you're right." Bell leaned forward.

Chris relaxed.

"How would you feel if Roger got the job and you had to take his instructions?"

Chris blinked.

"The thought had never even occurred to you before, had it? Are you so convinced of your own case?"

"I have more experience than he does. They even call me The Professor; I'm respected," he smiled. "Surely you wouldn't..." Chris nipped at the stitching around his cardigan's elbow patches. "I could take his orders, of course I could, and don't get me wrong, he's no fool, he won't foul up, so there'd be no need to put him straight, which of course I'd be happy to do, you know, to help out where I could."

Bell laced his fingers. "I think you'd struggle taking orders from him."

"No, no, that's wrong, Den— Mr Bell. I respect him, I *could* take orders."

"The successful candidate would have to be a good all-rounder, be an approachable manager and yet be forceful but tactful with those above and below him." There Bell paused and analysed Chris's reaction.

Chris's eyes narrowed into slits. "What's with all the messing about? I mean, how come..." Below the level of the desk, Chris curled both hands into fists. He teetered on the edge of his cheap fabric seat. "Do I stand the remotest chance of getting this promotion? Am I here just to... why *am* I here? Mr Bell, tell me why I'm here?"

Bell glared. "You're here to make my job of selecting the right man easier."

Chris bit down on his tongue hard enough to make his eyes water.

"Look," Bell said, "I don't know who'll get promoted yet. But you're going to have to raise your game. You need to study interpersonal techniques."

"What?"

"Things have moved on since your interview for SOCO, and now we look at every nuance of behaviour; better get used to it."

"Whatever happened to scene skills? Don't they count?"

"We're looking for a more rounded personality, someone good at interpersonal skills. You know the kind of thing, like speaking to your Head of Department with some *respect*." After a pause, Bell said, "They call this four-week period a trial, I believe. Think of it like that; think of it as a test."

Chris's head bowed; bowed to shield his tightening lips and the colour rising in his cheeks; bowed to hide the hatred in his face.

Bell leaned forward again. "One more thing."

Chris didn't look up, didn't see the point.

"The mobile phone you were given. It is not for personal use."

Now he did look up, struggling to think of a plausible excuse. "I've had a problem with my landline. I've tried to sort it out but..."

"A problem with your landline?"

Chris nodded, but couldn't maintain eye contact.

"The mobile phone is for when you are on call or for when you need to make calls of a business nature." He raised his considerable eyebrows. "Understood?"

Chris stood and left, closing quietly the office door behind him.

— Two —

In Wood Street Police Station, officers busied themselves in the Report-writing room, and next door to that, the Casebuilders and File Prep's office buzzed with the chatter of bored transcribers and harassed Witness Liaison Officers.

Farther down the corridor, tranquillity briefly touched the Scenes of Crime Office. Roger was trying to write a statement for court that covered his examination of one particular burglary scene he'd attended last month, one of sixty-nine burglary scenes he examined last month; a scene that yielded fingerprints good enough to implicate two youths and start the Casebuilders preparing a file for court. This statement was part of that file. His mind was on Weston though. If only he'd barged out into the traffic… but the bastard would have seen him for sure.

Like a block of well-weathered stone, Helen Gardener nestled in the darkest corner of the office.

Paul Bryant sat nearby, head propped up on a hand, CID6 crime report already written, waiting to update the Crime Information System with the results of his fire scene examination. He was frustrated; those around him seemed competently engaged in their tasks.

Jon Benedict, twisted by cynicism and tainted by a disregard for authority, had beaten Paul to the steam-powered computer, and was trying to upload his day's work. A sticker on the monitor read, 'Year 2000 Compliant'. Below it, someone had stuck a note: 'Year 1999 Incompliant'. It had frozen again, and Jon banged his head against the grimy screen. "Pissin' thing," he said. "Hey Roger, you got any spare coal?"

Tranquillity vanished.

Every time Jon cursed, Roger paused and let the noise settle before his hovering pen returned to the statement.

Jon stabbed the reset button. "Know anything about computers, Helen?"

"They're like men," she snapped. "Untrustworthy."

"That helps."

Paul bumped his chair over the linoleum to Roger's desk.

Roger put down his pen, resigned to finishing the statement another day. He crossed his feet on the desk and hooked his thumbs into the pockets of his burgundy waistcoat. "What's bothering you?"

Paul whispered, "I took a glass sample from a burglary scene yesterday. I don't know what to do with it."

"It'll come," Roger headed for the kettle.

"If I can't handle a burglary, what will I do at a major scene? Seriously. What if I can't remember something, what if I screw up or I find myself—"

"Whoa, whoa, slow down," Roger said. "Don't let it faze you. No one's going to throw a major scene at you and walk away. Well, maybe Jon would."

"Oi," said Jon.

"Drink, Helen?" Roger asked.

She ignored him.

"Well, if you're sure." He turned three mugs the right way up.

"Will you see him again today?" Paul asked.

"The Professor?" Roger slid his glasses back up the bridge of his nose. "He's at a Supervisors' meeting. Probably go straight home." The kettle boiled. "And that's where I'm going soon."

"Thought you were playing squash," Jon said.

"In a couple of hours."

Paul asked, "So you won't see him tomorrow?"

"Hope not. I'm on nights tomorrow," Roger handed Jon a mug of tea. "Won't see him unless he's called to a major incident that I happen to be covering. Something you need help with?"

In a hushed voice, Paul said, "I wanna know how I'm doing. I'm still on probation and—"

"I remember asking Chris for some constructive criticism years ago when I didn't know the pointy end of a squirrel brush from the furry end."

"So what's new?" Jon spilled tea on the floor.

"He told me I was shite," he said, "and that sort of broke the ice. He helped me begin learning the job rather than simply being afraid of it, or even worse – being afraid of never *understanding* it."

"What do *you* think of Chris? I've heard he can be a bit harsh," Paul asked.

Jon interrupted. "If he gets Lanky's job, I'm putting in for a transfer."

"You should make up your own mind," Roger sipped coffee. "He's not so bad."

"Who died and made you boss, Conniston? Oh, yeah, I forgot, Lanky did."

Helen didn't move until the phone rang. She whispered into it, nodded, and then asked, "Anybody free to photo a gun?"

Jon's head sank into his shoulders.

"Jon," Helen held the phone out, "stop ignoring me. Go photo the gun."

He looked hopefully at Roger.

Roger shook his head, handed Paul a coffee. "I'm off duty. Anyway, guns frighten the crap out of me."

"Come *on*," Helen raised her voice. "Officers are waiting at the scene."

Jon snatched the phone, and the lacklustre curtain of hair fell again over Helen's face.

"What's so scary about guns?" Paul asked.

Roger put his index finger to his lower lip and looked at the ceiling. "Er, they fucking kill people. Have you seen the mess a bullet makes of flesh and bone?"

"Only in photos."

"Next time you see a story on the news where some kid has been shot dead, think about it. Don't just sit there waiting for the sports news to come on; really think about it: what it does to the family, what are they going to do with his bedroom, his belongings, who arranges the funeral, who tells the school and the doctors and the clubs he was a member of? Who tells the grandparents…" Roger stopped.

Paul was staring at him. Even Helen raised her head, looked intently at him.

"I'm lecturing, aren't I?"

"Tell him," Helen said.

"Tell me what?"

"I didn't lose anyone to a gun if that's what you're thinking; nothing quite so drastic. But it ain't nice when a round flies so close to your ear that you can feel the heat coming off it and hear it purr before it sinks three inches into a breeze block wall. It can make you a tad nervous of them. Makes you *really* think."

"Someone shot a gun at you?" Paul sat forward, made himself comfortable.

"I went to a scene like the one Jon's going to. Straightforward photography job. Nothing snaggy. But before you can photo the weapon, it needs making safe. That means an AFO, an Authorised Firearms Officer, has to empty the thing, make sure there isn't a round still in the breech, and then sign a label accordingly. To 'prove it safe', it's called."

"Yeah?"

"So, I'm in the same room as the gun, the same room as the AFO and he's doing the business. He's gloved up, and I'm on my knees setting the camera up, getting the flash and the scales ready, that sort of thing. Anyway, he's fumbling with the damned thing when the fucking door behind him flies open and smacks him in the arm." Roger rubbed the scars on his fingertips. "The gun fired. The next thing I know, I'm on the floor on my back, the tripod's on top of me and there's screaming and pandemonium all over the place." He smiled, as if visiting a pleasant memory. "I soiled myself."

Paul dangled between horror and humour. Humour won evidently, and he smiled. "Sorry."

"So I think it's fair to say that guns really *do* frighten the crap out of me."

Paul laughed. Roger jumped as Jon, finally on his way to the job, slammed the door behind him. They could hear him cursing all the way up the corridor.

"It's frightening to have a gun go off in your face."

Paul became serious again.

"There's a flash first, and your instinct is to close your eyes and put an arm up to protect yourself. Of course, what could your arm do against a bullet? But before you've got your eyes even half closed, the thing is either rattling around inside your skull or it's in the wall. If you're lucky.

"Then there's an almighty bang – I mean a *crack* louder than anything you've ever heard and it's the crack as much as anything that scares you."

"What happened to the firearms man?"

Roger shrugged. "It didn't do much for his confidence. He's back on the beat somewhere in Dewsbury, I think."

"So what happens if a firearms job comes in, and you're it?"

Roger locked his desk drawer. "I put on my incontinence pants and go and do it. But I hate guns." He looked at Paul, a barely concealed fervour in his eyes. "I really hate them. And I think anyone who uses them, or deals in them, ought to be locked up forever. *Anyone.*"

Chapter 4

— One —

DESPITE THE FREEZING TEMPERATURE outside, Wood Street police station's Number One squash court was hot as hell, like a sauna but without the steam, and Roger's t-shirt clung to his body. Sweat matted his spiky hair and trickled down his plum-red face. He scrubbed it away quickly, hovering over Lenny Firth, wondering if he really was hurt.

"I think it's broken, Roger," Firth said through clenched teeth. "Might need an ambulance, mate."

"Shit, Lenny," Roger said. "I'm sorry, I didn't mean…"

Firth opened one eye, and as he opened his other, a grin framed a sly laugh.

"You bastard."

Firth laughed. "I got you, didn't I?"

"Prick."

"I did, didn't I? I had you hook, line and whatsit."

"You're just a sore loser, Lenny Firth; thought you'd bail out 'cause I was whooping your arse." Roger opened the court door, and the cool air from the myriad concrete passageways wafted pleasantly over him.

Firth stood up, scooped his racquet off the floor and limped out of the court. "It does hurt, actually. Twisted it or something. Anyway, that was obstruction."

"Bollocks, obstruction," Roger said. "Come on, I'll buy you a pint and you can cry into it."

Their voices echoed around the concrete stairwell.

Firth grinned, "I saw Weston giving you the eye on the way down here. And I'd take a wild guess it wasn't 'cause we nicked his court."

"He'd have a coronary just thinking about playing squash; maybe I should offer him a game," he laughed. "He only knows where the changing rooms are because they're joined to the men's toilet." As he rounded the next flight, Roger waited for Firth to catch up. "And you know why he's pissed off at me, Lenny."

"Didn't send you a Christmas card this year?"

"He won't speak to me unless he has to, so it's not all bad."

"A man of great taste, then."

"Like you'd know taste." Roger stopped again. "You ever had someone look straight through you?"

"Part of being a copper, mate."

"He looks right through me all the time. There's something malicious about him that says he'd love to get me alone for ten minutes and beat the crap out of me for exposing his scam."

"It would take an hour or more to beat all the crap out of you."

Suddenly the stairwell erupted with voices and hurried feet, and Roger pulled back out of the way as DCI Mayers and his squash partner sprinted past without even a second glance.

"Sir," Firth saluted the empty air and waved two fingers at the disappearing blur. "See, I told you people look right through me all the time." He listened to the retreating voices. "He was involved with it, wasn't he?"

"Mayers? He took my report to the ACC."

Firth stared and Roger detected a slight shake of the head. "And you can go fuck yourself."

"What did I say?" Lenny shrugged

"Think I should have kept it to myself?" Roger asked.

Firth didn't reply.

"You think it's okay for a copper to do something wrong and get away with it? Everyone's accountable, Lenny. Including inspectors."

"I just can't believe you had the balls to go through with it."

"You've got it all wrong; you've got *me* all wrong. It takes balls to do nothing." His face was dead straight. "How can I grass on one of my own? That's what you're thinking, Lenny. That's what's trickling through that shallow little mind of yours."

"Fuck off, Roger."

"Well, he's not one of my own—"

"That's perfectly clear now. The gap between civvies and coppers just got wider."

Roger nodded. "Would you have felt this way if they'd found him guilty?"

Firth walked on.

"It's not my fault they're incompetent."

"What's that supposed to mean?" Firth turned.

"They had him under surveillance; don't tell me you didn't know—"

"Yeah, I knew—"

"And so did Weston." Roger thudded on.

Firth laughed, "So, he's clean then?"

"And the Pope's a lesbian drag artist from Venus."

Oblique light from the car park flood lamps made it through the grimy windows and spilled onto the landing. They turned a corner, the light disappeared, and they walked along in a shade that was deep enough to lose sight of your hand in, heading for the changing rooms. They pushed through the double doors onto another corridor, more darkness.

Firth said, "If he is running guns, he must be worth a fortune."

"Seen the gold on his wrist? Never the same piece twice," Roger said. "And you can't afford the house and the cars he's got on an Inspector's salary."

Firth began to laugh.

Roger stopped, looked back at him. "What's so funny?"

"You! I can't believe how seriously you're taking all this shit. Christ, Roger, you're like a Man on a Mission."

"Ex-fucking-scuse me," he said. "He's bent, Lenny. He's selling weapons—"

"You don't know that."

"He's selling weapons; he's as good as killing people. I examined his Armed Response Vehicle; the whole job was a bake. How he wriggled out of it I'll never know."

"Okay then, so what made you think it was a bake?"

"I fingerprinted it. No marks other than his and two of his men showed up – I mean no other marks at all; no smudged marks and not even any glove marks. Two men threatened and beat him, but there was barely a bruise on him. He made it up."

Firth shook his head, stood before Roger. "I can see why they let it go. In fact, I *can't* see why they put obs on him in the first place. Negative evidence means shit."

Roger glared at Firth. "This is bollocks, mate. I don't know what kick you're getting out of bringing all this shit back up again—"

"I'm interested."

"In what? It's over. He won." Roger smiled, "You just want to know whether you should be seen hanging about with me, eh? Especially in here. Where all your mates can see you; fraternising with the enemy." He turned away, "Very shallow, Lenny."

"Shallow my arse, I'm just—"

"You got a promotion board coming up? Eh? Worried what the other Inspectors will say?"

"Hey, that's not fair, Rog."

"Fair? Fair! Two men got away with thirty weapons and all the ammo they could wish for. 9mms, 45s, Glocks, rifles. *Allegedly*. And any fool knows you're not supposed to carry weapons *and* ammo in the same vehicle; everyone knows that, even *me*. Apparently Weston must have forgotten." Roger turned and began striding. "None of it made sense. Think about it, Lenny, if you had that kind of firepower in your vehicle, would *you* stop at a petrol station for cigars on the way to the armoury?"

"But they must've put all that to him in interview?" Firth tried to catch up.

"I'm sure they did."

"Then how did he get out of it?"

Roger shrugged.

"Friends in high places?" And then Firth added, "Or not enough evidence."

"The petrol station attendant didn't see anyone else... And something else that struck me as wild: would you refuse an escort when you're carrying all this firepower, and send your men away on a false recce? I know he's not in line for Mensa, but come on."

Firth patted Roger on the shoulder. "You're all strung out over this shit, aren't you?"

"What I find strange, Lenny, is that you're not."

"What's that supposed to mean?"

"Work it out."

"Why don't you let it go? They held their enquiry, they found him innocent – stupid, but innocent – so let it ride, what's it matter to you?"

"I already told you why it matters."

"But—"

"And what do they do? Rather than risk Weston announce in public that he, a man with years of loyal service, was dismissed for being robbed and beaten while on duty, they transferred him back inside and closed the file. Sick."

"If you feel so strongly that he's escaped justice, and he hates you enough to make your life miserable, why don't you put in for a transfer?"

Roger stopped and turned. "Why should he escape justice, as you say?" He looked at Firth long enough to make him back up a pace or two. "You trying to warn me off, Lenny?"

Firth gently held Roger's arm. "But justice found him innocent! It's you with the problem, Roger."

Roger snatched his arm free. "He got to you, didn't he? That's what all this is about."

"You were proved wrong, and you can't leave it alone. No such thing as 'double jeopardy' yet, mate."

"Won't need 'double jeopardy' when he kills some poor bastard, will we?"

— Two —

The door marked 'male changing room' sighed closed and a solitary figure glided discreetly inside. He entered the first toilet cubicle and locked the door behind him. It smelled of bleach and air-freshener. He checked his watch. Conniston had been playing squash for twenty minutes, he guessed, which meant he had another fifteen or twenty minutes remaining. Plenty of time.

Calmly, he sat on the toilet, placed the black cotton bag on the floor beside him, then listened and waited.

Someone entered the room and made for the urinals. After a while, a zipper jerked up and footsteps approached the sinks. A moment later, they headed away and the door squeaked open. Noise from the corridor briefly leaked in.

From the black bag, he took a pair of latex gloves. Snapped them on. Then he took out a white mask and stretched it over his face; it covered his mouth and nose. Finally, he pulled on a further pair of gloves. Nice and easy, he thought. Don't forget your procedure. Just do it as you rehearsed, slick as a greased eel.

He unbolted the cubicle door and stepped out, about to go around the urinals and into the locker room when the door opened again.

He retreated inside the cubicle. Locked it, eyes rolling upward.

This time he did not sit, but stood there silently cursing, counting the seconds, ticking off the minutes with trembling fingers. Sweat glistened on his forehead.

Again, the door opened.

Now it was just him, the auto-flush, and the hum of an extractor fan.

Holding his breath, he left the cubicle again and hurried around the corner and into a long aisle of monotonous grey lockers. At the aisle's end were the double doors leading down to the gymnasium and courts. The doors' glass showed only his reflection; blackness in the corridor beyond them.

Around him, he saw that most of the locker doors were insecure, half of them were wide open like dark mouths draping their clothing tongues. There were slacks, shirts, clip-ties, body armour and boots lying all over the place, messy as a kid's room. Other bits of uniform and civilian clothing littered the damp floor tiles and the slatted wooden benches over red plastic duckboards. Wallets and warrant cards on full display.

How trusting, he thought, finally letting out the breath.

It took only moments to find Conniston's locker. Inside was an Adidas sports bag. He grabbed it, unzipped it and pushed aside socks, jeans, a checked shirt, before finally finding it. From the black cotton bag, he pulled a clear plastic bag with a built-in sealing strip across its neck. He reached back inside—

A noise. He stopped. Listened.

Rippling through the doors to his right was the confused echo of chatter.

He watched his own startled reflection in the doors, saw himself freeze. Then he dropped the bag, lunged for it, and knocked it further away. "Shit, shit!" he mouthed between clenched teeth.

The voices grew louder.

Quickly he retrieved the bag.

Voices. Conniston's voice.

From the Adidas bag, he seized it and thrust it inside his plastic bag. To his left, the door opened. Someone whistling walked into the toilet area. He was trapped.

He rammed the plastic bag inside the black cotton bag, the mask too. He felt sick.

The whistler stopped. A cubicle door closed and its latch banged across. The whistling, quieter now, resumed.

Still shaking, he moved, half running, half sliding around the corner and back into the urinal area, panting furiously. A moment later, the double doors swung open. The incoherence of the voices became clear and distinctive. For a while, he stood with his hot back against the cold tiled wall, and tried to bring his breathing and heart rate under control. Silently he removed the gloves, wiped a sleeve across his forehead and left the room before anything else could go wrong.

Chapter 5

Late Sunday 17th into Monday 18th January 1999

— One —

IF YOU WORKED FOR the police and you worked alone, Turner Avenue was a place you stayed away from at night. Tonight, Roger had no choice, but the consolation was he wasn't alone.

He brought the van to a halt and took a moment to think calmly about the scene. He made a note of his arrival time, and watched blue strobes flick across the wet bricks of a rundown terrace. At both ends of Turner Avenue, police cars blocked the path of restless on-lookers.

It wasn't working; he still didn't feel calm. He hated dead bodies. Despite the cool exterior, underneath he was dreading it. Sometimes, just sometimes, he hated this damned job. Roger shuddered. "Welcome to Wakefield's Wonderland," he mumbled.

This was Kirk Steeple; one of a dozen tiny villages spawned by coalmining that lay on the south edge of the otherwise resplendent and progressive city of Wakefield. And since mining died of heart failure fifteen years ago, these villages were growing septic, supported by nothing more than grants, welfare, and meagre helpings of stubborn Yorkshire pride.

Kirk Steeple's main street was about three hundred yards long, with ten rows of dishevelled terraced houses shooting off at right angles on either side. From above, it looked like the skeleton of a cartoon fish.

Drugs were like profanities: dwelling in every home and used as often as required and in anyone's company. But if drugs were common, then robbery and prostitution were rain and wind. Kirk Steeple was miles from anywhere, largely devoid of proactive- or community policing, and like an old Wild West town with tumbleweed scooting down the road, it was essentially free to govern itself.

On a grassed verge, at the end of town nearest Wakefield, was the dead colliery's twenty-five foot winding wheel, sunk into the earth and painted black and gold; a new-world crucifix. 'Welcome to Kirk Steeple' a ceremonial sign declared. 'Please drive carefully'. Across it in white paint someone had sprayed, *FUCK OFF*.

Good advice, Roger thought.

He turned off the wipers and the grim scene melted into the misty windscreen. The van window thudded and he jumped hard enough to bang his knees on the steering wheel. An officer peered at him through the fogged glass.

"Micky," Roger smiled reticently, "you prick—"

"Come on, Weston's waiting for you."

"I don't remember running over a black cat." Reluctantly, Roger climbed from the warmth of the van, watched the rain dripping from Micky's helmet. "Where is he?" he said, pulling up the collar of his old waxed jacket.

"This way."

Roger locked the van door and followed Micky under the blue and white cordon tape that marked the scene's perimeter. It whipped in the wind like bunting on a second-hand car forecourt.

Surrounded by bouncing rain, by intermittent police noise and by the hostility of the residents' hand gestures, they walked around dancing puddles, past shabby front yards littered with broken bottles, disposable nappies and animal faeces, moss-covered flagstones and dirt-smeared windows as neglected as the garden gates swinging on rusty hinges.

It was almost two o'clock Monday morning, and the rain came heavier. It always rains, Roger thought, when I'm on nights. He gripped the Mars bars residing as emergency rations in his jacket pockets.

"Drinking tea in the back of that Transit."

"How come he's out at a scene? Thought he was a desk Inspector now."

"Short staffed, I suppose," said Micky. "Don't think he had much choice."

"Somebody holding a gun to his head? Oops, shouldn't say things like that, should I."

"Say what you like. The man's a waste of a perfectly good uniform."

Roger turned his face to the rain and pulled his jacket across his chest. "If I had my way, he wouldn't be in a uniform."

"Yeah well, better luck next time, mate."

"Conniston," Inspector Weston jumped from the van, "glad you could make it." Weston put on his peaked hat, thick grey hair sprouting from the sides, and stared at Roger with barely concealed distaste. "Hope we haven't inconvenienced you?"

"I was planning a rather indulgent game of *Twister*, but how could I refuse your kind invitation on such a fine morning."

Weston wasn't amused. "Tell the ACR he's here, Micky."

"Sir," Micky said. "XW from 2894."

"2894, go ahead." The radio crackled and then gave out the familiar pips telling other users that a transmission was in progress.

"Yeah, SOCO 10-6, over."

"2894, 10-20. Control to stand-by." The radio and its pips died.

"Are you acting as Deputy SIO?" Roger asked.

"Till Shelby arrives. Got a problem with that?"

"Not at all. I welcome your experience," Roger tapped his fingers against the squashed Mars bars. "Who has the incident log? I should let them know I'm here."

"Micky," Weston stared at Roger, "start a scene log."

"Retrospectively?" Micky asked.

Rain dripped from Weston's peak. "Yes. Retrospectively," he said, quieter this time.

Micky sauntered away, cursing the task under his breath.

Roger closed up to Weston until they were less than a foot apart. "How about we just stay out of each other's way, so we can get this job sorted?"

Weston put a firm hand on Roger's shoulder, and whispered, "My time will come. I'll fucking have you." He raised his hand and Roger flinched. Weston adjusted his cap, smiling at the reaction. "Know what I like about you? You're just an average coward."

"And you're just an average arms dealer."

Weston stared.

"And do you know what I like about you?" Roger smiled, "Absolutely fuck all."

Weston's eyes twitched. "Watch your back."

"Why, is that where you shoot people?"

"You cheeky—"

"How far have you got with the preparations?"

Roger's question put Weston on hold, and he evidently appreciated it. He grinned, "I've got something lined up for you."

Bet it's not a weekend in Corfu, Roger thought. "I said how far have you got?"

"Look around you, Conniston. It's cordoned off, there's a log running, we've begun house-to-house enquiries—"

"Who found the body?"

"A neighbour."

"At this hour? What would a neighbour be doing—"

"He found her a couple of hours ago but didn't come forward for fear of being done for damage – he kicked the victim's door in when she didn't stick to a prearranged meeting."

"How was she killed? Gun, knife, glass, rope, needle?"

"Knife."

"How, a stab, a slash? Have you seen the body personally?"

"Yes."

"Did you wear a scene suit?"

"Well, no, but—"

Roger gawped.

"I only peeked into the lounge. Anyway, don't know why we're going to all his trouble," he said, "she's a whore."

"Definitely dead, is she, this *whore*?" He could feel Weston making another slip in Major Scene Protocol coming on like a migraine, and he loved it.

"Well, she...she's covered in blood, her neck's been slit."

"*Definitely* dead, is she?"

"Well she will be now, Conniston, it happened fucking days ago!"

"How do you know?"

"She hasn't been seen since Friday. Anyway, I've seen dead bodies before."

So had Roger. And he'd never found one yet he liked the look of. "Your call."

"Don't mess with me. She was dead. Alright?"

Roger folded his arms, "If you say she was dead, then she was dead." He didn't give Weston the chance of a retort before saying, "I'll go make some notes about the scene as I found it, and then I'll get to work. If you don't mind."

Weston turned and stormed away. "You're on my list," he called over his shoulder. He aimed a finger gun and pulled the thumb hammer.

"Bit late for a Christmas card," he yelled, "but I appreciate the sentiment." And then Roger turned away, and swallowed. He felt unwell, and successfully ignored the tremor in his fingers as he dialled home to leave a message for Yvonne to wake up to, just in case she was worried for him.

At two-thirty, the rain had turned to snow flurries, and the wind blew in from the north, cold and icy. The blue strobes still flashed. Micky stood at the victim's gate, a clipboard in his damp hands ready to note the names of people who would enter and leave the scene. So far, it was a very short list, but it was about to grow.

The police surgeon, an on-call doctor, arrived at 02.40, the same time as DI Shelby. And ten minutes later, the doctor, dressed in a scene suit and overshoes, came out of the house and discreetly nodded. Detective Inspector Edward Shelby recorded 'life extinct' at 02.55.

"Right, Roger," said Shelby, a pleasantly rotund man with large ears and flabby cheeks, and with a neck that cascaded over his collar; he had the presence of a truck served up with typical Yorkshire brusqueness, "progress report, if you please."

Roger took the scene suit from the doctor, thanked him and bade him goodbye. He turned to Shelby. "Not much to tell. Give me another half an hour and we'll get you started." Roger pushed the doctor's scene suit into an exhibit bag with 'Police Evidence' written across it in large blue letters. Wearing the suit and overshoes helped prevent inadvertent introduction of anything foreign; losing or disturbing as little evidence as possible.

"Make that fifteen minutes," insisted Shelby. "Where's the coffee?"

"Coffee? No time for a break yet, you've officers to order around and... and whatever else it is you do." He smiled at Shelby's crumpled face.

"Coffee first, orders second, and whatever else can wait until I've thought of it." Shelby reached deeper into his pockets, trying to keep the chill away. "You called a Supervisor out yet?"

Roger taped a yellow Criminal Justice Act exhibit identity label to the bag, initialled over the tape and the bag's seals, and threw it into the back of the van. "He's on his way, Graham. And he'll have coffee with him."

"Good. Who is it?"

"Chris Hutchinson."

"The Professor? Your *Supervisor*?"

"Acting Supervisor; he's on four weeks' trial."

"You got some real competition there."

"Don't remind me." Roger paused by the van door, shielding himself from the wind. "I miss Lanky, Graham. Things are going to change radically at Wood Street SOCO now."

"You enjoy your month of playing God? I hardly saw you."

"Different. It's all paperwork, stats and shift rotas. And just when you think you've caught up, they call you out to a major scene." He smiled, nodding, "It was a challenge."

"I thought it'd be right up your alley."

"I ain't out of the race yet." Roger swept water from his glasses with a numb finger. "But I don't have as much going for me as Chris does."

"You'll be fine." Shelby moved closer and whispered, "You know, Roger, I have a bit of sway with Denis Bell. I could always lean on him a bit."

Roger slammed the van door, eyes squinting against the wind. "Well, I appreciate the offer, Graham, I really do. But if you don't mind, I'd like to see if I can get there on my own. No offence."

"None taken." Shelby cringed as icy water dribbled down his neck. "Bastard weather," he cursed. "So come on, what's your plan on this?"

"I'll begin with the external photos, by which time Chris should be here. Then we can go in, have a look around and decide whether we need the pathologist to attend. I expect we will, though. Maybe a biologist too."

"Yep, okay. By the way, Lenny Firth's on his way down to act as Exhibits Officer, so liaise with him when he gets here. If you need anything, you let me know, okay?" Shelby walked a few paces, stopped, and then came back. "But be careful with him, he's hurt his ankle somehow."

"Really? Clumsy sod."

"And Roger?" Shelby tapped his nose, "Keep my little offer between ourselves."

"Forgotten it already."

Snow flurries and darkness enveloped Shelby. Roger opened the van doors again, pulled out the tripod and unclipped the camera case. Snow wetted his stubbly face as he screwed the camera to the tripod, and switched on the flash with fingers that wouldn't work properly. He thought of Weston, and his back prickled.

He finished the exterior photographs without hindrance from anyone. And then he took shelter, leaning into the back of the van while he scribbled notes with shaking hands that would help him compile his CID6 and statement later.

Dull, lifeless water dripped from the Mamiya's lens cover and then sparkled as the headlights of a large white van approached. The Major Incident Vehicle slid on ice at the end of the street before an officer waved it through. It pulled up alongside the flaying barrier tape, a Supervisor at its wheel. "Roger," Chris Hutchinson shouted as he closed the van door.

Roger clicked the film carrier onto the Mamiya and wound to frame '1'. "Hey, how did the Supervisors' meeting go? Anything juicy happening?"

Chris eventually replied, "Nothing that concerns you."

"What, nothing at all?"

"You done out here?"

Roger let it go, wasn't worth it. He grabbed the camera and began walking. "I've taken the exterior shots."

"Then I don't need to tell you we should go in now." Chris was soon at Roger's side. "You know the drill."

"Shouldn't we wait until—"

"Wait until what?" Chris said, pulling Roger to a halt, circling around him, getting into his face. "Do you have a problem taking my instructions?"

Roger looked at Chris, unsure if he was having a laugh. But Chris's expression remained as cold as the weather. "What's wrong?" Roger dropped the flash bag and gave him his full attention, trying hard to smile. "Bell been on your back? Look, we might be rivals for the same job, but I know a thing or two... if I can help with anything."

"Back off, Roger. Save your helping hand for the newcomers, okay? You're *my* competition. I'm *your* competition."

Roger stared through the snow at Chris. "Hang on; we're friends first, aren't we? No matter who gets the job, we'll always—"

"Whoever gets the promotion will be top dog. The one who comes second is the loser, the also-ran, the one everybody forgets. He'll still be just a SOCO. Nothing more."

"It's only a fucking job; why are you so hostile over this?"

He offered Roger a thin smile. "I learned something recently; that I can do this new job of mine. I can *really* do it. I'm motivated and I believe in myself."

Roger laughed. "That's amazing; you're still dreaming. You drove all the way here in your damned sleep!"

"Not funny." Chris turned away. "Let's get busy. I want out of this pissing weather."

"Just waiting for the word to go, *boss*." Roger wiped his glasses again, blinked snow from his eyelashes and smiled at Chris.

"Who's SIO?"

"Shelby," Roger pointed. "He's deputising."

Chris wandered off into the sodden night looking for Shelby, leaving Roger shaking his head. He called back, "Get the stepping plates ready."

Roger took the interior photographs; shots of the body in situ, shots of blood spatter patterns on the wall unit and floor, with and without scales; photographs of any item deemed foreign to the scene, though he found it difficult to discern what belonged and what didn't.

Under Chris's barked instructions, Roger photographed condoms, spectacles, pornographic literature, underwear, foil wraps, burnt spoons and the like, and acting under further instructions, bagged them and sealed them ready for Lenny Firth. He photographed anything that could assist the investigation, including the partial footwear impressions in blood on the lounge floor. No significant tread pattern though. There was also a photograph of the deceased girl holding a young child – it had a smudged footwear mark across it, and Roger seized it for future examination.

"What about trying some reagent on the footwear marks in blood?" Roger suggested. "We might be able to pick out more detail."

"Waste of time. We'll concentrate on the body."

"If I'd said let's concentrate on the body, you'd have wanted to do the footwear. Argumentative git." Roger got busy and carried on taking photographs, did his best to ignore Chris.

At 4.30am, Shelby escorted the Forensic Pathologist, Bellington Wainwright, into the scene. Chris joined them in standing around the body, arms folded, silent in contemplation. "If it was summer," Shelby said, "she'd be a sloppy mush by now, and you wouldn't be able to see her for the maggots and bluebottles."

Wainwright nodded his agreement. "Friday, you say?"

"Last seen about 4.30pm." Shelby glanced at his watch. "Back soon," he said.

The girl, a twenty-one year-old bleached-blonde, lay on her back among mounds of litter. Seeping blood had formed in a thick and lumpy pool around her head, reddening her hair as it escaped the gash in her throat.

Roger padded around the house, looking, and feeling. Absorbing. He checked out the bedrooms. They were a shambles; clothes and soiled bed linen scattered over the floors, inch-thick dust on rotten chipboard furniture, graffiti on holed doors and smashed windows covered by sheets of damp wood.

There was only one half-decent room in the whole house – and that was home to a well-worn double bed. The bedroom smelled of lavender massage oil, it smelled of perfume – cheap stuff but a welcome change from the rest of the house. On a dusty bedside stand, among cider bottles and ashtrays, were packets of condoms and tubes of KY Jelly. The carpet was sticky underfoot.

The bathroom, stained with black mould around the sink and bath, smelled of excrement and, strangely, of laundry. In the bath, a pair of pink jeans was soaking in some pre-wash solution. Back downstairs in the kitchen, it was the same filthy story; washing-up piled high in the sink, fat splattered across the wall near the cooker and a black bin bag overflowing with rubbish festering in the corner. After a while, Roger got used to the stench, and almost stopped feeling sorry for her.

Roger arrived back in the lounge. While the pathologist deliberated, Roger looked around at the nicotine-stained ceiling, at the furniture unfit for the tip. He recalled the ashtrays full of cigarette ends, and the foil wraps and needles hidden behind cushions on the sofa, and the empty lager cans under the chair. All were now in evidence bags leaning against the wall unit, ready for logging and removal.

No one mentioned the sad piece of tinsel, naked in places, hanging across the chimneybreast, nor that Twelfth Night was a week ago. No one mentioned the two Christmas cards on the mantelpiece. No one mentioned them because inside they were blank.

Clipboard in hand, Wainwright inspected the corpse, scribbled notes about the girl and her immediate surroundings.

Roger asked, "What do you want me to do, Chris?"

Chris dabbed a length of adhesive tape across the dead girl's exposed flesh and secured it onto a thin acetate sheet for later laboratory examination. "Bag her, please. Start with her head." He didn't look up.

Roger saluted.

Beneath the mask, he grimaced as he guided a plastic bag over her head, watching clots of blood slide away like cold prunes off a spoon. He pulled it down over her neck, watching it drag bloody hair over her face, watching it flatten her petite nose and squash her blue lips. In order to preserve whatever evidence might be in her hair or on her face, he tied string around the bag, well below the wound, and loosely so as not to leave a ligature mark on her throat. His gloved hands glistened red. He hated this.

"Van keys, Roger?" demanded Chris.

"What?"

"Where are your van keys? I need more acetates."

"I'll get them. I don't mind."

"Just tell me where they are, for Christ's sake."

They stared at each other. "Jacket pocket."

"Where's your jacket?"

"Hallway. Slung over the exhibits case."

"In the hall? Christ, Roger, you should know better than to leave your bloody jacket in a murder scene! Nothing," he shouted, "gets *dumped* in a major scene!"

Everyone looked at Roger.

He shook his head, made sure Roger saw him too. "Anyway, you'll be itching like hell the next time you wear it. Haven't you seen the fleas in here?"

"No," Roger said. "Guess I missed them. Looks like it's going home for washing, again."

"Prat! Don't do it again." Chris left.

Roger and Wainwright exchanged glances. "Where was I supposed to leave it? It's fucking snowing outside." Roger puffed beneath the mask, tried to pretend that the air in here was odour-free, and tried to pretend that Chris's conduct didn't bother him.

"I don't think he appreciates the value of a little etiquette."

Roger changed his gloves and looked at the pathologist, at his smiling eyes.

Wainwright lowered his gaze back to his clipboard. "Sorry," he mumbled.

"Don't be, you have a fair point."

"Is he under some kind of pressure perhaps?"

Roger bagged her right hand, the one easiest to get to. "It's no excuse for losing it like that."

Shelby accompanied Chris back into the scene, a fine powdering of snow already melting on their heads. Chris threw the van keys onto Roger's jacket and dropped the acetates onto a redundant stepping plate.

Roger looked up in time to see Weston peering into the lounge, curious like a rubber-necker watching the aftermath of a road accident. He was staring at the exhibit bags. Then he was gone.

They gathered again in the lounge, and discovered that, apart from the obvious neck wound, the girl had suffered an abdominal puncture, caused by a single-edged blade. Her off-white blouse hid it, and the blood spatter from the throat injury masked it, until Roger moved the body in order to get a plastic bag over her left hand. Then watery blood began seeping into the fabric like crimson ink into blotting paper, also highlighting the stab wound in the blouse itself.

"Could it be a post mortem wound?" Shelby asked.

Wainwright cleared his throat. "It's not easy to speculate."

"No," Roger interrupted. "Sorry, but I think it's ante mortem; she's on her knees by the time he stabs her in the neck. Look at the blood distribution on the floor."

Shelby nodded and looked at Wainwright. "Well?"

"That's a fair point."

"I think our murderer's new to this," Roger said. "I think he stabbed her in the gut but she doesn't die. Now she's screaming like hell. The murderer wants to shut her up and goes for the throat."

Chris was quiet, listening, watching Roger with interest. So was Shelby.

"When you pull the knife out of the stomach," Roger said, "the skin acts like a squeegee, sealing itself up, which explains the lack of blood. But there's lots of pain."

Shelby nodded. "Makes sense. Bellington?"

"A distinct possibility," he said, almost whispered. "It's true that a stomach wound sometimes won't bleed unless aggravated in some way; but it is hugely painful." And then he turned to Shelby. "I'd like to inspect both wounds more carefully before I commit myself. See how much blood is in the abdomen."

"I need a coffee." Roger strode past Wainwright and Shelby, wanting to be free of the house and the damned carcass for a while.

Chris sighed and said to Shelby, "He's right. I need a break too. Want a coffee?"

"No, you go on."

When Roger stepped back into the street, the snow had already stopped but the wind was ever persistent. Part of him felt cheated that there was no white covering, and the other part just felt glad he wouldn't end up on his backside. When he pulled off the latex gloves, his clammy hands discovered that the MIV door handle was carved from ice. He tossed the gloves and mask somewhere near a battered cardboard box on which someone had scrawled, 'bin'.

Shivering, Roger opened the side door and sighed into a bench seat behind a small foldaway desk; and from a green cool-box by his feet, he lifted out a flask and two beakers. Chris slumped into the seat at Roger's side, cursing the weather as he closed the door. "Well?"

"Yes, I am, thanks for asking." Roger poured the coffees.

Chris rubbed his hands with a disinfectant wipe. "What's wrong?"

Roger looked out of the rain-dappled window, tapping his beaker. "What a way to go. Very undignified."

"Seems to me she didn't give a shit about being dignified."

Roger just looked at him.

He slurped his coffee and mumbled something that sounded like, "Anyway, she's only a fucking whore."

Roger said nothing, watched the rain droplets on the window dance in the wind.

"Now drink up; we'll bag the stiff and get the body snatchers in. Shelby wants us out so he can search."

The undertakers, also wearing white scene suits, stood in the doorway and watched as Chris and Roger prepared the plastic-wrapped body for transit. Weston gazed over their shoulders. Minutes before, he had been enquiring of Firth what evidence they had found.

"Right, lads," Roger said, "she's all yours." Stifling a yawn, he turned to DS Firth. "How's your ankle, Lenny?"

"Oh, that's it," Firth said, "laugh at a cripple, why don't you?"

Chris asked, "You locking it down now?"

"Might as well, can't do anything more here tonight. We're leaving a guard front and back."

The foldaway gurney punched a splinter of wood from the doorframe and dented the front door's metal skin. It was Sally's final trip out of her house.

"Anyway, PM's arranged for six," Firth added, following the body.

"Who's SIO?" Chris unzipped his scene suit and buttoned his cardigan up to the neck.

"Detective Superintendent Chamberlain. We've informed him, but he's in no rush to come out at this hour. Apparently, he has great faith in Inspector Shelby."

Chris patted Roger on the back. "So, old chum, you and I will do the PM together. When the day crew comes on, they can do the fingerprinting here. What do you say?"

Roger shrugged, "Fine."

"And if you're not tired by the time we've finished at the mortuary, it'll be time for a hearty English breakfast. I'm buying."

— Two —

Beaver lay on his back, hands under his head, tattooed elbows out like butterfly's wings. In the darkness, the bunk below him rocked as Pinhead tossed himself stupid, grunting every now and then. Beaver listened for a while, sick at the thought of what was happening three feet away. He kicked the bunk's frame. "Pack it in, will ya; some of us are trying to sleep!"

"I thought you'd be asleep already. Lights went out hours ago."

"Yeah, well I'm not, so pack it in or I'll make you pack it in."

"Bet you can't wait for tomorrow, eh?" Pinhead's high voice rattled around the cell.

From further down the landing, Beaver could hear one of the new intake crying. He cried, it seemed, as often as Pinhead masturbated – and Pinhead always masturbated. "Today, you mean," Beaver's luminous watch told him it was after two in the morning of the day of his release. "Fuckin snowing. Just my luck." Condensation dulled the cell's window and diffused the bright light of the spot-lamps across the exercise yard, made them appear almost mellow for a change.

"You're lucky; I've got another year to do."

"Do you think your dick will last that long?"

"It's my wrist I'm worried about," he laughed. "I still think you're a lucky bastard."

And he was. Until seven days ago, Beaver looked forward to nothing. He envisioned traipsing out of this shithole the same way he entered it: broke and without hope; the pockets of his torn jeans rattling with just enough change for a bus ride to hell and then what, back to burgling the same tired shithole estate that he lived on, and a poke in the ribs from a stuck-up parole officer once a week. O joy.

All his mates were in here; none on the outside to speak of. None he could trust, anyway. In here, he'd met a bloke called Jess. Jess had become his best buddy; they had got along fine for the last eight months of Beaver's three year stay. And in the final week before Beaver's release, Jess had spoken the magic words: "I got a job for you".

Jess had sparked him up, made release something to look forward to. "It'll be piss easy," he'd continued. "One quick job, take you half a day, maybe, and then you're in the crew, guaran-fuckin-teed! We'll fix you up with a place to kip – won't be no Hilton though – and then you'll get regular work; shitty to begin with, but once he trusts you," Jess had nodded, "things'll get better."

"Once who trusts me?"

"Never mind just yet. You'll find out when he wants you to know." Jess had winked.

But it was that phrase, *things'll get better,* that drew him in like water down a drain. A life, things to do, things to look forward to, a guaran-fuckin-teed crewmember. Money, a car maybe... Hope.

The new kid down the corridor still cried.

"Like I said, I've got another year to do."

"What you got planned when you get out?" Beaver's indifferent voice echoed.

Pinhead was silent for a long time before he answered the question with another, "What's the chances of you recommending me? I mean, I could do it, Beaver, whatever they asked, I could, I've thought it all through, every job they could possibly throw at me: burglary, assault, robbery... You name it, I'm your man."

Beaver said nothing.

"Beaver? Well? What do you say?"

"Fuck off, Pinhead. You're just a wanker."

"You've got me in stitches, Beaver."

"You're full o' shit. You're hot air. They want someone with guts, someone who'll do what he's told." Beaver thought of the gun. But he kept his mouth shut. The fewer people knew the better, is what Jess had told him. "When I threaten something, I always see it through. Always."

Beaver slept for an hour. He dreamed of the crew, of having genuine comradeship for the first time in his life, looking forward to regularly seeing a friendly face that didn't belong to a stuck-up parole officer. Beaver, as they say, was made up.

He would never join the crew. And he'd see Pinhead again in less than a week.

At 3am, Pinhead made the mistake of grunting again. Beaver's eyes sprang open and he leapt off his bunk.

"What you doing?"

Beaver was putting on his trainers.

"Where you going?"

He almost replied that he fancied going for a walk. But he didn't. He turned, lifted a leg and brought his foot down hard.

Pinhead screamed.

Chapter 6

Monday 18th January 1999

— One —

In 1964, THE MANAGEMENT at Pinderfields General Infirmary had tucked the new mortuary well out of the way on what appeared to be little more than levelled waste ground. Buildings of a more acceptable nature surrounded it as though offering protection to those who couldn't bear to think of death just yet.

The mortuary was a single-storey building with moss-covered roof tiles; a rutted dirt track led up to the overgrown 'delivery' entrance; cracked windows at the back, and clunking refrigeration equipment slung up over that entrance on rusting metal girders. Old doors with flaking paint over chipped wood; chipped by equally old gurneys with stained frames and gnarled, squeaking wheels.

It was wintry enough in the car park to nip Roger's finger ends, but as he carried the tripod and camera case, and Chris carried the flash into the mortuary, it felt bitter, eye-wateringly bitter. They set their equipment down in the area where the freezers and fridges hummed directly outside the examination room's double flap doors.

Roger slung his waxed jacket over a gurney.

A whiteboard, scribbled with names corresponding to the numbers on the fridge and freezer doors, glowed under bright fluorescent tubes. Above the board, an Insectocutor radiated ultra violet, and below it on a shelf, cans of fly spray and several whiteboard markers. Someone had used the markers on a girlie calendar nearby.

He heard the detectives' voices echo, and peeked inside the examination room before Chris pushed past him. Inside the examination room was a cupboard with stacks of protective clothing. The detectives were already suited and booted.

White tiles and stainless steel, sluices, tubs of formaldehyde, handsaws, power saws, knives, scalpels and rib shears, the furniture and fittings of the Pinderfields General mortuary. Clinical waste bins stood in a row alongside floor squeegees; a stainless steel sink, a rotary floor scrubber for when things got really messy, and tucked under a bench was a small pile of cadaver head supports that looked like a nest of giant dead spiders. The smell of disinfectant was strong and the floor still shone from a previous hosing down; the grate in the centre and the gridded drains running to it were still wet with diluted blood.

Roger and Chris donned flimsy blue elasticated over-shoes and green plastic smocks.

They all awaited Shelby and the pathologist. Chatter among the detectives intensified as they began making preparations; clipboards were out, pens lay nearby, boxes of latex gloves, rows of plastic sample bottles, stacks of evidence bags, exhibits books and piles of yellow CJA exhibit labels were all on view. The second exhibits officer, DC Clements smeared Vicks across her top lip, and held the jar out to Chris.

"No, thanks," he grinned, nudging Roger. "We're used to it, aren't we, mate?"

Roger raised his eyebrows, "You going to be okay?" he asked Clements.

Just then, the doors swung shut. "Hiya, Chrissy." Ann, the mortuary tech, blew a kiss.

Chris turned away; his saggy cheeks lost the grin, and they reddened as the officers made fun of him. The more they teased him, the more he seemed to regress into the taciturn mood he adopted on their way here. He tried to smile, but was obviously desperate to be away from their attention.

"Oi!" Roger shouted. "Enough, prick."

"Why? You gonna run to Mayers?" A detective leaned out of the group, smirk on his face, staring at Roger.

"Leave it, Haynes," someone whispered, could have been Firth.

Roger peeled his eyes from Haynes, tied the green plastic smock over his waistcoat and finished setting up the camera equipment. Sally Delaney's body craved his attention. White pallid skin. Stained red.

Chris said, "You okay, Rog?"

"Tired."

With a clipboard under his arm, Wainwright entered the room, pulling on his latex gloves. Shelby and the coroner's officer, Jacob Cooper, followed, the voices hushed. "And just how professional do you lot think you sound? I could hear you from up the sodding corridor!" Shelby stared directly at Haynes.

Roger's work consisted of photographing the features of the body as a whole and those of the wounds it had sustained to the abdomen and throat, before and after cleaning. Under Wainwright's instruction, they paid particular attention to the depth of the cuts, the angles at which they were made and the damage each wound had caused. When Roger had taken all the external shots, he stepped away to the back of the room, avoiding Haynes's occasional glances, and waited for Wainwright to take all the necessary hair samples and intimate swabs, keeping DC Clements busy with sealing up bags and noting down times and exhibit numbers.

Using a scalpel, Wainwright made a 'Y' incision beneath the corpse's throat, and slit through the soft skin between her breasts and down, through a constant and thin layer of fat, towards her pelvis, avoiding the stab wound just below her rib cage. It appeared that he was drawing with a thick red pen, leaving a crimson trail as the flesh parted. He peeled the skin aside, using the scalpel to sever the link between it and the flesh beneath. And that was when something more powerful eclipsed the smell of disinfectant.

"Roger," Wainwright said, "photograph, please?"

Roger closed up to the body; felt the cold steel of the table against his thigh, felt the abnormal coolness of Sally Delaney's blood-splashed arm against his plastic apron as he leaned over to where Wainwright's bloodied glove pointed.

"There," he said, "the incision into the small intestine." And then quietly, as if to himself, "Through into the ileum."

The smell was noxious, and Roger's throat closed up. "Right," he said, aiming the flash. Then the camera's bellows floated outwards until the image of the wound was sharp on the ground-glass screen. Regaining his composure, he knocked the f-stop down to 5.6, pressed the shutter release, and then exhaled.

"Thanks," Wainwright said.

"Another, with a scale?" Roger asked.

"Please."

Later, Roger photographed the body's organs to indicate the damage caused to them by the attacker's blade or simply by over exuberant living, forcing himself to ignore the smell of the gutted corpse. They always said the only way to get used to the smell was to breathe it in deeply as you would the air in a rose garden or a freshly mown meadow. Never worked for him; they always smelled just like someone else's shit.

Wainwright collected blood samples for toxicology and forensic analysis by severing the femoral artery, and ran his hand along the inner thigh to force the coalescing blood into a plastic bottle, which he handed to DC Clements. Using a syringe, he took a urine sample from the bladder and filled another plastic bottle. DC Clements cringed each time a bottle of body fluid or a smeared swab came her way.

Firth looked away from the carcass and said, "Stinks like one of your farts, Roger."

"Strange that, Lenny, I was just thinking that about your breath."

Shelby looked on impassively, arms folded; there in the role of deputy, he gathered pertinent information for Detective Superintendent Chamberlain.

Wainwright rinsed and dried his gloved hands and diligently updated his notes. Then, he stripped away the skin around the neck wound, scaled it, and called for more photographs. And then Roger watched as he carefully sliced away the surrounding muscle until—

"There's our fatal wound."

Shelby stepped forward, leaned in, and noted the partially severed artery.

The flash fired. Mumbles among the CID.

Much to Roger's relief, Wainwright signified the end of the examination, and gave permission for Ann to dump the black plastic bag containing sectioned organs back into the cadaver's abdominal cavity. She then packed the brainless skull with cotton wool, pulled the scalp back into position and began sewing. Quietly, she whistled.

Roger took a deep breath and took the dead girl's fingerprints. With fine particles of aluminium, he powdered each digit, rolled a strip of adhesive tape, called an Austin lift, across its wrinkled bulb and placed the lift onto a clear acetate sheet, about the size of a piece of A4. He turned the sheet over so the fingerprints were the correct way around, and labelled them 'right thumb', 'right index', 'right middle', and so on.

She was cold and had become stiff again now. The skin of her abdomen that wasn't streaked with blood, had a green caste to it; the colour of decay.

He never got used to touching a human being and discovering its hands were not warm; that they lacked the ability to flinch when he cracked the fingers out straight so he could do his work, and how they were like raw chicken legs: how the skin, wrinkled and lifeless, slid over the gristle and the bone and the muscle—

"You okay, Roger?"

Roger smiled, "Looking forward to the full English."

Chris said nothing, just wandered away.

Ann, whistling loudly now, threw the bloodied rib shears and other assorted tools into a steaming sink of detergent. Around the room, voices grew, laughter began. DC Clements wiped her top lip. Bags were zipped up, clipboards, pens and labels packed away ready for the next body.

The fingerprints were now an exhibit, and for the sake of its integrity, Roger slid the acetate into a clear plastic bag, sealed it and signed over the seal before attaching a CJA exhibit label and a length of biohazard tape. And for the exhibit's continuity, he made a note of the time of exchange, and handed the bag over to DS Firth.

"You still want that breakfast I promised you?" asked Chris.

"Mind if I cut and run? I'm knackered."

"Quite glad, really." Chris moved in a little closer, away from the others, and whispered. "I'm a bit skint, actually. Can't wait for pay day." He stood there expectantly.

That was the kind of comment, thought Roger, you might expect from Hobnail, who at least was upfront about his fiscal situation, but there was something about the way Chris looked at him furtively, as though he should be honoured to dip into his pocket and help him out. Roger closed the latches on the aluminium camera case, looked up at Chris and asked, "You want to borrow some?"

"Get out of here," he whispered, "I wasn't…"

Roger stopped the embarrassment; he was too tired and it would lead to the same conclusion as it did last time. And the time before. "If you're really in a fix, I could run to twenty."

Chris's mouth snapped shut at the offer. "You don't mind? I'll make sure you get it back. Promise. I think I lost some, you know, that's why I'm skint."

Roger said nothing, but wondered on which three-legged horse Chris lost his money.

More rain accompanied Roger as he drove home with the heater fan on full and the wipers grating across the windscreen. Pink Floyd played *Comfortably Numb* on the stereo. Under his reddened eyes were dark bags; around his face the earlier five o'clock shadow had matured into a nine o'clock beard. He yawned constantly and sighed in between.

Even as Roger pulled onto the drive outside his home, the scene at Turner Avenue continued to buzz with police activity. Two SOCOs, one upstairs and one down, brushed aluminium fingerprint powder over every suitable surface, and three gloved-up detectives pulled out drawers, read bank statements and love letters, lifted scraps of carpet, and searched in the loft.

They were being thorough. Thorough enough to find eventually the late Sally Delaney's diary in the dust up on top of the wall unit.

— Two —

After a thin and fitful sleep, Roger was back in the office, feeling as though he had never been away. His shift began at six o'clock in the evening, always a busy time. But by ten, the calls had dwindled, and when he closed his fingerprinting kit on the last burglary for the evening, he made straight for Weston's house.

He drove past at speed. Then he drove past slowly. Then he parked the van and walked past. Weston was at home, Roger saw him in his spacious lounge, with his feet up and what looked like a glass of whisky in one hand and the TV remote in the other.

And that always dismayed him. Weston was running guns, and all Roger needed was to catch him just once; it would blow the death-dealing bastard right out of the water. In the last six months of improvised surveillance, he hadn't even come close; never saw so much as an air pistol, never mind a Glock! He'd seen him go fishing once down at Bretton Sculpture Park, west of the city centre, saw him again twice more, just going for a walk there.

Roger suspected there was something illegal inside the tackle box or the rod case, and if there wasn't when he went down to the lake, there sure as hell would be on the way back. And so Roger had followed. For three hours, he had crouched by an oak and watched. But Weston was as good a fisherman as he was a diplomat. He had caught nothing and left with the same gear he'd taken.

It was now midnight, the waxy smell of aluminium powder filled his nostrils and the clinical smell of detergent filled the SOCO office. From the exhibit store, he booked out the photograph he'd seized from Sally Delaney's lounge floor, the one with a smudged footmark on it. And he stared at the picture: a smiling teenage girl and a small child in a blue woollen hat. Sad.

The mark on the photograph was fragmentary, and it was in dust which meant any attempt to apply powder would destroy it. He shone the office torch across the mark and noticed even more detail than before. "Hush Puppies." He decided to photograph it.

It worked well, and half an hour later, he dropped an envelope containing the negatives, into the secure internal mail tray, and wrote his report.

The last he heard, CID still hadn't found Sally's murder weapon, presumed to be a three-inch, single-edged, non-serrated knife – something similar to a penknife, something that everyone from Boy Scouts to bus-drivers carried. This nudged the morale of the investigation lower still because everyone knew that the chances of nailing a murderer declined rapidly after the first couple of days of a fruitless investigation.

And then the press got hold of Sally's details, her circumstances. Easy enough to do: throw a tenner to anyone on her street and you'd get an instant report of her being Mother Teresa if that's what you asked for. They needed an angle that would sell papers and the one they chose described her as a lonely single mother attacked in her own home for no apparent reason. It sold more papers, but it also put the police under more pressure to catch the killer quickly before public apprehension increased, before the fear of crime gained more prominence than the crime itself.

And fuelled by those newspapers, that apprehension manifested itself in the question most heard by officers on the beat: was this the beginning of another serial killer; a second Yorkshire Ripper, someone who targeted women because he was sick in the head. The police officers had responded with cautious statements along the lines of it being highly unlikely something similar could happen now, twenty-odd years after Sutcliffe; technology and hard-learned lessons made that kind of thing almost impossible. But what frightened Roger most of all, was the word *almost*. Almost impossible. And since no one had been arrested for Sally's murder yet, offering unofficial statements like that, though well-intentioned, seemed a little reckless.

Even the reports on Shelby's desk, of a white middle-aged man, well built and wearing a dark overcoat, seen at Sally's door sometime in the afternoon, did little to raise Shelby's optimism. He was heard to say, 'Well that fucking narrows it down, doesn't it!' before slamming the office door on his way out.

The Town Hall clock chimed twice. Gratefully, Roger switched off his mobile and pager, and shut down the computer and the office lights. He traipsed through the security gates to the staff car park, a yawn never far from his mouth and thoughts of bed comforting his mind.

The security barrier was still open, and he drove straight out of the car park.

Later he would recall this night, and others like it, and would wish he *had* gone home to bed.

In 1888, Wakefield matured into a City, stealing northern eminence from Pontefract, but lying blissfully in Leeds' shadow. More than a century later it gained a reputation as a historical locale with a modern outlook. Wakefield blossomed. Socialising boomed.

The club scene promoted Wakefield with the panache of a sledgehammer crushing a fly. A night out here was an event big enough to attract the youths of surrounding villages and even those of nearby cities. It promised an unrivalled array of pubs, each advertising an 'Unrivalled array of beers', 'Happy hour, eight till eleven', topless barmaids, ear-crunching 'music', stomach-crunching cuisine and all the flesh one's bleary eyes could consume.

Bass permeated the cold air, belched from dark doorways manned by large men who wore long black coats and dicky bows. Westgate alone boasted twelve such doorways, some marked with flashing neon lights, others more discreet, more choosy of their clientele.

Police officers in liveried cars and vans, strategically sited wherever a space was available, observed the doorways too.

Occasionally, boy racers in GTIs and lowered, blacked-out Escorts with drainpipes for exhausts, thundered up and down the drag hoping to catch the eye of the dolly-birds while avoiding the eye of the law.

The earlier rain had gone, and the night was clear, the air heavy with cheap scent and cheaper aftershave. It was approaching the end of the revellers' evening, it was nearly 2.30 – but still the profound thud of bass escaped every club door, as did groups of staggering men and giggling women. They were a throbbing crowd jostling on slick pavements.

Most headed for the hot-dog stands and mobile burger bars, some stumbled towards the taxi ranks, some walked away merrily, others threw up in the gutter and a few, of course, started trouble. The cumulative screams, shouts and singing, were louder than a pneumatic drill.

Shooting off Westgate like the branches of a tree were cobbled alleyways wide enough for only one vehicle, and in the nineteenth century given names such as George and Crown Yard and Woolpacks Yard. Another was Thompson's Yard, rich with history, but now bursting with trendy solicitors' offices. Thompson's Yard led travellers through a brick archway between The Imperial Bank and Tony's Pizza Emporium, and out onto Westgate. The archway, a tunnel beneath the buildings' first storeys, was sufficiently long to be cosseted by an eerie darkness.

Tonight, a lone car occupied Thompson's Yard, lights off, a man at the wheel watching provocative, and sometimes alluring, young women stumble by. This was not a regular habit of Roger's, since he worked evenings only one week in five; but when he did, he made a concerted effort to go 'cruising', as he called it. This was the 'official business' he had told Hobnail of.

A young couple in the throes of sexual excitement chose his archway to begin kissing and fondling each other.

As Roger became engrossed, the sudden belch of a siren made him bang his head on the side window. The police car was big and menacing in his rear view mirror, and the officer at its wheel waved furiously at him. The young couple rearranged themselves and left. Roger crunched first gear and nearly stalled in his rush to depart. He turned left, gazing hopefully in his rear view mirror. The police car turned right and sped off down the street after a GTI.

Roger exhaled with relief, and felt his hands trembling.

The bed was warm. Yvonne snored in a rather feminine, petite way that somehow endeared her to him. She was disabled now, her quality of life outside home reduced, spoilt, dictated by where there were stairs and where there were not stairs, dependant on ramps and ease of access, jostling with indifferent and ignorant people. It was easier on mind and spirit to stay at home.

Rheumatoid arthritis had come along and savagely twisted Yvonne's beautiful body until it would fit quite neatly into a small box.

She had every right to resent her life, he thought.

Roger climbed into bed next to his wife.

Eventually, sleep carried him away into another nightmare.

Chapter 7

Tuesday 19th January 1999

So the nightmares are still—"

"I took Valium last night. I stole a full strip of them from Yvonne's medicine box a month ago. They've nearly all gone." Roger breathed away the tension, tried to relax in the chair. A finger traced the dial on his watch, over and again. "I dread going to bed after I've worked on a body." He laughed but it was derisive, hollow. "I just can't sleep, can't get their faces and their damned smell out of my mind."

"And—"

"And I'm worried."

Alice Taylor's office, like the rest of the Occupational Health Unit, was pastel green, quiet calm ruled, patience and understanding were always plentiful. It smelled of forests in springtime, and her desk was not a barrier between herself and her client, but was pushed back against the wall so together they could face each other unobstructed, sharing the problem. Gentle lighting created a soothing atmosphere, but simply her presence helped relax Roger to the point of being high. The worry slipped away – for the moment at least.

"Have you told anyone about the nightmares; except me, I mean?" Alice asked.

"Are you kidding? And I'd appreciate it staying between just us two."

"You don't think I'd—"

"No, no. I don't think that at all. Sorry." He rubbed the tiny scars that ran along the tips of the fingers on his left hand. It was as though they itched.

She put down the pen and the writing pad. The page was thick with elaborate doodles – from an earlier meeting, she assured Roger. "I think we've exhausted all my suggestions," she said. "The only thing to do is wait. I know it's a cliché, but time really does heal - eventually."

"I'm not sure I've got enough time left in me for an 'eventually'."

She squirmed in her chair. "You know, sometimes I have to put suggestions forward that..."

"Go on, Alice, don't be shy."

"Is this job right for you?"

"What! Of course—"

"But every time you see a dead body—"

"I know. *I'm* the one living through it. Shit! I'm the one who sees that dead body all through the night. I sleep with the damned things." He stood, walked away from her and took in the view from her window, his fists resolutely planted on his hips. "I... This job is everything to me. I can't do anything else. I don't *want* to do anything else." He tried to laugh again, but this time it just sounded feeble. "I feel like I'm a world class butcher, only to discover I'm allergic to meat, or a prize-winning hairdresser with a phobia of hair." He felt like punching a hole in the glass.

"Is that the only thing worrying you?"

His fists curled tighter. "That's not enough?"

"Look, I'm trying to—"

"I know!"

Alice leaned back in her chair, took a moment for Roger to compose himself, then asked, "How many bodies have you seen, and over how many years?"

"Countless," he stared into the grey clouds over St John's churchyard. "It's been nine years."

"There's something else, isn't there? You've been having nightmares for about four months, so what's happened in that time?"

"Us," he said. "We've happened."

"No, no, apart from us. Come on, Roger, you know the answer already."

His back still to her, he shrugged. Weston? he thought. Then he stiffened, "Promotion."

"Go on."

"Ever since I put the application in, went for the aptitude tests and the interview," he turned around to face her, "I haven't slept soundly."

"Voilà," her voice was calm, not at all patronising. "Pressure. That's all it is. You're worried about it."

"It's close." He glared at her, "I have a good chance of getting it."

"That's what's worrying you."

"Getting it is worrying me?"

"Sounds that way. After nine years of doing the job, I'd have to say you must be competent at it, but somewhere up there in your head, you're worried that if you get the promotion, you'll foul it up. You're not sure that you can take the responsibility or the pressure."

His eyes fell away from hers. "Thanks for your vote of confidence."

"It's true."

"If it was true, why the hell would I attack myself like this, why would I..."

She said nothing, only looked at him and raised her eyebrows in a question.

He turned away again, his head bowed. No fists this time.

"You were about to ask why you would decrease your own chances of getting the job?"

"So I would never find out if I could do it or not."

"So you would never *need* to find out."

"But I need this promotion." His voice had conviction, and his eyes mirrored it. The window was there, inviting, daring him.

"Of course you do. It's vital you have it. You can't live without it."

"Don't take the piss."

"You have a decent salary, a good home, and it's obvious you still enjoy the job. So why do you *need* this promotion badly enough to put yourself through hell?"

Roger slumped into his seat and rested his elbows on his knees. He stared at the floor, fingertips playing with each other. "Nice. Never noticed that before. Your anklet." He smiled at her. "Suits you."

"You think I'm a tart?"

"I like it is what I meant. No underlying meaning, Alice; just a couple o' words, that's all."

She leaned in closer now, forcing him to look at her. "Are you going to tell me why it's so important you get this promotion?"

"My dad," he whispered at last.

"I thought your dad was dead, we went through your family already."

Roger's face was ashen. No emotion pulled its features one way or the other. Impassive. "He *is* dead. But that's not important. I still need to prove myself to him." He tried a smile to cover his growing embarrassment, but it felt awkward.

"He's dead? And it's not important?"

Roger thought of looking out the window again, and then changed his mind. It was just games, just bluffs. He sat there and let it out. "My brother and sister were born with business wings, highflying accountant and highflying solicitor. They're both senior managers in London now. Whenever visitors came to our house, Dad always bragged of their successes in Eton and Cambridge but somehow forgot about me, about how I was getting along at Bristol University doing my engineering course." He looked back at the memory, and it hurt. He still wanted to smash the window, just to get the poison out. "And when I told him I…" he stopped, hung his head.

"Go on, it's okay, Roger. You've come this far, might as well finish it."

"I had prospects. That's what he said. But I always struggled with figures and equations. When I was young, I'd pull radios apart just to see how they worked. Of course, they never worked again once I'd finished with them. But I was inquisitive. Practical, not academic.

"When I enrolled at Bristol instead of Cambridge, the old man couldn't hide his disappointment, didn't even try to, really. But you should have seen him when I told him I'd flunked out, and that I'd met a girl." He looked up at Alice, smiled and said, "He punched me. Can you believe it; he freaked out and punched me. Eventually, he came around and tried to talk me back 'on track'. He said there was still time if I applied myself.

"My dad wasn't a bad man. I made him like that, I guess. He nearly had a fucking heart attack when I told him I was marrying the girl I'd met."

"Yvonne?"

"Christ, you're sharp today, Alice."

"Hey—"

"Sorry, sorry, I'm... Anyway, he was disgusted, and that was one thing he *did* say about me. Actually, he said it frequently. Annoyingly so." He tried to appear nonchalant, as though none of it bothered him. "At least when I moved out he didn't have to hide me anymore when The Influential came around. Didn't even say goodbye."

"Were you around when he died?"

Roger shook his head.

Alice clamped her bottom lip in her teeth, and stared at him. "And you want promotion to make up for that?"

And then he did laugh. Loudly, as if purged. "I see you attended the same diplomacy school as Weston."

"Who's Weston?"

"Never mind."

"I don't understand your position, Roger."

"Me neither. It's stupid, isn't it? But it won't let go; *especially* now he's dead. I can't change the 'Yvonne' part of my past, but I can show him that I have wings too." He realised how pathetic he must sound, and sat up straight, taking a moment to calm down. "You know the infuriating bit? I don't know who I detest more for making me do this: him or me. My motives have turned me into the very person I hate. I'm doing something like this... I'm busting my arse to be something—"

"You don't want to be?"

That capped it. Roger stopped dead as though slapped in the face with a breezeblock. His eyes were still and his jaw slack.

"You want to be a pretend manager, a phoney, a fake?"

"You know how to cheer—"

"Shut up, dammit! Stop being the jester, Roger, just for ten minutes."

Her hands were together as though in prayer, their bright red nails pointing at him, and he was tempted to say something humorous, but thought better of it.

"Put all those poignant thoughts of your dead dad to one side for a moment and think about the job you'd be doing if promotion were offered. *Think* about it! You could *actually* do it – for *you*, Roger." Alice pulled closer, tugged at his sleeve, and made him look at her. She nodded, "You could do it for you."

"I could do it for the glory, for the fame. Imagine the autograph-hunters and the magazine journos camping on my doorstep—" Alice slapped his face, and the breezeblock stopped him dead again. "Ow! You slapped me!" he laughed. "I'm your patient and you slapped me."

"You needed it."

"Do you slap all your patients?"

"Only the annoying ones."

"Do I pay extra for that?" Smiling, Roger straightened his glasses. "I thought you were supposed to be helping—"

"That's exactly what I am doing." She stood, smoothed out her tight skirt, hands flustered, attending to her well-kept hair. She opened a window and let in a rumble of traffic noise, embellished by a distant siren. The smell of Wakefield, of industry, commerce and learning, encroached into the room.

The rain had stopped, but naked trees still danced in the wind.

"Let your siblings lead their own lives, Roger. And if you want to honour your dead father, take some flowers to his grave. You can't live your life for someone else," she looked as though the thought repulsed her. "Don't waste this chance you've got trying to prove to distant relatives something that doesn't matter. Prove to yourself that you can do it." And then her face relaxed. "I think you'd be very good at it, too."

"Thanks."

"Don't do this for the wrong reasons, Roger. If you do, it'll find you out and it'll knock you off your pedestal. You can't use it to get back at your family."

Roger sat in silence. He considered her words, and in a weird kind of way he supposed, they actually made sense. "Thanks."

"That it? Thanks?"

"No, I mean it. Thanks." He reached up and held her hand. "Does this mean the nightmares will stop?"

She shrugged, didn't pull her hand away. Instead, she retook her seat and shuffled nearer, knee to knee, and she leaned forward, closing her eyes and kissed him softly for a second before withdrawing. "I don't know. We can only hope…"

"How long can we keep these visits under wraps?"

There was noise in the corridor outside Alice's office; and though it was nothing of concern, they separated. Roger stood, fingers tucked into his waistcoat pockets, admiring prints on the wall that held no interest for him. The noise was Melanie, but her voice, a length of razor wire wrapped in a soufflé, eventually faded.

"Why the paranoia about your counselling, Roger?"

"Allegedly, it has no bearing on promotion, but I think it does; I know how people's minds work, even if I don't know how mine does. Bell and his colleagues wouldn't want a SOCO Supervisor who's mental."

"You're not—"

"You know what I mean. They'd frown upon it. That's why I don't want any record of it. They dredge files from everywhere when making a promotional decision. And that's why I can't afford to have Chris finding out."

She appeared perplexed. "What's Chris got to do with it?"

Roger shook his head, "Look, it doesn't matter."

"I'll judge that, thank you. Go on."

Sighing, Roger said, "He made it plain that I'm his opposition. And something like this... well, he'd swing from the chandelier if he found out because he'd win on a technicality."

"You think he'd try to sabotage your chances?"

"You don't know how important this is to Chris."

"That's irrelevant, Roger. If you want the job, you have to pull yourself together. You can do this job better than anyone can. But you have to believe in your own ability. Otherwise you may as well retract your application and start getting some sleep again."

Her hair shone in auburn waves around her slender neck; her petite hands toyed idly with the pen as she looked at Roger. "It's about time you went shopping and bought a truckload of self-confidence."

Eventually, he grinned. "Can you get that at Asda?"

"That's the good news. The bad news is that we only have another two weeks to see each other as we please before Angus comes home."

Chapter 8

THE MAN STOOD IN the doorway, leaning against the frame, and he looked into his own private room where nobody was allowed. He listened to its silence. He observed the scruffy old school desk. It was gouged, beaten and scribbled upon. It sat beneath the small window, an equally scruffy stool nearby. By the rear wall, furthest from the window, was a comfy chair, one of those old padded things that's far too grubby for the lounge but which is far too comfortable to throw away. Its springs groaned each time he sat in it. Above the chair, three Escher prints nestled among the small room's darkest shadows.

In here it smelled of dampness; it also smelled of sweat despite the deodorant he sprayed. Most of all, it smelled of alcohol. Putting his glasses on, he came into the room, drew the thin curtains and sat on the stool in front of his desk. Towards the back of the desk was a six-inch magnifying glass with a fluorescent tube around its periphery, all mounted on a spring-loaded arm. He pulled the magnifying glass over his working area and pressed the switch. The fluorescent blinked into life.

He focused his mind, prepared himself for payback, and removed his jewellery. From a sealed box, he put on a pair of latex examination gloves, and removed a single sheet of A4 paper from a fresh ream. He folded it into quarters, then unfolded it and spread it before him.

Shit! "The bloody mask."

He screwed up the paper and tossed it aside.

From a new 3M box, he took out a facemask; the type used by workers in dusty environments, pulled it on and pinched the metal band across the nosepiece to ensure a good seal. This done, he shook his head, forcing himself to think of the details. After all, it was the details and only the details that would keep him out of jail.

A new sheet of creased paper lay before him.

From the black cotton bag, he pulled out a sealed plastic bag, and carefully took out the garment.

The illuminated magnifying glass cast a clinical light over the faded cloth. Relentlessly, he searched, pulling the material, tugging it, scrutinising it.

The light caught it, and for a moment he held his breath, brought the lens closer. He saw one hair, one single hair – complete with root. The surgical spirit sloshed around the beaker as he stirred a pair of metal tweezers. "Yes," he whispered. "I've bloody got you, you bastard." And just then, his eye slipped and he saw another hair protruding from a seam. A root on this one too.

Using the tweezers, he pulled both hairs from the garment, placed them carefully on the white paper, and folded it back up. Though he tried to keep his hands steady, they shook. A further meticulous search, lasting ten minutes, produced nothing further except a headache. It was a slim harvest, but it would be enough. It would have to be enough.

Finally, he gathered the equipment he would need, along with three pairs of latex gloves and put them all carefully inside the black cotton bag.

He put the garment inside the desk, and replaced the tweezers into the beaker of alcohol. Now he felt prepared for the event.

At last, he removed the mask and gloves, felt the nervous sweat cool his newly exposed skin, and sighed for a moment, closed his eyes and thought of the task ahead. It held nothing more for him than a slight trepidation, since he had already proved himself.

Then he ran a cold bath and lit the candles surrounding it, one at each corner.

Chapter 9

— One —

THE SCENES OF CRIME office was freezing. The heating was still dead and Roger sat alone at his desk with a thick woollen sweater on, head pulled into his shoulders, blowing breath rings through his nose. He detested working nights; sitting here waiting for the phone to make him jump, wondering what abhorrent mess the caller would send him to. Damned nights.

All was silent. The computer was blank, life signified by a blinking cursor. For once the telephone was quiet, the fax machine also, just one of many inanimate shadows in a room full of hollow stillness. The entire police station seemed asleep as though on standby, waiting for its own abhorrent mess.

It had been a long night. Roger spent the first two hours spreading dust and lifting fingerprints and footwear impressions at three domestic burglaries in the poorer districts of Wakefield, working by torchlight while the complainants stood over him with their arms folded, stern looks on silent faces, as if they blamed him for the burglary, pointing out every surface the intruder could have touched, every dirty mark they hadn't noticed until now, suddenly becoming aware of the place in which they lived. He could have written a book on the cunning of burglars. And another two on the complacency of occupants.

Roger spent a further hour at an aggravated burglary in a Normanton Post Office. He stood outside for a moment and held his breath, listening to the shrieks and wails of the Post Office staff who lived above the premises, and who were sleeping as the attack took place. Upon entering, and learning the details of the crime, his frustration grew; frustration at the people who did this, frustration at those who staggered home from the nightclubs of Wakefield, too drunk to be of any use as witnesses, and frustration at coppers walking through his damned scene. Roger screamed. Everything stopped.

They locked the doors. The officers took statements from the distraught counter staff in a back room. The examination then went smoothly. Fortunately, the burglars didn't fire a shot, and fortunately for Roger, they took their weapons with them. The burglars stole £28.10.

After leaving, Roger wondered where the burglars got their guns.

And then the long night became a quiet night. Back here at the office, he completed the associated paperwork: the fingerprint envelopes, the CJA exhibit labels, the exhibit book, the photographic paperwork and the statements to accompany the films, and then fed the Crime Information System computer with the results of his examinations. By a quarter to one in the morning, curiosity overcame him. He convinced himself that Weston was on a treasure hunt tonight, that he was digging up guns now by torchlight.

He couldn't sit in the office any longer.

The slush of dead leaves in the car park was a rigid white mass now; crisped by a sharp frost. He drove the unmarked scenes of crime van up to the wealthy end of town, to a place called Sandal, where the battle of Wakefield was fought sometime around 1490, during the Wars of the Roses. He drove past the ruins of Sandal Castle silhouetted against a dark sky, past grand houses where the councillors and the architects, the surgeons and the solicitors lived. And he tried not to think of his siblings.

Weston lived there too, able to afford splendour to an impressive degree compared to other Inspectors. Guns bought death, true; but they also bought sports cars and detached stone-built houses near medieval castles. But money never generated decorum or respectability, Roger thought.

He travelled with high expectations, but two slow drive-bys, with the van lights off, told him that Weston was home. The first showed his and his wife's cars on the drive, the last saw Weston in person in his lounge, reclining in a brown leather chair, phone to one ear, and the reflection of the TV on his reading glasses. The house was ablaze with lights; even the small attic window glowed, curtains drawn.

In a dejected mood made more so by the spreading frost, Roger drove back to the station noticing the city's drunks staggering about near the subway, and wondered if Hobnail were among them; he noticed the prostitutes loitering in the sink estates at the southern entrance to Wakefield. He passed the boarded up ABC cinema plastered in advertising posters, saw, and then smelled, the fast food shops with broken windows, junkies wobbling about outside waiting for someone to mug.

After a coffee and a natter with the Help Desk staff, he read the remnants of last Sunday's papers. Pictures of Sally Delaney and an infant looked expectantly back at him. He screwed up the newspaper and tossed it aside.

A second coffee steamed in front of him. He pondered how long the affair with Alice had been going; three and a half months, and Yvonne hadn't the slightest inkling of what was going on. You clever, *clever* adulterer, he concluded. He wondered if it was the shame he felt, rather than the cold, that made him shudder. The coffee skinned over.

Hands in his pockets, chatter in his teeth, he stared through the rippled glass and out across an empty Wood Street. The occasional taxi drove by, its headlamps illuminating powder-fine snow and the superfluous Christmas lights that still, two weeks after Christmas, swung in a light breeze.

Roger gazed into the Wakefield night. Golden floodlight bathed the cathedral's spire, and Alice's face floated before him like a ghost. Everywhere he turned this evening, she was there beckoning with a finger, lips pursed Monroe-style.

Time trickled around to one-thirty on Wednesday morning; only eight and half hours until he was back on duty and only half an hour until he dare leave the office, confident that no one would require his services at such an hour. Except maybe Alice.

But this time he wasn't looking forward to meeting her.

"Bollocks to this." Roger hung up his sweater and his waxed jacket, and buried himself in his overcoat. He collected his car keys, turned the lights off and left the building. After scraping the windscreen clear, he closed the car door and all the noises of the night fell silent. A moment later, thoughts gathered, intentions clear, he turned on the stereo to Fleetwood Mac singing *Go Your Own Way*.

Back in the dark office, the ringing telephone went unanswered.

— Two —

Alice beamed, "You're early."

"I couldn't wait any longer." Roger's response, he realised, sent out entirely the wrong signal. He trudged after Alice as she hurried along the hall, through a grand archway, and into a lounge decorated with red velvet and gilt inlay. His gaze barely left the carpet except to briefly admire her anklet, and the shape of her beneath that white silk dressing gown.

Alice shook her hair loose, and it fell in waves over her shoulders. "You randy little SOCO," she smiled.

"No, when I said I couldn't wait any longer, I meant—"

"Shall we...? Or should we begin with coffee?"

"I'm drowning with coffee."

"Something stronger perhaps, to get you in the mood. Although you sound as though you're already in the mood..." She stopped by the oak drinks cabinet. It was the size of a small wardrobe. "What's wrong?" she frowned at him.

"Nothing. No, I'm fine."

"Quiet night, was it?"

"Listen, Alice, I just wanted to say... I thought I'd come over to—"

She was on him, not in a vulgar way, but seductively. Lust drove her. He could smell brandy on her breath and tasted it on her glossy lips. She peeled off his coat, nuzzled his neck and Roger caught the odour of that same expensive perfume she always wore.

He buzzed with the thrill.

Pathetically, he attempted to fight her off and because it was so pathetic, she saw it as a preamble to foreplay, removing his waistcoat, unbuttoning his shirt, ripping off his tie. She traced a red fingernail down his chest. He said nothing.

Semi-naked he trailed her like a lost puppy across the room to a large brown leather sofa, its opulence unexceptional, even modest, in here. And whether he liked it or not, he found himself erect.

The scent of lavender candles lingered in the air, and for a moment it reminded him of Sally Delaney's bedroom. Her anklet glinted. Alice finished stripping him in a way only she seemed able. She used her teeth and her lips to free him of his garments and then beckoned him to make her naked too. He took only a second to respond. The sight of her full, rounded breasts and glistening thighs made him almost forget the guilt lying within him. Passion gripped them both but for Roger it was short lived, cold and impure.

Afterwards, the deep-seated shame, the thoughts of Yvonne and even concerns about work, slammed rudely back into his consciousness. He lay there motionless, thinking.

"Are you okay, Roger?" She wore a frown again.

He put his glasses on and folded his arms across his chest. He did not look at her.

"Talk to me," she coaxed as she tied the belt of her dressing gown.

Without a word, he climbed off the sofa, pulled his slacks on and found his socks and shoes. He looked across the room at Alice, and her piercing stare made him look away.

"Why won't you look at me?" she asked.

Reluctantly, he did.

She studied him for a moment. "It's over, isn't it?" Her voice began to rise, to take on a shrill quality. "That's what you wanted to say when you first arrived. Isn't it?"

He didn't answer. Fumbled with his fly.

"Isn't it!"

"Yes." He continued dressing, now with some urgency.

"You spineless bastard! You couldn't go through with it, could you? You didn't have the guts to call it off. Instead you left it to me to find out!"

"Alice."

"You were going to go and never come back, weren't you? How dare you use me like that?"

"Alice… I was going to have a chat with you about it. I was going to—"

"You were so convincing; all that shit about us being together, about us *staying* together."

"Now wait a minute." He pointed a finger. "It was never a permanent arrangement. You knew that and you were happy. I'm not prepared to give up—"

"You bastard—"

"You're not prepared to give up all this," he threw his arms wide, looked at the money dripping from the walls, leaking in large denominations from the stitching in the sofa, "for what I could offer you."

"I would—"

"Bollocks, Alice. I'm sorry you're hurt, I really am, but I think we both enjoyed ourselves and we should call it quits, go back to our old lives." He swallowed. "We're even."

She laughed. Cold. "Even? Even? I haven't begun to get even with you, Roger Conniston." She marched across the room and stood before him, arms like rods by her side. "Wanting to finish our relationship is one thing," she said, "but *fucking* me first? Why *was* that? Huh? Just as a reminder for when Yvonne turns her back on you? Or perhaps it was for old time's sake?"

He promptly tied his laces.

"You thought this whole thing was a sham, a put-you-on until your marriage got back on line and your ridiculous nightmares went away. Well I'm not going to be used by a waster like you as some kind of fucking sex therapist, or a fucking marriage guidance counsellor!"

"Look, I can—"

Alice leapt at him, knocked him onto the floor. Hysterical, hair a thorny nest, lips a dog's snarl; she threw a fist into his shocked face. The blow skidded from its intended target – his nose – but her thumbnail gouged across his cheek.

"Get out!" she yelled, pointing to the door. "Get out of my fucking house, now!"

For the second time that morning, he closed the car door and let the silence wash over him.

He turned the ignition and drove along the drive, the gravel crunching and popping beneath the tyres. Before he even reached the road, he decided to see Alice again; had to. Tomorrow he would finish work early somehow, get into OHU and sort this shambles out. He drove away from Alice's house.

When he reached home, Roger pulled himself awkwardly from the car, making as little noise as possible. At this hour, putting a key into a lock sounded louder than putting a brick through a window.

Avoiding the parts of the floor that creaked, he eventually entered the bedroom. He set the alarm for eight, undressed, having already checked his clothes for signs of lipstick and 'foreign' hairs, and climbed into bed, pulling the duvet tight around his shoulders. Yvonne stirred and murmured in her sleep.

The old shadows and the familiar glow of the street lamp through the curtains felt comforting. As his eyes grew accustomed to the darkness, Yvonne's silhouette acquired distinction against the white of her pillow. The sight was comforting, homely.

He determined that in future he would treat her as a woman, as his wife and not simply as an individual with an illness.

"I'll not let you down again, my love," he rubbed the graze on his cheek.

Yvonne opened her mouth to make breathing easier and quieter. Another tear dripped into her damp pillow. Tomorrow she would check his collar for lipstick and for hairs to confirm her suspicions. As Roger turned over next to her, a waft of Ysatis stung her nostrils.

Chapter 10

Wednesday 20th January 1999
0100hrs

LIGHTS OFF, HIS CAR crept over the cobbles of the back street. A faded sign proclaimed it as Thompson's Yard. Bass thumped from the Westgate nightclubs, and he could feel the vibration through his seat. The music, the shrieks and laughter of the merrymakers flooded into the car when he wound down his window. A stench of burgers and beer seeped inside too; the smell, he thought, of corruption.

Earlier it had snowed lightly, now ice formed between the cobbles, yet the women saw fit to bare as much flesh as possible without actually revealing nipple or bikini line. He stared in astonishment.

A misty layer of cloud hung low over the rooftops, pierced by the cathedral's spire two-hundred yards further up Westgate. And its flood lamps shone at the clouds' underbelly, made it look like the setting for a ghost movie. Concrete, tarmac and plate glass mingled with carved stone, cobbles and stained glass in Wakefield's blend of modern and ancient. The ambience, the lights and sounds of rowdy but controlled youthfulness, created an atmosphere conducive to his quest: uninhibited, spontaneous even.

Queues were forming at mobile burger bars, and the pizza- and kebab houses were filling up. More people were emerging from nightclubs than entering them. The streets throbbed with jostling bodies, hot and sweaty from their exploits on the dance floors. Laughter was everywhere, drunkenness followed it around, and then the police followed that around too.

The nose of his car edged from under the Thompson's Yard archway. From here he could see the brawl at Biggles' doorstep across the street. Fists flying, blood spraying onto white shirts, polished shoes scuffed. Police were there in seconds, and battle scarred bouncers gave assistance with filling their liveried transport.

He noted just how many sexy women there were around, flaunting themselves.

They're all the bloody same, he thought. Nothing has changed since my youth except the clothing covers less. And they wonder why they get raped and murdered.

He looked around those buildings he could see for signs of closed circuit television. Just below the gutter line of the building adjoining Biggles, one camera. Of course, there would be others, certainly one on the front of The Imperial Bank to his right. If he stayed where he was, however, the shade of the arch would conceal him from the camera facing him, and he wouldn't even be seen—

"Are you a taxi?"

He jumped and then caught his breath.

Leaning in, almost touching his face with hers, was a blonde whose smile at his obvious shock, caused him to stutter, "Christ. I wish I was, dear." She leaned further in and even in the half-light beneath the archway, he could see straight down her flimsy white top and out the other side to her tight black jeans. To his delight, she wore no bra.

"Aw," she cooed, "my friends are staying out all night again but I have to be up for work tomorrow. It'll be ages before a taxi comes," she winked. "Actually, I was hoping you could give me a... ride."

"Where do you live?" His nails dug into the steering wheel, heart racing.

The blonde didn't answer. Instead, she hurried around to the passenger side, wobbling her chest on purpose, and grinning as she closed the door. "Ooh, it's freezing out there," she rubbed her arms briskly and smiled across at him. "Nice and warm in here, though."

Once inside, he quickly appraised her, and his situation. She was drunk, fine; he had no problem with that. In fact, if he was hoping to accomplish anything at all tonight, then it was a help that she was. Anyway, he acknowledged, would she have jumped in a stranger's car with sex on her mind if she were sober? She was cute. He guessed she was maybe twenty, twenty-one, roughly the same age as Sally Delaney, only not in the same league at all.

"What's your name?"

"Nicky," she smiled.

"Well, Nicky," he followed her curves again just to make sure she was real, "where *do* you live?"

"Barnstones Estate. It's just off Aberford Road actually, near Pinderfields."

That was all he needed for the time being. He looked around, flipped the car into reverse and pulled slowly further up into the shade of the archway.

"Aren't you going the wrong way?" she said with a tipsy smile.

"I just don't want people to see us. I mean, they may get the wrong idea. A young girl hitching a lift with a bloke she doesn't even know. They might think I'm a murderer or something," he joked.

"People won't know anything of the sort. I'm not out very often. No one actually knows me, except my friends, that is."

He could not have chosen a better candidate if he'd read her CV.

"Anyway," she hiccupped, "they'd probably think you're my uncle come to give his niece a lift home." Together they laughed. "Because, do you know how many weirdos are out there? Every fourth person is a weirdo, actually; let me tell you, it's true. It's a fact. I read it somewhere. There are more weirdos kicking about than you think. Can you imagine how many weirdos are running the country? How many are treating you in hospital?"

He made no reply.

"Frightened? You bet your arse I'm frightened. I mean, through that arch, there must be six or eight police cars with two coppers per car..."

He thought of the police. Swallowed.

"...that means there are... well, there's loads of 'em, at least a car-full."

"It makes you—"

"One in four," she pondered. "You can't be too careful. Well, that's what my brother keeps telling me, actually."

"Your brother?" He slowed the car's retreat.

"Yeah, I live in his house."

He brought the car to a halt. "And he's waiting for you?"

"No, no, silly. He's in London, lives there. I just rent his house from him. It's not much of a rent though, because he says I'm doing him a favour by looking after it while he's away. Suppose I am, really, aren't I? I mean if he—"

"You're a wonderful person, Nicky." The car continued uphill again, but its retreat was thwarted. A car rumbled down Thompson's Yard towards the archway, towards his car. Reflecting from the rear-view mirror, a pair of headlamps painted a white rectangle across his face. They flashed at him, blinding him. "Can't they see I'm trying to go—"

"You'll have to go out through the arch," Nicky said.

The car behind flashed its main beam again and then the horn sounded. He began to feel flustered, agitated. Panic touched him. "You'll have to get down, Nicky; I mean I don't want anyone to get the wrong idea."

"What do you mean, I'll have to get down?" she giggled suggestively.

"No, no. I mean you'll just have to bend over so that you're not seen. I wouldn't want anyone to think..." His words stalled; she ran her tongue delectably over her upper lip. Then without another word, Nicky bent low in the passenger seat.

The car rolled forward out into the bright lights of Westgate. He was right; there *was* a camera to his right, far above him, and another pair of cameras constantly monitored things up and down the street from their vantage point over the bank's main entrance.

He turned on the headlights and pulled out onto the road, looking around all the time, yet trying to be inconspicuous. The street was busy even for this hour; traffic buoyant, noisy with music and affluent with speed. Police vehicles were in abundance, marking their presence on the corners of Westgate, casting shaded eyes over the throng of youth. Some had their windows down, eyeing-up or talking to girls who dared to stop for a chat. Either way, he thought, they're paying no particular attention to me: just a middle-aged male, in an average car, proceeding at a modest speed with no one else on board.

When he turned left at the end of Westgate, right at the traffic lights on Northgate, and over the roundabout onto Aberford Road, he invited Nicky to sit back up. She grunted as though nearly asleep, and then sat up obediently. He liked that, because it lent to him a feeling of power over her, the passenger no one knew he had.

Flashing orange lights of a lorry sparkled up near the hospital. As they neared, he saw it was a gritter, scattering rock salt on the road. He slowed down and kept his distance.

"You've got strange eyes," she said thoughtfully.

He said nothing, only watched the blinking orange lights.

"So, what's your name, then?" she slurred.

"You're drunk, aren't you? I bet you stopped drinking when you were tipsy, but it's catching you up, isn't it?"

"Hmm," she sniggered, "Actually, I think you're probably right! And it feels good, too. I may even have a swifty when we get home." She appeared slightly confused, and then nudged him with her elbow. "Did I say swifty, then?" He nodded and she laughed again. "How presumptuous of me." Slowly the laughter drooped into fits of giggling but her perpetual smile remained. "Anyway," she said, "stop changing the subject, what's your name, Mister Mister?"

He thought about it. "Roger," he said. "You can call me Roger."

"Oh yeah? And what does everyone else call you?"

He looked across, snatched glances at her. "Why? What do you mean?"

"Hey," she giggled, "I'm only kidding."

"Oh," he said, relieved.

"Roger. Are you jolly?"

"What?"

"It's a joke, silly. Jolly Roger?"

"Very good," he said. "Very funny."

"Oh, Roger. And what does my chauffeur do for a living?"

"Nothing exciting really. What about you?"

"I asked first."

"You'd better tell me where you live, Nicky. I know you said near the hospital, but where exactly."

"Oh, sorry. It's over there. We passed the actual turning already. I'm sorry, I was too busy chatting, I suppose."

He pulled the car to a halt and saw the gritter disappear over the crest of a hill. He reversed into Pinderfields entrance and re-entered the main road. "Potter Lane?" he asked without any hint of the frustration or the nerves he felt.

"Yes, yes. That's the one. Potter Lane. Forty-two to be precisely-type-thingy. Hic!"

"No problem. And what was it you said you did for a living, Nicky?"

"I'm a bank clerk, that's all. Nothing very glamorous, I'm afraid, but I suppose it pays the bills, you know."

He turned down Potter Lane and drew the car to a halt beneath the cover of a willow tree. On both sides of the road were large grassed areas populated intermittently by trees, and a tiny, unlit playground. Further down the hill, perhaps a quarter of a mile, the houses tipped gradually into a form of slight disarray before finally giving onto the council-owned Barnstones Estate, a community that thrived in the mining days.

"Why are we stopping?"

"Well, Nicky, I don't know about you, but I need some fresh air. And I could do with a little exercise, you know, to ward off that tired feeling and bring me round a bit."

Nicky surprised him when she said nothing, just opened her door and climbed out.

He got out too, locked the car and saw Nicky tottering off down the street without him, her arms wrapped in an embrace against the cold. He didn't shout because it wasn't worth the risk, but instead plodded quickly after her. "Nicky, Nicky, wait." He caught her and gently took hold of her arm.

She spun around, staring coldly at him. "I've got pride, Roger. I actually know when I'm being given the brush-off."

"Whoa, whoa, Nicky. This is no brush-off, dear. I meant what I said; I need some air and a stroll. I need to wake up a bit, that's all."

She squinted up at him. "You sure?" Breath clouded before her.

"Take me to your house, some coffee wouldn't go amiss."

Nicky's smile reappeared and she walked unaided, though still shakily, down the hill to her house for the last time. The sky was a clear and desolate black. No breeze blew and all was still.

As they strolled down the path towards Nicky's side door, the security light came on and lit up the whole driveway and next door's house as if they had their own private patch of daylight. Silently, he cursed and walked ahead of her so she partly shielded him from the street. A shiver ran up his back and his concern returned to Nicky's hand as it tried to get her key into the lock. He felt like shouting at her to hurry the fuck up and get inside, but he forced himself to remain calm, taking long slow breaths. Over her shoulder, he looked around the cul-de-sac; only a few lights were visible, and no curtains twitched.

"At last," Nicky said, hopping up the step into the short hallway between the kitchen to her left and the lounge on her right. "You go make yourself at home, Roger, and I'll fix us a drink."

"Just coffee for me, please," he said.

"Oh, go on. Have a vodka. I love vodka."

"I'll stick to the coffee. Don't forget," he said with a sickly smile, "I'm driving."

"You er, don't fancy staying the night?"

"See how it goes, eh. Just coffee for now."

"Okay." She winked. "I suppose it could actually work to my advantage, if you know what I mean."

"I know what you mean." With his elbow, he turned on the light switch and assessed the lounge, its floor covering, and even the fabric of the sofa, revising and amending his plan as he went along. He chose not to sit down, but he did choose to step out of his shoes by the fire and lay his folded coat carefully over them, being aware, even at this stage, of leaving fibres and footwear evidence. He couldn't know if her bedroom was carpeted or whether it had that same fake wooden flooring the kitchen had.

He patted the bulge in his hip pocket.

The lounge was small but sparsely furnished, giving it a more spacious appearance, despite an abundance of whale and dolphin posters. A glass-topped coffee table took centre stage. A small TV stood in one corner near to a mini stereo. In the magazine rack were copies of *Bella*, *Hello* and a mail order catalogue, no TV magazines or newspapers.

From the kitchen, a cupboard door closed, a teaspoon rattled in a mug, milk bottles clinked, and Nicky mumbled something and giggled.

At the back of the lounge, a pair of curtains drew his attention. He pulled one aside to reveal French doors looking out onto a small overgrown garden that hadn't seen a mower for a couple of seasons. Frost glimmered white on the long grass and the nettles illuminated by the sliver of lounge light. Beyond the broken wooden fence at the foot of the garden, was total darkness. He let the curtain swing back over the doors, and turned around. Opposite was the staircase winding tightly away into the shadows.

So far, so good, he thought. He fumbled with the small package.

Nicky reappeared with a tumbler of vodka and a steaming mug of coffee. "Why don't you sit down?" she asked.

He gestured at the stairs, "Well, I thought…"

Nicky grew excited. "You are an eager beaver, aren't you?" She thudded his mug onto the coffee table hard enough to spill its contents down her hand and onto the glass. "Oops." She licked her fingers, sucked them. "Clumsy me." Then she downed her vodka, hissing as it stung her throat.

"Come on, sexpot." She hurried to the threadbare stairs and climbed them two at a time; peering under her arm to make sure he followed.

He followed.

As he ascended, he could see up her white top, and watched, almost mesmerised, as her breasts oscillated beneath their gossamer shroud. At the head of the stairs, she turned left down a pokey little landing. Two steps later, she stopped and twisted a dimmer switch just enough to illuminate what was a small but tidy room with a double bed beneath a dark, curtained window. The only other furniture was a single wardrobe, a cheap metal-framed chair, and a four-drawer chest with a white-framed mirror and a scattering of cosmetics.

Nicky pulled the curtains open and turned slowly around to face him. She drew the flimsy top up over her head and exposed her breasts. "Let me take your clothes off."

"No," he snapped. And then, "I'm sorry. I prefer to strip quick and watch you strip slow, is what I meant to say."

"Fine by me."

Her smooth skin, embellished with subtle touches of make-up, her dark eyes edged with mascara and her full lips coloured a deep red, looked oh-so inviting to him, but still he kept his distance as she unbuckled and let fall her black jeans. She wore no underwear.

"Come on, Roger, you're lagging behind, you know."

"I know, I know."

"Actually, I could give you a hand?"

"No."

"Aw." Nicky was disappointed, but undeterred; she became even bolder in her attempts to coax him from his apparent shyness. Her fingers glided around her chest, stroked her thighs; her expression changed as her eyes closed, and she uttered a groan of pleasure.

The dull twinge in his crotch grew only to a tepid erection, but he knew that control was essential. "Lay down, Nicky."

"That's more like it," she said, eagerly bouncing onto the bed like a kid until she settled down on her back.

"Draw the curtains, will you?" he asked.

"You *are* shy, aren't you?"

"Mind if I turn down the light some more?" he said.

"No, go for it. I sometimes leave the curtains open and the light on when I'm getting undressed or when I feel like a little solo fun; I dunno, it sort of adds excitement wondering if there's someone outside actually watching. Well, it does it for me every time." She pulled the curtains closed again.

While Nicky's back was turned, he fumbled in his pocket and from a plastic bag, pulled a pair of latex gloves. He quietly slipped them on, and using the back of a finger, twisted the light switch until the darkness intensified, creating deeper shadows.

She was back on the bed. "Hurry up, Roger," she teased. He could hear her groaning. "I'm waiting."

He turned around and shuffled to the side of the bed. Being careful not to brush against the chair, and minimising contact with the duvet, he stood at her right side and watched as she tugged at her erect nipples. Her legs moved erotically back and forth, supplying glimpses of the delight held between them. She groaned. He licked his lips, but took no further notice.

"Okay," he whispered, "I'm going to undress now, Nicky."

"'Bout time, too."

"Now, I want you to put your hands over your eyes for me," his voice quivered only slightly.

"Aw, I want to watch. You watched me," she reminded him.

"I'm shy, Nicky. Please, just while I undress."

She tutted and then obliged.

"That's better," he said, and then wished he'd brought a plastic smock, just in case things became messy. Hands behind his back, he silently pulled out the blade concealed within the knife's handle.

"I can't hear you."

"I'm working up to it. Any second now." His breathing became rapid, shallow. With great deliberation, he reached over her. He raised the small knife towards her left ear.

Nicky's hands began to slip. She tried to peek.

He thrust the blade into the meat of her neck, having to fight her thrashing arms. A steaming gush of black fluid pumped from her throat, soaking his gloved hand and the pillow, flowing like hot mud across the bed. He could see steam.

She arched her back. Her eyes pleaded with him, and even in the half-light, he could see the look of misunderstanding, of misplaced trust in her eyes. She gasped for air, swallowed and then began choking on her own lifeblood.

For only a short while did her arms and legs continue thrashing but not once did she catch hold of him or his clothes or even go near the embedded knife. She seemed afraid to go near it; preferring to accept whatever lay before her than risk finding out what was causing the pain and the encroaching blackness.

As the life seeped from her, he could see the opaque glaze of death growing on her half-opened eyes like ice crystals forming on glass. Now who's got weird eyes, he thought. The sound of her final breath, a burble of air in thick liquid, left her body and suddenly the room was silent save for his own hushed breathing.

Now began the clear-minded process of departure, while leaving behind nothing of himself, nothing that could incriminate him. He removed the gloves, the hot liquid that covered them already beginning to cool, and laid them on the quilt as if he'd done this a hundred times before.

From his coat downstairs, he took out his glasses, unfolded their arms and put them on. He retrieved a black cotton bag and from it took two fresh pairs of latex gloves, a pair of sterile disposable tweezers, a plastic bag and the small white paper package. Returning upstairs, he pulled on a new pair of latex gloves and while holding his breath, used the tweezers to place the contents of the paper package into the mound of her damp pubic area.

He stepped away from the bed, exhaled and took a moment to recover a little of his composure. His mouth was dry.

Kneeling beside her, he took out a new disposable pen and wrote 'Roger 710961' on the back of her left hand. From Nicky's equally neat bathroom, he used a dampened face cloth and rubbed most of the writing off again, leaving only the slightest trace in the creases of her skin. He returned to the bathroom, wrung out the cloth and then wiped the tap from which he had drawn the water, free of the faint bloody streaks.

He tried to swallow, but his throat clacked.

For the last time he entered her bedroom, folded the plastic bag inside out, used it as a sheath to withdraw the penknife from Nicky's neck, closed the blade, and pulled the bag the right way out again. With care, he slid the face cloth in and his first pair of dripping, bloody gloves, followed by the tweezers and the paper. Then he pulled off his current soiled gloves, pushed them in also and sealed the bag's end. Nicky's blood smeared his right thumb and the bag's inner surface.

Without blinking, he put his third and final pair of latex gloves on. Everything then went inside the black cotton bag. He smoothed out the creases on the bedclothes where he had laid his instruments, looked around to make sure he had left no traces of himself behind and then exited, turning off the light with a nudge of a gloved finger.

Quietly, he lumbered back down the threadbare stairs, being careful not to trip during his unsteady descent. For a while – it must have been at least a minute – he stood in the lounge, aware that he was alone, but strangely sensing a companion of sorts, a dead companion, maybe.

Should have brought a smock, he thought, noticing fine droplets of blood on his shirt. But how could he have unfolded it and put it on in silence, he reasoned, without her hearing him.

It had all gone according to plan, just as he'd imagined it would in all the rehearsals in his mind.

He put the black cotton bag and its scarlet contents on the floor, stepped into his shoes and took the gloves off so he could tie the laces. Next, he put his coat back on and was about to bend and retrieve the black cotton bag and the gloves, when he saw the mug. He allowed himself a brief moment to calm down, slurped a drink of warm coffee to moisten his parched mouth and his clacking throat, and then carried the mug into the kitchen. He knocked off the light switch with his elbow and poured the remainder of the coffee down the sink, using the light from the streetlamp outside to see by. He used a tea towel to cover his left hand and turned on the tap, rinsed out the mug, and still using the towel, opened a few cupboard doors, found the correct one and put the mug away.

As he entered the short hallway, he noticed the heating thermostat and though it wasn't in the original plan, he switched on the heating to warm the place up. He knew this would extend the window of error surrounding her estimated time of death by making the body cool down slower than it would naturally.

Before collecting the black cotton bag from the lounge, he removed his glasses, folded their arms and tucked them away into his breast pocket. And then he stopped, had a last look around, found Nicky's keys and let himself out. The air was refreshingly cold and he felt pleased to note that things out here were still quiet, quieter even, if that was possible. There were no police cars, no barking Alsatians slavering all over his Hush Puppies, no helicopter overhead, its searchlight pinning him to the doorstep. It was as dark as a power cut and quiet as a corpse. The sky was an endless black. Orion peered down on him.

And when he turned, closed and locked the door, the security light over Nicky's door clicked on and saturated the driveway with a white brilliance. He walked away, taking the long route back to his car. He laughed as he walked.

At last, he was sitting in the tepid warmth of his car beneath the willow tree, looking at the passenger seat and retracing the route his eyes had taken as they trailed over her curves earlier that night.

He started the engine, checked his rear view mirror, indicated, and pulled out onto the road.

At 02.15 on Wednesday morning, he closed his garage door and prepared a small bonfire. The plastic bag and its gruesome contents joined his coat, trousers and shirt in the flames. At three, he extinguished the smouldering ashes and, clad now in an old boiler suit, packaged the charred remains into an old shoebox. Then he brought his car into the garage, vacuumed the foot wells and seats. Finally, he cleaned the offside and nearside external and internal surfaces of the car, being careful not to forget the seat belt buckle.

After all this, he locked the shoebox in the boot of his car. On the way to work, he would visit at a restaurant or some other establishment with large wheelie bins outside, and dump his ever-so-private waste in there.

Business attended to, he thought.

At four o'clock, he climbed into bed and slept until six.

Chapter 11

At 6.10am, Yvonne could stand the pain no longer. In frustration she threw back the covers and bit down on a scream as her skinny legs tipped out of bed; and she gradually stood upright, reluctant to let go of the bed, looking like a woman testing to see if the floor would take her weight. Part of the scream escaped anyway, but Roger slept through it. During the night, her right knee had locked solid, and the pain had increased with every thud of her heart. She knew that when eventually the knee cracked free, it would be as if someone had taken a swing with a lump hammer.

She saw herself reflected in the mirrors on the wardrobe doors. The frown, the narrowed eyes, the bags beneath them. "Not pretty. You look like shit," she said, and then her image drifted out of focus. Into focus came Roger; his uncontrollable mop of hair sprouting from the quilt. An arm floated over the edge of the bed.

They had an arrangement: when he anticipated being late home, he would ring and leave a message on the machine. Should she wake up at three or four in the morning worried by the unusual amount of space she had, she would check the machine for messages. But last night she didn't need to check the machine because last night she didn't sleep; the ceiling and the gentle swaying of the curtains entertained her mind, as did the luminous clock on Roger's nightstand and the incessant throbbing in her knees.

There was no call, no message. And seeing how there was no sleep either, Yvonne elected to call him at the office and then on his mobile to see how he was doing. And was she surprised when he didn't answer? Well, yes, she was, at first. Suppose he could've been busy or had left his phone in the van but...

When he finally did come home, smelling of perfume, she solved the puzzle.

Yvonne made it to the bathroom and then downstairs. On her way through the lounge, she stopped in front the 10x8 of their wedding day. How pretty she looked back then without the need for makeup, and how... young. No bags, legs in fine working order. How much in love she was. All smiles, all love, all promises.

All broken.

In the kitchen, she grabbed the kettle, almost threw it into the sink and wrenched the tap on. Water sprayed off the lid, soaked her nightie and splashed across the floor. "Fuck!" she yelled.

Roger woke as downstairs the kettle switched off.

He noticed Yvonne was up already, and then headed for the bathroom. He sat on the toilet seat, waiting for the bath to fill. He added bubble bath, sat down again and sighed. The Fleetwood Mac song from last night floated around his mind.

The bath filled, he checked the temperature and then turned off the taps.

"Coffee, Roger!"

"Coming." Dressed in boxer shorts, he scooted down the stairs and entered the lounge as Yvonne struggled into her seat.

"Bath's ready."

"Coffee's in the kitchen." She didn't even look up, merely dropped her makeup bag on the floor beside her chair.

He went back into the lounge, sat opposite her, rested his coffee on a convenient shelf in the bookcase and nervously ran fingers through his hair.

"Got a bit rough did she?"

"Sorry?" And then his hand went to his cheek. "Oh, this. I told her if she did it again I wouldn't pay her." He grinned, rubbed his glasses on the leg of his shorts.

"Roger, my body may be disabled, but I promise you my eyes and my mind are still in good working order." Her stare remained hard. "Please, don't lie to me, and whatever you do, don't patronise me."

"Yvonne, I... I was only kidding, for God's sake."

She raised her eyebrows.

"Oh come on; since when could I afford a prostitute?" He couldn't help it; he burst out laughing.

Yvonne did not. "Careful, now."

His laughter settled, and eventually stopped completely, about the same time that he stopped looking at her and started looking at the carpet. He continued rubbing his glasses. "I don't know what all the fuss is about, Yvonne. I was at a burglary where the intruders had broken a kitchen window, see." He sipped the coffee and began miming. "You would have laughed – well, maybe you wouldn't – I powdered the outside and then put my head through the broken window to look for..."

Yvonne folded her arms. "Now, is this a lie or are you patronising me?"

"Neither!" His reaction was so good that he almost convinced himself.

"Carry on."

"Well," he became unsettled and tripped over his words. "I, well, as I was saying, I poked my head through... and there was this piece of glass protruding from the frame..."

"Yes?"

"Well, that's about all really. I cut my cheek on it."

"Oh really?"

"Yes, really."

She still appeared unimpressed.

Roger grew desperate. "That's how I cut my fingers, remember, lifting broken glass?"

"And since when did you use your face to lift broken glass?"

"Oh, how droll."

"Where was this burglary?"

"Why?"

"Where?"

"Castleford. Just a domestic burglary in Castleford."

"You'll rub the lenses through to nothing if you don't stop now." She stared at him. "Did you know, apart from cleaning powder off your glasses, you only ever clean them when you're lying?"

"Hmph."

"Hmph, indeed. Maybe it's so that you can't see properly, so that your eyes don't give away the fact that you're lying." She smiled at him, but it was surgical. *Knowing.*

He put his glasses back on and folded his arms, still not looking at her.

"What time was this?"

He picked up his coffee again, needing to hold something. "I don't know, half-one, two-ish. Why?"

"Such an urgent job was it? Couldn't leave it for the day staff?"

"No, well, you see, they wanted to board it up—"

"I see. So, let me get this straight; you're definitely not lying to me, and...you're *definitely* not patronising me?"

"Yvonne? What's the matter? Your bath will be getting—"

"Sod the bath!" She threw the plate of half-eaten toast at the wall next to his chair. It shattered, and both stared at the fragments. The toast clung to her needlework stretched taut on its wooden frame. She scowled at him.

"You were not at the office after one-thirty last night. Your mobile was switched off after one-thirty last night. A simple domestic burglary would have been left for the day staff. Should I continue?"

Roger looked stunned. Couldn't think of a reply. His jaw hung slack.

"Even you wouldn't be so clumsy as to cut your face on glass. And anyway, am I to assume that expensive perfume had been sprayed around these premises? To be even more patronising," she said, "should I assume that on the way back to the office, perhaps, you were accosted by several females who needed a flat tyre changing and one of them happened to work in a cosmetics shop and just happened to have a free sample on her which you thought you'd try out to see if I cared for the aroma, and so rush out this morning and by me thirty fucking pounds worth!"

Roger thought for a moment. "Now you're being silly, Yvonne."

"I might've run out of plates, Roger, but I still have a cup in my hand."

"You'll get tea on your tapestry."

"Watch it, Roger. Don't be flippant."

Any thought of approaching this with humour finally keeled over and died. His face straightened.

And that's when Yvonne put down her tea and stood. She limped over to the 10x8 wedding photo. Roger opened his mouth to speak, but nothing came out as she took the photograph down. She stared at it for a brief moment and then walked to the kitchen door.

"Yvonne?"

She bent down, grunting and puffing, and carefully placed the picture, smile side out, upright against the doorframe.

"What are you...?" Roger stood and he almost managed a step towards her before she took the edge of the door in both hands and slammed it. Glass exploded, gold-painted wood splintered and the door bounced back, its handle banged against the wall.

Yvonne turned, staring at him. "Tell me," was all she said.

"That," he pointed, "it was our—"

"I know what it was," she shouted, "and if you don't tell me, I'll put your nuts in there next time!"

"What do you want me to say?"

"Take a wild fucking guess. What do I want you to say! Hell, Roger, the bastard truth might be a good place to start. What d'ya think?"

"I've broken it off." The words just tumbled out of his loose mouth.

Her eyes sparkled at the discovery. Or was it the beginning of hatred? "Aha. Now we're getting somewhere. So, you're starting at the present and working your way cautiously into the past, am I right?"

"Yes, Yvonne. You're right!" Defeated, he flopped down in the chair. "This cut on my cheek... I've broken it off. She was none too pleased."

"Were you going to leave me for her? Is she married and was she going to elope with you?"

"No, I was not going to leave, and I can't answer for her."

"She was, wasn't she? She was disappointed; that's why she came at you."

"I don't know, no, yes. I don't know."

"How long has it been going on for? And I want, no, I *need* to know the truth, Roger." Yvonne looked at the broken glass, then turned and hobbled back to her seat.

"Three months or thereabouts."

"Do I know her?"

"No!"

She actually laughed at him. "Why so astonished, I do know police officers, Roger. Sometimes some of them even stop here for a cup of tea."

"I know they do. She's not a police officer."

Yvonne drained her cup. "Don't worry," she said, "I'm not going to throw it at you. I merely wondered if you would fill it up for me."

He grasped the cup, but she did not let go. Their eyes met, and she held his gaze this time.

"I knew you were lying."

"I... You said already: the glasses, right?"

"And because you stopped reminding me to take my tablets."

Just for a moment, Roger Conniston wanted to be someone else, anyone else, just as long as he didn't have to endure this awful feeling any longer. He felt like a drunk who just ran over some kid's puppy.

"I think you should leave, Roger."

"But..."

"But what?"

But I haven't made your cup of tea yet, he thought, and then hated himself even more. He stared at her for a long time, and noticed she'd already put makeup on again. "I've been stupid. I'm truly ashamed of myself, Yvonne."

Even though he wasn't on duty until ten o'clock, he showered and dressed ready for work, selecting one of three identical pairs of navy blue slacks, a blue shirt with crisply ironed sleeves and a crumpled torso, his only tie, faded grey with aluminium powder embedded in the material, and his burgundy waistcoat. He was coming down the stairs when Yvonne shouted for him to take his toiletries and spare clothes with him. He stopped on the stairs, rocking, nearly falling forward with the impact of the words.

No humour occurred to him now.

Nothing would ever be the same again, he thought.

Chapter 12

— One —

CHRIS ARRIVED EARLY AT the office. Today he felt fine. Today, he felt in charge.

A rape had come in overnight and officers were still guarding the scene. He allotted the job to Jon who expressed his dislike by slamming the office door in Chris's face. Tough, he thought, someone has to do it.

Now it was time he got to know his new member of staff a little better, and he told himself it had nothing to do with Roger quietly suggesting he had a talk to him and reassure him. "Bring your coffee over here, Paul. Come on, pull up a pew and have a chat with your boss." He rolled the sleeves of his grey cardigan up, creasing the brown suede elbow pads.

"Have I done something wrong, Chris?"

"I don't know, have you?"

"Well, not as far as I know. I mean, I began to fingerprint some recovered property before I'd photographed it, but seriously, I think that's about all."

"Well then, you've done nothing wrong. And," he sipped his coffee, "if you *had* done something wrong, we'd talk about it, help you avoid the same error again."

"I know. I guess I'm just a worrier."

"I don't like errors, it must be said; I demand a high standard from my team and that includes thoroughness and accountability beyond reproach. There's only one way of doing that: be professional. Tell me, if something comes along and you're not sure how to handle it, do you have a go, or do you seek help?"

"Well, I think I—"

"Think? Come on, Paul. What *would* you do?"

He tugged at his purple tie. "I'd follow my intuition. I'd do what I thought was right."

Chris saw something spark in the lad that impressed him. He was enthusiastic. "Good. So would I."

Paul's relief was evident. His hand went to his tie again.

Chris aimed to make himself approachable to Paul, but spoke firmly, laying down his own methodology and expectations. It was important that he had Paul on side, important that he could take orders, but think for himself too. "Right, sit back, sit back and tell me your worries, your aims or whatever else you want to talk about."

Paul thought for a while and then said, "I've set certain goals for myself. I thought I'd encounter these things fairly quickly, but—"

"Like what?"

"I want to do a post-mortem. I want to photograph a night-time RTA. And there's all the complex stuff: murders, rapes, you know. I don't want to let anyone down."

"I have a feeling that you'll do just fine, Paul. I like the zest you have. Wish more people had it. And I wish you'd mentioned the rape earlier, you could've gone along with Jon." Maybe not, he thought. He banged the coffee cup on his desk, "How about a fresh one?"

Paul nodded, stood and reached for the cup.

"No, I'll do it," Chris said. "Fair's fair." He grabbed the cups and then asked, "Is there any piece of kit you're not sure of? The ESLA perhaps, or the fingerprint camera?" The fingerprint camera was difficult to use – and it was guaranteed that new staff would struggle with it.

"Ah, yeah. That was a nightmare, awful thing, that. Couldn't grasp it."

"Go get it from the van. I'll fix the drinks, and we'll practise. How's that sound?"

They found a scrunched up newspaper in the bin, and taped it to the floor around the office doorframe, put masks and gloves on. Chris stood back with his arms folded, "Go on then, let's see your technique."

Using black powder and an old squirrel brush, Paul examined the office doorframe, and developed a quantity of marks. Black powder fell in clouds onto the paper, onto the surrounding floor and all across Paul's shirtsleeves. "That's it, apply it liberally," Chris boomed. "Okay, get a clean brush and gently – you know how fragile a black-powder mark is – brush along the ridge detail, just try to clean the mark up a bit before we photo it."

Paul took off the gloves and under Chris's guidance, loaded film into the cumbersome fixed-focus fingerprint camera, and then prepared some blue labels. The labels had spaces for information that should be caught on film alongside the mark it was meant to identify: the name of the SOCO, the mark number, its location and the date.

"Let's add a touch of realism here," Chris said.

"How do you mean?"

"Okay, you're at a rape scene, you're all suited up, the pressure's on to bring home some top-notch evidence. The SIO is tapping his fingers waiting to see what you find. Imagine this is a lounge doorframe, or a bedroom doorframe. Yes, a bedroom doorframe. Er, let's say you've photo'd another eight marks so far, we'll make this one number nine," he said, and Paul wrote out the label. "Okay, good. Don't bother with the date for this exercise, but up in the top right hand corner, yes, that's fine, write B/W."

"B/W?"

"Yeah, it's just to let the Photographic Studio know we've used black powder so they can make a diapositive."

Paul sighed and gave away his ignorance.

"When you powder with aluminium or white powders, they can simply photograph the mark and ship it through to the Fingerprint Bureau as it is for them to search, but when you use black powders, or sometimes when you photograph marks in grease or in blood, they have to make a double negative so as to correct the troughs of the fingerprint into peaks and visa versa. Get it?"

"Yeah, I think so; I wish it would all just click into place, though."

"It will, it will. Anyway, that's a diapositive."

"Shall I do the honours?"

"Be my guest." Chris put his reading glasses on and studied the developed marks carefully, checking them with a pocket magnifying glass, and pointed to the ones he deemed good enough to warrant all this trouble; those marks where he could see sixteen clear ridge detail characteristics. "It's a standard imposed by the courts. Find sixteen," he said, "and no one can challenge that fingerprint – it belongs without doubt to the suspect."

Paul stuck the blue label alongside the ridge detail of Chris's selected fingerprint. "It's just strange that there's no viewfinder on this thing."

"The beauty of fixed focus. Get the mark and the label inside that metal framework, and you've cracked it. "Okay, got it on f16, 125th shutter speed?"

"Yup."

"Go on, then. Go on."

He pressed the shutter release. The small flash popped, the camera clicked and Paul waited for some sign, some kind of approval. Chris eventually nodded and Paul relaxed.

"Well," said Chris, "what exactly was so tricky about that?"

"That was good. In fact I quite enjoyed it."

"Good. Right, I'll develop it and we'll see how well it worked, shall we?"

"Fancy another coffee?"

Paul sat before the computer, watching as the Open Incidents screen unfolded real life, real-time stories of domestic violence, damage to motor vehicles, minor road traffic accidents, and reports of theft, shoplifting, and burglary. He was so engrossed by what he saw that he almost screamed when the door banged open and a police officer stormed into the room like a truck with no brakes.

"Where's Chris Hutchinson?"

He had skew-whiff eyes, Paul noticed. "Er, in the darkroom."

"Who was on late turn last night? As if I need to ask."

"I don't know. I'd er, I'd have to look at the duties."

"Look at the duties!" he barked. "Don't you know your duty roster by now, lad?"

"Well," he quivered, "I've only been here a few weeks—"

"So look at the damned roster, then," the officer snarled at Paul.

Paul leapt from the seat, circled wide around the office, nervous of the officer and his uncoordinated eyes, and quickly thumbed through the roster trying not to look at all that gold jewellery. He must be the Bulldog I've heard them all talking about, Paul thought. "It was…it was—"

"Conniston?"

Paul looked at him, "Yes, it was Roger. He was on duty until—"

"Two. At least he was *supposed* to be on duty until two." The Bulldog marched to the corner of the office and banged on the darkroom door. "Chris? How long you going to be?"

"Give me a bloody minute, will you!"

Paul stood perfectly still, hands behind his back, avoiding the Bulldog's eyes.

"What exactly are you doing here?"

"Well, I work here—"

"I mean with the black powder, stupid."

"Training exercise. Chris is developing the negatives now."

The officer's eyes skimmed the blackened doorframe, and then he looked closer. He bent over and he looked very close.

Chris held the film up to the light. Water cascaded down the strip of celluloid and then slowed to a casual drip from his fingers. He moved the film along, glancing at- and then studying each frame closer. The results were satisfactory. Each one had developed perfectly, bore superb ridge detail and more importantly, each one had a completed label on it.

Paul had done well.

Between his fingers, Chris squeezed as much water from its surface as he could before hooking it, weighed down at the bottom, into the drying cabinet next to another strip of negatives. Eventually, he opened the door to the office and flooded the small hot room with the dazzling white light. Before him stood Inspector Weston, arms folded, agitated – as usual.

"Put the kettle on, Paul. I believe Inspector Weston takes his coffee black." He turned to Weston and said, "Colin, social call?"

"The night sergeant left a note on my desk. I don't like walking into this kind of shit first thing on a morning. A fatal occurred last night, and I think you may be able to help with my enquiries."

Chris caught his breath. "In what way?"

"I've already established that Conniston was supposed to be working last night when this smash came in—"

"Accident? Road accident?"

"Yes, road accident. What did you think I was talking about?"

"Go on with your, er... enquiry."

"At one-thirty-four, an RTA came in at Lofthouse at which a mother and child died. Despite attempts to locate Conniston, he could not be found. The Traffic sergeant had to turn out another, more reliable SOCO from Morley to do his work. Not only did this cost road-closure time and officers' time at the scene, *and* recovery garage time, but it made this Division look foolish!" Weston's well-upholstered jowls reddened and his eyes narrowed to threatening slits. It was only Paul handing him a steaming mug of black coffee, and Chris beckoning him to sit, that calmed him.

"Well, it's not like Roger to go AWOL. I expect there was a good reason for him not being here."

"Not good enough as far as I'm concerned." Gold rings clinked against the mug.

"All I can say is that I am really sorry for any inconvenience. I *really* am; the last thing I want to do is sour relations between our departments, and of course I'll be asking some searching questions when he shows up this morning."

"When does he come on?"

"Ten o'clock."

"I'll be back when he gets in. I want some input into this meeting." Weston slurped coffee, grimaced, and then stood. "Next time," he glared at Paul, "don't give me coffee with aluminium powder floating on it or I'll snap your pissing legs." He stormed out every bit as quickly as he had stormed in, cursing, "Fucking civvies," as he went.

An uncomfortable silence fell on the office before Paul asked, "Are my negatives ready yet?"

"I'll get them." Chris peered at Weston's steaming mug. "You should turn the cups upside down after you wash them out. The air's always full of powder in here. You'll learn," he said, walking away. "Second nature to us." He was about to refill the kettle when he heard his name grate over the Tannoy in Sergeant Potts' rough voice. Chris stopped dead. He seemed as worried as a man about to have all his teeth removed without anaesthetic.

Paul was about to ask if he was feeling okay, but he daren't. Chris left the office without a word, and Paul returned to the Open Incidents computer, and had read each story before Chris came back in. And if Paul hadn't seen Chris's teeth as he sighed into his chair, he would have said that he *looked* like a man who'd just had all his teeth removed without anaesthetic.

— Two —

Roger locked the car door, saw the green checked bag on the backseat and wondered how long he would have to live out of it. Like the weather, life was perpetual greyness. He looked around, expecting to see Hobnail waving him over from somewhere near the main gate, but he wasn't around today; having a sleep-in, maybe. And he wondered if this was how Hobnail had begun his career as a vagrant. It didn't make him feel any better. But, would anything? He approached the magnetically operated doors and swiped his ID card through the adjacent reader.

As he crossed the threshold into the office, he saw smears of black powder, like deep shadows on the floor by the doorframe. Chris was in his chair, eyes unfocused, staring off into the distance; fingers laced together tightly until the knuckles were white. His face was white too and he looked a dozen years older, slumped in his chair like a man made of rubber. A copy of *The Racing Post* was folded on his desk, reading glasses open on the cover.

What's up with you, he thought, being Big Cheese leaving a bad taste today, is it? Whatever it is, bet I can beat it, my old pal. He hoped Yvonne was okay.

Paul was sitting at his desk staring forlornly at a strip of negatives and cradling a cup in his hands. There was a nasty edge to the office this morning, and Roger felt like turning right around and leaving again. "Much on?"

"Jon has it under control." His eyes came back into the office, he blinked and turned to Paul, "Go up to Sunways, there should be a couple of cars that need examining."

"But—"

"Do as I say!"

Paul set his cup down, grabbed a set of van keys and left.

Roger took off his coat, and slung it around the back of his chair. "I said he needed your guidance, not a—" Chris just looked at him.

Chris said nothing.

"Should I borrow a stab vest?"

"Get an extra thick one, especially around the back." Now Chris swivelled his chair around to face him, and folded his arms.

"Someone filled your toothpaste tube with badger shit?"

"Never mind me; you've got the Bulldog coming towards you at sixty miles an hour."

"What am I supposed to have done now?" Roger kicked his forensic kit and then bit down on his lip. "I'm pissed off this morning already, I don't—"

"No, you don't need any more crap. *I* don't need any more crap!" A malicious stare smacked Roger full in the face, and then it was gone.

"I don't follow," he said walking to the kettle.

"Well, you can tell *me* what's going on, or you can wait," Chris glanced at his watch, "for another three minutes and tell Weston all about it. He's after your balls. Sounds to me as though he'll get them, too."

"Is this because he has none of his own?"

"It seems your absence last night has landed him in a little hot water."

Roger busied himself with the coffee, making no attempt at a reply.

It was all Chris needed. "Listen Roger, sometimes we all knock off ten minutes early if it's slack, but you knocked-off half an hour early."

Roger heard the kettle click, but ignored it and instead thudded into his chair, waiting for Chris to begin. He squeezed the bridge of his nose and wished today would just fuck off and leave him alone.

"Hey, you didn't go cruising again—"

"No," Roger gave him a reproachful look. "No, I didn't." He hooked his thumbs into his waistcoat pockets and waited for the knives to fly.

"They were trying to reach you for an RTA, but couldn't find you." Chris sighed, "Go on, then; where were you?"

Roger was about to clean his glasses, but drummed his fingers on the desk instead. "I went home. It was quiet, and to be honest I didn't feel too good, so I thought I would slope off."

"Is that why you didn't book out?"

He nodded.

"When Weston gets here, you'll just have to take it. I mean, we can say you were unwell...but he won't like it. And since you told no one you were leaving..."

"I know."

He didn't have to wait long; Weston punched his way through the door like a pound of nitro-glycerine. He only stopped when he reached Roger. "Where the *fuck* were you last night!" Spittle flew. "You were supposed to be on duty in this police station, or on the other end of a fucking phone—"

Roger's mouth fell open.

"That's enough," Chris said. "If you want to come here and interview my staff then you will do it in the proper manner. You will not use foul language and you will not raise your voice."

Weston took a step back, the fury still bubbling. "If you were on my rota, I'd kick your—"

"Well, I'm not on your sodding rota. And yes, I'm a civvy bastard; so go on, get it out of your system and then we can sort this out." Roger's heart nestled somewhere in his groin and he pressed his fingers into his waistcoat so no one could see his hands shaking.

Weston leaned forward, inches away from him. "When police officers did your job, they had respect—"

"When police officers did my job, they did it wrong."

"Watch your mouth, Rog. I don't care where we are or whose company we're in." He leaned closer, brought the stench of old cigar smoke right up to Roger's nose, "I'll pull your fucking tongue out and then feed it to you. Got it?"

"Why do some coppers think we're the enemy?"

"Because you are."

Roger tried to smile. He couldn't manage it.

Weston straightened. "Where were you at 0134 hours?"

"On my way home," Roger croaked.

"Why?"

"Ill."

"Did you report your 'illness' before you left?"

"Mr Weston—"

"Inspector Weston, to you!"

"*Inspector* Weston," Roger tried again, "if you have a complaint about my behaviour, I request that you take it up with my line manager, so that he may deal with the matter in the appropriate way."

He pointed to Chris, "You're gettin' a minute sheet about this." Then he left the office, cursing civvies, and shouting, "Lazy idle waistcoat wearing civvy bastard."

Roger turned to Chris, "I like my waistcoat. Do you like my waistcoat?"

"You know he'll go straight to Denis Bell, don't you?"

Though he still shook, relief pumped through Roger as his heart clambered back into his chest. "That's what I'm worried about."

"Yeah, well, I think there was a personal element to that attack, don't you?"

"Oh, you noticed," Roger said through a laugh.

"Maybe if you left him alone…"

"He'd leave me alone? Don't think so. Anyway, I can't leave him alone. He's scum, Chris; the man is scum."

Twenty minutes later, when a little colour had returned to his face, Roger stirred the drinks and laughed. "Did you see the black powder on Weston's hands? It'll be all over his white shirt and his face in no time."

"Talking of faces," Chris said, "what happened to yours?"

"I was an inch from having my tongue pulled out and fed to me and you wonder why I'm pale."

"The scratch?"

"Oh that. Gardening accident."

"In winter?"

"No, I only have a garden in summer," Roger said.

Chris stared. "Right."

Roger stirred the drinks some more, cheeks throbbing as he ground his teeth. "Thanks for that, by the way."

"For what?"

"For not capitalising on a... on a lapse of duty."

Roger sat at his desk, thumbs again in his waistcoat pockets, trying to gauge Chris's mood. It was foul and had been from the moment Roger came into the office. But he didn't know why it was foul. Surely, it had nothing to do with Weston; that was gone now, passed an hour ago. There was something else. "You okay?" Chris's mood was an important factor when it came to asking for time off.

"No."

"What? Weston?"

"He's a prat. I ignore him."

"Wish I could." Roger contemplated leaving the subject and just asking for the favour he had in mind. But he couldn't. "You know, if I can..." he took a breath and just said it. "Do you want me to help you?"

Chris turned in his seat, dragged his wrist beneath his nose and eyed Roger with a curiosity reserved for intellectual dunces. "Beg your paradox."

"I knew I'd offend you. Forget it, I didn't mean."

"You really want to help me?"

"What's bothering you? You're twitchy as a hare these days; seem to be on your guard all the time."

"My corns hurt."

"Fine." Roger turned away.

Chris straightened in his chair, cleared his throat and then swept his greying hair down the side of his head the way a teddy boy would. "Actually, I *could* use your help."

"Shoot."

"I'm struggling, if you must know. My car tax is due, I've got a mound of fucking bills at home... I'm stuck, Roger. Till payday, I mean; I'll be hunky dory after pay day." He smiled warmly, and Roger could feel the heat of embarrassment from ten yards away, could see the squirm. "What is it they say? Why is there so much month left at the end of the money?" He laughed as though it was nothing.

But Roger could see it was more than nothing.

And this presented Roger with another problem: how to help a friend out with a loan when he would be sleeping next to smelly old Hobnail tonight, watching every penny for when the maintenance payment was due. "How much do you need?"

"I don't like to ask—"

Roger waved the protest aside. "Don't worry about it; I have a favour to ask in return."

"I'm already into you for twenty quid."

"You're into me for forty quid, Chris, but don't worry about it. How much?"

"Three hundred."

Roger closed his eyes. How the hell was he going to explain that to Yvonne? She really would think he was seeing a prostitute then.

"I know it's a lot," his voice was quiet, shame brought the volume right down, and his eyes came down with it. "I wouldn't ask, only I'm living like a tramp as it is just now."

"I'll help if I can; might not be three hundred though."

"Anything..." And then Chris looked up, pointed at Roger. "Shit, speaking of tramps, that pet of yours, Hobnail, pulled me again this morning—"

"I *told* him not to bother—"

"He stopped me to pass on a message to you."

"Oh yeah? What's he say?"

"He needs to speak to you urgently," Chris said, "wouldn't tell me what it was about."

"Where?"

"He didn't say. I thought he'd wait for you like he always does."

"When was this?"

"When I came in to work, about 7.30 this morning. He said he'd been trying to get hold of you all week."

Roger wore a pensive look; it went well with his troubled heart and his solemn thoughts. Apart from Yvonne, all he could think of was Hobnail. Maybe he was ill and needed someone to get him to the hospital; it would explain why he hadn't been there when Roger came into work.

Chris asked, "Why do they call him Hobnail?"

"He wore hobnail boots for twenty years as a miner. Even wore them out of work, down the club, shopping, out playing football, everywhere. Now he wears old trainers, has done for years, but the name stuck." He resumed his thoughts.

"Go on," Chris said, "you've got twenty minutes. Go see if you can find him."

There was the slightest chink of sun fighting through the tarmac-coloured sky in Wakefield centre: Hobnail's stomping ground. Eventually the cloud won and the sun retreated. The multi-layered greyness matched Roger's mood as he stretched his long legs through the busy streets, avoiding the crowded footpaths and walking on the gritted roads, his long raincoat floating out behind him like Dracula's cape, the tuft of black hair bouncing on his head with each elongated stride.

This was Roger's patch too; this was his city and he knew it very well. Wakefield was compact, and at a brisk pace, one could walk north to south through its very centre in just fourteen minutes, twelve minutes east to west.

He checked the municipal bins around the back of The Ridings shopping centre and those behind the Burger King in the precinct, and the small brick alcove in the bank of air-conditioning units behind Boots where the homeless gathered.

With watering eyes, he walked the periphery of the Bull Ring. He walked slowly past people huddled on benches, while above them on the ornate lampposts, posters advertising Wakefield's second Rhubarb Festival flapped in the wind like trapped birds. He peered into the Black Rock pub, named as a tribute to Wakefield's mining past, and The Fleece, and finally The Joker, on his way back into the office.

Hobnail was missing.

Back in the office, still desperate to know what had become of Hobnail but unable to do much about it, Roger got on with the business of asking for a favour. "I don't suppose this is a good time to ask for a couple of hours off this afternoon, is it Chris?" He bowed with his hands together in prayer.

"You've got more neck than a bloody giraffe. Go on, enlighten me, what's it for?"

"It's another of Yvonne's appointments. I said—"

"Yeah, of course you can." Chris's face straightened, "Just one thing puzzles me, why didn't you tell Weston that Yvonne was poorly and that you had to leave early? Maybe he would have been more lenient on you."

Roger said, "I couldn't use her illness as an excuse or an alibi; I'd rather take the shafting, I think."

"Very noble."

— Three —

At last, the SOCO office was empty. This was good.

He worked quickly. He found a roll of rubber lifting tape in the store cupboard they kept by the door. He snatched a length. It made a sound like ripping paper. He took the lifting tape to the doorframe, glanced down at the covering of black powder and searched for the fingertips, the ones that were easy to spot.

There they were. The tiny scars along all four fingers. He smiled and stuck the free end of the lifting tape to the doorframe and smoothed it across the prints.

He crouched, peered and then smiled. All was good. Gently, he peeled away the tape and the black ridge detail parted from the doorframe. He lifted the tape up to the light, and briefly inspected the fingerprints. They looked fine to him. Once he'd mounted the lift onto an acetate sheet, he slid it into his back pocket.

Next, he walked over to Roger's desk, inserted a house key past a crusty old Mars bar, and into Roger's jacket pocket. Then he forced them through the lining, ripping the fabric inside.

The scene was set. Now all he had to do was wait. Wait and forget the details.

Chapter 13

"XW to 2894, receiving?"

Micky wound down the window of his patrol car, flicked his cigarette into a large puddle, and put aside thoughts of a full breakfast in a bread cake. "2894, go ahead."

"2894, just received a report of a misper who hasn't shown in at work today. Are you available to check it out, please?"

Micky's mouth fell open. "XW from 2894, isn't this taking the nanny-state thing a bit too far?"

"2894, 10-20 that, but there is reason for concern." There was a distinct edge to the operator's voice. "A colleague of hers noted her absence and is at the misper's address now. There's no sign of life there and the misper is not known as a prankster. Are you in a position to check this out? Over."

"I'm en-route to take a statement. Is no one else free? Over."

"Negative. You're it."

I'm it, I'm it. I'm always frigging 'it'. Micky sighed into the mike. "10-20, pass details."

Micky drew up to the house on Potter Lane and noticed a Rover parked on the drive, a lone woman at the wheel. She got out and was approaching before Micky had even turned the engine off. "XW from 2894, 10-6, over."

"2894, 10-6, 10-20."

Reluctantly, he climbed from his warm patrol car and sauntered towards the ashen-faced young woman. He forced himself to smile, despite the rumbling from his stomach.

The woman, dressed in a dark suit, introduced herself as Joanne Philips from The Imperial Bank on Westgate. She said that Nicky was rarely late to work, "And if ever she was, she would always ring in. We all went into town last night for a knees-up; it was the Assistant Manager's birthday—"

"Miss Philips," Micky interrupted, irritated by the tale already and still eager to visit his favourite greasy spoon, "are you sure that she didn't stay at someone else's house last night and perhaps felt too hung over—"

"No!" Miss Philips shouted. "Sorry," she said.

Micky nodded.

"She left earlier than the rest of us, she's not a big drinker." She followed Micky round to the front of the semi where, unusually, the kitchen was located. "I mean she was tipsy, maybe even a little drunk, but she wasn't slaughtered or anything like that."

Micky didn't appreciate her choice of words. The curtains were open. "What time did she go out last night?"

"I'm not sure."

"Roughly."

"Sometime before seven, I don't really know."

"That helps," Micky said sarcastically. He shielded the kitchen window with a hand but could see nothing of note.

"We all met at Yates's around seven, but I don't know what time she left home; I mean, she could have gone for a drink before..." Miss Philips followed him around to the side of the house. "She's a good kid, and well, all I'm saying is that this is so out of character."

Micky grunted and peered through the letterbox, the leather kit on his utility belt creaking as he bent. He saw nothing out of the ordinary, certainly no signs of disturbance. He could smell nothing odd either. "Well, I'll file a Missing Person's report," he straightened up, "but I don't see that there's a whole lot more we can do."

"How about looking round the back, there might be a broken window or something."

Without a word, but cursing inside his head, Micky unlatched the wooden gate between the house and the concrete garage, and headed a few steps into the back garden. Surrounding the knee-high weeds and scruffy, yellowing grass was an old fence, broken and orange with fungi. "No," he said, "there's no sign of disturbance here either; look, no tracks across the... lawn. The curtains are all drawn tight upstairs." Before she could respond, he was heading back around the front and hopefully back to the comfort of his patrol car.

She scurried after him and then overtook him, held onto his arm and brought him to a halt. "But—"

"There are no signs of disturbance anywhere," he said, too firmly, "and you have to admit, she's a young girl out on the town last night and, well, she could have stayed at someone's house and maybe she feels a little too tired to come in, or maybe," he winked, "she's still enjoying herself."

Miss Philips erupted. "I beg your fucking pardon!"

Micky stepped back, hands outstretched, "Look—"

"She's a good kid and *I'm* concerned for her safety, even if *you're* not. And I don't think you're taking this as seriously as your sergeant would like you to take it."

"You want me to break the door in, don't you?"

"How perceptive."

Ouch, thought Micky. Again, he bent to the letterbox and shouted, "Hello, in there. This is the police, would you please respond?" Nothing. There was nothing but dead silence. He looked up at Miss Philips. "Really, breaking down her door is a bit drastic when she might show up at any time."

Miss Philips's voice grew louder, "Would you please be a hero for once in your life and break down the door for me?"

"Hey," Micky danced backward, "I can't just go around kicking in people's doors, despite what you might see on TV—"

"Listen, I'll accept responsibility for the damage, I promise. I'll pay for it all."

Micky admired her. "This goes against all the rules, Miss Philips."

"I know," she whispered, "but I stand by my promise."

"Okay," he stood back, "here goes." He aimed his boot at the upright below the mortise lock, and kicked. Two more blows and the door crashed in; shards of white-painted doorframe scattered around the tiny hallway, but the glass remained intact.

Miss Philips beat him to the entrance and was in the hall before he grabbed her gently by the arm. "Now listen," he said, "I've done you a favour, you do me one, eh? Let me have a look round first, and I'll come and get you. I promise too." She reluctantly agreed and Micky left her on the doorstep. He didn't bother checking the kitchen; it was small and appeared in order from outside, and anyway he knew Miss Philips would crane her neck while he searched the rest of the house. "Oh, and don't touch anything," he called back.

When he entered, a wave of heat prickled his face.

The daytime noises drifted away as he carefully walked through into the lounge, eyes flicking left and right, and even behind the door, glancing at the ceiling where the centre light still shone. He touched the long low radiator against the back wall and got burned fingers for his trouble. "Bastard," he said, shaking his hand. "Why put the fucking heating on so high," he whispered. "Is she fucking anaemic or something?" He felt clammy under the arms, and shuddered as rolling sweat tickled down his back.

Satisfied that the lounge was all clear, he took to the stairs, noticing that the bare bulb hanging from the ceiling was on too. The drawn curtains over the large landing window were thick, and despite the light bulb, it was like twilight in here.

He checked the bathroom, then the smaller of the two bedrooms. All was in order. Slowly now, he walked across the landing towards the master bedroom. It was even hotter up here and tiny beads of sweat congregated beneath Micky's wide eyes. The floorboards creaked.

"Can I come up, yet?"

Micky jumped, "Fuck!" he whispered. "Not yet, Miss Philips," he called back, maintaining a friendly tone.

He listened at the closed door of the master bedroom. Deathly silence greeted him. Micky turned the handle.

She decided to go up anyway.

Her way lit by a naked bulb dangling from a flex high above her head, she mounted the stairs. And as she neared the top, the heat became almost intolerable; her head prickled and her throat glistened. Everything was quiet. Eerie.

Joanne looked left and saw the officer disappear into the darkness of Nicky's room, and silently followed. There was a slit of daylight between the drawn curtains, and it shone directly onto the bed beneath it. She could pick out individual shapes among Nicky's bedroom furniture, the wardrobe, chest of drawers and chair, and only a moment passed before she saw the darkness on the bed surrounding a small naked body.

Her world spun into a heat haze and she fell backwards onto the threadbare landing carpet.

Chapter 14

— One —

IT WAS WEDNESDAY 12.30; Chris lowered his head and took a large bite from his burger. He chewed and swallowed hurriedly as the phone rang. Wiping a hand across his shining lips, he picked it up. Meat juice trickled down his chin and landed with a splat in the centre pages of his Racing Post.

"Log number? Right, I'll print it off and we'll head out. Oh, who's SIO? Right, right. Well who's deputy SIO, then? Yep, okay. I'll be taking Paul with me. Okay." Chris replaced the receiver and said, "Better chew and drink fast, Paul. That's your last meal for a while." More juice dripped onto his cardigan.

Before Chris could satisfy Paul's curiosity, Roger strode into the office and declared there had been another murder. "They're wondering if it's connected with the one on Turner Avenue."

"Why's that?" Paul stammered.

"Both young females—"

"No comparison," Chris blurted out. He swigged tea. "Look where they happened, Roger: Turner Avenue and Potter Lane. It's like comparing Beirut with Florida."

"Potter Lane's near the Barnstones Estate, Chris, and that's like the Turners in places. Rough as a bear's arse. And they both happened indoors; both women lived alone. They're seriously considering them being the start of a serial."

"Anyway, we'll soon see. Won't we, Paul?" Chris wiped his hands down his trousers.

"Yeah," was all Paul could say.

"You're not concerned about contamination?"

He screwed the burger wrapper up, dragged a sleeve through the grease on his chin. "I think we're safe on that score. But thank you. Anyway, it's on my patch and I'm going."

"It's your call," Roger said. "You still okay with me having a couple of hours off?"

"Go for it. The job would be easier with you *and* Paul, but I think we'll cope. You go and look after your lady, and give her my best, won't you?"

"Course I will, and thanks, I appreciate it."

It was raining again when Chris climbed from the MIV. He instructed Paul to set up the camera equipment, and sought the deputy SIO. "And don't forget to sterilise the tripod's feet," he called over his shoulder. "And then document the fact."

Shelby, in the end found Chris. "Did you come via Brighton?"

"Traffic was—"

"Never mind," Shelby smiled. "I took the liberty of commencing a scene log and erecting barrier tape, Chris," he said, "though if you need it moving—"

"It's fine, thanks. Saved me a stack of bloody time, it has." Both men ducked beneath the tape and strolled towards the house, getting a feel for the job, summarily casting a glance over the windows and doors for anything obvious. "What's it all about then?"

"I've got to say, Chris, this is a peculiar one."

Shelby pulled up the collar of his big camel hair coat, something all detectives of Shelby's generation seemed to wear. Maybe it was part of the entrance criteria, Chris wondered.

"The girl, Nicky Bridgestock, has no enemies that we know of, and she's clean as a whistle as far as drugs and men go.

We've run her details through all our systems: bugger all. And according to her friend," he flipped open a small black book and scanned the scribbles on the last page, "Miss Joanne Philips, Nicky is a really good girl, rarely goes out, though she did last night, and..." Shelby paused, closed the book, "Well, she's the typical girl-next-door."

"So how did she die?"

"Dunno; I've not even been inside yet. You know me with scenes like this. I stay clear if there's a chance of contamination. I won't go in until you guys have put stepping plates down and I'm wearing a silly-suit."

Chris offered a wry smile, "But you're already wearing a silly suit."

Shelby feigned dismay. "Don't let my wife hear you say that."

"Go on, then. What have we got?"

"Micky Harris forced entry since Miss Philips was concerned by Nicky's absence from work."

"And?"

"According to Micky, she's got a big hole in her head or her neck; he didn't want to get too close. And Miss Philips was having a fit on the floor behind him so he didn't have the chance anyway, he says."

"Right."

"Nicky seems to have come to a rather sticky end, starkers on her bed with a gunshot wound or similar, to her head. So far, all I can say is that she was out clubbing last night, left early because she was up for work the next morning – told you she was Miss Prim-and-Proper – but didn't show in because of the massive headache she had this morning. Don't yet know who did it or why."

"No forced entry?"

"Won't know until the PM."

"No, I meant the doors or the windows."

"Ah. No, they're all in order, no damage at all, except Micky's."

"Have we pronounced life extinct yet?"

"Doctor Rahall's on his way; shouldn't be more than a few minutes."

"Paul," Chris called, "get the gunshot residue kits to hand, will you?"

"We don't *know* it's a gunshot wound," Shelby pointed out. "I mean, none of the neighbours we spoke to heard a bang of any description, we're only going on what Micky saw in her dark bedroom."

"Preparation is nine-tenths of the game."

"Fair enough," Shelby said. "I'll get out of your way and let you get on. Though if anything shows up, let me know, okay."

"You can come and have a butchers yourself when we get the stepping plates down, only be twenty minutes. Oh," he clicked his fingers, "have you sorted a pathologist yet?"

"All in hand."

"Not that prat, Dwight Thistlethwaite-Smythe or whatever his bloody name is?"

"Bellington Wainwright? Yes, it is," Shelby said.

"And Jacob Cooper, is he aware?"

"Yes, the Coroner's Officer is aware. I'm reasonably up on these things, Chris."

"It might be worth putting a ballistics expert and a biologist on standby."

"It's not amateur night, y'know."

"Point taken. Right, if you'll excuse me, I'll get suited up now and go and play."

"By the way, I thought Roger was working today."

"He is, but he didn't fancy coming out to this for some reason."

"Oh. Why?"

"Don't know," Chris said. "Anyway, it'll give young Paul there an insight into how to do the job properly."

Shelby walked away shouting, "Back soon for a look around then, Chris."

— Two —

Kensington Road, an upmarket street in St John's, not far away from HQ, was where the Occupational Health Unit had its base. Roger sat outside in his car watching the wipers flick back and forth, oblivious to the wind as it rocked and jostled him; hurling leaves and long-dead tin cans down the pavement. Pink Floyd played *Comfortably Numb* again, quietly in the background.

He had two important things spinning in his mind.

Hobnail wasn't missing after all. On the way out of Ward Street car park just ten minutes ago, Roger had almost knocked him over. His mind, he told Hobnail, was working on other things. But what Hobnail had said in reply blew him over, sent his thoughts skittering down avenues not previously hoped for. His brain worked on Hobnail's news like it was all-consuming. It was good news. In a way.

But it would have to wait until later for full consideration, until Roger had attended to the other thing on his mind. He closed the car door against the force of the wind, and then allowed it to blow him towards OHU's glass fronted reception. Inside the reception area, Melanie busied herself with files and invoices, yet she stopped her work when Roger politely coughed.

"She's out."

"Her car's outside."

"She's still out." Melanie went back to her invoices.

"Why so hostile?"

"I know what you did to Al—"

"Come through, Roger." Alice stood in her office doorway, arms folded.

As Roger sat, Alice closed the door and stood before him, business-like. The atmosphere, so calming the last time he was here, felt unfriendly, and there was a distinct chill in the air. "I hope that you're here for professional reasons."

"I wanted to apologise for the other night," Roger said.

"How sodding gracious of you. Would you like to bend me over the desk while you're here, just as a PS to last night?"

"I am truly sorry for not coming clean with you when I first got to your house, but I wasn't strong enough to just come right out and finish it; I...I still have feelings for you."

"I shall do my best not to shout, here. Are you intimating that you would like to recommence our relationship?"

"No," he said quickly, "no, I'm not saying that. I'm saying that I handled it badly and would like to apologise for that. I still think we have no future together."

"You used me in the most repulsive of ways, and for that, I'm not sure I can forgive you." Her eyes were dark, menacing, and her pale lips a tight line on an unemotional façade.

"I can understand that, Alice. I came here to say I'm sorry; to say I'm *genuinely* sorry, and that I hope I can still come to you with my problems."

Alice sat opposite him, this time with the desk between them, still business-like but with arrogance attached. "I accept your apology, whatever the motive behind it is, but I will never forgive you. You know that, don't you?"

"I am sorry—"

"Stop saying you're sorry; you're beginning to annoy me," she said. "As far as our professional sessions are concerned, I will continue to counsel you for your own good. I want you to know that I could refer you to another counsellor, but it would mean you starting from scratch again, and I don't think that would benefit you at all."

"That's very kind."

"No, it is not." She stood again. "Above all, I am a professional, and I could not let something of a personal nature interfere with my professionalism, no matter how intense that 'nature' once was. When you next come to see me, neither of us will mention anything relating to our previous out-of-hours experiences together; it will be purely to help you with the nightmares adversely affecting your bid for promotion. Is that clear?"

"Yes, Alice, that's very, very clear."

"Now, if that's all, I am busy."

Roger left the office, closing the door behind him. He didn't stay to chat with Melanie, who ignored him anyway. He just quietly left and let his concerns drift over towards Yvonne.

Alice left it five minutes and then called, "Melanie, bring me Roger Conniston's file, will you?"

"Okay, Alice."

"I have a few backdated entries to make."

— Three —

Doctor Rahall pronounced life extinct; he saw no reason to move the body, merely felt for a pulse and studied the girl's eyes. Nothing else was needed. He couldn't give more than a very loose approximation of the time of death because of the heat. It slowed the body's rate of cooling and therefore made any measured body temperature uncertain. It seemed to him, however, that rigor had only recently begun to set in, and "that usually happens about twelve hours after death," he said. "The air temperature is almost thirty degrees. I'll make a note of it and of the body temperature, and file it for the pathologist. Okay?"

Chris instructed Paul to seize the doctor's scene suit as an exhibit, and then turned the heating down. Cursing and sweating, he opened as many windows as he could without risking loss of evidence. But he could still see the heat haze wafting off the bedroom radiator.

And now, dressed in their white scene suits, white overshoes, facemasks and latex gloves, they stood on stepping plates and leaned over Nicky Bridgestock's body. Chris peered at the girl's white face, studied its features as he would a natural history exhibit. "Right," he turned to Paul, "can't take any more photos at this stage. We'll take some after the body has gone."

"So what's next, Chris?"

"Well, it's perfectly clear that she hasn't had her head blown off, so we can forget the gunshot residue kits. She's been stabbed in the left side of her neck."

"How many times?"

"Just once."

"Go on, then, enlighten me."

"Come round here and I'll show you."

Paul did, being careful not to disturb anything lying on the floor, especially the girl's underwear.

"You see she's been stabbed in the first quarter of her throat, that's where the carotid artery runs. The carotid artery supplies the brain with blood, which is pumped under tremendous pressure directly from the heart. Now," he pointed at the wall beside Nicky's head, "see all the blood, how it has spurted from the neck in ever decreasing arcs across the wallpaper?"

"Yeah," Paul said.

"That's arterial bleeding. She's been stabbed once because we can see only one initial, or primary, arc. See? All the ones below it are subsidiaries of it. They're decreasing because her blood pressure's dropping all the time." He swept a finger through imaginary arcs, dropping it a couple of inches each time. "If there had been more than one penetration into the neck then we could expect to see separate arcs, like tiny teardrops, created by the knife, or whatever, as it was pulled out, leaving behind its own small track on the wall. That's called cast-off spray. This is the art of blood spatter interpretation and something you could expect to pay hundreds to the labs for."

"But seriously, couldn't you tell she'd only been stabbed once because she only has one puncture wound?"

Chris blinked. "That as well." He straightened. "Anyway, until we begin hacking and slashing in the mortuary, it's still unclear how many times she's been stabbed. There's too much blood around to see the wounds clearly." He checked his watch. "Okay, come on, it's twenty past three and there's work afoot. I want to take you right through this scene and on to the mortuary if I can. But we'll have to get a move on. So, go grab a body bag, two or three acetates and some poly bags for her head, hands and feet. Oh, and some adhesive tape. And some string."

They peeled Nicky's head away from blood-soaked pillow, noting how the blood beneath her was still in its slimy stage while the exposed blood on the bed and that caught in her hair was dry and as flaky as dandruff. Chris held the head clear of the pillow while Paul slipped the plastic bag over and then pulled it down before tying it around her neck with string that glistened red.

"You okay?"

Even with a mask to hide behind, Paul looked queasy. "I still feel seriously too hot, that's all."

"You're not going to puke, are you? Tell me you're not going to throw."

"No, I'll be fine."

"We'll take a breather soon."

Both changed gloves, throwing their old pairs into a black bin liner that was already half full of empty film boxes and cellophane wrappers. Next, they tied bags around her stiffening hands and cold, clammy feet.

"Right," Chris said, "tapings next, I think."

"Shouldn't we wait until the pathologist gets here?"

"Yes, we should. Shouldn't have bagged her head either, but we have things to do, and we can't wait around all bloody day for him to finish his round of golf. Anyway, when he gets here, he'll ask if we've taped the body, so we may as well get on with it."

They completed the tapings, twelve in all: two for each limb and four for the trunk: two front and two back. "Okay, go and ask Shelby where the bloody Exhibits Officer and Pathologist are?"

"Right."

"I'm gonna start taping the inside of the body bag."

Paul stopped and turned. "Why?"

Though he didn't have the time to educate him on every point, Chris told him anyway. Knowledge belonged to all, he remembered. "If we find any hairs on her at the mortuary that don't belong on her, where could they have come from?"

"From the murderer," Paul said.

"Correct. But they could also have come from Mrs Bloggs in China or bloody Japan, or wherever it is they get this cheap crap from, whose job it is to inspect these bags and then fold them into the nice neat little square of black plastic you've just unwrapped. See?"

Chris knelt beside the bag and half-heartedly dabbed sticky tape around its inner surface. His attention was yanked from the task by noise on the stairs, of scene suits crackling, latex-clad hands creaking on the banister. Chris stood with anger in his eyes as Shelby and the Pathologist entered, the Exhibits Officer behind them, and a couple of DCs behind her. Paul was last in, standing out of the way. Chris said, "Please tell me none of you used the banister on your way up here?" He looked at the ensemble. "Well?"

"We might have grazed it," one of the DCs said, eyes squinting in a grin.

Chris recognised those eyes; it was Haynes, the dick from Sally Delaney's PM. "Don't you know anything, *anything*, about murder scenes?"

Haynes looked away.

Chris screamed to everyone, "Touch nothing! This is my bloody scene and you go nowhere unless I or the DI say so. And just to make sure we understand each other: keep your bloody hands by your sides!"

"But we all have gloves on," Haynes said.

"Whoopee-fucking-do."

"Chris, that's enough," Shelby warned.

He glared between Shelby and Haynes. "Sorry." And then, just for the officer's benefit, "What happens to the murderer's fingerprint, which is made of nothing more substantial, nothing stronger, than oil and water, when a clumsy—" he checked his language, "when a clumsy soul like you drags his hand, his *gloved* hand, right through the centre of it?"

"I'm sorry," Haynes said. "I'll bear that in mind."

"Super," Chris said. "Super."

Everyone remained quiet, successfully chastened. Bellington Wainwright inspected the body, made scribbles on a dog-eared note pad of the blood distribution patterns on the wall, and of the body's position and surroundings. "No Conniston today?" he asked Chris.

"He has other commitments."

Wainwright seemed pleased that he was absent. He took the names and designations of those present, then asked Chris, "Have the tapings been done?"

"Yes. And head and hands bagged, and scaled photos of the blood on the wall and the bed, and photos of her clothing..." Chris trailed off, bored by the man.

"And we taped the body bag, too!" Paul chipped in; hoping to sound like an old hand.

"Of course, your blood splatter photos won't be perpendicular." Wainwright stated.

"We'll be doing them again when the body's gone and when we can pull the bed away from the wall." Chris's gloves creaked as he clenched his fists.

"Good. Splendid." Wainwright studiously – and slowly – took measurements, made more notes and peered at the girl's fingernails through the crinkling plastic bags. He ignored Chris's constant and rude sighing. "Do you think," he turned to Shelby, "that we could arrange the PM for about seven-ish?"

DC Clements, a slip of a girl with hair the colour of ginger biscuits and with Chanel No. 5 leaking into the room, perked the place up a bit and helped Paul to bag up the girl's belongings, which included her black jeans, flimsy white top, several sets of underwear lying across a chair, more underwear on the floor, and her shoes. They took further photos of the room now Nicky had been taken away, including the pools of blood she had left behind, and the duvet with its indented mark. Then DC Clements bagged that too, and with some regret on Paul's part, left the scene, taking her fragrance with her.

Within fifteen minutes, they had marked the height of the bed on the wall and pulled it far enough out of the way to get the camera in so they could take perpendicular scaled, arrowed and measured photographs of the blood distribution patterns on the wall. Chris said nothing throughout the operation.

"Are we having a biologist, Chris?" asked Paul.

"No need. The photos are good enough." Chris put a fresh 3M mask over his face, pulled up his hood and opened the lid of his fingerprinting kit. "Anyway, it isn't going anywhere; if we change our minds later, he can come out and see it in the flesh." He wore new latex gloves and began brushing black powder over all the surfaces he deemed suitable for this technique: doors, doorframes, windows and sills, and even the unpreserved banister rail. Not surprisingly, few marks developed. She was obviously a clean girl, and probably had visitors infrequently.

Black powder, like soot from a freshly swept chimney, still floated around the room when Chris took out his clipboard and began drawing a plan of where each mark was located.

"Chris?" Paul was signing over the seals of a brown paper sack with police evidence plastered across it. "I thought you were going to let me do that?"

Chris stopped sketching. "You're right; I did say you could do this, didn't I? Bloody hell." He stroked an arm over his glistening forehead, and left a black smear. "Look, Paul, for the sake of speed, I'll do the upstairs part of the fingerprint photography while you start powdering downstairs – which,

I might add, could prove to be equally important, and then you can do the fingerprint photography down there?"

"Yeah, okay." Paul mumbled as he plodded across the aluminium stepping plates, heading dejectedly for the stairs.

"Stop. You're right, come back here." He held out a sheet of labels and smiled. "Fuck the time, Paul, write out some blue labels; you can do it."

Like a small child given the sweets recently denied him, a grin burst back onto his face. "Seriously?"

"Don't look so bloody happy," Chris said, "it's tedious work."

"It doesn't bother me."

"Good, 'cause it would bore me stupid."

"Where shall I stick 'em?"

Chris raised an eyebrow, then showed him where the marks were and handed him the fingerprint camera. "You okay with it? Want me to watch over you?"

"Might be an idea, just for the first few, at least."

"Go on, then, get on with it."

The flash popped, and as he wound the film on, Paul asked, "I wonder how your horse did."

"What?"

"Your horse. The one we stopped at the bookies for on the way here."

"Keep your damned voice down!" Chris growled and then jumped as Shelby peeked his head around the door.

"Progress report, if you please, Chris."

"Start downstairs now, Paul."

Paul tutted loudly enough for them to hear, set the camera down and without glancing up, he pushed past Shelby and thudded down to the lounge.

Chris watched him go, shook his head. "A few marks in here that we've just photo'd, a couple on the landing; er, the girl's clothing and photos of the scene. That's really about all, I'm afraid."

"Can't say I'm not disappointed. I expected far more evidence than this." Shelby strode into the centre of the room, perched on a stepping plate, his mood heavy. "Did I tell you that we pulled Richard Andrews in?"

"Who's Richard Andrews?"

"Sally Delaney's pimp."

Chris became attentive. "No, you didn't. Has he coughed to it? Have you found the weapon?"

"No, and no. He didn't do it. His alibi checks out."

"What alibi?"

"He was in the cells at Wood Street. Drunk and disorderly."

"Can't get a better alibi than that, can you. Any other leads?"

"We've interviewed a dozen or so of Sally's known associates, had two other pimps in for a chat. Zilch. I got a Prison Intelligence Liaison Officer trawling through Wakefield and Armley's files just in case some known associate pops his acne-riddled face above the parapet, and I've got three Informant Handlers scouring her locale. Bugger all so far. But I'm keeping my fingers crossed on the cash."

"What cash?"

"For a hard-up prostitute, she had a large amount of cash in the lounge—"

"But we searched the lounge."

"Not well enough, Chris. Anyway, it's gone away for chemical fingerprinting now, so we'll soon see."

"Well, you won't find anything as lucky here, I'm afraid. All very straightforward."

"You call this straightforward? It's not straightforward from where I'm standing. I have nothing to go on, Chris. I've got a dead girl and bugger all else." Shelby strode to the window, looked through the rain and out on the fields.

"Nothing from house-to-house?" Chris asked.

"Nope." Shelby sighed. "I had a full OSU team on it. But Chamberlain bawled me out, said it was misuse of resources, that I should use divisional coppers." He folded his arms and added, "Tosser."

Chris stared at Shelby's back.

"I need a leak," Shelby made for the bathroom, already pulling at the zip on his scene suit.

"Whoa, no you don't, Graham."

"What? Why?"

"You don't use the facilities in a crime scene. Rules."

"Whose rules?"

"Mine. Oh, and ACPO's too. You'll have to use a neighbour's house." There was no room for negotiation in Chris's voice.

"Thanks." Shelby went back to the window. "Do you think the attacker was forensically aware?"

"Well, I don't know. I mean, the marks we've developed *may* belong to the offender and so we might already have him in the bag." He pulled his hood back and lifted the mask up. Sweat clumped his grey hair. "Then again, they may all belong to her or even Micky, in which case—"

"We're shagged," he shouted. His voice boomed in the silence, and then his volume shrank back to a whisper, "Correction, I'm shagged." There were no familiar crows-feet visible on Shelby's friendly face now. He looked only a day away from haggard. "You know, they say 'find out how they lived and you'll find out how they died', and until now I thought there was some validity in that. I think there *was* with Sally Delaney's case, even though we're no further forward with it yet. But this... Nicky Bridgestock just blew that theory right out the fucking water." Shelby pulled his mask off too and wiped a plastic sleeve across his face. "You know what I find the hardest thing?"

"What?"

"I haven't got a hypothesis for this. It's motiveless as far as I can see. And they're the worst bloody ones to solve."

Chris relaxed again. "Are you going to send her clothing away? Maybe that could give us an idea."

"Oh, I've already got some ideas," he huffed. "I've got hold of the CCTV footage from Wakefield town centre."

Chris paused, "Well, that's good, isn't it?"

"Half of the bloody cameras around town are out of order, some of the loop tape in the others is only fit for cross-stitch, and some of the bloody things are dummies! Which I did not know about, and..."

"And," Chris prompted.

"And the rest, which are in fine working order, are pointing in exactly the wrong fucking direction. We know she came out of Biggles' at about one-thirty-ish and one witness – who was totally paralytic at the time – said she was talking to someone in a dark car. A *dark car!* I ask you, a dark car?"

Chris felt almost sorry for him.

"Well that narrows it down a bit," Shelby said.

"Neighbours not heard anything, then?"

"There's still three or four to contact yet, travelling salesmen, long-distance truckers and the like, oh and next door-but-one set off for Wales in the early hours of this morning. Still out on that one." Shelby rubbed his lips with latex-clad fingers and then inspiration struck him. "Couldn't we use the Fingerprint Development Laboratory here? I mean is it the right kind of wallpaper, the type that works with their chemicals?"

But Chris seemed to have drifted off at this point, mind on other troubles.

"Snap out of it, Chris. I'm on a tight enough noose already without you pulling on the other fucking end."

"Sorry."

"I asked if FDL would be any good here." Impatience rattled Shelby and he closed in on Chris, ensuring his full attention.

"By all means get them out, you never know, we may find the mark that cuts you down."

Shelby rubbed his plump throat and looked not at all amused as he thudded past Chris. "I'll get them involved," he growled. And then he stopped before even reaching Nicky's bedroom door. Without turning, he asked, "Not found any keys, have you, Chris?"

"Keys?"

"Funny shaped bits of metal that make you feel secure at night, or that can lead to you getting stabbed in the throat if you turn them for the wrong person. Yes, keys!"

"No, no keys."

Shelby seemed to contemplate Chris's words as though they were a riddle unlocking the secret of life. Or the secret to this investigation.

"You think she let someone in after she got home then?"

"Just another option," was all he said.

He walked from the room and before long, Chris heard Shelby and Paul talking in the lounge, heard Paul quoting a magazine article to Shelby, about every fourth person being a weirdo.

With the room now clear again, he continued his work, applying lifting tape to all the black finger marks that Paul had previously photographed. When he finished it was past 6pm.

He lifted each mark and laid it on to an acetate sheet, labelled it with a consecutive number, matching those on Paul's blue labels, and asked Paul to complete the other details. From the fingerprint camera, he wound off the exposed film and sealed it with the adhesive strip. All this went into his clear plastic folder to be processed back at the office when the pressure was slightly less intense.

— Four —

It was ridiculous, and he felt embarrassed. But he'd been kicked out, and it was only polite—

Yvonne answered the back door.

Her hair still hung across her eyes, unintentionally eighties style. Quite provocative, attractive; and she had made her face up, made her eyes more pronounced, more…

She didn't look so angry any more, and though she was obviously in pain – still unable to stand fully erect, always bent slightly at the knees as though stuck in some bizarre curtsy – she appeared a whole lot calmer.

Roger fumbled, trying to get his sprouting of hair to lie flat, but it and the wind had other ideas. He contented himself with letting his eyes float over Yvonne, and rubbed the small scars on his itching fingertips. "I hope you don't mind, but I wondered if you'd allow me to have a shower. I mean, I could use the ones at the nick if you'd rather."

"Another one?" she raised her eyebrows. "You'd better come in, Roger. Close the door behind you."

Although he only left home this morning, he felt like a stranger already, as though an old memory had grown a layer of dust that hid all the details but kept the rough outline so it wasn't completely foreign. He half expected to see the lounge a different colour, or the furniture moved around or, or even a new man installed in his comfy chair. No, he thought, nothing is the same.

"If you want a drink," Yvonne said, "you'll have to fix it yourself."

"No, I'm fine. Thanks. Unless you want one," he blurted. "I'll make you one if you want one. Do you want one?"

Yvonne flicked a finger at the stray hair that partly covered one eye. And she smiled at him. A friendly smile. "I rang you at work. They said you'd left already."

He returned the smile, tentatively. Was it the first stages of mockery? He didn't think so. "Yvonne, I—"

"I think I understand your motives. I can't forget what you've done to me. But given time, enough time, maybe I can forgive you."

"What?"

"You've stood by me and although I don't want you to think I've been keeping score or anything, you've accrued some kind of good will." She frowned. "No, shit, that's not the right way to say it." She paused and thought deeply, offering only, "I owe you a lot. And I understand why you... why you did it; it can't be easy living with a cripple."

Roger's eyes grew damp.

"I know we haven't been happy for some time, but I was hoping, after you lied to me and patronised me this morning, that we would be able to pull our marriage back out of the grave. A new start. I'll try not to be so demanding, I'll try not to hate the way you fuss over me, if you promise not to hurt me again like you hurt me last night."

"Yvonne, I—"

"I need to trust you again; you know that, don't you? It's not like just turning a corner and forgetting all that's gone before, there's always an element of doubt there..."

He nodded slowly, "I'll do—"

"We're not finished yet, Roger. There's something else I want from you."

He looked at her again, a dread behind the tears.

"I want you to love me again instead of simply caring for me."

Roger cried then.

Chapter 15

Drizzle, thrashing windscreen wipers and a haunting blaze of red taillights in the darkness. Tyres on wet tarmac and loud traffic noise roared into the van as Chris lowered the window and dumped a handful of empty chocolate wrappers out. "You should carry your own emergency supply of these. You never know when you're gonna need 'em." He offered Paul a chocolate bar. "You sure you don't want one? Could be a while before your next meal."

"No. Ta."

"Could be a while before your next breath of fresh air, come to think of it."

Within minutes they were bouncing up the rutted mud track leading to the mortuary building. He parked the van, switched off the engine and watched rainwater running down the broken drainpipes.

"Shouldn't someone else be doing the PM?" Paul asked.

"Why?" Chris got out of the van in a hurry, still shaking his head, only now it was because the kid was starting to annoy him.

Paul stuttered, looking for a good reason not to be here. "Contamination?"

Chris closed the van door, "Bring the camera gear and hurry up about it."

Chris held open the exterior door for Paul who slovenly ambled in, head down, huffing. He walked past the wall of twelve refrigerators and three freezers.

The door swung shut and quietened the hum of the refrigerant machines outside.

It was nearly 8.30; Bellington Wainwright's timing for the PM was hopelessly optimistic. When the entourage arrived at Pinderfields mortuary, Ann Halfpenny was still tying off the beautifully neat stitching on the chest of a heroin victim. She didn't look up and she didn't stop her happy humming.

The large, well-lit room was clean, smelled of pine disinfectant, and was cool and echoey. A ceiling-mounted fan blew a breeze in Chris's face and if he closed his eyes, he thought, he could be in a Norwegian forest... "I wish," he whispered.

A stainless steel workbench complete with sinks and sluices filled one wall. Fluorescent lights peered into the deep scratches of polyethylene chopping boards set beside digital scales. These scales were used for weighing the organs as they emerged from each cadaver. Over the chopping boards were clear Perspex sheets designed to prevent blood from spraying into the pathologist's face as he cut the organs to inspect their interior surfaces.

At the other side of the room, a similar workbench was partly hidden by a congregation of police officers, all suited up in green disposable aprons and white rubber gloves. As with Sally's PM, some were there in an observational capacity, gathering information about the girl first-hand to pass onto the briefing and the SIO the next day. Others were there performing the role of Exhibits Officer, collecting items from the pathologist, samples of all body hair, nail scrapings, blood samples for toxicology and DNA use, urine samples and anything else that may lead the investigation in an appropriate direction.

Chris watched the Coroner's Officer, Jacob Cooper, standing silently, seemingly unable to penetrate the cliquey circle of detectives.

At 8.50, Ann laid Nicky's body on one of the three stainless steel tables. At one end a drain hole, similar to that found in a bathtub, caught her slim trickle of redness, and over it was a dripping showerhead.

Paul rigged up the tripod, affixed the Mamiya medium format camera to its head, while Chris busied himself loading film into the spare camera backs in readiness for a quick changeover. Some PMs were performed at a startling rate, and some pathologists became irate if their proceedings were affected by ill-prepared SOCOs having to wind-off and reload film. Then Chris flicked both Metz flashguns into life, listened to their high-pitched whine and watched their LEDs flash.

Between them, they photographed the body from both sides; general shots, not concentrating at this stage on any detail, before having Ann turn Nicky's body onto its side so they could photograph her front and back.

All the while, the detectives spoke quietly amongst themselves and did so in a suppressed and respectful way as they would, for example, in a library. Their banter was hushed not out of respect for the dead, but because while they stood temporarily idle, others were performing their own work and it would be impolite to disturb them.

What a change from Delaney's PM, Chris thought. Haynes seemed subdued.

Bellington Wainwright entered the room dressed in a green cotton smock, heavy-duty rubber gloves, and white Wellington boots that squeaked on the tiled floor. In one hand, he carried a facemask with a clear visor – rather like a welders mask – and in the other, a clipboard. "Right..." he said.

The echoes in the room hushed further.

Chris had worked with Wainwright only once before, and wasn't too impressed by the thoroughness or the methodology he employed. He was on the Home Office books though, and so should be up to the standard, but Chris thought he could certainly tighten up his routine, and not miss so much bloody evidence!

He was a quiet worker who would timidly ask for a photograph here or a swab there, rather than yelling orders like a Sergeant Major, as would some pathologists.

Wainwright began his autopsy by carefully removing the plastic bags covering the hands, feet and head. These he handed to one of the Exhibits Officers, who began her routine of packaging and labelling. He then made more notes of the deceased to supplement those he made at the scene, and sketched any unusual markings to the skin, scratches or abrasions on the wrists or hands that may have indicated signs of a struggle. Defence wounds, they were called.

He checked her eyes for obvious signs of drug abuse, illness or the like, and her arms and legs for tracks. There were none. She did indeed appear to be a clean young lady.

By the end of this preliminary stage, half an hour had passed and people began chattering again. Chris was not optimistic of an early finish. The Exhibits Officer, DC Clements, flicked a pen against her bottom lip, her top lip shining with Vicks; Haynes rapped his fingers on the bench, and Paul, Chris noted, looked away from the body; not just slightly away, coyly like he was pretending to be busy, but 180 degrees away, arms folded, stomach rumbling.

Before Wainwright put his clipboard down, he again picked up the girl's left hand and studied the back of it quite closely. When, after a moment, he failed to put the hand down, the chatter gradually ceased. Pens, fingers and feet stopped moving and attention grew. Wainwright looked up. Shelby glided to where the pathologist stood and looked at her hand. "Chris," he said, "can we have a picture of this, please?"

"Sure," Chris snapped a shot of the blue-ish smudge on the white skin. "Looks like it says something to me," he said, more to Shelby than anyone else. There were two faint lines of blue smudge running roughly from her wrist to her knuckles.

Ann rigged up an illuminated magnifying glass over the dead girl, and Wainwright peered through it at her hand. Distinct letters and shapes appeared. "Strange," he said.

"What, what?" Shelby said, hoping for a lead.

"Well, the writing, if we at this stage may call it writing, is angled peculiarly."

"How do you mean?" Shelby asked.

"If for example, you were to write upon your own hand, chances are it would go in a straight line roughly from the inboard part of your wrist towards the top knuckle of your index finger, following the line of the tendon. But as you can see, this goes in a straight line from the base of her thumb toward the knuckle of her middle finger, possibly indicating that someone else wrote whatever it is, and not the girl."

Shelby nodded, and DS Lenny Firth made notes in a green-backed pad. "S'cuse me, boss?" Firth chipped in. "I don't think she wrote on her hand. She's left handed."

"Are you sure?"

"Yeah, yeah. I took her watch from her right wrist; and back at the house there were left-handed scissors and stuff in the bathroom."

"Okay, then. So, we have some illegible writing on her left hand probably written by someone else. Photo, Chris, if you please."

Chris photographed her hand with and without grey measuring scales, and then re-photographed it using a slow speed black and white film, hoping to provide better contrast.

"What can we do with that, Chris, to bring it out more?" Shelby asked.

Just as he was pulling the camera out of the way, tripod legs hopping across the tiles, Chris paused. "We could try Quasar," he said. "It's a high intensity light which, if the right wavelength is selected, should get the ink in her skin to fluoresce, but I don't think that will be available until tomorrow; it needs specially trained staff from the Fingerprint Development Lab."

"Okay, good."

"Oh, we could also use a plain old-fashioned UV lamp and photo the results."

"Good, good, any ideas, Chris, keep 'em coming." He finally smiled and the crow's feet surfaced. "Well," Shelby said, "let's bag her hand up again so the writing doesn't get washed off or rubbed out altogether, and we'll get FDL here tomorrow."

He was about to ask a question of Firth and then said, "Never mind, I'll arrange it."

"Well, let's see if we can't get some under-nail crud; paring stick please and a Beechams," Wainwright said.

"A what?" asked DC Clements.

"A folded piece of paper," Chris whispered, "to catch the nail scrapings in."

"Right." And then quietly, "Why didn't he say than in the first place?"

"It isn't going to be easy," Wainwright examined her fingers, "she was a nervous little thing; bitten most of her nails away."

Shelby moved closer, peered at her ragged nails. Some were so well chewed that they had dark deposits – dried blood – up by the quick.

"But we'll try." He did, but unsuccessfully.

The hand re-bagged, Wainwright moved on to take other body hair samples. These were primarily in order to link her with another scene, to place her in a car or perhaps another address, if the full story of her last night alive ever became known.

He plucked and cut head hair, and placed it into a plastic universal container held in the Exhibits Officer's shaky grasp. Then he passed her some eyebrow hair, then eyelash hair, and then nasal hair. When he moved down to the pubic region, Wainwright stopped in his tracks, tweezers poised. "Inspector Shelby."

Shelby moved over, accompanied by Firth, and saw that her pubic mound was sheathed in fine light ginger, almost straight, pubic hair; downy to the touch.

"What am I looking at, Bellington?"

"Can't you see it?"

Shelby looked harder, moved even closer. "I haven't a clue what you want me to look at."

"There," Wainwright pointed with a gloved hand. "The black hair amongst her own?"

"Photograph, please, Chris."

Chris photographed the hair, and then again with an adhesive arrow pointing it out in case the jury couldn't make it out either.

Wainwright's tweezers shook as he handed the hair to the Exhibits Officer.

"I want that treated as a priority," Shelby said sternly to her. "We should be able to get DNA from that, right?"

"Hopefully," said Wainwright. "If the root is still in good condition, yes. If not, then we should be able to extract mitochondrial DNA from the hair shaft which will enable a maternal strain to be identified."

"A what?"

In his wonderfully rich, public school voice, both aspects of which annoyed Chris, Wainwright explained that, "Mitochondrial DNA is unlike the nuclear DNA fingerprinting one hears of on the news occasionally. It has less of a distinguishing property in that all the mitochondrial DNA from siblings is identical, and furthermore is only carried down from the mother – hence, maternally-passed down."

"Thank you," was all Shelby said.

"Problem being though," Wainwright continued, "is that mitochondrial DNA is not compatible with the National DNA Database. That means, I'm afraid, you will need a suspect to match it against. Or access to his mother."

"Fucking marvellous," Shelby said.

Wainwright took a sample of her own pubic hair as a control. Next, two sets of oral swabs: one from around the inner region of the lips, and the other from around the tongue; and then he performed upper and lower vaginal and anal swabs before concluding, "I would say that no sexual penetration has occurred recently before death."

"But plenty afterwards," whispered Haynes, who thought Shelby couldn't hear him. He was wrong, and reddened when Shelby strongly intimated demotion.

"What?" asked Shelby, returning his attention to the pathologist, more confused than ever. "You mean to tell me that a pretty girl was found dead in the bedroom of an otherwise unoccupied house," he pointed, "*and* she was naked, let me add, and you say she hadn't been...she hadn't had sex?"

"That's right, Inspector."

Shelby muttered, "What *is* the world coming to."

"Possibly the offender, er..." clearly embarrassed, Wainwright looked at DC Clements, "I mean, perhaps he was unable to er, to fully er—"

"He couldn't get it up?" Clements suggested.

"Well, I just think it's something you ought to bear in mind, Inspector."

Next, Chris took more photographs of the neck wound before and after cleaning. They discovered that a single-edged blade had penetrated her neck by nearly two inches, severing the carotid artery and nicking the jugular vein. It was the sort of blade found on a million penknives, and that similarity with Delaney's death wasn't lost on anyone.

After Wainwright weighed and dissected each organ, everyone stood back and watched Ann place them in a black plastic bag and shuffle them into Nicky's gaping abdominal cavity, humming *Bring Me Sunshine*. She didn't sew Nicky up at this stage, as there was a chance of a further PM carried out by another pathologist under the instructions of the Defence counsel – if one were ever needed.

"Briefing at oh-eight-hundred sharp, Chris."

A light snow began to fall.

Chapter 16

Thursday 21st January 1999

— One —

ROGER COULD BARELY KEEP his eyes open. It was only the turbulence from buses and large lorries passing his parked van and rocking it, that kept him awake.

He had been here for two hours. Here was sixty yards away from Weston's front door and about two hundred yards from the silhouetted ruins of Sandal Castle. The dashboard clock said it was 08:32. It was four degrees outside.

The meagre snowfall that littered crevices yesterday evening, that hung around in the corners between pavements and walls like a work in progress, had vanished overnight. Cloud was thick today, and even now the sky appeared in tumult, shoved around by the strengthening wind. It still wasn't fully light, the earth had a bubbling ceiling and it appeared there had been a celestial power cut.

Roger had been on duty since six o'clock. He had rushed to work, dumped his sandwiches and his Adidas bag, and printed off the jobs for Jon and Helen who would arrive at eight. He made sure there was nothing urgent that required immediate attendance, left a brief note for Chris in case he showed up at the office, and then brought his van here, his mind rattling with Hobnail's words and soothed by Yvonne's compassion.

It began to rain as Weston's BMW nosed out of the drive.

Roger's eyes sprang wide and for a moment he didn't know what to do, had forgotten everything he had rehearsed last night while he should have been sleeping. He buckled his seat belt and fell in behind Weston half a dozen cars behind. The rain grew heavier the further out of town they travelled. The windscreen misted up.

For twenty minutes, they travelled, with the cars between them leaving, others joining. The gap remained constant. The traffic lights at Durkar, where you could turn left towards Newmillerdam, caught Roger out. Weston scraped through on amber and Roger could only watch from behind a red light, as the BMW slipped out of sight around a corner. He panicked then, knowing this was the big chance, maybe his only chance to prove what a dirty bastard Weston really was. He felt the bulge of his compact camera in his coat pocket: no, not good enough evidence for a conviction in court, perhaps, but good enough to get the ACC or Mayers to sit up and really take notice this time.

When the lights changed, Roger craned his neck, brought the van over to the right and saw Weston's car in the distance, stuck in a queue of traffic by a roundabout. He pulled up four cars back. And he swallowed, felt the sweat on his palms, and peered through the dirt-streaked, misty windscreen at the man who dared call *him* the enemy. The BMW took off, Roger willed the cars in front onward, grimaced at their inability to pull out into the main flow of traffic, and that's when his mobile phone rang.

Steering with one hand, he struggled to get the damned thing out of his other coat pocket and answered curtly. It was Jon, and through his continual splutter of bad jokes and awkward questions, Roger kept his attention on Weston. "I really have to go; speak to you later." They were well out of town now, heading along the dual carriageway towards the M1.

Where the hell are we going? he thought.

"You heading somewhere?" asked Jon.

"I'm on a job."

"What job? I don't see your call-sign in—"

"It's more of a personal job." He passed beneath the motorway, which from down here looked like a sea wall with a barrier of spray running its full length. The wipers scraped across the windscreen, the road noise blotted out Roger's loud breathing.

"Ah. I see."

"I don't think you—"

"The Bulldog?"

Roger paused. "Keep it to yourself, Jon."

"Just be careful, you stupid man, and don't turn your phone off. Where are you now?"

"Heading towards Bretton Country Park, looks like."

"Okay, I have to go now, Helen's coming back. Take care of yourself; I don't want to trail out there to rescue your sorry arse."

"Has Chris come in?"

The line went dead, and Roger turned on the phone's silent function.

On a narrow road, hemmed in by naked black trees, and by hedges covered in grey road dirt, Roger peered through the spray, trying to sight Weston's car. There it was, two cars separating them.

Suddenly, Weston turned right into the Bretton estate and Roger carried on, skidding the van into a narrow dirt lay-by thirty yards past the entrance. The van slid to within two feet of an overflowing concrete litterbin. He climbed from the warmth, out into a tearing wind that pulled at his coat, rippled his trousers against his long skinny legs, and nearly snatched his glasses from his face. The rain came heavier, almost horizontally. He squinted over the rough hedge to watch Weston's car splashing through puddles towards a small gravel car park by the wooded hillside. Water ran down his neck and dripped from his glasses. Cars sped past him, throwing up clouds of dirty water and drowning thought with noise.

Roger locked the van, tucked the keys safely away, and pulled his collar up, making a dash for the far side of the road and the entrance to Bretton. The gullies at either side of the tarmac road bubbled with storm water, and overhead, power lines hummed and phone lines whistled.

The tarmac road became a potholed gravel track after thirty or forty yards. Another hundred yards after that, it divided left towards the house and gardens, or right towards the woodland, the lake and stone-built boathouse further down the valley, and the picnic areas and sightseeing trails. A generous car park, also gravelled, accommodated only three cars; one of which was a black BMW. Empty.

Hurrying, Roger left the harsh noise of traffic on the wet road, and swapped it for harsh winds tearing through trees, barging into them until they sang like perpetual thunder. Cold wind-blown rain stung his face until the skin was numb and blotchy red; eyes screwed up, coat fastened to the neck, hands rammed into pockets and wrapped around the disfigured Mars bars.

He turned into the woods, hurrying silently among the turmoil, through towering trees, shiny with rain, through mounds of slippery leaves, navigating minefields of snagging bracken and fallen trees, and over tributaries whose banks were a mire of clinging mud. He looked down at his shoes, and merely tutted at the muddy water soaking into his socks.

Whipping branches plucked at his coat and trousers, attempted to steal his glasses, and made grabs for his hair. Still the rain pierced the naked canopy, and still Roger headed deeper into the woods, well away from the marked nature trail, lower into the valley and closer to Weston.

And the truth of it was, the closer he came to Weston, the more his footing slipped, the more his hands came out of his pockets to regain balance, the harsher his breathing was and the more unsure of his quest he became.

Not for a moment did he consider that this time Weston was going fishing in the lake, or was taking a walk in the woods for no more sinister a reason than to work off some of his weight and enjoy a minor struggle with nature. He wasn't in this for the pleasure, wasn't Weston: he didn't look up at the trees, didn't admire them or the knee-high foliage or the bracken, or the fungi growing on dead wood, or the squirrels that darted into places of greater safety every time their tree shook.

He was here for a specific purpose. Such as digging up some guns, or *a* gun, and he was going to take it back to his car, and he was going to meet someone at twelve o'clock, and he was going to sell them that gun at a place called Harvey's Table. And then in the months to follow, that gun would kill people, maim people; and the money would buy Weston more cigars and beer, and would fund the deposit for a two-week holiday in Spain in April. How nice.

That's what he was doing.

The noise was incredible. It was like standing next to a Boeing as it prepared for take-off, and even in here, covered by the woods, he was violently whipped about, found walking difficult, found it a real effort one moment and then a real effort to keep from falling flat on his nose the next. Mud seemed to grow up his trouser legs. His fingertips were numb, his nose was leaking, eyes streaming.

Roger thought of Hobnail, how he'd finally met him outside the station, and he thought of what Hobnail had told him, how he said he'd seen Weston enter The Joker – "couldn't bleedin' miss him," he said. "I'd recognise the fella who nearly mowed me down a few days ago, no problem. And he walks the same as he drives: aggressive."

And Roger had been enthralled by Hobnail's tale, eyes had never moved from the tramp's, nose completely ignorant of the smell, ears hearing nothing except the old man's coarse accent and his regurgitation of the words he had heard, about how Weston "Was meeting a beaver at noon, Thursday. So he was gonna dig up the metal before then."

"He said that? He used those exact words?"

Hobnail had looked worried, as though maybe they weren't those precise exact definite words, and he'd made a right balls up. His eyes had moved away from Roger as he dug around in his memory. At last, he'd stared back and nodded. "Oh aye, mentioned metal, he did."

"Thanks, Hobnail, but you can't remember where—"

His hair had blown about his dirty pate in thin wisps. "No, no idea. All I know is the man what I couldn't see says to Weston, 'Final, Harvey's table'. Now, maybe it's in a restaurant or..." he shook his head, "I don't rightly know." He'd shrugged. "But I remembered you sayin' he was bent, this Weston, that I should steer well clear of 'im—"

"You should, he's dangerous." He had thanked Hobnail and paid for another liquid lunch.

Then he saw Weston, and gasped. He froze, didn't know what to do.

He remembered the last time Weston caught him. He'd snarled at Roger and said next time he would pull his innards out through his arsehole. Roger swallowed hard, fingertips trembled.

Weston was fifty yards further into the woods, striding unheard ever inwards, wading through the undergrowth as though struggling through a deep snowfall. The wind tugged at his hair and pulled his coat out behind him and then threw it back at him; the wind came from everywhere all at once, and its noise in the dense trees was massive. Roger moved to his right, slipping down a shallow, muddy embankment and lost sight of Weston. He stood, craned his neck and then scrambled back up, mud and wet foliage slick between his cold fingers. He took a couple of strides closer, and Weston's fawn coloured coat came back into view.

His heart raced, and he tried desperately to close the gap between them down to something the camera could comfortably handle. Oh, for a telephoto lens. Weston had stopped in a small clearing, the wind making him squint, as was Roger, against the onslaught of spinning leaves and twigs. His gold bracelet looked bright against the darkness of the trees behind him.

He seemed to be looking for something.

Roger continued to move closer; he took out the camera, turned the power on and felt, but could not hear, the lens motor working. He was forty yards away, and he almost cried out as Weston spun a full 360, quick as a gyroscope, scanning the woods for... well, for spies, Roger guessed.

He panted. Had Weston seen him?

There he was standing out in the open for all to see; might as well staple a neon sign to his head that flashed on and off: *I'm here! I'm here!* Even so, Weston hadn't stopped to scrutinise; he carried on turning, didn't flinch. So maybe he hadn't seen him.

But Weston *had* seen him.

And now Roger crouched breathless behind a wide oak, his back to the wet bark, and waited, taking the opportunity to clean smears and specks of mud from his glasses. Roger needed to catch his composure. It was nothing to do with fear, he told himself, he wasn't the least bit worried about Weston, possibly armed, finding him in the same stretch of woodland. No, not worried at all. But he might have been holding his breath. And his fingers may have trembled slightly.

Roger was about to pull the camera up to shooting position. But he didn't get the chance.

— Two —

She had been right; the pain *was* like someone hitting her knee with a lump hammer. Yvonne screamed and flopped onto the hallway floor with a sickening crunch. She screamed even harder and beat at the carpet with feeble fists as her eyes screwed shut against the pain.

Agony ruptured the bubble that Yvonne had created to hold her breath in. Another scream exploded into the hallway. This one caused by a torture as bad as she could remember, and suddenly her head hit the carpet and her fingers dug in.

Five minutes later, or it could have been fifty-five minutes later, Yvonne held her breath again and pulled herself into the lounge with fingers the nails of which lay in tatters in her wake. Her makeup had run in great black streaks down her face, the trace of blue mascara looked like a four-year-old had applied it with a pasting brush. Her lipstick was on the hall floor, though a streak of it remained in the cleft of her chin.

Dignity, Roger. That's why. "Couldn't you *see* it?" It didn't matter. What mattered was the phone. And there it was, on Roger's table next to his easy chair. It was close, only a few yards away. Another few minutes…

— Three —

He pressed ok.

"Yvonne?" It was a shout, but in this wind he supposed it was more like a whisper. His wet hair whipped about his head, and his coat collar was like a very small boat's sail, how it flapped against his neck as he crouched behind the oak, exposed knees tucked up, rain dancing on their shiny sodden surface.

"I need you," she said.

He buried his finger in his spare ear, and said, "Speak up, what did you say?"

She told him that she had fallen. Yes, she said, it was serious, how the knee seemed to grind as she hit the bottom stair, and how "I've never felt pain like it, Roger. I'm in agony!"

"I'll call an ambulance."

"No!" she shouted. "I've freed a seized joint, Roger, that's all. Hurts like a bitch, but it's not worth getting them and hospitals involved."

"You sure, sweet?"

"Please, just… Soon, Roger."

He closed his eyes, dragged a wet hand down his wet face and stared off into the woods, back the way he had come, and he watched eddies, trainee whirlwinds, throw leaves around, trying to screw them into the woodland floor. How the naked branches were tossed about by the wind like blades of grass to a child's sigh; and they were clashing, having a thousand simultaneous swordfights.

Roger had a choice. Stay with Weston, wait for him to find the site, wait again while Weston checked and made sure all was okay, perhaps take out a cigar and have a smoke while he assured himself no one was around. And then he had to wait for Weston to bring the gun out into the open, whether this involved him digging the thing out of the earth, or reaching inside the hollow trunk of a dead tree, he would have to wait and see...

But there was the problem. That one word: wait.

He couldn't wait. Even if he were sitting inside his van at this very moment, it would take him twenty, maybe twenty-five minutes to get home. If he waited until Weston got his shit together, he would be here at least another half an hour. And that alone put waiting out of the equation. He wouldn't leave an injured pet in agony for over an hour, so why would he leave Yvonne?

Roger turned the camera off, threaded it back into his pocket and then hooked the phone back on his belt and zipped his coat up against the infernal wind. "Next time," he sighed. "There'll be a next time."

He fixed his eyes on a point in the woods; a far off red painted marker, one of the Estate's nature trails, and he'd seen it on his way in. A man throwing sticks for his Labrador was over there, oblivious to the conditions, one of life's outdoor people. Anyway, the red marker, that was his trail of string, it was his way back out of here, and he focused on it as he stood and strode unheard away from the oak.

Weston watched him go.

— Four —

He got home at 10:15; Christ knew how, he thought. It was as though someone had fitted a turbocharger to his van while he was ensconced in the woods. Anyway, Yvonne was suffering, smeared makeup right across her face told him that as soon as he entered the lounge.

But he restrained himself. He thought he acted with perfect etiquette but with the required amount of familiarity thrown in too. He had promised to stop treating her as a cripple, and he achieved it, though it tore tiny shreds off his heart to do it. He sat shivering on the edge of the bath as it filled, rain still dripping from his hair, toes and fingertips that were fresh out of the freezer. He got a handful of colourful drugs together in a small plastic pot, and offered her a glass of water. He then turned on the radio for her.

"How come you're wet through and plastered with mud?" she asked. "Someone been mugged while potholing?"

There was disappointment on his face and a distinct lack of a smart response.

"You've followed him again, haven't you? Inspector Thingy."

Roger shrugged.

"You should leave it alone, don't get involved."

He kissed her.

"It's not healthy. I mean, throwing darts at his photo? Following him around? Come on, Roger, you're a bit old for playing James Bond, don't you think? Anyway, it's not your problem; you did the right thing, now it's up to them to sort it." She stared him right in the eyes. "Okay?"

"It's about time I just dropped it, eh?"

She nodded. "Good. I'm glad that's sorted."

Roger towel-dried his hair, pleased the subject was closed and he hadn't agreed to anything.

Yvonne wanted to have the bath and come straight back downstairs. "I have jobs I need to get done," she said.

"I'll cancel squash and I'll do the jobs when I get home after work."

"I want to do them. And I want to do them today. Thank you." Steam dulled the bathroom echoes and her face grew red and moist, her hair clung in ringlets to her damp forehead. "I love you, Roger."

He was about to bend and kiss her, when she said, "There is just one thing you can do for me before you go back to work."

"I don't have to go back, Yvonne."

"I'd like you to get my makeup bag and the small hand mirror and put it on the kitchen table on your way out." She still looked at him. "Yes. I think I'll do it there. Make things easier, I suppose."

"Makeup bag," he said.

"Yes, it's the blue and white—"

"I know, I know." He stood up to leave. "I'll do it. Sure there's nothing…"

She was already shaking her head. "That'll be just fine, Roger. I'll have a meal ready for you about 4.30. So if you could be home for then."

After a hurried change of clothes, he was back in the office for 11.00, and as if by the magic of television, it felt like he'd never been away. Roger dived for the phone book, thumbed through it looking for a restaurant or a pub called Harvey's Table. He knew Weston was destined to meet someone there at noon to sell a weapon, and Roger wanted to be there too. But there was no such place, he even rang the Force's directory enquiries but had no luck there. Resigned to defeat on this occasion, Roger sank into his chair when there was a knock at the office door.

The desk sergeant, Sergeant Potts, poked his head into the office. "Chris, can you photo a bloke's injuries for me, please?"

Roger looked up, scanned the office, and then gazed at Potts.

"What's up?" Potts asked.

"How long have I known you, James?"

Potts' eyes rolled up. "Dunno, ten years?"

Roger nodded thoughtfully. "Wheel him in, James, I'll do it now."

"He's at the front counter; I'll nip and get him."

The man had been punched in the face and then glassed. He had a bruise over his closed-up eye the colour of an overripe plum and a gash across his nostril you could park your bike in. Distractedly, Roger took the photo in seconds, walking around him to make sure there were no further injuries. He squelched as he walked.

"Just one punch," the man said, listening to the noise, confused by it.

"Really," Roger said. And then, as though realising how rude he sounded, "You've seen a doctor?"

"Eh," said the man. "Don't be a fucking nonce!"

Roger's mouth fell open. "Right," he said. "Nonce."

"Come on, Mr Nesbit," Sergeant Potts held an arm out to guide him to an interview suite for a statement, "I'll lead you back out."

Mr Nesbit walked from the office like a guerrilla, looking back over his shoulder. As he rounded the corner, Roger heard him ask the sergeant, "Why's he got fucked-up hair?"

Roger closed his mouth.

He removed the film from the camera and sat down to write the paperwork that would accompany the film to Headquarters Studio for developing. He filled in his CID6 book for the appointment and then dumped it in the wire tray labelled 'Lord Lucan Files'.

After Sergeant Potts left, Roger opened his sandwiches, took a bite and then removed his shoes, the ones he had worn while following Weston that morning, the ones that were still wet, and turned them upside down on top of the mildly warm radiator, padding around the office in his socks, and leaving a trail of damp footprints on the linoleum.

The office felt quiet, and again he was alone with a problem that followed him around like a hyena tearing at his heels and giggling as it scurried out of reach: Weston. He was so damned fucking close today that it was cruel.

He fixed a coffee and sipped as he munched, tutting at the aluminium powder floating among the bubbles. The ringing phone diverted his mind from Weston. "Conniston of Wood Street," he croaked. Then, "Chris, what's up?"

"I need you to come down to the scene on Potter Lane and help out with the Quasar when it finally arrives."

Roger looked at his watch; it was 11.15. "Do you want me to give Paul a ring and ask him to come to you instead?"

"Why the bloody hell do you think I'd want him? I'm asking *you*, aren't I?"

"Chris, I'm due off at two and I've got a stack of paperwork to do."

"Look, I've bent over backwards to help you recently; I can't be in two bloody places at once, I'm needed here at the scene *and* down at the mortuary. Now how do you suggest I accomplish that little feat?" There was a pause, "I want you here please, Roger, if it's not too much trouble."

Anger sharpened Roger's drowsy eyes. "I'm not coming down to the scene; I've been on duty since six. Quasar-ing a house will take the best part of five or six hours and I'm not working a thirteen- or fourteen-hour shift when there's other people available. *And* they'd be fresher than me, *and* they could do the sodding job just as well!" He suddenly realised that his voice had risen to a furious climax.

When Roger realised his outburst was leading him towards disciplinary action, he quietened his trembling voice. "And then I suppose the house will need treating with ninhydrin, would you like me to stay for that too?"

"Forget it," shouted Chris, "I'll do it all myself. You and I will be having a discussion."

"Fine," Roger hung up.

Chapter 17

— One —

THE BRIEFING WAS DUE out of the blocks at eight, but it was twenty-past before everyone hushed and Shelby cleared his throat. He stood at the head of the room in his customary weathered brown suit. Chris, who overslept, had held up the procedure. He told people he hadn't heard the alarm, and it was a fair excuse, he had worked long and hard yesterday, and everyone seemed to accept it without doubt.

Of course, it was untrue, Chris never overslept: the job first, sleep second. At the breakfast table, already dressed and ready for work, he had mulled over the evidence they had so far, the implications of that evidence, and how the investigation was likely to proceed. He thought of his performance too; thought he'd done rather well, but spared little time congratulating himself. Instead he dreamed of the top slot.

Now he sat in the briefing, noting how accurate his 'mulling' had been.

The grey-painted room was the size of an average classroom, lit with banks of twin fluorescent tubes. An overhead projector pointed like an accusing finger at the whiteboard, and on the table next to it was a projector of the kind that casts a picture of a photograph or plan, rather than a transparency. Yesterday's briefing saw it used for the scene photos now lying on Shelby's desk.

Around the remaining three of its four walls, the investigating officers sat, with more standing at the back of the room, arms folded, leaning against the wall and each other. Maybe thirty people in all, chewing pencils, doodling, or reading previously gathered statements, propped on small arm-desks. Most of them seemed relaxed; gassing with their neighbour, sharing jokes and snippets of gossip, but some were edgy, preparing themselves for the time when they would be speaking to the team, to Shelby, to the SIO – Detective Superintendent Chamberlain.

Not all of them were field personnel. A few were charged with indexing the process of the investigation, collating information, producing Actions, updating HOLMES 2, keeping Nicky's brother informed, and liaising with agencies within the Force and external to it. Each had a vital role to play in solving the riddle, in catching the killer.

Behind Shelby, sitting at a small teak effect desk, was Chamberlain, a man who rarely ventured further than his office door and a man who reputedly never ventured more than ten minutes away from his next cigarette. What an honour then, that he should be here at all.

Chris didn't like him, had never spoken to the man; he thought Chamberlain was shifty, slimy. Detective Sergeant Lenny Firth, Shelby's right hand man, had been relegated to the peripheral chairs.

Shelby sought a nod from Chamberlain before commencing. "Okay, ladies and gentlemen. First things: turn any mobiles onto silent and turn your radios down. Right, I don't have to tell you how important this case is. I shouldn't *have* to tell you how important this case is. But I'm going to."

As if wanting to illustrate his point, Shelby turned the projector on. All eyes looked at the rectangle of white light before it vanished, replaced by a picture of Nicky; young, smiling and happy.

"Nicky Bridgestock lived alone, as we ascertained yesterday. It's become apparent, through OIS and PNC checks that

A LONG TIME DEAD

she's never had cause to be involved with the police." His tone suggested that this was a 'bare facts' briefing, nothing revelatory to follow. "As we know, she was a typical girl-next-door who did not partake in the misuse of drugs, was not a member of any criminal fraternity of any description, was not a known member of any religious sects, or subscribed to any extreme political persuasion. She didn't even have a boyfriend. She drank rarely, seldom partied and kept herself very much to herself."

"What convent did she go to, boss?"

Some in the room laughed aloud, others tittered, and some turned away.

Shelby did not even smile. "I will thank you, Detective Constable Haynes, to keep that kind of remark to yourself, because if I hear any more along those lines, or similar to the ones you made at the PM yesterday, I will send you back to division with a slapped arse and a note for your Inspector!"

Haynes bowed his red face. Chamberlain did not move, Chris noted.

The room was again silent. Shelby paused, daring any dissension. He removed Nicky's photograph from the machine, and a new rectangle of light barely had the chance to dazzle the audience before another picture took its place. "This may seem funny to you," he continued in a calmer vein, treading across the creaking floor and back again, "but that girl could have been your sister, or your cousin. I don't want to preach or prophesise on natural law, but in my opinion, she was the kind of girl who shouldn't have died like that; she was the kind of girl who should have been given a chance. She was clean." Shelby cleared his throat again.

Smiling and youthful, the photograph on the wall. An image of Sally Delaney.

He paced again, hands clasped behind his back. "We found fingerprints at the scene yesterday and they're on a Fingerprint Expert's desk at the bureau as we speak. I'm having FDL out to the scene today. Though they don't know it yet. Chris Hutchinson, there," he nodded at Chris, "tells me there could be valuable fingerprints on the walls, and we can get them using some kind of laser tool. It all sounds very *Star Wars* to me, but I've heard of startling results from it before, so we'll be trying it here." Shelby stopped pacing and gathered his thoughts. "After that, we'll use, er...help me out here, Chris."

Everyone turned and looked at him.

Chris tapped a pen on the desk and in a quiet voice began, "We'll use the Quasar first of all, because it's non-destructive." The pen slipped and fell on the floor; he felt the weight of the room on his shoulders. "Using a high intensity light source, we can cause the contaminants within a fingerprint to fluoresce and then we photograph it. Simple. Its only real drawback is that it takes a long time, perhaps five or six hours to cover only a few rooms." He pulled at the cuffs of his grey cardigan, and continued more confidently, "If Quasar produces no satisfactory results, we'll decide whether to move up to iodine or ninhydrin treatments. These methods don't take so long to apply, only a couple of hours, but they may take a day or two, depending upon ambient temperature, to finally show any marks up."

"Want me to arrange the Quasar, boss?" Firth asked.

"No Lenny, leave it to me, please. I have a feeling that it'll be a bit sticky asking them for at least one member of staff for a full day, and then I've got to organise a fingerprint expert to view the marks and that's like prising a limpet from the arse of the Titanic."

"And a photographer," Chris reminded him.

"Yes, and a photographer," Shelby added.

"If it takes these chemicals a day or two to work, boss, are we keeping the scene guarded?" Clements asked.

The spotlight off him, Chris licked his lips and retrieved the pen.

"We might not need the chemicals yet, but if we do, I'll arrange uniform cover with Inspector Weston. Chris and I are also arranging a similar kind of laser device to examine the body, hopefully this afternoon, again depending on staffing levels at FDL and Scenes of Crime. Are you all aware that on Nicky's right hand—"

"Left, boss," Firth corrected.

"Sorry. On her *left* hand, we found smudges of blue ink that may be letters or figures of some description. Well, we're hoping to decipher them this afternoon and with a bit of luck, we'll have something to tell you at the five o'clock briefing." He paced the floor, hands behind his back, studying the walls, thinking. "Lenny, I want you to arrange a recent reverse phone subscriber history from BT."

Firth made notes.

"Gez, have you managed to contact the neighbours from No.76 in Wales yet?"

Gerard, one of the more timid of the assemblage, said, "No, not yet, boss, but we have a lead on their last whereabouts. A local sergeant is on with it and he'll let me know when he's made contact."

"Keep me posted. Lenny, anything of value from PNC or DVLA regarding cars parked on Barnstone Road that night?"

"No, boss. They all check out."

Shelby circled the room. "Have we visited all the local taxi firms yet, Lenny?"

"Clive Worrall's still on with that."

Shelby stood still, facing the white board and then, as if on a parade ground, spun on his heels and gazed at the meeting, making sure he had their attention. "Key," he said. "Missing. I want a top priority Action raising for Nicky's house key. Joan Philip—"

"*Joanne* Philips, boss," Firth butted in.

"*Joanne* Philips, Nicky's colleague from the bank, says her key fob was quite distinctive. It was a small naked man, with a hard-on a little disproportionate to his stature." A giggle, of a volume acceptable to Shelby, spread across the room. "Made of pink rubber, it is a small, three-dimensional figure measuring approximately an inch and a half in height. The figure, that is, not the hard-on."

Shelby continued to walk the floor. "Unfortunately, no one seems to have a bloody clue where or when she bought it. If indeed she *did* buy it, it might've been a gift or whatever. Anyway, it seems that the fob is very rare, certainly everyone I've asked has never seen one, and obviously if anyone has knowledge of a single Yale key with such a fob attached, it could produce another lead." He stopped. "Did I say 'another'?"

His audience giggled again, even quieter this time.

"I want an Action to find such a fob." He stared intently at the Incident Room Sergeant and the two female Indexers, "I want as many resources throwing at this as you can spare. Check out the card shops, the little gift-type places in the Bull Ring and the markets, whatever you think. Just get me a bloody fob like it, get SOCO to photograph it and then get the negatives to HQ Studio asap."

He turned to the Press Liaison Officer, "By lunchtime today, I want a picture of that key fob on local television news and I want the local radio stations to broadcast a description. Mr Chamberlain's holding a press conference-come-appeal at lunchtime." He smiled at the SIO, "Fame at last, sir." The room giggled, though Chamberlain did not. Shelby hastily continued, "He'll display the fob and appeal for any witnesses from the town centre nightclubs to come forward. Gez, I'm putting you on this one as well. I want results. Go see Inspector Weston; he'll help out with manpower."

"Inspector Weston's not here today, boss."

Shelby appeared puzzled, "Okay then, speak to Inspector Banner."

"What about the girl's clothes, boss? Shall I get them to the lab?" Firth asked.

"Absolutely."

"Right, I'll get SSU authorisation."

"Bugger the Scientific Support Unit, just get them there yesterday. I'll authorise it."

"Right, boss."

"And take that pubic hair with you, too."

"Right, boss."

"Fast-track 'em all."

"Okay."

Shelby strode with determination around the room, barking instructions, his voice commanding and receiving the focus of everyone's attention.

"Anything to add, sir?" Shelby asked of Chamberlain.

Chamberlain, shaking his head, stood to leave.

"Right, listen up, you lot. H2H Sergeant, Management Team Sergeant and Search Team Sergeant, stay behind please, I need to check your progress. The rest of you... what're you still doing here? Go on," he shouted, "get on with it."

Just as the officers prepared to leave, Shelby yelled over their mumbling voices, "Oh, just one more thing." There was a brief flash of light. "Look here." Chris's photograph, from the PM, showing Nicky's half-open, glazed eyes and her seeping neck wound, greeted their attention. "Just a reminder of why we're doing this."

— Two —

Shelby was still on the phone to FDL, trying to secure the services of the Quasar and an operator. He told Chris that normally he delegated this kind of job, but the pressure was bearing down on him like a lead weight, so now he was using his own weight to get results. Today the Fingerprint Development Laboratory was receiving some stern words.

Sitting on an easy chair in Shelby's office, facing the big man, whose complexion was decidedly ruddier of late, Chris punched buttons on his mobile phone, but continued to watch Shelby with concern. Shelby was struggling, and he would jump at the chance of an imminent arrest.

Shelby laid into the technician on the other end of the line, telling him that he would be at the scene by 11.45 or he could start looking for alternative employment – *he* would see to it personally. And no, he didn't care what workload he had, nor what he would have to postpone in order to furnish Shelby's request, and no, he certainly didn't give a shit how much hot water it would land him in with his line manager. Regulations regarding job suitability and grading could go to hell.

Chris pressed call on the phone and heard the tones as it dialled the office number. After a while a mouth full of food said, "Conniston of Wood Street."

"It's me."

"Chris, what's up?"

"I need you to come down to the scene on Potter Lane and help out with the Quasar when it finally arrives."

Shelby put the phone down and groaned, anticipating more problems.

"Why the bloody hell do you think I'd want him? I'm asking *you*, aren't I?" He slid a thumb over the mike and whispered, "I feel a fob-off coming through."

Shelby went to fill his recently drained cup.

"Look, Roger, I've bent over backwards to help you recently; I can't be in two bloody places at once, I'm needed at the scene *and* down at the mortuary. Now how do you suggest I accomplish that little feat?" It seemed the harder he pressed Roger, the more he dug his stubborn heels in. And that was fine. No, really; that was just fine.

He covered the mouthpiece and whispered to Shelby, "He's fucking me off." He shrugged at Shelby, "I want you here please, Roger, if it's not too much trouble." Chris held the phone away from his ear so Shelby could get a feeling for the volume of Roger's unhappiness.

"I'm not coming down to the scene; I've been on duty since six. Quasar-ing a house will take the best part of five or six hours and I'm not working…"

He let Roger rant, sighing an apology at Shelby for his disinclined staff. "Forget it, Roger," he shouted, "I'll do it all myself. You and I will be having a discussion." Chris pressed end and threw the phone on Shelby's desk. "We'll have to go to the scene," he began, "start them off there and then I'll head down to the mortuary and fanny about with the PolyLight."

Shelby, unimpressed, slurped coffee.

"I don't know what's wrong with Roger these days," he began. "I know his wife's ill, but he doesn't usually act like a prick. He jumps at the chance of working a major job."

"I know; I've worked with him a lot. Bet he wouldn't turn it down if he were Supervisor, would he?"

"Wouldn't dare." Chris could feel himself creeping just a little closer to the finish line. Tantalisingly close.

"Who did he suggest came along and helped instead?"

"Paul. You know, the lad who was with me yesterday." Shelby slurped.

"He's not up to speed yet, I don't want him getting under my feet really, and he'd be no use at all with the Quasar or the PolyLight, let alone photographing the bloody marks." It was getting hot in here, and Chris rolled his cardigan sleeves up.

Shelby slackened his tie. "We're investigating a top notch stranger murder here. This is a priority one; do I have to organise every fucking thing myself these days? If you want Roger there, Chris, then bloody well order him there!"

"Calm down, Graham," Chris said in a smooth, almost condescending voice.

"Don't tell me to calm down, man. You know the kind of shite that's falling from above and right now, I don't need it. I have to produce answers, I have to put a man – a person – at the scene, and I have to prove beyond reasonable doubt that he killed an innocent girl!"

Shelby stood and began shouting down at Chris. "The papers are going ape-shit about this killing, wondering what the recent hike in Council Tax has produced and suggesting that the police are wasting resources – making comments like 'This doesn't happen in America', and 'The Feds do it like this'…and…"

He went to the window, shook his head at people taking photographs of the old Crown Court building and the Barbara Hepworth statues, and watched the flag on the Town Hall thrashing about in the wind. He turned back to Chris. "Chamberlain has ranked this as a Category 'B' murder; which means staffing levels are stretched on this side of the line as well as yours. He's given me a HOLMES Sergeant, two Indexers and six Receivers in the office. How can I manage on that?" He scratched the back of his head, "Still, it's more than I got for the Sally Delaney murder; they didn't seem to care a toss about her, she was Cat 'B' too but without the heat, you know… But *this*," he pointed at the scene photographs strewn across his desk, "they're going mad over. She was the original angel, just about the cleanest kid on God's earth and some bastard killed her – on *my* patch!"

"I still think you should calm down."

"I've got two fucking murders running at once, Chris. Not because I want two, but because Chamberlain won't let me off-load one of 'em."

"He thinks they're linked?"

"There's a good chance, wouldn't you say. Anyway, that means I'm playing mother to two Incident Rooms and... I don't know my arse from my elbow. But what I'm hoping for is this: solve one murder, and the other solves itself." He slumped in his seat and rested a leg over the corner of his desk. "I don't know what's happened to this Force. I've been here twenty-odd years. And back in the old days there was discipline, there was respect for authority. But now it's all wishy-washy bollocks, where people's feelings have to be taken into consideration, where solving crime comes second to... I don't know, comes second to public image. It's all 'let's sit down and have a chat about our corporate performance and where the public thinks we ought to be heading'. Fuck the little chats and fuck the corporate performance, what about reassuring the public, what about *seeming* to reassure the public? What about catching a *murderer*?"

Chris sat there dumbfounded.

Shelby looked up, his face red. "So stop pissing about, and get Conniston to the scene." Nicky's photographs stared up at him. He tried to turn away, but Sally's photographs got him. A moment passed before he opened the lower drawer of his desk and pulled out half a bottle of Bells and a plastic cup. "Want one?"

"No, it's a bit—"

"Early?"

The sadness in his old eyes pricked Chris.

"You're right, it's too early." He put the liquor back. "We'll save that for when we've got ourselves a killer, eh?"

"Yes," Chris whispered, and looked away.

"Well, are you going to summon Conniston or what?"

"Nah. He's got a point. I'm punishing him because he's good at his job. I'm relying on him too much, when I should be spreading the work around."

"There you go again, with your wishy-washy bollocks. If you want him, get him!"

"No. I can manage. Honestly."

"But if you're worried about overworking him, look at yourself. Look how much you've done and *you're* the Supervisor. For Christ's sake, supervise!"

"I could say the same," Chris retorted. "You're panicking over this murder, and it's only been running two days. The bloody Press have got nothing more substantial than a 'body'. Whoopee-fucking-doo. Yet you run around like a blue-arsed fly, doing all the bloody work yourself when you, as a Senior Officer, should delegate."

Shelby closed his mouth. "Touché," he said. "Okay, then, if you think you can manage, Professor, then do."

Chapter 18

THROUGH GO-BETWEENS, THE TWO strangers had arranged to meet at a derelict farm. Its rutted cart road had a healthy growth of weeds topped with a frost that lingered on the high ground up here north of Castleford. Long ago, vandals had shattered the farm's windows, the remaining ones clouded by cobwebs; flaking, cracked doors hung from seized hinges and the thin sleet blew unobstructed around the stack yard carried on a biting wind. Rotting wooden gutters spilled water down moss-covered stone walls. The smell of decay hung in the air like a ghost.

This particular brick shed was dim. It had only one window and a silted-up skylight. It was oppressive. Musty. The lingering smell of cattle and of old diesel oil was choking. A damp odour saturated the air too, seeped from the dirty whitewashed walls.

"You got a name? They call me Beaver." He stood opposite the stranger, a rusty waist-high filing cabinet between them, not really knowing if he could trust the man or not; not knowing if he would actually walk out of here or meet his end spitting oily dust with the smell of frozen cow shit in his nostrils. He chewed gum. All he wanted was to get his stuff and be away from here *and* this creep as quick as he could. Beaver buried his tattooed hands into the pockets of his denim jacket, and tried but failed to see through the man's sunglasses and get a look at his eyes. He was short, wide as a house, crooked nose like it had been broken several times.

"I'm not interested in what they call you, or even who *they* are."

"Fine," Beaver said. "What you got for me, then?"

"You got a good memory?"

You bet your arse I have, Beaver thought. When it came to information like this, his memory was spot on. "Just tell me." Beaver stared at the man, hoping to see some sign of weakness, a long swallow, or the slip of a smile. Nothing; there was no detectable emotion. No weakness.

"Thirteen, Wedgwood Grove, Wakefield."

"What's he look like?"

The man's leather jacket creaked. "He lives alone with his crippled wife; they don't get too many coach parties dropping by. Shouldn't be too difficult to work out."

"Good description," he chewed.

"His hair's a mess."

Beaver laughed. "Is that it, his fucking hair's a mess?"

"Tall, six foot, maybe six-one. Slim, wears glasses."

"Well that's better than 'his fucking hair's a mess'."

"You don't want to fuck with me, kid. You might have a skin-head and tattoos all over your neck, but it doesn't make you hard."

"What time's he usually home?"

"He works shifts. Better hunker down and prepare for a long wait."

Beaver's eyes sparkled. "Who are you?"

"Someone you need to stay on the right side of."

Out of the two, Beaver turned away first. "The equipment?"

The man in the scuffed leather jacket reached inside a pocket with a massive gloved hand, pulled out a gun and placed it on the filing cabinet. He slid the weapon over towards Beaver.

'You need the right equipment, Beaver,' Jess had said, 'and I know someone who knows someone with just such equipment. Get it, learn how to use it, and blow the fucker's mind away. If you do a good job, you'll be hearing from us'.

He picked it up, felt its weight, and curled his hand around its knurled grip. He admired its dull shine by the diffused glow from the skylight. He sniffed it. "It's brand new," he said rubbing oil from the trigger into his fingers. "How come it's brand new, I didn't expect a brand new weapon."

"So give it back and I'll be on my way." The man held out his hand.

"Can it be traced? I mean, it's brand new; a used gun can't be traced."

"You're new to this game, aren't you?" The man mocked.

"What's that supposed to mean?"

"You *need* a brand new weapon." He spoke slowly and deliberately. "Suppose you get caught with a used gun, suppose the police send it to ballistics—"

"Now you're talking shit!"

"Am I? I know a bit about forensics, kid."

Beaver looked at the gun; saw the obliterated serial number. He felt its weight again and adored the power it gave him. He almost had a semi on. "Go on."

The man's lips barely moved when he spoke. "If a gun is tested forensically, they can match it to any crime it was used in. You're caught with a used gun, kid; you're caught for its crimes."

"They can't prove—"

"Listen to yourself!" He slapped the filing cabinet and dust bounced into the air. Then he said, "You're a bright kid, you've been away, you know what it's like to have a record; it would be down to *you* to prove that you didn't do whatever the gun says you did."

Beaver thought it over. It made sense.

"Do you want to spend your time looking at it, or do you want something to fire from it?"

"It don't come with bullets?"

"I never transport weapons and ammunition together."

"You don't want to piss me about or—"

"Put your fucking mouth to sleep, boy." The man pointed a finger right in Beaver's face. "Remember this; I'm doing you a favour, I don't normally deal with street shit like you. So mind your tongue before I pull it out through your fucking nose. Clear?"

Beaver stopped chewing, "Where's the clip?"

The man in the black leather jacket and dark glasses walked away from Beaver, heading for the door. "It's in a brown paper bag hidden in the grass by the left gate post."

"Which gate post?" Beaver strode after him, but the man turned and stared. Beaver thought it would be a lot healthier to stay just where he was.

"At the entrance to the farm."

"And what do I do if I need more ammunition? How did you know I'd only need one clip?" he shouted. A gloved hand pulled the creaking door closed behind it, and left Beaver alone thinking he'd just been rogered wholesale.

He smacked the clip home with the heel of his hand just like they did on TV, and then slipped the weapon into the front of his belt, paused, thought better of it and tucked it into his back pocket.

Beaver walked further into the harsh countryside, Jess's instruction being to practice. He would fire half the clip and hope that would be enough. If nothing else, it would get him accustomed to the gun's kick.

Chapter 19

— One —

WHEN CHRIS ARRIVED AT Nicky's house, Gareth, the technician from the Fingerprint Development Laboratory, was waiting outside in his car, the engine running, heater on full and wipers intermittently flicking rainwater from the screen.

Chris recorded his time at the scene with the log-jockey, who told him that Shelby was already inside awaiting their arrival. Chris thanked him, then shook Gareth's hand – a soft, wimpish shake, and exchanged the usual inter-departmental pleasantries. "Have you booked in?" he nodded towards the officer with the clipboard.

"Oh yes, done that," Gareth said. "Are we suiting up?"

"No need. I think we have all the trace evidence we're likely to get."

"Okay. Which room are we starting in?"

Chris said, "This way. I'll give you a hand with your kit." Struggling with an umbilicus, something similar to a thin vacuum cleaner hose, two large aluminium boxes, a transformer and a further plastic box of goggles and black sheeting, they made it into the lounge and then stopped and listened to the shouting coming from upstairs. "Just follow the noise," Chris said.

"Lenny, just write the bloody thing!" Shelby was screaming.

Chris looked at Gareth and saw the worried look on his face.

"It's a simple report, for God's sake. Yes. Yes! You know the headings, I left you a pro-forma." Shelby sank into the monotonous tone of someone reciting a list. "What risks did the offender take entering the house or using an escape route? What physical or emotional aggression was required for her to become compliant? What? I don't bloody know; think of one yourself for a change. Yes, one more heading: Planning. Is it possible he used reconnaissance, or even had a rehearsal of some kind? And what did he do to avoid detection?" There was a growl.

"He's a pussycat, really," joked Chris. "Come on, best not keep him waiting."

They struggled up the stairs and into the bedroom. Shelby stood at the window, phone pressed awkwardly to his ear, fingers crawling through his thin hair. It was 11.35; results were slowly coming in, but not all of them were of the positive variety that Shelby wanted. The errant next-door neighbour had been located in Wales but could shed no light on any of their questions, more intent it seemed to carry on with his holiday. No results from house-to-house, zero from the taxi companies.

"Got that? Good. Yes. On my desk by 1600hrs because I have to have it on Chamberlain's desk by 1800hrs. What? Never mind bloody squash!"

Shelby hit end, rammed the phone into his jacket pocket and turned to face Chris and Gareth. He let out a sigh. "Thanks for coming," he said with no particular enthusiasm. He patted the phone through the pocket, "I hate these things. They always know where you are, they never leave you alone, and *ha*, Lenny Firth suddenly turned fucking stupid on me. One more IQ point and he'd be a glass of water."

Chris laughed, Gareth quietly set up the equipment, plugged it into the mains and selected a filter for the Quasar.

"All set then?" Shelby stepped aside, rubbing his hands. Chris was about to answer when Shelby's pocket rang. "Bear with me a minute." He walked from the room and yelled into the mouthpiece, "Yes!"

The machine hummed as Chris flicked on the light switch, taped a black plastic bag over the window to minimise ambient light, and waited for Shelby to finish his ranting.

"Is he always like this?" Gareth whispered.

"Is that why you looked so worried when I pulled up outside?"

"It showed?"

"He is when things don't go his way. And things are not going his way. Not these days, anyway."

Shelby came back into the room, his face long and full of disappointment. "Better find me some fingerprints, lad. Those *you* found, Chris, aren't much to go on, unfortunately."

"You are taking the piss, I hope!"

"Six of the nine you sent in were hers, one belonged to her brother, one was crap – Barry from the Fingerprint Bureau's words, not mine – and the other is unidentified."

"Has he fed it through the AFR system?"

"Yup, no joy."

"The NAFIS computer?"

"Give him time, man."

Chris muttered something about incompetence, and tutted to Shelby.

"Don't worry, I've asked him to do a manual search and then to check all attending officers. I've arranged for someone to go to the bank and get elims from that Joanne woman. I suppose he's doing the best he can, though it can't come quick enough for me."

"Me neither," echoed Chris. "Where's the photographer? He was supposed to meet us here at 11.45."

"Anyway, get on with it lad, let's see if we can't find a few for him to look at when he finally arrives."

Much to Shelby's disgust, Gareth placed a warning sign outside the room, closed the door and commenced the safety briefing required when using this apparatus. "This is a 400 nanometre-wavelength filter we're using, so we need...see here on the card? We need a filter of 380 or more. Let's check our goggles for the—"

"Oh, get on with it, man!"

Gareth put his goggles down and stared at Shelby.

"What're you waiting for, lad, get—"

"Listen, you dragged me out here to do you a favour, Inspector Shelby, and I'm doing you that favour."

Shelby's jaw went slack.

"This safety chat I'm giving is not only obligatory under Health and Safety, but I happen to think it's a good idea; I find being able to see quite useful. If I've read the card incorrectly or given you the wrong goggles – who's blind and who's to blame?"

"Okay, okay, now get on with it."

"Sir," Gareth said, "check your goggles for the correct frequency or I'll have to insist you leave the room while I carry out the examination."

He snatched the goggles and snapped, "What's the frequency?"

Gareth responded, "Thank you, sir. 380 nanometre."

Shelby shuffled his feet and pulled the goggles on, "Right, find me some marks."

Gareth put his goggles on and bid Chris do the same.

The room was in near darkness, only cracks and chinks of light slithered in through minute gaps around Chris's makeshift blackout curtain, and more poured in through gaps around the door. It was like staring up at a midnight sky on a clear winter's night.

The torch, fed by the umbilicus from the main machine, spewed a cone of yellowish light at the walls. The cone was six inches across, but was magnificently bright; even with the goggles sealed onto their sweating faces the glare was atrocious. When the light illuminated an area of contamination, its reflected hue was bluish green.

For several minutes, Gareth played the light between waist and shoulder height across two or more yards of wall before anything substantial showed itself. "Keep your goggles on," he crossed to the main machine and selected another filter of a different frequency. "I'm placing a 420 filter into the machine," he robotically recited, "and the 380 goggles are still safe." He returned to the mark on the wall, trained the cone onto it and four fingerprints from a small left hand shone back at the group, almost dazzling them.

Chris placed an adhesive arrow near the marks and that too, like the white shirts of nightclub dancers under fluorescent lights, gleamed a brilliant white.

They continued all along one wall, finding and arrowing marks until Chris stood, gripped the small of his back and said, "Right Graham, that's it for me. I'm off to the mortuary now; see if the PolyLight has shown up."

"Wouldn't fucking surprise me if it hadn't."

Gareth turned off the machine and then hurriedly gathered the goggles back into the plastic box.

Chris's forehead was wet through and an odour of rubber and moisture filled his nostrils. Again, the room appeared brighter, and the marks, which were so evident under the high intensity light, returned to complete invisibility again.

Shelby continued. "You've got my mobile number, haven't you?"

"Thought you didn't want people ringing you," Chris smiled.

"I want that poly thing there and working as arranged, I don't want anybody crying off. Understood?"

"I'll sort it. Don't panic."

Gareth skulked in the corner, cuddling his machine.

"And ring me as soon as you've got any news. Any news at all."

"I will, don't worry."

"Don't worry, he says," talking to no one in particular. "Where's that sodding photographer!"

— Two —

Chris headed for the mortuary, past the splendour of nineteenth century buildings in the city's centre, and out the other side where the quality plummeted into an abyss of red brick council estates.

The midday news spilled out of the tinny van radio. News of more job cuts at a local clothing manufacturer, news of men trapped in a pothole in the Dales. Then, the newscaster's crackling voice made an unusual appeal:

"Police are asking for help in the murder of a local girl, Nicky Bridgestock, from Wakefield. They are anxious to trace the key to her house, which was believed to have been secured by her murderer. The single Yale key is on a ring with a distinctive fob, showing a small male figurine about an inch and a half tall, in a state of sexual excitement. If anyone knows of its whereabouts, could they please contact the Wakefield Incident Room on..."

He parked the van in the mortuary car park and listened to the sports headlines. When they came and he heard the bad news, he screwed up the betting slip and tossed it on the van floor. He closed his eyes and banged the window with a fist. That was his last chance to make this week's payment without having to sell anything and without having them pay another embarrassing visit at work.

Absorbing the stillness for a moment, he collected his thoughts and prayed that his assiduous dedication came to Bell's attention. Quickly.

He rolled his cardigan sleeves down and covered the goose pimples on his arms, climbed from the van and trudged into the mortuary. Ann Halfpenny lounged in one of the side rooms eating a microwave lasagne and sipping coffee from a mug that bore the legend: 'Mortuary Technician – working with a stiffy!' It was supposed to be a rest room; it had an old black and white TV in the corner and copies of 1973 *Homes and House* magazines on a low heavily stained table. Torn chairs were scattered around the room, and overflowing ashtrays and countless cigarette burns gave the fawn carpet tiles a pattern.

"Hello Annie," Chris poked his head into the room. "Still taking the diet seriously, then?"

She waved two fingers at him. "Want some coffee?" she asked through a mouthful of pasta.

"Why not." Chris chose a seat facing the car park. "Might as well relax until the man from FDL decides to show up. Can't get staff these days."

"Funny, he said exactly that about ten minutes ago." She revelled in his embarrassment and passed the cup. "He's through there," she pointed at the theatre, "setting his gear up. You know, Chris, *he* refused a cup of coffee, said he didn't want to keep you waiting."

"Ah."

Ann laughed at the look on his face. "Drink your coffee; I'll wash up and then I'll pull her out of the freezer."

"Freezer! You've not bunged her in the bloody freezer?"

"No, I haven't. But I can't get enough of that face of yours, deary. She's in the fridge, you prat. Go on through, I'll be there in a mo."

"So it's just some writing on her left hand then?"

Chris stared at Peter Lord, Gareth's colleague from FDL, and thought his hair was too damned long. "Won't take us too long, eh?"

"It shouldn't be too taxing. Shall we make a start?"

They pulled back the cloth covering Nicky's body.

Chris winced. Her skin was not just pale any longer, but white, clammy like a bar of soap left in cold water. Her lips were blue, her fingers almost translucent, and she felt as cold as ice. Her breasts now sagged either side of her torn rib cage, sexless.

"Hello," said Peter, waving a hand in front of Chris's far away eyes, "Sorry, I didn't mean to startle you."

"No, that's fine. You didn't startle me," he began removing the plastic bag from Nicky's left hand. "I'll get the lights."

Ann drew down the thick black blinds and suddenly the room fell from brilliant white into mind-numbing blackness. Green shapes floated before Chris's eyes, but all he could genuinely see was a fluorescent marker by the light switch, another by the fire extinguishers, and blinking LEDs on Peter's flash pack.

"Shall we try low power UV first?" Peter asked. They did, but all it succeeded in showing them was the glowing hairs on her arms and dark patches on her grey neck and thorax where her blood had stained. "I thought we'd get better results than that."

"Don't worry; let's crack on with the heavyweight gear."

"I heard that!" Peter's voice boomed. No Health and Safety spiel this time; Peter threw Ann and Chris a pair of well-used goggles. "Ready?" he asked, grabbing a pair for himself.

"Go for it." Chris held Nicky's arm in gloved hands while Peter played the strong yellowish light across her dead flesh.

"If anything of value does show up, you'll have to hold the PolyLight and I'll take the snaps if that's okay, Chris?"

"Not a problem."

The light stroked her hand. The ink they had all seen yesterday with their naked eyes was even more discernible, appeared refined.

"Looks like…I don't know," Peter spoke his words slowly, concentrating on the light source, "Looks a bit like …'R'? Wouldn't you say?"

"Can't really make it out, do it again."

Peter did, and this time, he could see it quite clearly. The ink had penetrated the epidermis. The strength of the light permeating her skin reflected off the ink a slightly modified colour, giving contrast and clarity.

Chris studied the ink, came closer, close enough to feel the coolness of her skin against his own hot face. "Yeah, I see it now. Do you think that might be an 'o' next…or maybe an 'a', lower case?"

"An 'o', I'd say. Though I'm not totally sure."

"How about we try a different filter?"

"Yep, I'll go with that."

Another two changes of filter finally convinced Peter that he was seeing was an 'o', after all. They then identified the following letter, a 'g'.

They photographed her hand again, using ultra violet-sensitive film and a non-reflective sticky scale. A further thirty minutes of playing revealed four numbers of what could have been, according to Peter, a telephone number. They photographed the numbers in the same fashion with Chris teasing the light source around them as Peter struggled with the tripod's position. The rest of the numbers were indiscernible smears.

"Shelby will be well chuffed with this," Chris said.

Ann turned the lights back on and everyone blinked away the dazzle, stuffing the goggles back into a plastic bag.

"Good. I like it when you're in the thick of it, you know, when an investigation like this can leap forward three of four hefty places because of the information you've supplied to it."

"How long before we have the positives?"

Peter rolled up the mains flex and shut the portable machine inside an aluminium case. "I should be able to have them on your desk..." he looked at his watch, "by three."

"Excellent!" Chris had made a mental note of the findings, but confirmation by photograph would reassure Shelby. And that was all that mattered.

Chris set off back to the office, hoping against hope that Roger would come good with the three hundred. Quickly.

Chapter 20

— One —

BELL OPENED THE FILE marked 'Departmental Promotions' and scanned the preliminary pages before turning to the back and reading his summary of each player's performance, right from the application form stage, through the aptitude tests and the interview, all the way to here: acting up.

"Oh, I don't know," he rubbed his chin, slid his spectacles back up his nose and returned to the first page. Even now, after all the necessary 'evidence' was in, he had trouble making up his mind whom to appoint. It was a close call between both of them: Conniston and Hutchinson.

He gazed out through the blind and into the hibernating gardens that ambled gracefully along the HQ building on Laburnum Road. Directly below his first floor window, a small fountain trickled water into an overflowing stone bowl, though the incessant wind blew much of it away in a spray. Speckles of rain landing on the window distorted the view.

Bell liked Conniston, liked the way he performed at jobs and especially liked the reports he had accrued from Senior Officers and, ironically, from Hutchinson too. But something niggled him. He knew that Conniston's approach to discipline was softer than his own, and certainly more lenient than Hutchinson's. But Conniston loved the job, and that counted for a lot.

And, having considered all that, Bell was reluctant to pass such a responsibility onto Hutchinson for no other reason than the man was arrogant enough to consider himself a natural choice. Bell turned away from the fountain, retook his seat and searched the two names again, hoping for a clear answer to the dilemma.

Conniston had something even more persuasive in his arsenal than did Hutchinson. He had integrity and honesty. And of course, there was Hutchinson's inability to control his fiscal affairs. But in Hutchinson's favour were the years of experience, a sound understanding of technical processes and an undeniable authority figure that new-starters and wayward old-timers would take seriously.

Hopefully the answer would come soon, in less than an hour.

— Two —

Roger signed off the CIS computer and sat there staring at the screen wondering what made Chris so damned jumpy, so damned insistent he came to the Bridgestock scene. His shoes were still damp, and they made him shudder as he put them back on. He just towel dried his hands and mopped up the water that had squeezed out from the laces, when the phone rang. "Conniston of Wood Street," he said on autopilot.

"Roger," said Denis Bell. "Roger, are you there?"

"Yes, yes, Mr Bell, sorry, I was miles away."

"To be expected if you've been on duty since six."

"I've had a pretty—"

"What happened on your night week? I've had Inspector Weston complaining about something of which he thinks I should be aware."

Roger slumped back into his chair and squeezed his eyes closed. "Yes, Mr Bell, I can explain."

"Good. I am glad to hear it. You're off duty in twenty minutes. Come and see me now."

"Now?"

"What I have to say won't wait until tomorrow, I'm afraid."

He needed to get home for Yvonne, and then he remembered he and Lenny had a squash court booked. The two mixed in his mind as he fought for the excuse to give Mr Bell, and all he could think of saying was, "But I've got squash in an hour." And then he shook his head, couldn't believe he just said that.

"Never mind squash! I want you standing before my desk in fifteen minutes – get an escort if need be!" He hung up.

Roger abandoned the paperwork and the accumulated exhibits, picked up his old jacket for the wash, and squelched out of the office, chin resting on his chest. On the way over to HQ, he fastened the top button on his shirt and tweaked his tie into place.

— Three —

Denis Bell laid his gold-rimmed spectacles carefully on his leather-bound desk blotter. "Chris tells me that your wife is in a certain amount of distress."

"He does?"

"He inferred that this could explain your absence from the office around midnight."

"Yvonne has arthritis. It comes and goes in waves, changes as often as the damned weather. But lately her knees are inflamed and her ankles are beginning to twist inwards slightly." He tried to smooth down his tuft of hair, feeling suddenly self-conscious.

"I can sympathise," Bell said. "Both my parents suffered with it until they passed away. It's a debilitating disease." He studied his desk blotter for a moment, as though thinking of the past. Then he said, "So am I to take it that your unannounced absence was due to unforeseen family circumstances?" He raised an eyebrow, almost prompting Roger to agree.

He did, despite telling Weston that he was ill. "Yes, that's right, Mr Bell. I had to go—"

Bell palmed away Roger's words, picked up his fountain pen and scribbled on a sickness form. "You don't have to explain; I just need something to shut Weston up. Weston is a man devoted to paperwork and procedures. The more the better, I think; he wakes up on page one and only goes to bed when he has reached the end of the chapter. Do you follow me?"

"Yes," he mumbled, "I think so."

"Right, we'll say no more on that, then." He completed the form without another word. "How long have you worked for us, Roger?"

"About nine years. Ten in another three months or so."

"Do you feel that you've gained knowledge of a wide diversity of crime scenes?"

"I've handled everything from RTAs, arson, rape, to murder and suicide…" he wondered what Bell was fishing for. "I suppose I've done almost everything a SOCO could expect to encounter, except a bomb scene, and SO13 would deal with that anyway. But," he quickly pointed out, "that doesn't mean I'm perfect, and it doesn't mean I'm not still learning, because I am – willing to learn, that is. If you stand still in this profession, then you're going backwards. Look at DNA," he enthused, "when I started, they were only getting partials from large crime stains using Quad profiling, now with SGM they can get full profiles from next to nothing, with a probability of one in fifty-million!"

Bell leaned back in his chair, didn't stop Roger displaying his passion for the art and craft of the profession; he was enjoying the sight of someone still excited by it.

"How would you feel if I appointed Chris Hutchinson as Supervisor at Wood Street?"

Roger took a moment to think. He said, "Fine. I don't have a problem working with anyone, Mr Bell. We get along well anyway." He wondered where this was leading. "If you chose him," he continued, "then he must be right for the job."

"Conversely, how would you feel if I chose you?"

"Delighted," he said immediately, and then followed it after a moment's consideration with, "But I'd need some help with office management from other Supervisors. Lanky ran the office without letting anyone else help, so I'd need guidance."

"How do you think Chris would react?"

He'd blow a gasket, thought Roger. "Ah, the big question," he said. "I don't think he'd be too impressed. He thinks it's his already— sorry, that's just the impression I get. But I would hope he'd come around to the idea. I'm not an ogre, after all."

"Are you listening carefully, Roger?"

"Yes, Mr Bell."

"Roger," he said. "Call me Denis."

— Four —

Roger closed the back door and let the wind and the rain and the outside world dissolve. He had a grin across his face that made his cheeks ache, and he savoured the moment. He placed his old jacket in the utility room and customarily waved two fingers at Weston's photograph.

Yvonne stared at him with a mixture of surprise and curiosity in her eyes.

"How are you?"

"I'm fine," she said. "I see you beat Lenny at squash again."

He didn't correct her, merely widened his grin. "Is your knee okay now?"

"Roger, what's happened?"

Roger kicked his damp shoes off and swaggered through into the lounge where Yvonne sat before her needlework, lengths of cotton draped across her lap.

"We're going out for dinner tonight," he said.

She put down her needle, turned in the chair and paid him more attention. "Are you going to tell me—"

"Did you remember to take your tablets?"

"For God's sake!"

Roger sat in the chair opposite her and rubbed his nails on his waistcoat, a look of exaggerated pride smeared across his face.

Yvonne's mouth fell open. "You got it, didn't you?"

He nodded and began to laugh.

Yvonne screamed with delight, and then put her hands over her mouth while she briefly pondered the news. News duly pondered, she shrieked again and waved her arms in the air. "Come here," she called, "come here, you... you... Oh, just come here!"

Never had a meal tasted so good, but never had Roger wanted so much to be home. And when they came home, they shared a glass or two of champagne. "Are you proud of me now, Yvonne?"

She put her glass down and hugged him tightly. "Did you ever doubt it? But I hope you didn't do this for me, Roger; hope you did it for yourself."

He nodded. "I did it for both of us."

"What about Chris?" Yvonne asked.

"Nope, I didn't do it for Chris."

She prodded his chest, "You know what I mean. He's going to be distraught."

"Denis is going to sort it. I think he's having a meeting with him sometime tomorrow evening after Chris has finished with this murder he's working on."

"Oh, the Bridgestock girl? How's it going, anyone in the traps yet?"

Roger shrugged. "Not a clue; no one's spoken a word of it, which means *they* haven't a clue either."

"Hey," she said, "we'll have to get you a new waistcoat now you're a manager."

"I like my old one just fine. Don't want to change a thing. Though the idea of a pocket watch sounds good."

"You old man." She snuggled into the space between his neck and his shoulder. "Bet you can't wait to tell your family, can you?"

He thought about it, and then said, "They don't need to know."

"I love you," she whispered, playing with his mop of hair.

Chapter 21

Friday 22nd January 1999

— One —

DESPITE HIS TIPTOEING DOWN the stairs and the obvious care he took in closing the noisy back door, she still heard him go when the car pulled off the drive. Yvonne pulled back the bedclothes.

Her head ached from last night's celebrating. She smiled as she remembered his proud swagger. Yes, last night was good, and she thought of it as the first step she had to take in trusting him again. It would be a long time, she supposed, before things ever got back to how they used to be, before she could feel him crawl into the bed beside her after a late shift and not wonder if he'd crawled into someone else's bed earlier.

Once downstairs, Yvonne put the radio on and then put her makeup on. And after her daily exercises, she busied herself with the laundry, listening to the news. That's when she found the key in Roger's old jacket. He'd left it hanging over the director's chair in the utility room ready for the wash.

A routine pocket search located a couple of crumpled Mars bars and a hole in the lining. And when she poked her fingers through, they came back out holding a single key.

The key meant nothing to her, but the fob was amusing. It was a little rubber man with a proud grin on his face and a massive erection held in his right hand. She threw the jacket into the machine and giggled at the little man in his erotic pose. Why would Roger have someone else's key in his pocket; someone else's *house* key? Then she stopped giggling and her face straightened; she remembered the news and the appeal they had made yesterday. The appeal for an unusual house key.

— Two —

Chris sat in Shelby's hot office, fingers drumming on his knee, his mind at work praying that Captain Gemini won the 2.30 at Doncaster. This really was his last chance of staying pain free. Outside in the general CID office and across the hall in the Incident Room there was excited activity.

He knew the investigation was beginning to wind down and that's when things got like this: more people inside fretting about paperwork than outside making further enquiries and pulling the drawstrings of the investigation neatly together.

This morning, he had come straight to the Incident Room to update Shelby with yesterday's findings at the mortuary. Within minutes, the news had spread and the investigators' fervour boiled.

The door closed and Chris jumped. The noise from outside snapped away and Shelby stood in its place with an armful of folders. His complexion was a lot paler than recently, healthier, though his demeanour was sombre. He walked past Chris and dropped the folders on his considerably neater desk. "I'm processing Section 18 warrant paperwork, making sure it's all in order. We don't want to piss the magistrate off, eh?"

Deflated, Chris looked away. He knew it wouldn't be long before they asked him to leave the remainder of the investigation to them, and tell him not to discuss what he knew with anyone.

"Have you anything else to add, then?" Shelby asked.

"Like what?"

"I don't know, anything—"

"'That may assist with your enquiries'?"

"Something like that."

"You know the phone number might not even be his?"

"You done the maths?"

"What maths?"

"The probability that a man named Rog has the same four digits in his phone number that Nicky Bridgestock had written on her hand?"

"And you have?"

"No. But you're the statistician, you work it out."

Chris answered, blank-faced. "I can't believe it."

"*You* can't believe it? Think how I feel, I've never been so wrong about a person before. The whole station is on the back foot because of this. Fuck, I hate this job sometimes."

"The whole station doesn't know about it yet."

"Stop being pedantic, Chris, you know what I mean." Shelby slumped in his seat, rocked back in it and rubbed his eyes. "Wait till the fucking press get a hold of it. You've not seen shock till they get hold of it. You won't be able to walk into your local store without hearing someone slating the police. And Chamberlain is spitting blood—"

"Are you going to need a personal statement from me, you know, about his recent behaviour, his recent... misdemeanours?"

Shelby raised his eyebrows. "It's for CPS to decide, but I expect so, yeah. Anyway," he said, "what misdemeanours?"

"You can read it in the statement. It's not something I want to gossip about." He shook his head, looked past Shelby, and out of the window that framed a turbulent sky. "I just never suspected a thing."

"Look, I know it's not easy for you; you've worked with him for years, and so have I, come to think of it." Shelby pushed aside the files and the papers spilling from them, and leaned forward again, elbows resting on his desk. "It reminds me of the eighties when bad coppers were being pulled out by the scruff of their necks. Discipline & Complaints had never been so fucking busy with obs and court appearances, and they'd never been so hated by their own colleagues, because some of them were taking backhanders or turning a blind eye. Most of 'em had done nothing wrong. Nothing."

"Come on, Graham. You're saying your friends were innocent of taking backhanders, mine's guilty of murder! No comparison."

"Yeah, you're right. Bad analogy. But I also had friends I'd worked with for years exposed as rotten – and I never suspected a thing! Somehow, it turns your perception of the world upside down. It sends the black-and-white way that we see good versus bad into something grey and hazy where no one's really sure anymore. It's shitty when the good guys – aren't."

"Shit," was all Chris said as he stood up, ready to leave.

"Well, you know what I'm going to ask now, don't you?"

"I think I probably do, yes."

Shelby rose and stretched out a hand, his big round chin shaping his mouth into a pleasant smile. "Well, thanks for everything you've done, Chris. I can see why they call you the Professor; you've been a fantastic source of knowledge."

— Three —

Chris tried to distance himself from the dregs of the enquiry. He found himself perched on a plastic chair in the canteen. It was getting busy. Growing cold in front of him was a shepherd's pie and chips. He ignored it and sipped from a cup with the West Yorkshire police crest on its side.

Behind the counter, Kay, one of the kitchen staff, prepared food for the prisoners in the bridewell on the ground floor. She stacked the plates up in a pile of four using metal plate dividers, before backing out of the kitchens and heading for the lift.

Around him sat uniformed officers, CID and support staff, chewing the cud and chewing the fat with each other. Their mellow banter and occasional raucous laughter went unheard by him.

Over in the corner, the TV showed a sombre news reporter. His lips moved silently before the picture cut to an equally sombre Chamberlain, mouthing some silent plea before the camera panned down to a key ring, phallus and all, the same plea they ran on yesterday's news. A few of the officers in the canteen jeered at Chamberlain and laughed at the fob. As the Incident Room hotline flashed onto the screen, Chris wondered how the West Yorkshire police attained its straight-laced image with arseholes like this working for it.

"Still not found the key then?" Micky pulled up a seat and encroached upon Chris's space and thoughts.

"Don't know. And even if I did, which I don't, I couldn't tell you. I've been sworn to secrecy by Shelby." He watched the news, hoping Micky would get the hint and leave, or at least eat his meal in silence.

"Oh yeah?" Micky scooped up a shovelful of potato, "Must have someone in mind then?" He asked the question bluntly, not even hinting. It was Micky's way.

"Watch this space."

"So you *do* know what's going down then?"

He tutted. "I know nothing."

"Well," Micky looked around to make sure all those in earshot were engaged in their own conversations, "I've heard that it's someone close to home. Very close to home."

"Who?"

"Dunno. I was kind of hoping you could fill me in with that one."

"Can't. Sorry." He sipped more coffee, saw the queue forming at the counter. At its head was a tuft of hair he recognised. Stick around, Micky, you're about to be filled in. Chris watched Roger pay for his meal, gather a knife and fork and then walk into the centre of the melee looking for a friendly face with whom to sit. He approached Chris.

Chris's stomach heaved. He thumbed the crest faster.

Roger seemed unaware of the net closing in all around him, the 'drawstrings', Chris thought.

He pulled up a seat and sat opposite. "Look, Chris, about the Quasar job, I—"

Chris waved a hand. "Forget it. It was a stupid request in the first bloody place."

"You sure?"

"Don't worry about it."

"So how's the investigation coming along then? Any news?"

"He's keeping stumm," chirped Micky. "I think he knows, but he's not saying."

"I'm not *allowed* to say."

"Must be someone close or important then." Roger began to eat, but his eyes never left Chris.

Chris's head dropped.

"Micky, have you, er, have you spoken to Helen recently?" Roger asked.

Micky ignored him.

"Thought not. I think you should; she feels abandoned—"

"I didn't abandon her, she abandoned me!" Micky paused, and then his angry eyes softened. "It's not my fault she's a fucking psycho." He put down his fork, and sighed. "Maybe I'll talk to her, see if we can get back on track."

Roger nodded, smiled reassuringly. "She'd like that," he said. "She misses you."

"She said that?"

"Oh yes. She's so depressed these days. She mopes around in the office so much that we've rechristened her the Olympic torch."

"Why?" Micky asked.

"Because she never goes out," Roger laughed.

Micky stared at Roger with a blank face.

Chris didn't find it amusing; in fact he thought Roger, despite being close to Micky, was being intrusive. He couldn't wait to get away from both of them.

Only a few minutes passed before Roger's plate was empty and he slurped orange juice from a polystyrene cup. "Are you okay, Chris?"

"Tired."

"Not hungry?" Micky asked.

A group of three strangers entered the canteen, looking around their unfamiliar surroundings. They were CID officers from another division who Chris recognised from the briefing. They spoke to diners at the first table they came to. The diners searched and then pointed in his direction. This is it, thought Chris.

"Chris?" Roger said.

"What?" His eyes didn't leave the approaching men. The three CID men discreetly circled tables, moved apologetically around diners, but headed this way still, concentrating on Roger's back.

"What's bothering you?"

"I'm fine," Chris mumbled, knowing Roger wouldn't push any further.

Roger's concern was evident, but he changed the subject. "How's Paul getting along?" he asked, unaware of the men approaching only a few paces away.

"Roger Conniston?"

Roger stared up into the strong face of a very tall but equally thin grey-suited detective from the Criminal Investigation Department who leaned ominously over him. "Yes," he answered, waiting for some kind of punch line.

"Would you mind accompanying me and my colleagues to a more private area?"

"Why?" he asked, now on the defensive, but now also worrying about Yvonne for no logical reason.

"We have some matters to discuss."

"Look," he began, "if it's about a job—"

"It's nothing to do with any job."

"Then what's so important it can't wait until I've finished my meal?"

"We would prefer to do this in a more—"

"Whoa, whoa. Wait a minute. Do *what*, exactly?" Around him, the room grew quieter and stiller. People began to stare.

Chris watched the TV.

"Please, Roger." The suit used his Christian name. "All will be revealed. But can we please go elsewhere?"

"No." Roger faced front.

Micky stopped eating.

"Mr Conniston, I shall ask you once more to step into a more private atmosphere."

Roger ignored the suit and drank his orange.

Two of the three detectives hauled him out of his seat.

Chris saw a couple of uniformed officers rising to their feet, unsure of what was going on, but they were unwilling to see a much liked friend being upset by three unknown officers. Others among them pulled them back into their seats, saying it was none of their business.

Roger's shouting increased in volume and ferocity. Chris saw him look at Micky for support, but all Micky could do was sit there, dumbfounded; he recognised heavies when he saw them.

"Roger Conniston, I am arresting you on suspicion of the murder of Nicky Bridgestock…"

"What!" cried Roger. "You can't do this. I never…"

"You do not have to say anything…"

"…even met her. I don't even know where she lives."

"…but it may harm your defence if you do not mention when questioned something which you later rely on in court."

"I've never hurt anyone in my life. Chris, tell them!"

Chris sipped his coffee.

"Micky, you know me, I wouldn't—"

"Anything you do say may be given in evidence."

To Chris he looked afraid, had the big wide eyes of a cow being dragged into the slaughterhouse.

"Get off me!"

They pulled Roger through the crowded canteen. The silent, staring canteen. Officers made way for the struggling CID men and their newly acquired 10-12.

"Fucking get off me!"

The double doors swung shut and Roger's shouting died away in the same way a prisoner's shouting dies away when the cell door slams shut.

"You knew, didn't you?" Micky asked.

Chris said nothing, thumbed the crest again, slower this time. The room hummed into life as gossip rose to a crescendo.

"Why didn't you tell him, why didn't you go with him? You could've helped him, Chris; you could've saved his face," he scowled, "instead of having half the nick watch—"

"Shut up, Micky."

"There's been a fucking mix up, Chris. It's obvious, it happens all the time. He didn't kill anyone. You can't let him go through all this shit and not stand up for him; he's your friend, you Muppet!"

"Fuck off, Micky!" Chris threw the empty cup at the TV. The cup shattered. The room hushed again as Chris stood. Before he left room, acknowledging no one, he said to Micky, "The man is a murderer."

Chapter 22

— One —

"You okay?" Shelby asked.

"Take a wild guess," Roger replied.

"I'm sorry."

"Really? What are you sorry about? Are you sorry that I didn't get to finish my meal break or are you sorry that your imported gorillas hoisted me in front of the whole *fucking* station?" He calmed slightly when Shelby didn't respond.

The Custody Sergeant's fingers prodded the keyboard, a pen clutched between his teeth, busy booking a prisoner out.

Roger continued, "Graham, I've always liked you, you know I have; but I'm going to put you in a fucking sling for wrongful arrest, for unlawful imprisonment, and anything else I can stick on you!" Spittle flew from his mouth.

The prisoner looked across, smiling.

"Piss off!" Roger shouted.

The prisoner looked quickly away.

Shelby addressed the Custody Sergeant, "Book him in, Ellis," and then Shelby walked away. Roger watched the CCTV monitor by the sergeant's side. It showed the car park, only yards away in reality, through that gate and then an outer metal door that led to the van dock and freedom. Roger inched closer to the desk, peered at the buttons on the console, less than a foot from the sergeant's right elbow. Roger licked his lips.

"Don't even think about it."

Roger whirled around and came nose to nose with Inspector Weston. "Fuck!" he yelled.

"Indeed," said Weston. "How nice of you to visit us."

"Put him in Number 6 for us, Colin; I'm a bit stretched here," the sergeant said.

"Pleasure." Weston pushed Roger down the corridor. "I might pop in to see you in a bit. If you don't mind."

A shiver ran up Roger's back and the thought filled him with trepidation. Roger said, "You stay the hell away from me."

"Hey, it's no bother. I'd like to make sure you're settling in."

They reached the cell and Roger didn't even have the time to ask for water before he found himself skidding across the tiled floor on his belly. The cell door slammed and the locks turned.

Weston whistled a merry tune as he walked away.

Roger sat alone in the cell, staring at the plate of crusty food on the wooden bench beside him. He sipped a cool brown liquid that could have been coffee, and listened to the banter echoing up the corridor from the desk. He'd been photographed, had his fingerprints and DNA taken and then faced the indignity of having his outer clothes seized. He now wore a white suit similar to those he used at major scenes. His shoes were outside his cell.

Above him, a meagre light, shrouded by thick glass and further protected by a wire guard, almost begrudgingly spat a little light into his dark world. He surveyed the scratched cream walls, the damaged plank he was supposed to lie on, and the shiny but sticky tiled floor beneath his bare feet. In the corner was a stainless steel potty. On the floor, surrounding it, white alkaline stains of old piss.

It stank.

He thought about consequences: both of them. He thought about Yvonne, about how she'd just regained some of her faith in him… and he thought about his hard fought-for promotion, and how all this just blew both to shit.

The peephole in the door opened and a squinting eye peered at him. The peephole closed, and it took Roger a while to establish that the eye wasn't squinting at all, but was laughing. Laughing at him. His hands shook, and the coffee in the polystyrene cup rippled. His heart pounded and he felt sick. The lock turned and Roger's heart kicked up a gear. In the doorway stood Inspector Weston.

Weston checked up and down the corridor and then took a stride into Roger's very private space. He inched the door closed, and then stepped closer.

"Does the Custody Sergeant know you're in here?"

Weston shook his head, "Helped myself to his keys. I thought I'd have a little chat with my old mate."

"Well now you've had your chat, you can piss off and leave me alone."

"Not very friendly."

"Shock, horror."

Weston stood straight, shoulders back, neck swivelling, smiling, taking in the surroundings of the cell as though it was the luxurious lounge of a new show home. One of Weston's eyes focused on Roger, and then the other joined it. "No more following me, eh," he lifted his eyebrows and laughed like someone was tickling his feet. "I'm so happy you're here. I'm so fucking *happy* you got your just reward."

"I am not a murderer."

"Couldn't care less. You're here and that makes me happy." A large gold bracelet thudded against a gold watch. "You see, they do say that everything comes to those who wait. They do say that, don't they? I've waited a long time for this. And they also say what goes around comes around." He looked away, thinking. "Never really understood that myself, but I should think it means those who are slimy little wankers, such as you, will eventually share a shower with a slimy little wanker." And then he inhaled deeply as though taking pleasure from sea air. "Oh, I think they'll love having you in prison. I mean, they'll love *having* you, if you see what I mean." He came closer. "I er, I got friends in prison."

"Now why doesn't that surprise me?"

Weston twitched at that. "I think I'll get in touch with them, let them know you're about to come and live with 'em. I'm sure they'd welcome you." He stepped even closer, leather shoes squeaking, the smile elongating to a grin. "Ever since that firearms job that you stitched me—"

"I did not stitch—"

"That you *stitched* me up for," he continued undeterred, "I've longed for the day when you fell foul of the system. Really longed for the day." He whispered, "My life will be so much easier again, now that you're in here."

"When I get out of here, I'll fucking hound you so much you'll think you've grown a second shadow."

"Only way you'll get out of here is when you go to court."

"They'll release me by nightfall. And when they do—"

"If they do," Weston warned, "you'll be dead by daybreak."

And those words stopped him dead, as the slap from Alice had. But he couldn't let Weston see how shocked he was. His mouth continued all by itself. "You're lucky that you're not in the next cell."

Weston laughed, "Lucky? I don't believe in luck. I believe in planning. I believe in planning so much that I have every eventuality covered. And I believe I hate you more than I have hated anyone before; you started the enquiry that put me in an awkward position with people who depended on me. And I never forget them who cross me." Then he stood back as though admiring something of his own making. The sovereign rings on his club-like fingers caught the cell's light. "Bet you're pissed off now, eh? No more promotion, no more 'cruising'."

"How did you know—"

"You fucking sicko."

"If you don't get out of here now, I'm—"

Without warning, he slapped Roger across the right cheek. Then he swung a backhand across his left cheek. One of Weston's gold rings caught Roger's lip and blood flicked across the graffiti. Coffee splashed onto the floor and his glasses landed in it. Before Roger could react, Weston rammed a fist into his testicles, and scraped a boot down his shin. The man was crazed.

Weston glared at him, loathing in his dark eyes. "Nearly there," he said, "nearly there. One way or another." He reached the cell door and said, "Back in a bit. We can talk some more if you like." Then he just left and locked the door behind him. His shoes squeaked down the corridor.

Ten minutes later, the custody sergeant came in, already equipped to wipe the blood off the wall. Without looking Roger in the eye, he dabbed the blood from his chin. Then he mopped up the coffee with paper towels, and turned away, carrying the tray of crusty food. He never said a word.

"Ellis? Ellis, why are you doing this?"

The sergeant ignored him completely.

"What's Weston said to you, Ellis? I'm still the same old Roger, y'know."

Ellis locked the door.

"I haven't done anything wrong. They cocked up! What's he said to you?"

Weston had caused maximum pain and minimum injury. Roger's lip had bled but that was about it. His face would probably be red for a while but it wouldn't bruise and as for his shin, it would look like a graze many people carry around with them. But perhaps most dangerous of all, Weston had the custody staff under his thumb.

Roger sat there with his arms wrapped around his bent-up legs, rubbing his shin, feeling alone and fearing the future.

He concluded that his colleagues had obviously found physical evidence; maybe a 'witness' or two had been dragged up from somewhere to help their case. But, he thought, physical evidence aside, his track record for cruising, for having an affair, for lying to his wife, for lying to his employer, would all send him down for eternity. In that respect, Weston was right: what goes around comes around. Yet despite the underlying fear that kept him pinned to the wall, he knew it was an error and he knew it would be sorted out.

— Two —

In the interview room, just off the main cell area, Shelby sat across a small desk from Roger and said nothing.

It smelled of old vomit and disinfectant in here. The walls were stippled cream, the carpet a well-worn shit-brown, but the door was still police station blue. In the corner was a Pioneer twin cassette deck, specifically built for police purposes and housed in a metal frame to protect it from prisoners of a more disturbed nature. Around the room, as in the custody area, ran a pressure sensitive alarm tape; should the interviewee become a little irate, bells, gongs, klaxons and lights would sound and flash outside the door.

"You sure you don't want a solicitor?" Shelby finally broke the silence.

"I haven't done whatever it is you're accusing me of, so why would I need legal advice? Anyway, I won't be in here that long. Once your fuck up is uncovered, I'll be on my way, right to the County Court."

"If you're—"

"I *will* need legal advice in the near future."

Shelby began with a caution for the benefit of the tape. This was a legal requirement, and no questioning about his involvement with the specific charge could begin without it. "You do not have to say anything. But it may harm your defence if you do not mention when questioned something which you later rely on in court."

Roger's mouth fell open. The sombre words he'd heard a thousand times before were now aimed at him. He laced his fingers tightly together on the desk in front of him. The paper suit crackled. He could not believe this was happening.

"For the tape, I am Detective Inspector Graham Shelby, and I am interviewing Roger Conniston in connection with the murder of Nicky Bridgestock." He glanced at his watch. "The time is 1410hrs, Friday 22nd January 1999." Then a little less formally, "Roger, are you sure you do not want a solicitor?"

Roger shook his head.

"For the tape, please."

"No, I don't want a solicitor. Thank you for asking."

"Right then," Shelby opened a blue folder, quickly read its opening page. "Do you know a girl named Nicky Bridgestock?"

"No."

"Have you ever been to Nicky's house?"

"What's her address?"

"What?"

"I don't know if I've ever been to her house. Where does she live, what's her address?"

Shelby was puzzled.

"What's my job, Graham? I'm a SOCO; it's my business to go to people's houses. Now what's her bloody address?"

He returned to the opening page, embarrassed at being caught off-guard in the first minute. "Seventy-four, Potter Lane, Wakefield. Ring any bells?"

Earnestly, Roger thought for moment and then answered, "No, I've never knowingly been there."

"Did you have cause to go there while investigating her death?"

Roger shook his head, remembered the tape and said, "No."

"Can you explain to me how your fingerprints were found in her house?"

"What!" He propped himself forward on the desk. "My fingerprints were found in her house? Where?"

"Can you explain to me—"

"No! Now where the hell did you find my bloody fingerprints?"

Shelby was a wolf approaching its frightened prey, all too easily caught. This was the part he loved, and for the moment he put aside any friendship he may have enjoyed with Roger; this was the job, this was what he was paid for. "Two nights ago, you were supposed to go off duty at

2am, that's Wednesday morning. You actually retired a little earlier, one-thirty to be precise."

Roger flinched.

"Would you mind telling me where you went?"

Roger responded at last. "I went to see Alice Taylor."

"Who's Alice Taylor?"

"She's a counsellor, among other things. At OHU."

"Our Occupational Health Unit?"

Roger nodded.

"That was a yes," he looked at the tape recorder. "You said, 'among other things'. What did you mean?"

"We were having an affair," Roger lifted his chin.

"Is she married?"

"What does that matter?"

"Is she married?" Shelby repeated.

"Yes."

"How long has the affair been going on?"

"Three or four months, not that long."

"Where did you meet her?"

"Originally, you mean, or that night?"

"That night, Roger."

"Her place."

"Why did you not tell your superiors this when asked?"

"Weston's not my superior."

"Christopher Hutchinson was. I assume he asked where you'd been when Inspector Weston raised the issue."

"How did you know—"

Shelby raised his eyebrows. "Well?" he pressed.

"Would *you* tell your superiors you were having an affair with someone from OHU?"

"Did you meet her through a counselling session or through purely social events?"

"Counselling."

"Problems?"

"No, I liked the fucking furniture in her office!"

Shelby slammed a fist onto the desk. Pointed a chubby finger. "Don't keep on with the sarcasm, Roger. I don't like it and it's not helping you."

"Look, I didn't kill this Nicky girl; I *do not* know how my prints got into her house. I *do* know that I have never been there. Ever!"

"Okay, let's try another, shall we? And I'll have this checked out, Roger, so beware. You also left the office two hours early on Wednesday afternoon, a medical appointment for your wife you said. Is this correct?"

The cassette bobbins turned, catching each word, each sigh, each denial.

"No," he said. "I lied to Chris. Alice and I had split up…" He paused and then explained to Shelby's fierce eyes. "That night I took time off, I went to her house to break off our affair."

Shelby urged, "Go on."

"When I got there…I didn't really have the bottle, and… Let's just say that Alice's powers of seduction were irresistible to me. We ended up in the sack." His chin lowered again.

"So you didn't split up?"

"Let me finish. Afterwards, I said we should quit."

"*After* you made love?"

"I'm not especially proud of the order I did things."

"So why did you go and see her the next day?"

"After I said we should quit, she gave me this," he pointed to the fading scratch. "Needless to say, *she* wasn't entirely happy with the order I did things either. I suppose that was her leaving present to me."

"Roger is pointing to a scratch across his left cheek," Shelby said for the tape. "So why *did* you go and see her?"

"I'm going for promotion; well, I *was* going for promotion – and was told yesterday that I'd got it. Congratulations to me, huh." He sighed, and then continued, "Anyway, at the time I was still *trying* for promotion and so I didn't want Alice, who was pissed off at me, to mess up my chances by putting anything nasty into my personal file.

"I went to try and make up, as friends, nothing more. I went to smooth the waters. They say that your counselling sessions are in confidence anyway, that nothing is written down, and certainly nothing is transferred to Force Personnel files. But I know how this Force works; I wanted to hedge my bets."

"She'll corroborate your story?"

He shrugged. "Absolutely, she's no reason to lie."

"I'll check this out. So if you're spinning a tale I'd rather you came clean now."

"I can't believe I'm sitting here at all, Shelby. I can't believe I'm being accused of a girl's murder – a girl I've never clapped eyes on, and you say you'd rather I came clean! What sort of a man do you think I am? I've worked as a SOCO in this nick for years, I've worked for the Force for twelve years, and suddenly I'm a lying bastard with nothing better to do than 'spin tales' for someone like you who has got things just about as fucking wrong as they could be!" The tendons stood out proud on his neck, the skin so tight it looked on the verge of splitting.

Shelby straightened in his chair. His face lost its wrinkles and the colour filled his cheeks again. He continued, "We've already got your personal file and we've begun an informal interview with Mrs Taylor because of the remarks found within that file."

Roger felt panic rising in his chest. "I am innocent! Why won't you believe me?"

"Because you can't refute anything we have against you."

"You can't check my personal files. That's an infringement of the Data Protection Act, it's against Human Rights."

"Data Protection doesn't apply when I'm interviewing a suspect in a murder. And that's what you are, Roger."

"You're systematically ruining my career, shafting my marriage and now you're bringing the Force into disrepute—"

Shelby slammed his fist into the desktop again. "*You*," he roared, pointing a shaking finger, "shafted your own marriage as soon as you climbed into Mrs Taylor's bed – if indeed you did at all! And, *you* are the one bringing the Force into disrepute!"

"Read the sodding file, then. She told me she wouldn't write anything down anyway."

Shelby stood and hastily gathered the folder. "Interview suspended at 14.50."

Shelby stood in the corridor outside the cell area interview room, his starched face lit by the red ceiling light outside the room's door. He was trembling with anger at the man's attitude. The custody sergeant glanced up, saw Shelby's fury and quickly returned to his newspaper.

For a while, Shelby harboured doubts about Roger's guilt, fingerprints or not, but the way he was defending himself stank of guilt. Twenty-odd years of prodding and poking interviewees had taught him well. And those twenty-odd years went into his interview strategy – which now appeared slipshod, amateurish… Usually two officers interviewed but Shelby thought he'd handle it better alone. He was beginning to question that decision.

The cells' gate banged closed. "Boss!" Lenny Firth limped up the corridor towards him and Shelby pulled himself together quickly. "Got a statement from Alice Taylor," he waved the papers.

"What's she say?"

"She's had several professional meetings with Conniston, nothing on a personal level; in fact she was offended by the suggestion."

"Get to the point, Lenny."

"He's unbalanced."

"Aren't you his squash partner?"

"I'm being objective, boss, I'd—"

"I know, I know; I mean *you* should know if he's unbalanced, Lenny, shouldn't you, without recourse to Alice Taylor."

Lenny said, "He could be very emotive, very angry, and passionate even. But you never really know what's going on inside a man's head. That's where a counsellor has the upper hand over a squash opponent, she ought to know if he's unbalanced."

"Go on."

"Apparently, he has nightmares – every time he sees a body, he can't shake them off. She concludes by saying she thinks he's unstable and was about to recommend professional external counselling through his Head of Department."

Shelby began to feel better; Roger's innocence was something he could forget all about. "I want his DNA taking to the lab now; see if it matches the hair we found on Nicky."

"Already there, boss."

"You after Brownie points, Lenny?" And then he thought how enthusiastically Lenny was executing his duties towards his squash partner. He seemed to be enjoying this. With friends like you, Lenny…

Firth puffed out his nimble chest. "I've taken the liberty of Fast-tracking it; we'll have the results by close of business tonight."

"Good." Shelby said. "Not that I'm bothered, but what kind of a premium are they putting on Fast-tracking nowadays?"

"Two grand, plus the £247 for the sample."

"Shit. Discount for bulk analysis?"

"Don't think so, boss."

"Thought not." He turned to leave. "Oh, Lenny, does she seem…fair-minded, this Alice Taylor? Not the vindictive sort is she?"

"Straight as an arrow, boss, very nice lady."

"Bring us a couple of coffees in, will you?"

Shelby entered the interview room again. He pressed 'record' and gave his name and the time. "We've spoken to Alice—"

"Shouldn't you caution me when the interview recommences, advising again of my right to a solicitor?"

"Do you want one now?"

"No. Just making sure you know my rights."

He didn't feel better anymore. Shelby cautioned him in a low hypnotic voice. "Alice Taylor says that your relationship was entirely professional and that you are suffering delusions of grandeur to think it was anything more."

Roger felt alone again. "She's lying."

"Why would she do that?"

"Easy. His name is Angus. He travels a lot and she's the lonely one stuck at home waiting for a bit of weak flesh like me to come along and play with her. She said her husband wasn't the forgiving kind. Don't think he'd take it too well if he found out I knew more about his bedroom and his lounge than he did."

"She says you're unstable."

"At the moment, I'd say I have every right to be unstable."

A knock came at the door and Firth came in with two coffees on a plastic tray.

"Thanks, Lenny," Roger said.

Firth closed the door.

"My friends," he whispered, "suddenly aren't." He sipped the drink, looked back at Shelby. "Anyway, she *would* say that, wouldn't she? Don't forget, I'm the one who broke it off, I offended her femininity, she thinks she's an unpaid whore now, doesn't she?"

"Does she?"

"Well who do you think gave me this?" He pointed to the scratch.

Shelby's face was blank.

"Don't tell me; you think Nicky bloody Bridgestock gave it to me?"

Shelby blew at the steam floating over his coffee; he took in Roger's demeanour over its rim. At that moment, it provided the perfect cover for a flashback to the post-mortem. Back to where the pathologist, Bellington Wainwright, had extreme difficulty obtaining nail scrapings because Nicky had bitten them down almost to the quick. Hardly face-scratching equipment. Hardly *itch*-scratching equipment.

One-nil in favour of Roger's innocence, he had to concede. "She also says, and I'm pressing the point of Alice Taylor, considering she's your alibi, that you have dreams of dead bodies." Was this going to be one-all?

"She's no right to give away that kind of information," he whispered in a defeated slur. He took his glasses off and rubbed them against the suit.

"If this investigation concerned the Chief or the Mayor or the Head of the bloody Police Authority, we would dip into any available information we could, so cut the crap about rights to privacy, get on and answer the bloody question, man."

Roger put his glasses back on. "What question? You didn't ask me a question."

"What do your dreams consist of?"

"Are *you* offering me therapy?"

"Answer the goddamned question!"

Roger fell silent for a time and Shelby could see him thinking, could see his shoulders rise and fall inside his ill-fitting white suit as he considered his response.

"I suppose I saw one body too many. I don't know; that's why I went to see her in the first place to try to get some help with the ghouls floating around inside my head." He smiled at Shelby, making fun of himself. "She suggested I was putting an obstacle in my own path, an obstacle against my promotion."

"Why would you do that?"

"It's not something I planned, you know. I didn't sit on the edge of the bed one night and talk myself into having nightmares! I was afraid of getting the job, I guess. Afraid I wouldn't be able to do it. So subconsciously I tried to prevent it from happening at all."

"Did you dream of a dead body last night?"

"How sweet of you to ask."

"Did you?"

"No. But I was high; I'd had the good news of my promotion, and I'd had a drink or two to celebrate. I don't think I dreamed anything last night."

"You didn't dream anything last night?"

"You want a cracker?"

"For a man facing fifteen, you're very flippant."

Roger became thoughtful, lowered his eyes. "I still think it's a foul up; it'll be sorted by the end of today and…" he trailed off, slipped back into his thoughts.

"No, Roger. It won't go away. No one has fouled up and I think it's about time you started to take this seriously."

"I don't have to prove my innocence, Graham."

Shelby ignored the remark. "So, you have nothing to substantiate this feeling of depressive instability. Is this something to go hand in hand with nightmares, something you take with you to your counselling sessions, so you could continue to meet with Alice Taylor and fantasise about her?"

"You should be on telly."

Shelby waited there for a moment, studying the man, trying to destabilise him, waiting to see if Roger felt the need to fill the silence. He didn't. "Another thing I find a little intriguing, if not disturbing, is that a man of your status, married with good prospects, a man of the law, respected and middle-aged, finds it necessary to patrol the night-clubs of Wakefield looking at young women. Do you think I'm reasonable in finding that fact disturbing?" Shelby watched the shame crumple Roger's features, and chalked up another point in favour of 'guilty'.

"Yes, I do. I hold up my hand to that one. I can guess where you got your information, and Chris is right. I nicknamed it 'cruising', because that's what I did. After working late and finishing in the early hours of the morning, I would cruise slowly through the streets and yeah, I looked at the girls.

"My marriage was at a low point, and seeing young girls baring all put a little sparkle back into my life. I did nothing wrong, I broke no laws; I wasn't kerb crawling or stalking or harassing anyone. I certainly didn't speed," he almost smiled. "But I want to emphasise to you that I never picked anyone up. That I can promise you."

Shelby folded his arms. "You finish work early, and coincidentally of course, a young girl called Nicky Bridgestock dies at roughly the same time? Can you explain why we found your name and number on the back of her left hand at the post-mortem?"

"Maybe she wrote it herself—"

"She's left-handed. She wouldn't have chosen to write it on her left hand." He pulled a photograph of the strangely lit inscription from the folder and showed it to Roger, proclaiming the action for the tape. "It's not complete, I know, but it goes a long way towards your own details. Here's another photo, same hand, same writing, enhanced by PolyLight. Convinced?"

Roger accepted the evidence.

He was a scrap of the man he was ten minutes ago. Shelby expected the request for a solicitor about now, but it didn't come. Roger looked fraught, and Shelby thought he detected in him the first signs of real fear, though unusually for a fearful suspect, he didn't fidget much.

"I can see why you came looking for me," Roger said. "But I've never set eyes on her, never been to her house. Yet my name and number are on the back of her hand?" He appeared to surrender, and leaned forward submissively. "I can't answer you, Graham, like I can't answer the fingerprint. I honestly do not know how they got there." Then his posture relaxed, his shoulders slumped, as had become the norm for this interview.

"Have you ever suffered from black-outs?"

"No."

Shelby asked more questions, Roger grunted answers, occasionally expressing astonishment or wonder, but usually his eyes were pointing south. Now though, he didn't conceal his feelings, and Shelby noticed a sparkle of hope.

"*I know how all this bloody evidence got there, and I'll be fucked if it never crossed your mind as well!*"

"How?"

"Planted." Hope shone in Roger's eyes.

"Who by?"

"Who has a grudge against me?"

"You tell me."

The sparkle died. "It's obvious when you actually stop and think about it. Weston."

Shelby gave no reaction, perhaps a tinge of sadness, that was all. "Weston?"

"He hates me."

"The grudge thing?" Shelby asked.

"*His* grudge thing."

"Okay, for the tape: you suspected Inspector Colin Weston of stealing weapons that were in his custody, yes?" Roger nodded. "Inspector Weston was investigated and subsequently vindicated. Since then, you both share a mutual dislike. Is that a fair summary of the situation?"

"I reported him for stealing weapons and he was questioned about it. He objects to me having a heartbeat."

Shelby folded his arms, and said, "Roger, that was months ago. Everyone knows Weston had nothing to hide from that investigation. In fact, he's the aggrieved party in all of this, and he laughs about it now."

"You don't believe me?"

"You think a police Inspector would go to the trouble of killing someone and planting all your evidence around the scene because he was questioned about an *alleged* theft?"

Roger grabbed at straws. "He beat me in the cell, only an hour ago." His voice rose, his desperation made it to the surface, and that's what Shelby clearly saw. A desperate man.

"Okay, Roger," he said, "I'll look into it."

"You really don't believe me, do you?"

Shelby made no reply.

"Gee, thanks."

"How did he plant the evidence, how *could* he plant the evidence?"

Roger thought for a long time before looking back at Shelby, before looking through him. "I have no idea."

"Did you have sex with her?"

"Who, Nicky Bridgestock?"

"Yes, Nicky Bridgestock."

"I've already said I didn't know the girl."

"This is a picture of Nicky's face; perhaps she went under an alias." Shelby handed Roger another photograph.

"No, I've never seen her before." He slid the picture back across the table. "Why ask me if I've ever had sex with her? What sham have you come up with now?"

"It's no sham, Roger. We found a hair, a pubic hair in amongst her own—"

"Oh go on, you think that's mine, too?"

"Judging by the evidence we've collected so far, I'd say it was a pretty safe bet, wouldn't you?"

"But, just one?"

"Yes. Why?"

"It's a plant, Shelby!" Roger's arms shot outwards to emphasise his eureka moment. "I've never found only a single hair. Two, three or a clump of them, but never just one. Doesn't that suggest a plant to you?"

"It represents good, hard evidence."

"Go on, surprise me, it *is* my pubic hair, isn't it?"

"Don't know for sure yet. I was hoping you could save us a couple of grand trying to find out, really. All you've got to do to make things easier on yourself is admit having sex with her."

Now Roger's temper surfaced again. "I didn't have sex with her! Since I was twenty-three, I have slept with only two women: my wife and Alice Mary Taylor. Did you find any semen, any trace of lubricant from a condom?"

"What car do you drive?"

"Did you find anything? Answer me, Shelby, otherwise I stop being so fucking co-operative and demand a solicitor."

Shelby stared at Roger. "No, we only found the hair."

"Then it's a plant, man. Are you so blind? It all makes sense to me, but you can't see the weather for the twatting snow! Open your eyes."

"Calm down, Roger."

"Piss off with your 'calm down'. Put yourself in my shoes – wherever they are – would *you* be calm with someone's murder pinned to you? Well? Would you bollocks."

"What car do you drive?"

"Sierra."

"What year?"

"Ninety-five."

"Seats?"

"Four."

Shelby cursed under his breath. "What material?"

"Why don't you tell me what fibres you found on her clothing, I'll just agree with you and we can move onto the next load of shit you've got lined up." He slouched in his chair. "If I did kill her," Shelby sat up, "don't you think I would have cleaned the inside of my car to remove her fibres from them? Or if I was really clever, I could have used one of those polythene seat covers that mechanics use." He shook his head, rubbed his fingertips. "If you find fibres belonging to a Sierra on her clothes, bully for you, it proves she rode in a Sierra, it doesn't prove she rode in *my* Sierra." Shelby's face remained expressionless. "It's in the car park, impound it and SOCO it."

"Already done, Roger." Shelby flicked the corner of a file with a fingernail.

"So what's with the stupid questions then?"

"Answers, that's what's with the questions."

Suddenly Roger beamed. "I had a pair of underpants go missing."

"What?"

"It all makes sense now."

Shelby said, "What the hell are you blabbing on about?"

"I know where Weston got my pubic hair. You can ask Lenny Firth."

"Ask Firth what?" Shelby couldn't understand where this was going.

"Last time I played squash with Lenny Firth, we got back to the locker room and a pair of my underpants had been stolen."

Shelby barely managed to conceal a smile, but he got the impression Roger detected it anyway.

"Go on and ask him if you don't believe me." He sat back quickly and folded his arms like a chastised child, and it wouldn't have surprised Shelby if he stuck his tongue out.

"Someone stole a pair of your underpants from the locker room?"

"Correct."

"Why would they do that?"

Roger faced forward. "To plant evidence on a fucking corpse? I thought it was someone taking the piss at first, and eventually I forgot about it; but it all makes sense now."

"To you maybe."

"Weston must've rooted around in my locker, stole things that didn't belong to him, and then planted them on the body. I think that makes a whole shit-load of sense. Don't you?"

"Incredible, I'd call it. Weston stealing your pubic hair?"

"That it belonged to me hasn't been established yet."

"I'm assuming that it's yours since your fingerprints and your name and number have been found around the scene. A fair assumption, wouldn't you agree?"

Roger said nothing.

"So, Weston placed your fingerprints at the scene as well, did he? Explain it to me. Go on, I'm all ears."

"Tell me and then we'll both know. But someone sure as hell did, didn't they?"

"Yes. You!"

Roger offered a weak laugh. "You know, this whole thing is preposterous. You'll accuse me of killing Sally Delaney next."

Shelby stopped flicking the file. He blinked, sat up straight and watched the smile fall off Roger's face. "Did you?"

"No! I did not."

"They were both stabbed in the neck."

"So you're sharing info with me now, huh. Hoping I'll slip that little nugget into the interview somewhere? Well, I didn't know Nicky was stabbed in the neck—"

"But if you *did* kill her, Sally I mean, the scene's messed up now; you've contaminated it since you were there to examine that scene. You had legitimate access," Shelby suggested.

"Ah, but I didn't do Nicky's scene, did I?"

"Exactly. And we found your evidence at Nicky's scene."

"If I wanted to corrupt that evidence, supposing I did kill Nicky – which I did not, I would have volunteered to do her scene with Chris."

"No, no; Chris Hutchinson said you had other commitments. Like visiting Alice, we've since learned."

"If I had killed Nicky Bridgestock, I would have gone to the scene to nullify the evidence. If I'd wanted to ruin the fingerprint theory, I would've accepted Chris's invitation to do the PolyLight."

"Your marks were already at the bureau by then."

"That's my proof! How would I *know* that?"

"But even if you visited Nicky's scene, you couldn't eradicate your name, number and hair, could you?"

Roger sat back in his flimsy plastic chair, sweat glowing on his forehead. "If I was going to kill Nicky Bridgestock, why would I write my details on her hand and then kill her?"

Shelby kept the distance between them constant; he leaned forward, laced his fingers and grinned an old dog grin, eyes twinkling. "Double bluff."

"Bollocks. I've heard of kids doing that sort of thing with graffiti, but come on, this is murder. I wouldn't do it, Graham. I wouldn't take the risk."

"I don't think she was your intended victim. Maybe you met her in Wakefield, exchanged numbers and then you ran her home. You wanted sex then, and maybe she did something to offend you, just as you were close to penetration. And you lost it, Roger, you lost it big style and you stabbed her in the neck!"

"I did not!"

"It's rough, I grant you. But I was hoping you'd fill out the details for me."

"Fuck, Shelby, make 'em up. You're pretty good at storytelling."

Chapter 23

— One —

CHRIS FOUND FIRTH IN the Major Incident Room. It was a large office attached to the briefing room, and set up specifically to deal with the murder of Nicky Bridgestock and nothing else. When the investigation was complete, the room would be mothballed, HOLMES 2 would be shut down and the team disbanded back to whatever division from which they had been abstracted, resuming work of a more routine nature.

Taped to the Incident Room walls were plans of Nicky's house, maps of the surrounding district, dates, times, names, associates, her recent whereabouts, her last known activities – everything that was known about the short life of Nicky Bridgestock. And next to the whiteboard at the head of the room, there was a blown up photograph of the girl herself, smiling, happy and young.

And dead.

"Lenny, have you got any news about the interview yet?" Chris asked.

"Nope, not a sausage."

"Well," he whispered, "I think it's only fair to go and tell his wife what's going on. It's four o'clock; he's due home in an hour and when he doesn't show, it's going to worry her."

"Oh, no, no, no," Firth wagged a stern finger. "That's part of my job. In fact, after I've been to OHU, and got this Section 18 search warrant authorised, that's just where I'm heading."

"Shelby working you hard, then?"

"I can handle it."

"I'll be out of your way before you get there," Chris said, about to leave.

"No you're not—"

"Come on, Lenny, give the woman a break. She's not well. Let her hear the news from someone she knows and trusts. I'm their *friend*. I—"

"No!"

The Indexers and HOLMES Sergeant looked around at them.

Chris lowered his voice, "I promise I won't ask her any questions or give away any of your information, I just want to be the one who tells her. I've known her for years. Anyway, you won't even know I've been."

"I can't let you do it, Chris."

"You owe me, Lenny," he whispered.

"How the fuck do I owe you?"

"I bagged you a bloody killer, didn't I?" His whisper grew menacing. "And anyway, I'm off duty myself soon; are you going to stop me popping in there for a coffee?" He smiled reassuringly at the Indexers. They went back to work.

Lenny gave it some thought. "Okay," he conceded, "but if you find any sniff of evidence, or she tells you anything of interest, firstly you get out of there, and secondly you tell me. Understand?"

"Deal."

"You say nothing about—"

"I'm not about to piss on your bonfire. I won't give away any operational secrets. I simply want to be the one to tell her. We're good friends, you know."

"Okay. Like I said, I'll be paying her a visit myself later, but maybe you're right; it would be a good idea for a friendly face to see her first. What's wrong with her, anyway?"

"Arthritis."

"Ouch. My gran had that; nasty business."
"Yeah, nasty," Chris said.

— Two —

It was Friday. Beaver's big day. He had 'borrowed' the pool car from an associate, and then he stole a Wakefield street atlas.

The car, an old Escort, was on false plates, used illegal red diesel and ran out of tax about the same time its tyres ran out of tread. It hadn't seen an MOT station in years. Water dripped onto Beaver's skinhead from the so-called sunroof. The wipers worked when they felt like it.

He drove through town, past French-style cafes, the trendy wine bars and then out of Wakefield, up Leeds Road past the drive-through chippy, past the video and hardware stores and pulled into a lay-by so he could double check the map. Nervously, he chewed gum. He turned to the page he'd folded over, found his location with a dirty nail-bitten finger, and made a mental picture of the directions to follow on foot.

"Wedgwood Grove. Next left, left again and then right. Next left, left again and then right," he repeated. "Shouldn't be too difficult." If there were any witnesses to the killing, they would see him leaving the scene dressed in a red coat and blue jeans. He planned on turning the corner and reversing the coat, pulling it inside out, so black showed, giving himself sufficient time to get back here at a leisurely pace. He climbed from the car, slammed its door and crossed the street.

Beaver took his first left and almost fell onto the baby as a pushchair took his feet from under him.

"Sorry, sorry," said the young mother. "I'm lethal with this thing. I haven't passed my test yet." She smiled shyly at him, waited for a jovial response.

Beaver glared. He regained his balance, and carried on walking, glancing back over his shoulder. Clumsy fucking bitch! How's that for blending in, he thought.

He took his next left and then crossed diagonally over the quiet suburban street, turned right where kids threw ball and cycled around in the rain, where dogs barked at the fun and where elderly neighbours stood chatting beneath golfing umbrellas, plumes of hurried breath pulsing out of their gummy mouths. The sun was twenty minutes from being dead, and high in the third quarter of the sky, a translucent half-moon dangled in a solitary patch of clear sky.

Beaver kept on walking, the wind in his face, watching the house numbers roll by. He looked at the smudged number written on his hand: thirteen; unlucky for some, he mused.

Thirteen came slowly up on his left side.

He continued walking, taking several lengthy glances at the house. He could see no one through the lounge or hall windows, he could see no one upstairs, and the drive was empty except for a few oil stains and a ragged cat taking shelter under a handmade wooden bench. He decided to continue his walk for another hundred yards and maybe select a vantage point from which to view the house without being the centre of attention himself. He spat out the gum and fumbled through his pockets for more.

— Three —

"Boss, boss." Firth closed the cell area gate and walked down the corridor to meet Shelby as he came out of the toilet.

"Can't I even have a leak without—"

"Two bits of news."

"Hurry up, Lenny; I don't have time for 20 questions."

Firth calmed down, took deep breaths. "They found another hair. The lab, they found a second hair in the body tapings from the scene."

Shelby stuck out his rounded chin, stood upright for a change instead of slouching under the weight of a lopsided investigation. Wait till Conniston hears this, he thought. Plant indeed. "And?" he said.

"Oh yeah, she lied to us."

"Who? What are you talking about?"

"Alice Taylor! She's been telling us porkies." Firth was excited about his 'find'. "I called around at OHU to speak to her again, and of course I got chatting to the secretary, Melanie."

"Lenny—"

"Just a second, boss. Melanie told me she thought it was common knowledge that Alice and Roger were shag— were having an affair; they certainly didn't keep it a secret from her. She says how bad she felt for Alice when Roger came round to try to patch things up. Said Alice was close to tears that morning because Conniston had his wicked way with her the night before and then broke the relationship off in the very next breath!"

"That's—"

"*Then*, after Roger left OHU, Alice called for his file."

"Are you saying we have a witness who can testify to Alice Taylor's evidence being a sham?"

"I am indeed, sir."

Shelby exhaled like a man smoking his last cigarette, and he closed his eyes, trying to think. Bitch, he thought; Alice Taylor was a liar. But he would keep it to himself for the time being.

Shelby retook his seat in the interview room and continued where he'd left off.

Little over half an hour had passed and there was a knock on the door. "Sir," said Firth, "can I have a word?"

Shelby grabbed his jacket from the back of his chair, and ceased the interview formally. "Time for a break anyway. You've got about thirty minutes, Roger."

"I don't want a break."

"Well, *I* do."

"No, please, let's just keep going." His wide eyes flicked between Firth and Shelby.

"We're taking a break." He summoned the custody sergeant, and Roger was escorted back to his cell.

"What's wrong now, Lenny?"

Firth watched Roger go. "What's the matter with him, not wanting a break?"

"Who knows. Now tell me."

"You asked for the DNA results from the pubic hair."

"Get on with it, Lenny."

"It's Roger Conniston's. Probability of one in fifty-thousand."

Thank God for that, Shelby thought. "I'm glad I didn't count my chickens."

"I got the statement from Melanie, too, boss. Apparently, this isn't the first affair Alice has had. For want of a more appropriate way of putting this, sir, she's the OHU bike, and everyone with a problem and a dick qualifies for a ride."

Shelby's hopes took a nosedive and the slouch reappeared. "I see. Thank you, Lenny." Then he banged a fist into the interview door.

Firth walked away. Shelby called him back, and with spittle flying from his lips, said, "I want you to get straight onto Discipline and Complaints, hear me? I want her arse in a sling and I want her P45 in the fucking post. First class. Got it?"

"Right, boss, I'll get onto—"

"Are you still here, Lenny!"

Firth trotted away, his ankle regaining the limp it had only recently lost, and Shelby left the cell area and walked up the corridor over to the front counter, where he beckoned old Sergeant Potts over. If anyone knew anything of interest, illicit comings and goings, it was always the desk sergeant.

Potts smiled, "Sergeant Shelby."

"I'm an Inspector now, James."

"Oh that's brill news, is that. Congratulations." Potts held out a hand.

"I've been an Inspector for... oh forget it."

Potts appeared confused, as though he'd missed the punch line but would work it out later in private.

"Just out of interest, have you noticed anything strange about Roger Conniston over the last couple of months? You know the kind of thing, skulking out of the office, looking flustered, that kind of thing?"

Potts thought for a moment, pursed his lips. "Who?"

"Roger Conniston? The SOCO?"

"Oh yes, I know who you mean."

"Well?"

"I get messages," he raised his eyebrows.

From the dead? Shelby wondered. "What kind of messages? Who from?"

Potts came closer, lowered his voice. "Bookies. He comes out here and places the odd bet, even has his friends from the bookies show up sometimes. I don't mind, really, I mean if he wants to keep his private life a secret from—"

"Roger Conniston, James? You sure?"

"Oh yeah, the cardigan man. I never understood why folk wore cardigans with them silly elbow patches—"

Shelby closed his eyes and sighed. "Thanks, James. Sorry to have troubled you."

— Four —

"You're not planning on taking a break just yet, are you, Ellis?"

The custody sergeant ignored him and let go of him as they were half way up the corridor, and Roger dejectedly wandered into his cell and he stood there as the door closed behind him, the lock turned and footsteps echoed down the corridor. He wondered when Weston would appear. Butterflies smacked against his ribcage.

He cradled himself on the wooden plank, knees tucked up, lying on his side rocking slightly, waiting.

And then he heard it. He held his breath and listened. There it came again, a sort of hissing noise, a whining. And then he saw the eye at the peephole; and the noise stopped. The peephole cleared, the flap swung shut and the door lock banged open. Roger's heart kicked and his fingertips tingled right along the line of scars. Weston stood in the doorway, arms folded, and hissed the same hiss, the sound a chuckle makes when forced through clenched teeth.

"Fuck off."

"Now, now, let's not be like that," Weston said. "I relieved Ellis for ten minutes so we could have a little chat." He cracked his knuckles and the rings gleamed again.

"I'm onto you. I nearly had you this morning," Roger's eyes were slits, he wanted this piece of shit to know that they might have closed the file on him, but it was still very much open as far he was concerned. He sat up.

"That right?" Weston smiled in return.

Roger gawped. Not the kind of reaction he hoped for.

"You stood out like a karaoke singer in a fucking opera. If you want to come and see where I take my country walks, that's fine by me."

"It won't work, you know."

"What's that then?"

"They'll find you out, Weston. They'll find the evidence."

"You're off your fucking trolley, you piece of shit."

"They know you framed me for murder, Weston." Roger smiled nervously. "They're working on it right now."

"Eek, I'm scared." Weston let his arms drop. "Don't be like that," he crept into the cell, away from the open door, "don't be hasty with this 'framed me for murder' shite." He laughed again, quieter this time, "You don't want to go blabbing things like that around; people might start to believe you," he laughed, "and then those people might commence investigations. Tut-tut. We can't be having that now, can we?" His shoes creaked as he stepped further forward. "Anyway, Shelby already thinks you did it, you know that, don't you? And do you know what clinched it, do you know what made him change his mind about you?"

"Change his mind?"

Weston said, "he thought you were innocent when it all began, but you've succeeded in changing his mind for him; he now *knows* you're fucking guilty." Weston came closer, eyes peering at Roger like he was a strange exhibit in a museum. "Protesting your innocence like that did it; you know, when you scream someone's name the way you did, and especially when the name you scream belongs to the bloke we all know you hate, that's when people begin to see people like you as… what's the term, *unstable*, I think," he winked. "They think you're a fucking nutter, a man full of sour grapes, out for revenge." His black eyes sparkled in the meagre light.

"Bollocks."

"Sounds like you're going through hell in there with Shelby. I've been listening. Hope you don't mind."

"What do you want?"

"What do I want?" He contemplated the question for a while, seeking the answer in the cream-painted ceiling. "What do I want? I want to see you squirm, you cock-sucking piece of civvy shit." He flicked change in his pocket. "And I want to see what your face looks like when I tell you who else thinks you're guilty of murder."

"Just turn around and go away."

Weston asked, "Not interested, huh?"

"No," he lied. "Now fuck off."

"I know where your boss has gone."

Roger said nothing, only looked at the walls.

"He's gone to visit your wife. Yvonne, isn't it?"

Roger paid attention now.

"That's right. He's gone to tell her the good news. You won't be home for tea; for about fifteen years." He laughed; the sound echoed around the cell. "Wouldn't be surprised if he didn't slip her a length while he was there."

Roger kept quiet.

"She'd probably be glad of it too; make a change from seeing a shrivelled dick like yours—"

Roger edged forward; his body poised for an attack, eyes though, still looking at the black leather shoes.

"Go on," Weston said, "go on; give in to it. Lunge man; let's see how yeller your blood is, eh?"

"How did you get hold of my fingerprints?" Roger asked.

"You fucking coward."

"Come on, how did you get them into the girl's house, huh?"

"Yeah, I can see it now; Chris Hutchinson cuddled up nice an' cosy on your settee with Yvonne by his side. He slips an arm around her neck, slips a hand up her skirt." Roger flinched. "She coos at him, and starts groaning as her bra strap falls away—"

Roger leapt from the plank and ploughed into Weston. They fell to the cold floor, a whiff of piss and disinfectant stung in Roger's nose. Weston's fist caught Roger around his left ear. His glasses skittered across the floor. And Roger was on his back, looking up into a blurred image of Weston.

A roomful of shouts, echoes, and screams. Of fists and bared teeth.

Weston grabbed Roger's neck, gold-encrusted fingers digging into the flesh. It felt like Weston's thumbs were touching the front of his spine. Roger began turning red; his eyes closed and seconds later, his pawing hands fell away from Weston's arms.

"Got you now, you wanker." Weston's words echoed in the silence. His thumbs relaxed.

A whistle of cool air poured through Roger's clenched teeth, and as Weston tried to regain his grip, Roger smashed his arms down, breaking Weston's hold. They rolled, and Roger had Weston's head in his hands, rammed it into the sticky cell floor. He lifted it, screamed into it and rammed into the floor... and then he stopped.

Weston's body relaxed.

Panting, Roger saw the blood on the cell floor; droplets had sprayed outwards, and there were more droplets on the knee of his white suit. He let go of Weston's head and fell off him, rubbing his burning neck.

The cell door was open.

Fifteen years.

It kept bouncing back like an echo. Fifteen years. Could he really hack fifteen years inside? And if it *was* a fuck up, it had already gone this far, who was going to stop it going all the way through the courts?

The cell door was wide open.

Weston didn't move.

Roger picked his glasses out of the piss stain near the toilet. Like a rubber man, he stumbled out of the cell and down the corridor. He heard other prisoners shouting, thumping their doors. At the end, he peered around the corner. The place was empty. Mercifully so. Or had it been planned like that? Roger wondered.

On the sergeant's desk was a phone. Roger grabbed it, punched numbers. He listened. "Come on, baby. Answer me, please." His heart banged and his neck throbbed.

Eventually, he dropped the phone, left a red smear across the handset, and got moving. Ellis could walk in any second. And that's when his troubles would truly begin. Roger staggered back up the corridor. The prisoners' shouts were dull echoes. When he returned to Weston's side, he searched his pockets, found his car keys, and his wallet. He closed the cell door. Locked it, feeling a wicked satisfaction, and put his shoes on. They were still damp.

Inside the cell, Weston's eyes snapped open. Through bloody lips, he croaked. "Don't let me down, Beaver."

The custody area was still quiet. But he knew it wouldn't be for long.

The monitor showed Roger the empty transit bay. He ran behind the custody sergeant's desk and smacked the door release button. Then he stopped. How much more trouble could escaping custody cause him?

Seconds later, he blundered through the iron door leading from the custody area into the transit bay. With a heavy metallic 'clang', the door latched behind him; its significance – no return – wasn't lost on him. In his panic, he dropped Weston's wallet. Store cards and credit cards scattered, spilled like playing cards across the gritty floor. "Fuuuck." He bent, dropped the keys. He scooped the keys back up, searched through the cards, found Weston's warrant card, and slid it through the transit bay's reader.

The roller shutter door creaked up. "Come on, come on." Rusty metal grinding on its spindle. Roger cringed at the noise and ducked beneath it, felt his tangle of hair brush against it, and ran up the ramp into the wet, floodlit car park. Icy air punched him. He waited by the concrete bulkhead as two officers locked their car and disappeared through the back entrance to Wood Street. He wondered when Ellis would return.

Stamped into Weston's brass key fob was a registration number. "P312SYG, P312SYG." He scanned the car park, head flipping around so quickly that he missed it twice. It was right in front of him. The car park was clear now. He ran.

With shaking hands, Roger closed the door and the world was mute except for his wheezing. He breathed the smell of stale cigar smoke. One last check around and all seemed clear.

He started Weston's patrol car, turned on the headlights and took it quickly around the bend, towards the erect barrier—

A dazzle of headlights blinded him. Roger stamped on the brakes.

The width of a matchbox separated the two patrol cars. Smoke and steam from the tyres drifted past his window. His heart hammered. And now he thought he was going to vomit into his own lap.

Micky looked at him through both windscreens. Expressionless.

Roger held his breath.

After what felt like minutes, Micky swung his car out and pulled up alongside, and wound his window down. He stared at Roger, and then said, "You're going to end up in some serious shit if they catch you."

He let the breath go. "I didn't do it, Micky."

"This isn't the way, mate. The system will—"

"Fuck the system! It's flawed, Micky, and it's going to send me down."

Micky thought for a moment, and asked. "What're you going to do, then?"

"Pay Weston's home a visit."

"What?"

"He's the key to all this crap, and I'm going to prove it."

"Roger, you can't just—"

"Any better ideas?"

Micky shook his head. "None. Just stay away from your home. They'll put a plain car somewhere on your street. Watching."

"There is one more thing you could help me with."

Micky didn't seem impressed, but he didn't seem surprised either. "What do you want?"

"Your mobile phone."

"My..? I want it back," he said, passing it through the window, "in one piece. It's my own personal phone, is that. Helen bought it for me."

"Thanks Micky. If I can ever..."

"I still think you're—"

"I know. I have to try." Roger revved the engine.

"Oh," Micky shouted, "and you never saw me. Okay?"

Roger could only nod his gratitude.

Chapter 24

— One —

Four minutes after Roger took possession of Micky's phone in the car park, Sergeant Ellis Coldworth swiped his card through the reader next to the custody area door. The gate closed behind him and he walked towards his desk, newspaper tucked under his arm, aroma of tobacco drifting from his face. He craned his neck to get a look up at cell 6, but couldn't really see too much without making a detour, and his paper was far more interesting than the goings-on inside a cell.

Ellis slid his chair back, filled it with his generous backside and put his feet up on the counter, shook the newspaper out, and started at the sports pages. On the desk just beyond his feet was his telephone. Smeared red.

Lenny Firth pressed the intercom button and called, "Let us in, Ellis." The cell area gate clicked and Firth swung it open, then let it shut behind him. He heard Ellis shake his newspaper. "Busy, then?"

"Aye. Always bloody am."

"We want Roger back through now. Break time's over."

Only Ellis's eyes moved. Then all of him moved – quickly. "Roger Conniston? The SOCO? In cell 6?"

"Problem?"

"Problem? No, don't be daft." Ellis excused himself. He marched up the corridor, keys swinging in his hand, glancing back.

Firth leaned over the desk to look at the paper. And as he did so, he noticed it. On the phone. It was a strange enough sight for him to forget the paper, to lean further over and look properly. Ellis shouted something from up the corridor. "Oh God. Now what?" Firth said, and walked up the corridor and in to cell 6.

Sergeant Coldworth looked up. "Call an ambulance, Lenny," he said.

"Shit," Firth stared at Weston's body, and then ran out of the cell, pulling his mobile phone from his jacket pocket. "Shelby's going to fucking kill you, Ellis."

"Oh thanks a lot, Lenny." Ellis put Weston in something approaching the recovery position, and then he scuttled back to the phone behind his counter, grimaced at the blood on the handset and called the ACR. "Yeah, it's Sergeant Coldworth from the cells at Wood Street— what? Yes, just listen, will you. We have an escaped 10-12— yes, dammit, are you fucking deaf?" And then he stopped. "Sorry," he said, "I didn't mean to— yes, you're absolutely right. I'm very sorry. He's called Roger Conniston..."

Firth told Shelby, and after he calmed down, Shelby gave the order to the patrol sergeant. Moments later twelve police officers dashed along the corridor towards the car park, pulling on their body armour. Firth flattened himself into the wall to avoid the stampede. "Oh, Christ," Firth said, and walked down the corridor to where Shelby stood, eyes blazing, jaw pulsing.

If ever Shelby wanted to thump someone, it was now. He knew it wasn't Firth's fault but that didn't matter. Right now, Shelby wanted to beat the living crap out of someone, anyone, and Firth was the nearest. Only the fear of Firth hitting him right back, stopped him.

"I found these," Firth held out a stack of credit cards and a brown leather wallet. A Gold MasterCard on show with Weston's name on it.

"So they're in the cells," Shelby said, "they have a fight, Conniston wins, takes Weston's wallet and uses his ID card to get out, right?"

He looked at the MasterCard, "These were in the transit bay, sir, so yes, we're supposing so."

"You're supposing so! What was Weston doing in there in the first damned place? Oh, don't tell me, I can guess. And now Conniston's gone."

"Long gone."

"How long, Lenny?"

"Custody camera says he went at 1644."

"Great. He's got a quarter of an hour on us."

"Weston's got concussion, and he's—"

"Whoa, Lenny. Hold it there. You're under the impression that I give a sideways toss about Weston." He glared at Firth. "I don't want to know. Okay?"

"Sir."

"Right, get a guard at Weston's bedside. And do it now. I don't want *him* doing a bunk as well. He's got some serious shit coming his way."

"There's er, there's something else too, boss."

"Am I going to want to hit you for this, Lenny?"

Firth nodded. "I think so, boss, yeah."

"I'm waiting."

"Weston's patrol car keys are missing."

Shelby closed his eyes, sucked in a deep breath and held it before saying, "I hate this job sometimes."

"I know—"

"Get the fleet number. Contact the Radio Custodian and ask him to disable the radio in that car, I don't want Conniston to know what's happening."

"Right, boss."

"And then get a car outside Weston's house," Shelby screamed.

Lenny stood there, stunned.

"Lenny?"

"Boss?"

"You're still here?"

Shelby knocked quietly, hoping Chamberlain wouldn't hear him, and he could creep away off the face of the earth.

"Come in."

He groaned and entered Chamberlain's smoke-filled lair for the hundredth time during this enquiry. He felt the heat prickle on his face as he stood at his desk while Chamberlain stubbed out a cigarette and opened a window.

"Sorry about the smoke," he said. "I thought it too chilly to open a window. Now I can barely see my desk," he giggled. "Suppose I'd better get cold, eh?"

"Sir," Shelby said.

"You seem pensive, Graham? Is everything in order with the Bridgestock case? Haven't come to beg more staff, have you, because if you have—"

"No, sir. I haven't."

"Has he admitted to Delaney's murder yet?"

"Well, sir, I'm still—"

"Never mind," Chamberlain waved a hand, "put it in the report and we'll convene a meeting on Monday."

"Sir—"

"I'm on with the Home Office paperwork now, Graham, so I trust your report will be forthcoming before the end of tomorrow?"

"About the report, sir—"

"Interview strategy working the way you hoped?"

"Well, I—"

"Good."

Shelby closed his eyes and counted to ten.

Chamberlain retook his seat, folded his arms. "But something is wrong, Graham. I can tell, because you are not creeping around me. Do you have a telephone directory down the seat of your trousers in preparation?" Chamberlain smiled. Then he gripped the desk, "Conniston has hanged himself hasn't he? I *knew*—"

"He's escaped custody, sir." Shelby braced himself.

It took a while for Chamberlain to react. From his drawer, he pulled a packet of cigarettes. He lit one, breathed deeply, exhaled and then screamed, "How?"

"We're not entirely sure yet. Inspector Weston was found unconscious in Conniston's cell—"

"What on earth was *he* doing in there? He's not a gaoler!"

"Don't know, sir."

"Don't know? *Why* don't you damned well know, Inspector Shelby?"

Shelby shifted his weight. "Weston's patrol car is missing, sir."

Chamberlain spat smoke out and broke into a coughing fit. Shelby moved to slap him on the back and then thought better of it. Instead he stood uncomfortably still until his senior officer stopped coughing and his colour approached normal again. "You are trying to get me into medical retirement, Shelby, aren't you?"

"No, sir—"

"Now you listen to me, man." Chamberlain stood up and pointed aggressively, "You get me Conniston. Summon the

Chief's Reserve, get them involved, get... get *everyone* involved." Chamberlain appeared unwell, eyes red, face green. He kicked his chair aside and marched around to Shelby.

Shelby twitched but stood his ground.

"What have you done so far?"

"We have a team at his home address and we have four patrols – all our available early turn staff – and three CID officers on the road searching."

"What about the helicopter?"

"In the air now, sir."

"Now let me be clear about this; you find Conniston before this gets out." He stepped closer. "If the press gets hold of this, Shelby, I will do my best to have you looking for another job within a month."

"But it was Weston who shouldn't—"

"Stop passing the buck, man!" Chamberlain sucked on his cigarette, turned abruptly from Shelby, stood by the open window and said, "That is a sincere warning. Now get out."

Shelby got as far as the door.

"I expect you to report back in *two* hours. Let the news be good."

Shelby stepped onto the carpeted corridor and reached all the way to the double swing doors at its end before he breathed out. He felt like putting his fist through the glass. He took his jacket off, slackened his tie and wafted his shirt against his hot skin. "Firth!" he called as he reached the CID office. "Where's Firth?" The three people left in the office all replied, "Toilet."

Shelby waited outside, teeth grinding together.

Firth stepped out and almost collided with him. "Get the helicopter up, Lenny," he said. "Broadcast the ID number of Weston's car. Then get me the Chief's Reserve. I want Wakefield crawling with uniforms. Understand?"

"Yes, boss."

"Then get back to me quick. I'll be in the canteen preparing for my nervous breakdown."

"Right, boss."

"Are you waiting for that in writing, Lenny?" Shelby watched Firth trot out of sight. It was 1710hrs. Dark outside.

— Two —

Shelby replayed Chamberlain's words and especially the threat that he was more than capable of fulfilling. But he couldn't really blame him for the outburst; it was a shitty situation.

His chubby hands caressed a mug of black tea, and he considered the evidence. Roger's version of events, of it being some kind of elaborate set-up, had begun to gain credence – until he ran away, that was. And if that *was* the case, that it was a set-up, who would have cause to do it and why, were the extremely big questions.

The fibre evidence from Nicky's clothing finally came back as late model Ford; Roger drives a late model Ford. But so did half the bloody population, Shelby knew. And really, even a trainee barrister could pick holes in the name and number evidence; they could be there merely as pointers in the wrong direction.

He could imagine Chamberlain's reaction to a 'wrongful arrest' suit. Oh yes; he would kick Shelby's head around his office for a few hours and then play golf with his testicles. And all that before sacking him.

"Sir?"

Shelby jumped. Firth walked toward him alongside a man he didn't recognise. "Lenny, just give me ten minutes to think through my bloody strategy, can't you?"

"Boss, this is the Fingerprint Expert who checked the scene marks."

"Did you do as I asked, Lenny?"

"I got the helicopter—"

"Just a yes or no will do, Lenny. In fact, just a *yes*, forget the *no*."

"It's a yes, boss," and he added, "I think you ought to hear what he has to say." Firth turned to the man who waited patiently in the background.

Shelby stood and shook his hand. "More tea, Lenny, please. Would you join me...?"

"Barry Goodwyn, sir. We spoke on the phone a couple of days ago. And yes, please, I'd love one," he said to Firth, "white, no sugar."

"Right, what have you got for me?"

"One of the marks from the scene, the one matching Roger Conniston, has traces of paint on it."

"Is that supposed to mean something?"

"Well...oh thank you." Barry took the tea and moved aside to let Firth sit between them. "Sometimes, when fingermarks are lifted, unsound paintwork can also come off with the mark. I've often said we use tape that has far too strong a tack value—"

"Barry, please, I don't have time for riddles. Tell me what you've got."

Barry blinked. "The paint on the lift is blue. I discussed this with Gareth, who used Quasar at the scene, and he insists categorically, that all the paintwork in Nicky Bridgestock's house was white."

Shelby absorbed the news. Then, "What? You're saying the mark is foreign to the scene. Are you telling me it was planted?"

"Well... I don't see how blue paint could—"

"Fuck!" Shelby stood, knocked the table and Barry's teacup hit the floor with a wet thud. "Get that new SOCO here now, Lenny. He's fucked up somehow. And then get that mark across from the bureau. Now!"

Shelby stormed out of the canteen and hurried to the SOCO office on the ground floor. He barged through the door and found two people in there. Helen had her head down, studying the grain on her desk it seemed, and Jon, eyes buried in a newspaper.

"Where's Paul?" Shelby asked.

Helen didn't move. Jon took his feet off the desk, thought about the question, and answered, "Don't know. Must've gone home."

"Thanks for all your help." Shelby slammed the door and shouted at James Potts on the front counter, "Put a call out for Paul Bryant. Tell him to come to the front counter immediately. Okay?"

There was no answer to the Tannoy, and Shelby excused himself, unable to tolerate James's incessant chatter. Firth had no luck in any of the men's rooms or the CJSU office. He found out Paul's address and was about to send a unit from Killingbeck in Leeds to call at Paul's home. But Shelby commandeered him first.

"Lenny, come with me."

"But, I—"

Shelby pounced into the SOCO office again. Jon's newspaper remained obstinately before his eyes. "Jon, what car does Paul drive?"

"Aston Martin Lagonda."

"Right," Shelby said. "Do you know the... Are you taking the piss?" The newspaper dropped, Jon's smile died as Shelby snatched for his neck with fingers like claws. "You think this is funny?"

"What," Jon pushed his chair backwards. Shelby followed still reaching forward. "Do I think what's funny?"

Helen looked up only briefly.

Shelby grabbed Jon's shirt, and yelled, "What fucking car does Paul drive, and what's the fucking number?" He lifted Jon part way out of his seat. The newspaper fell to the floor.

"I think it's a VW, a white VW Golf."

"It's a Polo," Helen said.

"Number?"

"I don't know. Sorry."

Shelby dropped Jon and dragged Firth back out into the corridor. "I want you—"

"I know. You want me to check the car parks for a white VW Polo."

"So exactly what are you bloody waiting for?"

"Boss."

"And when you've finished, back to my office, sharpish. And check with the patrol sergeants, I want an update from their search."

Chapter 25

— One —

Roger was half way to Weston's house when he stopped at the side of the road and forced himself to think. He knew that Shelby would put men on *his* house, but he'd probably put them on Weston's house too. And he'd do that because he knew Roger would go there, he knew Roger wouldn't be able to keep his nose out of the investigation.

The metal streetlamps wobbled in the wind, illuminating horizontal rain. The wipers screeched across the screen and rush-hour traffic flowed past. Roger immersed himself in thought.

Visiting Weston's house could wait until later in the evening when full darkness would provide more cover. Weston would be in hospital by now, hopefully with his wife by his side. And later, Roger would find a way into the house around the back, he hoped, out of sight of the guard. So he reluctantly turned around, took back roads out of Wakefield, heading not towards home, but to a safe place that held no connection to anyone involved with this case: a village called Outwood, filled with terraced houses and neat gardens, where the Post Office was also the library.

It was 1718 when the UHF radio died. Roger couldn't raise anything except static. He sat in the patrol car, parked around the back of a petrol station in Newton Hill facing the main

Leeds Road. His nerves were jagged. Frightened. But angry too. He thought the time spent here alone might clear his head, might produce some inspirational thought that would get him out of this mess. It didn't happen.

The rain slackened off considerably, a mere drizzle spitting on the screen.

Roger picked up Micky's phone and dialled home, praying Yvonne would answer this time.

After a while, she did answer by saying, "You're going to be late again, aren't you? I said I'd prepare a meal—"

"Is Chris there?"

"Whatever happened to 'hello'?"

"Please, Yvonne. Is Chris there?"

"No," she said, "why would he be?"

"Okay; he'll be there soon, Yvonne, and he's going to give you some bad news."

"Why? Roger? What's happened?"

"Hey, I'm okay, I'm okay. Really, it's nothing like that. I've... Yvonne, they've arrested me."

"What!"

"It's a bake, Yvonne. Listen, I'll tell you all about it later, but you have to trust me. Yvonne," he asked, "you do trust me, don't you?"

There was a pause, long enough to have Roger worried. "Yes," she said at last. Then, "Why have they arrested you?"

"Never mind. It doesn't matter. But Chris is coming to see you; I need his help, he's the only one I can trust—"

"Why's he coming—"

"Probably to give you the bad news. Just... please, will you tell him to meet me at his house, I need his help; I need his advice."

"Okay," she said. Her voice was subdued, a little shaky. "I'll tell him. Answer me this though, Roger; is it something to do with that dead girl, Nicky Bridgestock?"

"I haven't got much time."

Yvonne paused, and then said, "I found her house key, Roger. In your coat pocket."

"What!"

"It's here. On the table. Large as..."

The bastard. Oh, you're a clever man, West—

"Are you going to tell me what's going on, Roger?"

"Get rid of it, Yvonne. They're part of the bake. If they find that key, it'll make things harder for me."

"But I don't understand why they were—"

"Planted, Yvonne."

"Who the hell would do that? Come on, this is not a soap opera."

"Damned right it's not. It's real, Yvonne. Weston's out to get me."

"The dodgy Inspector? The one you should have left alone?"

"I'm begging you! Trust me on this one. I've screwed up in the past, I know, but not this time, Yvonne. I'm being straight here. Please," he urged, "trust me." Another patrol car passed by. Roger gasped. "I have to go, have to get away from here; they're out looking for me." Without giving her the chance to respond, he ended the call and threw the phone onto the passenger seat.

He started the car and headed for Chris's house.

It was a newish estate, maybe ten years old; one of those designer dreams where the access road meanders gracefully between the semis and the bungalows, where each bowling green front lawn stands next to its partner with no separating fence, just a row of immature ferns. Roger parked the patrol car close to Chris's house and climbed out. He jogged past a For Sale sign sticking out of the front border, down the short drive and around the back.

He peered through the kitchen window, hoping Chris was already at home and that maybe the car was in the garage. He banged on the back door, idly kicking the step, hoping for a response. None came and now Roger suddenly felt vulnerable, isolated and on view in his white plastic suit. Across the back of the garden grew a line of conifers that swayed in the wind. Only Chris's garage afforded any cover on the third side, and even that was intermittent: there was no fencing fore or aft of it. None standing, anyway. It was horizontal, long grass growing through it, a victim of the winds suffered on Wakefield's higher ground. And separating Chris's house from his neighbour's was a five-foot lap fence. Their rotary washing line, weighed down by clothes, tapped annoyingly on the fence top.

Roger crouched at the fence and peered through a knothole into the neighbour's back garden. It, and the kitchen window, was clear, no one about. And on the line near to the fence, within grabbing distance, was a black t-shirt. Shame there were no trousers.

He pulled the damp t-shirt on, mouthing an apology for the theft, and then ripped the white arms off his suit and stuffed them under the overblown fence. The icy breeze bit instantly. A few minutes later, he returned to the car, unable to risk waiting out here any longer.

Roger parked the car in the gloom of an alleyway behind a snooker hall, an Italian restaurant, and a used car pitch. The heater was on full, trying to dry his damned shoes out. No foot traffic and no vehicular traffic so far. All quiet. And when he turned off the headlamps, a deep blackness descended, only a crack of light showed from the restaurant's door. The wind threw twisting sheets of dirt at the car. A smell of rotting vegetation wafted in shortly after each gust.

The force helicopter swept over him once, but Roger guessed that the pilot would have to know exactly where to look. Ten minutes passed, tapping the steering wheel, fidgeting, before the idea struck.

From the passenger seat, Roger took Micky's phone, pressed call, and listened to the dialling tone.

"Paul Bryant, Scenes of Crime."

"Paul, don't say my name. Are you alone?"

After a considerable pause, Paul answered. "What the hell's been going on? The whole station's seriously freaking out. There've been red faces and raised voices all afternoon around here. It's fucking crazy. Where are you?"

"Listen, Paul, I have something important to ask you. But before I do, I want to know who you're going to tell about this conversation." There was another moment where white space filled the earpiece.

"You came that close to me hanging up then, you know that, don't you? That close!"

"Great. I'm glad you were offended."

"I could be in big trouble just for talking to you."

"Where's Jon?"

Paul glanced at Jon's desk. "Out. Gone home. I don't know." There was a scribbled note on the floor below Jon's chair; it began: 'Chris, Denis Bell wants you—'. Paul ignored it.

"And Helen?"

"I think she's out on a job. Why?"

"I'm pleased you chose not to hang up. I need a favour."

"Why did you run, Roger—"

"Paul! Don't mention my name, dammit. You don't know who could be listening."

"Okay, sorry, sorry." He whispered, "Tell me, then; why *did* you run? If you're innocent, I mean, why leg it?"

"It's because I'm innocent that I *did* run. Weston's stitched me up tight, and I could see where it was all heading. Straight to jail."

"And that's where I'll go if this favour you need is crooked." Paul's voice tightened.

"It's not—"

"I know what you're going to ask," he continued to whisper, "and if you're wrong about Weston, I seriously could go to jail right alongside you."

"I'm not wrong, Paul. I'd risk everything on it."

"Even me, you'd risk me?"

Roger held his breath. "I'm not wrong."

"Where are you, anyway? Rumours are flying that they've got you cornered, that you've taken a hostage, that—"

"What! Now stop there," Roger said. "Calm down. You're more nervous than I am – and I'm the one they're chasing! I haven't got a damned hostage."

"I heard—"

"No one has caught up to me yet. I'm not cornered, and I definitely haven't taken anyone hostage, okay? I thought coppers weren't supposed to jump to conclusions."

"No, this is from the girls at CJSU. Think they're running a book on you."

Roger thought for a moment. And then he just said it. "So what's your answer? Do you fancy some overtime?"

— Two —

The call from Roger was over, had been for ten minutes or more. But Yvonne sat in shadows at the kitchen table staring at the phone, tapping the dead girl's house key on the table. Tears brimmed in her eyes.

The front door banged and Yvonne jumped, dropping the key onto the table.

Chris stood on the doorstep all nerves and twitchy feet, with eyes that flicked only briefly at her.

"Come in," she said, peering up and down the road. She led him through into the kitchen, and turned the light on. There was still a pile of dirty laundry on the floor by the machine in the utility room, its door stood open. The key was on the table.

"It's true, isn't it?"

"Yvonne..."

"He called," she said, "not long ago. He said they'd arrested him for her murder. Nicky Bridgestock. Have they?" She sat at the table, fumbled with the key.

"Yes, they have."

"Jesus," she sighed. "Do *you* think he did it, Chris? Do you think Roger is capable of killing a young girl?"

Chris leaned back against a worktop and folded his arms. "We found things at her house that suggest he had an involvement, yes."

"But—"

"It's for a jury to decide, Yvonne. Whether I think he did it or not doesn't matter a damn."

"It matters to me," she said.

"Where did you find that?" he nodded at the key.

"In Roger's work jacket. He said it needed washing, that it had been in a house where there were fleas." She laughed, it was hollow, depressed. "I suppose he forgot to ditch the evidence, eh? This could nail him for a long time, couldn't it?"

He didn't answer.

"Will you take it?"

"Found it in his coat, eh? Good evidence, Yvonne." He shook his head, even tutted a little. He took the kettle. "Tea?" He held it under the tap.

"No I don't want tea! I want some pissing answers!"

"They won't be far behind me, Yvonne, CID I mean. A few minutes, fifteen, maybe. If they have warrants with them, they'll want to search the house, see if they can—"

"So take the key."

"Can't do that, Yvonne." He looked across at her, glanced at the key. "What else did he say?"

"He's broken out."

Chris dropped the kettle in the sink. "What the... *why*? He can't do a stupid thing like that!"

"He already has. He needs you to help him."

"Me? What the hell am *I* supposed to do?"

"He says you're the only one he trusts; he says you can give him advice."

"I don't care what he says, the man's gone crazy." Chris stopped. "I'm sorry, I shouldn't have said that."

"No, you shouldn't. You have to meet him at your house, Chris. You have to sort things out."

"I can't aid a..."

"Murderer?"

"Does he know what he's asking? I should go straight to Shelby with this."

"You can't! He trusts you, at least listen to him, for Christ's sake."

Chris was silent for a while. He plucked the kettle out of the sink, filled it and stood in the centre of the kitchen. "Okay," he said at last. "But when Shelby gets here, promise me you won't mention this to him. It's my job, Yvonne; it's my promotion, everything I've worked towards."

She stared at him. "You don't know?" she said. "No one told you?"

"What? Told me what?"

"I thought you were having a meeting this afternoon—"

"What! Spit it out, woman."

She shrank back into her chair and quietly said, "Denis gave Roger the promotion. Told him yesterday."

Chris stared at her in disbelief. "No," he whispered. *"No!"* He threw the kettle into the far corner of the kitchen. The bread crock smashed, the lid snapped off the kettle and a shower of water sprayed onto the wall.

Yvonne shrieked, holding her hands to her mouth.

Chris stood perfectly still as though thinking hard. He turned to her and calmly said, "If that's his decision." Water dripped.

She stared at the kettle and the smashed bread crock. And then looked at Chris, emotionless. How do you dampen a fiery temper so quickly? "Chris? Are you alright?"

"Yes, yes, I'm okay," he said. "I'm sorry, I'm okay. Really." He hovered right over the key. "I'll go and help him. I don't know what I can do, but I'll try, yes I'll go and help..."

"Thank you."

"Just promise me, no matter what happens, you'll say nothing of this."

She paused, gauging his words. "Okay," she said slowly. "I promise."

— Three —

"Get on to North Yorkshire, South Yorkshire, GMP and Humberside; tell them a patrol car's been nicked. Make sure they have full details, the fleet number, the ID number, everything."

Shelby paused, listening to the question from Force Control. "Yes, yes. Tell them about him, but... ask them to be discreet." He hung up and said to no one in particular, "If that's possible."

He slid his fingers through his hair, and then dialled Chamberlain. "Sir, it's Graham; I need RIPA authority for a landline. It's for Conniston's home phone." He listened, slackened his collar and felt the heat in his face. "I realise that, sir; but better late than—" he reached inside his desk drawer, his hand hovering over the whisky glass, and then picked up the forms instead. "I understand, sir. Thanks, I'll bring the paperwork up."

Chapter 26

— One —

It was dark now, but the security light was on, and it illuminated the fine drizzle that fell on the patrol car's roof. From the back garden, overgrown with weeds, Roger peered along the length of the garage at the car and watched the smoke from its idling engine turn red in the glow from the taillights. Moments later, Paul's van came into view, turned in the road and halted in front of the police car. Paul climbed out, arched his back and yawned, appearing wonderfully blasé about the task in front of him. The police officer guarding Nicky Bridgestock's scene met Paul at his van's rear doors. They exchanged a few words, though Roger couldn't hear them, and shared a joke.

Paul and the officer looked at Nicky's side door, and they both walked over to it, shielding their eyes from the glare of the security light. Paul, who knew Roger was watching, didn't let his eyes roam in search of him. From his stab-vest pocket, the officer pulled a set of Yale keys attached to a large plastic fob with wyp stamped across it, followed by a four-digit number. They deemed the scene important enough to sheet Nicky's damaged door with a metal skin, and leave an officer guarding it.

With a screech, the metal door opened and obscured some of the police car from Roger's view. His hand tightened on the fence, unlatched the gate. He saw both pairs of legs go back down the drive to the van, heard the van door open. Then Roger was running. He hit the concrete driveway as the police officer began to look around.

Just as Roger pulled his trailing leg in through the doorway, Paul dropped the camera case and shouted loud enough to reclaim the officer's attention.

Eventually Paul stepped inside the house wearing a scene suit, carrying the aluminium camera case, the tripod, flash and a Maglite. The officer put his forensic kit onto the hallway floor, and from the lounge, Roger watched his hand pull back out into the brightness of the security light.

"Thanks," Paul said. "There's too much shit to carry around these days."

"No problem," said the officer. "If you want a loo, the old lass at 69's pretty obliging. She'll probably be out in ten minutes with a cuppa. Bless her."

"Ah, none for me, thanks, I got water with me. And anyway, I really should be getting on."

"Righto. Leave it with you, then."

Using the forensic case, Paul wedged Nicky's broken door closed. He hung a scene suit over the hole where the lock used to be, and turned on the hall and kitchen lights.

"Nice one," Roger stepped out of the lounge. "We'll make a murderer's accomplice of you yet."

Paul stood up straight, the large purple knot of his tie visible through the V in his scene suit. "Don't ever joke about that again. If you do, I'll walk. Then I'll talk."

"You're right. Bad taste. I'm sorry. I'm a bit stressed..." He was suitably chastened. "I should be thanking you for doing this for me, not—"

"It seems you're important, Roger. The officer out there says Shelby's paying overtime for off-duty coppers to return to the station and go out looking for you."

"What an offer; it's nice to be wanted," he said. "Listen, before we start, I want to know why you're doing this."

"You still don't trust me?"

"Of course I do."

"Then why do you ask that?"

"Because I'm depending on you, that's why. My future is in your hands, and... and I'd like to think you're on my side."

"I wouldn't be here otherwise."

"No, fair enough. Just thought I'd check."

Paul's straight face began to soften, and a smile grew. "Because Weston called me a fool, and he threatened to snap my legs after I'd gone to the trouble of making him a drink."

"What? You're doing this because—"

"No," he said, serious again. "I'm doing it because if it's a choice between you killing a girl or Weston killing a girl, my money'd be on him. Anyway, I figure if you're guilty, you'd have run far away, you wouldn't bother trying to prove your innocence. Am I right?"

Roger nodded. "Spot on right."

"But if this goes wrong, I lose everything, Roger. Do you know what a big deal that is? Everything."

"I'm there now, mate. I know exactly what you mean."

Then the tension fell out of Paul's face. "I see the weather hasn't improved your hair at all."

Roger smiled, then glanced around the lounge.

"Nice t-shirt, by the way."

"Okay, Paul, let's get started. I want you to tell me what you and Chris did when you got here. It'll take a while, but I'm patient, so... in your own time."

"What happened to your face, it's seriously smashed."

"Weston happened to it. Now tell me."

Paul told him everything he could recall right from stepping out of the MIV. This was his first murder, his first proper body, he said, so his recollection of the details was sharp enough to impress Roger. He remembered Chris in the bedroom, and how he taped the body sheet and the girl's bare flesh. He mentioned the fingerprint camera, the clouds of black powder, which even now shadowed the carpet they stood upon, as though it was smoke damaged. The drag of feet across the pile signified by clean scrapes.

"What are you— what are *we* looking for?" Paul asked.

"Would you be annoyed if I said I didn't know? However, Weston's not a forensic man, so maybe he's made a mistake somewhere along the line. And this is the only part of the line I can deal with. *We* can deal with, sorry."

"You *hope* he's cocked up?"

"If he hasn't, then I may as well get in that patrol car out there and introduce myself."

Paul continued his account. He remembered taking control samples of lounge, stair and bedroom carpets, he recalled packaging them, attaching CJA labels, signing them over to DC Clements and then later, more exhibits to Lenny Firth. His memory was accurate and full of details, such as how Clements smelled of some exotic perfume, and how Firth just smelled.

Roger didn't interrupt, merely listened, sitting cross-legged on the lounge floor, his hands double gloved already, tugging at the stitching around his overshoes. He had questions and theories queuing.

There was that moment, Paul continued, when Nicky's body lay tied up in the black body sheet; how small she looked, how valueless she seemed. How much like rubbish ready for disposal. Then he explained how Inspector Shelby and Chris talked for a while, before he came downstairs to do the fingerprinting.

"Who did the bathroom?"

"Who fingerprinted it?"

"Yeah."

"He did. Chris."

"Any marks?"

"That I can't remember. Don't think so. Don't remember writing them up if there were."

He stopped tugging the seam. "What? If he did the exam, he should write them up."

"He mentioned that, but said it would be quicker this way."

"He's a funny bugger, is Chris. He really is an old Professor, and old fashioned too; I mean, you wouldn't catch me using black powder here."

"Why?"

"Well, the paintwork looks sound, it hasn't oxidised; nice flat surfaces, not too many blemishes. It would hold good fingerprints," he said. "I would've gone straight to aluminium powder and lifted. Quicker, easier. No messing about. And anyway, if you apply black powder incorrectly, you can damage the mark, even rub it out altogether; black powder fingerprints need a one-brush application, any further brushing will just smear them away. Now with ali, you can bring the mark up with your first application, develop it and then clean out the ridge detail with an empty brush. What could be simpler?"

"Well, yeah," Paul leaned against the lounge doorframe. "I thought that."

Roger rested against the coffee table. It was wooden with a glass top. On the glass was a fine layer of black fingerprint dust, almost unnoticeable; but in the centre of the glass top was a cleaner circle, about the size of a tumbler. Next to it, a coffee ring. He looked past Paul, and through into the kitchen. "Well, let's go through her last moments. Were there any signs of forced entry?"

"No. Everything was as it should be."

"Right, then; Weston picked her up, and she brought him back to her house – though God knows why, he must be twice her age. Anyway, they're here, alone. She invited him in. We know she came from Wakefield town centre, from the nightclubs, so he probably picked her up there. Okay so far?"

"Sounds fine. Go on."

"She's drunk, or she's tipsy—"

"More drunk than tipsy. Toxicology said so."

"You've seen the pathology report?"

"Heard of it, more like."

Roger tugged at the stitching. "What's the first thing a newly introduced couple do when they get here?"

"You're jumping to conclusions, Roger. I mean, he might have knocked on her door after she got home—"

"Any taxi firm come forward to say they remember her?"

"Don't think so," Paul said. "But I'm not sure."

"Was any request made to examine a taxi, you know, for fibres, hair?"

Paul shook his head. "Don't think so."

"Okay," Roger stared at the coffee ring, "you're right; I'm assuming a lot. But it changes nothing really. Nicky came home with Weston, probably with the intention of spending the night with him. Let's say they're both in here, in the lounge; she's drunk, he's not."

"How do you know?"

"Because he's about to kill her, Paul. You'd want to be sharp if you're going to get away with murder. And I'd also guess that you and Chris found almost nothing? Right?"

"Only evidence that you killed her."

"Another good reason to stay sharp then. And that alone should tell you it's a premeditated attack; there was no bloodbath, no signs of disturbance, no signs of a fight."

"Quite the opposite. She was seriously naked on her bed."

"There you are, then." He gently dabbed a gloved finger at the coffee ring. It was still tacky. "So, back to our scenario. Let's assume Weston brought her home; what's a good hostess do first?"

"Drink?"

"In one, Paul. A drink. They have a nightcap."

"No, that's wrong, we only found one glass."

"Did anyone check in there," he nodded, "in the kitchen?"

Paul thought for a moment. "Not really. I remember Shelby took a step inside and said it looked completely undisturbed, and Chris agreed." He shrugged, "I'm just the hired help. I do what I'm told."

"Yeah, fine," Roger said. "But it stinks. Just because a room looks like it's come straight out of *Ideal Homes*, doesn't mean it's isolated from a major crime scene. They should know better."

"Chris wouldn't even let me have a glass of water from it. I was seriously parched."

"Good. At least he got that bit right. You can't use the—"

"*Facilities in a murder scene*. Yeah, I got that lecture a couple of times. So did Shelby."

"Apart from Shelby's step inside, no one went in there? No one at all?"

"No," Paul said. "Not unless Shelby sneaked all the way in while we were upstairs."

"Shelby can't sneak, it's impossible." The coffee ring stared back at him. Roger got to his feet. "Okay, you seem to have covered the rest of the house, now let's cover the only room no one touched."

"Now I'm confused. Why would you want to examine a kitchen that no one else thought worth the trouble?"

"She gave him a drink, Paul. The murderer put his cup back. Weston put it back."

— Two —

After Chris left, only a few minutes passed before there was another knock at the door. The dead girl's key was still on the table. There were key-sized indentations in the wood all around it. Yvonne let the doorbell ring a second time before dropping the key into a drawer, and heading towards the front door.

There were two of them; Lenny Firth and another, larger man, whom she didn't know. Both appeared serious, preoccupied even. "Yes?"

"Yvonne," Lenny Firth said, "how are you? Haven't seen you—"

"Have you found him yet?" she asked.

Firth looked at Shelby. "Yvonne, this is Detective Inspector Shelby, my gaffer. May we come in?"

She opened the door wide, and stepped back into the lounge.

"We won't keep you long, Mrs Conniston," Shelby said. "My name's Graham, by the way."

"Take a seat, Graham," Yvonne said. "Lenny, you too. Can I get either of you a drink? Tea, coffee?" And then she remembered the kettle was out of service.

"Thank you no," Shelby said. Firth closed his mouth, deflated. "You're aware of Roger's predicament, Mrs Conniston?"

"Which predicament are you referring to?"
"I take your point; Mrs Conniston—"
"Yvonne. Please call me Yvonne."
"You know he's missing from custody?"
"Yes."
"Has he been in touch with you?"
She hesitated. "No."
"When did he call?"
"I said he hadn't been in touch."
"You are lying, Mrs Conniston."
"I..."
"When?"
She played with her fingers. "About half an hour ago, maybe three quarters of an hour."
"Where was he calling—"
"He never said." Yvonne glared right at Shelby. "I think you've got the wrong—"
"Doesn't look especially innocent to me," Shelby said, "not after he half killed a police Inspector to break out of custody. Not the look of an innocent man, isn't that."
Yvonne's jaw dropped open. Then it snapped shut.
"What did he tell you, Yvonne?" Firth asked.
"He said you'd arrested him. For Nicky Bridgestock's murder. He said you had it all wrong. He said he broke out of custody."
"Did he say what he was planning to do now?" This from Shelby.
"No."
Shelby sighed.
"It's true," Yvonne said.
"He rang to pass the time of day?"
"Breaking out of custody after having been accused of someone's murder is hardly passing the time of day, Inspector, is it?"
"I can't believe he would ring you, tell you all that, and not elaborate; not tell you who he planned to see or where he planned to go."
Yvonne said nothing.

"You know, when this is resolved, Mrs Conniston, the courts may take a very dim view of your reluctance to cooperate."

"When this is resolved *correctly*, Inspector Shelby, there will be no need of a *criminal* court."

Shelby pulled his head back, the threat of civil proceedings obviously not lost on him.

"Will that be all, Inspector?"

Shelby stood. "Goodbye, Mrs Conniston. Hope to see you again soon with more news."

Lenny Firth remained seated for a moment longer. "Has Chris been over, Yvonne?"

"He kindly broke the news, yes."

"Did he arrive here before or after Roger rang?"

"Before." Yvonne cleared her throat.

"You sure?"

"Goodbye, Lenny."

"He didn't mention anything to you except news of Roger's arrest and escape?"

"He said nothing of Roger's escape, Lenny." Yvonne bit her bottom lip.

"Did he say anything else to you other than news of Roger's arrest, then?"

"No."

"Yvonne," Firth began, "you're not doing Roger or yourself any favours—"

"Get out please, Lenny."

"Perhaps you ought—"

"Perhaps you ought to leave, unless you have the proper authority to be here."

"Mrs Conniston," Shelby said from the hallway, "we are the police, investigating a murder and an escape. Believe me, that alone gives us authority enough. But we'll be back later with a warrant."

"The next time he calls her," Shelby said as they climbed into the car, "I'll have the bloody thing on tape, and with luck, I'll have a location. Mobile or landline."

"How can you get a location if it's a mobile phone?"

"Triangulation. They can pinpoint a signal between three masts, apparently."

"Right, I see," Firth said.

"I know what I meant to ask you," Shelby said as he turned the ignition, "do you know if Roger had any underwear stolen from the locker room last week?"

Firth looked confused. And then his eyes lit up. "Yeah, I do. Someone taking the piss."

"No. He says they were taking the pubes," Shelby sighed. "Wish you'd told me before."

"You never asked before. I mean, I expected to see them flying half-mast on the flagpole the next day."

"Lenny, I have to say that sometimes you are a grave disappointment to me."

"Why's that then?"

"Because you can be tactless, you are flippant, you didn't consider one of the largest pieces of evidence in the damned case. Roger's pubes? And how that might go hand in hand – so to speak – with a pair of missing *underpants*."

"Well, I…"

"Go on. I'm listening."

"Like I said, I thought it was a prank." He shrugged, "And then it just left my mind. I didn't expect them to be the centre of a murder investigation."

"Exactly. It never 'clicked', did it? And that's why you disappoint me, Lenny. You always have to be told, or you have to be shown. You never take it on yourself to find something out, do you?"

"Where are we going?"

"You tell me, Lenny. Where are we going?"

Lenny looked out the side window and chose to ignore Shelby.

— Three —

"Can I ask you something?" Paul said.

"Go for it."

"Why do you always wear a red waistcoat?"

Roger and Paul stood side by side in the kitchen doorway, looking into the small but orderly room. A large window looked out onto the sodium-lit road, facing a row of quiet houses. Framing the window were dark green curtains tied back onto gold-coloured hooks.

Paul waited.

The sink was clean, tea towel neatly folded on the empty draining board. Around the far side of the kitchen were sand-coloured worktops, equally empty of clutter, only a kettle, a toaster and a microwave oven, all gleaming and bright. A pair of fluorescent tubes lit the room.

"It's like a fucking show house," Roger said.

"Well? You going to tell me?" asked Paul.

"I always wear a red waistcoat because I don't like blue."

"Don't give much away, do you."

"To tell you the truth, I wear it because it looks smart."

Paul smiled.

"Well *I* think it looks smart. Plus, I only need to iron the sleeves of my shirts."

"Crafty."

Around the room, more worktops shone. A porcelain duck with stainless steel utensils poking out the top, and next to it, a stainless steel bread bin tucked squarely into a corner. Above and below this final stretch of worktops were fake oak-fronted cupboards, eight of them. They too were clean; no dark areas on the edges of the door, no dirt in the grain.

Nicky had pictures on the walls, framed prints of Pooh Bear and a dog with drooping eyes that reminded Roger of Weston. There was a corkboard with fast-food fliers and menus pinned to it. An Eeyore clock ticked on the wall next to it.

Only a few chips of white painted doorframe littered the otherwise clean floor. Like the fake cupboard doors, the floor was oak effect; a pearled finish. "Okay, what's the first rule of scene examination?"

"Photography."

"Good. But wrong. Think, Paul."

He did, but shook his head. "I don't know, then."

"Look, that's all. Nothing special, nothing scientific. Just look. Take it all in." Roger crouched in the doorway. "Pass me your Maglite." He focused the torch beam into a pencil point and swept it across the floor, gliding it slowly from side to side. The chips of wood cast long shadows, and hairs stood out brightly alongside chewed fingernails and crumbs of food near the edges of the floor. There was also a fine, almost indiscernible covering of normal household dust. Not as clean as he first thought. Roger passed the torch over again, and this time he saw it, narrowed his arcs until the light rested on a small area of floor in front of the sink. "Bingo." The light picked out signs of recent dust disturbance. "You got any ESLA?"

"I'll get it."

"Gel lifters?"

"Coming right up. You found a footwear impression?"

"Yup."

"Type?"

"Don't know yet, can't make out any detail from here." Roger turned off the torch and stood. "Are you okay with this?"

"Are you going somewhere?"

"This is your scene, Paul."

"But—"

"Remember me telling you that I would never throw you in at the deep end and leave you alone? I meant it. But you have to learn how to do this. It's important."

"Exactly," countered Paul, "it's *fucking* important. I can't—"

"Yes, you can. Get it right here," he said, "and it'll be a breeze forever."

"Yeah, but get it wrong and I could seriously balls things up for you."

"You'll do just fine," Roger smiled. "Seriously."

Paul photographed the kitchen. "Non-destructive evidence gathering," Roger said. "This is what the jury will see; they have to know the layout of the house, the layout of the kitchen, where the evidence came from, see?"

"You think we're going to find anything?" Paul loosened the knot of his tie.

"Wrong attitude, Paul. You don't go to a burglary or a rape thinking you won't find anything, do you? You have to look for it, if it's not there, move onto something else. There will always be something. But you have to work hard for it."

"You actually want me to ESLA the damned floor?"

"Problem?"

"I haven't ESLA'd since training school."

"Bit rusty? And the longer you leave it the rustier you'll be, and then you'll reach retirement having never used it, always wondering if you could have used it if push came to shove. Well," he leaned toward Paul, "I'm shoving you. Now unpack the zapper and the foil."

The foil's trade name was *Mylar* film. On one side it was shiny; chrome-shiny like kitchen foil and just as thin, and on the reverse side it was an endless jet black. And like kitchen foil, it came on a roll. "So just wind off six or seven feet," Roger said, "and roll it out across the floor." With the torch, Roger highlighted the area Paul had to aim for.

Paul unrolled the film, and seemed relieved when it was laid out on the floor. It was like a mirror, but all ripples and dimples that reflected the white ceiling and fluorescent tubes in a distorted fashion.

"Good, now for the zapper."

Paul cringed. "I'm going to get a belt off it, I know I am."

"You're not, don't worry." Roger took the zapper out of its packing.

It was a black box with its trade name, *Pathfinder*, emblazoned across it. *Pathfinder* was slightly bigger than an outstretched hand, had an on/off switch and a dial surrounded by a series of LEDs, going from green, through amber and ending with red. The zapper had what appeared to be three metal feet protruding from the base by a quarter of an inch, only they weren't feet at all, they were electrodes: one positive, two negative.

"Here, take it. Put the earth plate near the foil, but not touching it. Now put the zapper down so its electrodes are touching the foil and the earth plate."

He did, hesitantly.

"Good, nothing to worry about. Flick the on switch and turn the dial into the orange section."

All the green LEDs illuminated, and two orange ones. The film buzzed and as the power increased, it hissed, sucking down onto the floor as though attached to a vacuum cleaner. The ripples and dimples tightened up. "Now ease it up into the red." The film became a mirror, was sucked flat onto the floor, and became a truer reflection of the fluorescent tubes and the ceiling. The *Mylar* film hissed as static electricity chased the remaining air bubbles out at the sides, popping with relief.

Paul stopped breathing, and Roger nudged him. "It ain't going to bite you, Paul. Go on, turn it off, leave it a few seconds to discharge and then lift the zapper away."

"Why do they call it a zapper?"

Roger shone the torch and inched across the floor, keeping away from the film, seeing in the oblique light that he wasn't destroying any other footwear marks. "Go on, take a wild guess." When Paul lifted the machine away, the *Mylar* film relaxed, seemed to sigh as the ceiling reflection rippled into distortion again. Together they turned the film over so the black side faced up. "Because if you don't wait for the discharge, it'll sting you like you just poked your fingers in the mains socket."

Paul laughed, "So my hair would—"

"Would look just like mine, yeah, yeah." Roger waved the torch over the *Mylar*'s dust-covered surface and found a series of footwear marks. The static created by the *Pathfinder* attracted loose dust particles like iron filings to a magnet. There were obvious stiletto shapes, obvious slipper shapes, and bare feet too – even their ridge detail was visible. And then he saw the footwear mark from near the sink; a perfect negative of a, "Hush Puppies."

"Hush Puppies? Jesus, Weston's seriously gone down in my estimations."

"He couldn't get lower in mine," Roger said. "But even so, Hush Puppies?"

"You want me to gel lift it?"

"Okay, yeah. Then we'll check the rest of the floor and see where he's been. If we find anymore, we'll just gel them. Forget ESLA, it's taking too damned long, and I have to get to Chris's and lie low. I want him to go and see Shelby with these results."

"What about a plan?"

"Plan?" Roger laughed, "I'm making this up as I go along."

"I meant a plan of the floor."

"Hey, good point. Okay, tell you what, that's my job. You crack on with the gels and I'll sketch."

Paul peeled the clear plastic sheet away from the gel lifter. Like the *Mylar*, it was jet black on one side, but was self-adhesive across its fifteen-inch length. Its reverse side was white rubber. Paul used a small roller to adhere the gel to the floor and ensure no air bubbles were trapped. He left it in place for Roger to measure and sketch, and used the torch to find another four *Hush Puppies* impressions.

"They go right up to the cupboard," Paul said, staring at the lifters and then up at Roger. "And then they go back out of the room again."

"Okay," he said, "open it."

"You sure you don't want to do it? It's your—"

"Please, the fucking suspense is killing me; just open the damned cupboard."

— Four —

"Can you see anything?" Shelby walked around the back while Firth cupped his hands to the cobweb-covered garage window. It had a dull silvery sheen right across it. He tried the handle.

"I think he's got curtains up in there or a sheet across the window."

Shelby looked at Chris's back door, flipped the handle. He peered in through the kitchen window.

"Why are we here?"

"There you go again, Lenny. Letting your mouth go off on one all by itself."

"Is it 'Pick on Lenny Day' today?"

"Yes it is." Shelby turned away from the window. "Mrs Conniston said Chris had called round. Didn't she?"

Firth said nothing.

"Lenny, that was a question. It's traditional to provide a response after a question."

"Yes, she said that, yes," he sighed, squinting into the drizzle.

"Good. Then that's why we're here. They're good friends those two, Conniston and Hutchinson. Thick as thieves sometimes."

"You think he's hiding Roger?"

"Well, I don't know. Seems a bit strange that he should want to tell Mrs Conniston of her husband's misfortune, her husband's arrest, I mean."

"I'll double check round the front."

"They'll be together somewhere." Shelby followed at a more leisurely pace, giving the garage another cursory glance. "Best friends share no secrets, Lenny."

Chapter 27

— One —

WHERE ARE YOU, ROGER?

Chris turned off the engine, sat in the car brooding, listening to the cooling exhaust ticking in the darkness of the garage. After three quarters of an hour, it stopped ticking. Cool. Cold. He waited patiently.

How could Bell give Conniston the promotion? For fuck's sake, he still had another two weeks of acting-up to do. They were all square in the role-plays and the interviews. So how could he do that? And then, the real insult came when Yvonne Conniston told him the news. Bell didn't even have the fucking courage to tell him himself!

"'You'll have to work on your interpersonal techniques...' you fucking knew all along that Conniston would get it, you slimy bastard, didn't even have the decency to let me finish acting-up, didn't have the guts to give us a fair fight, a fair competition. I'd win then. Oh, you're damned right I would."

Chris froze. He saw someone through the corner of his eye at his garage window. A silhouette peered in, hands cupped to the glass, talking to someone else.

Burglars! They tried the garage door and Chris's heart lurched to see the handle flick up and down all by itself. For some stupid reason, he held his breath.

No, no, not burglars. It was those bastards from the bookies. Tony Paxman Bookmakers on the Bull Ring were fine bookies; great at extending credit, no problem, Chris, you're a good customer, they said. Hey, you can't do too much for a good customer. They were good lads who popped in here to see him once a fucking week regular as a clock with the trots, to collect their dues. Chris swallowed. He was going to disappoint them again. And he wondered how far they'd take it this time. He closed his eyes. Waited. Apparently, you *could* do too much for a good customer.

He listened to the voices, and thought he recognised them.

No, those voices didn't belong to Paxman's men, didn't even belong to Paxman himself; one of those voices belonged to Terry. Terry had no second name. But he came into the station every now and then to pay his respects to Chris personally, just to make sure Chris didn't forget him. Chris never had, though he'd been fifty quid short once. And that hadn't gone down too well. Luckily, only embarrassment gave him a red face that time. Next time would be worse. Nice man, Terry. He carried a shiny chrome knuckleduster for late payers. Chris had seen it, and being in this job, he knew what it could do to a mandible. The results were frightening. Terry always got his money before anyone else. Terry liked it like that.

Still sitting inside his car, afraid to make a noise, he wound the window down an inch and put his ear to the gap. The voices faded, and some moments later, they returned. One of the voices he knew well. And it wasn't dear old Terry at all. It was Shelby. The other voice belonged to Detective Sergeant Lenny Firth. He said, 'You think he's hiding Roger?'

'Well, I don't know. Seems a bit strange that he should want to tell Mrs Conniston of her husband's misfortune, her husband's arrest, I mean.'

'I'll double check round the front.'

'They'll be together somewhere'. Shelby's voice said. 'Best friends share no secrets, Lenny.'

Chris bit down on his lip. Blood landed in his cardigan.

He waited another half an hour.

"You're right, Graham; best friends share no secrets. Me and Roger, we share everything. Everything. I gave him my promotion. I gave him my knowledge too; he's damn nearly as good at the job as I am. But no match in a straight fight. He couldn't hack it at a major scene." He waved a pointing finger angrily at the air. "Not Roger. And what did Roger give me? Fuck all, that's what."

He got out, closed the door, and locked it. "What does Bell think Roger would do at a major scene, huh? When he's the one giving the orders and taking the shit from idiots like Shelby? Conniston would fold in ten minutes flat. He would, or he'd ask around, get a consensus of opinion!"

Where are you, Roger?

Chris unlocked the small wooden garage door and slowly stepped out, peered around in case Shelby and Firth were being cunning for a change, then locked it after him. The hinges creaked annoyingly, loudly. He tiptoed through the rain, across to the house.

He unlocked the back door, stepped in, locked it and kicked his shoes towards a pile of others. They missed, thudded the wall and knocked the bin over. He took off his jacket; let it fall on the floor. It was dark in here but he didn't turn on any lights.

He sat in the lounge, folded his arms against the cold, and thought of the absurdity of it all. He thought about Conniston, about how he had 'acquired' *his* promotion. And he was galled.

Still no sign of Roger.

Chris's toes hurt. In the darkness, he looked down to see his feet curled into the foot-equivalent of a fist. They dug into each other and they dug into the floor. His arms were still folded achingly tight across his chest. Like his toes, his fingertips hurt, and so too did his ribs.

He leaned back again in the chair, in the gloom, in his cold house, with his feet curled into fists, and another drop of blood soaked into his cardigan as he waited. He waited for Conniston, because his bitch of a wife – who tried to give him the dead girl's house keys – can you fucking believe it – who tried to pass him incriminating evidence – said that Roger Boy wanted a favour, old bean, old pal.

"Oh, I'll do you a favour alright," he mumbled.

The lounge was black. A putrid, meagre light came in through the window and glanced off the *Lucozade* bottles on the floor. People walked by, looking in, some peering in. Nosy bastards. "Fuck off!" Chris threw two fingers. Eyes front, the passers-by passed by quicker.

I could go to Shelby. When Roger gets here, I could tell Shelby. I could yell it, I could yell 'Shelby, I have your escaped murderer here in my house, take him away before…'

I'd get it then, the promotion. Bell would have no choice, would he? Chris smiled again, retrieved his jacket, and stuffed it behind the settee. He stood in silence, bit his nails and spat them across the floor before climbing the stairs, feeling his way. He paced the landing. Back and forth, back and forth. Wondering. Thinking. Cursing.

A thought bounced around his mind as though it were inside a pinball machine. It scored over a million before he could nail it down: it's all falling down around my ears.

But it's not.

It is.

No, you are the new Supervisor. Congratulations. Terry and Paxman will be pleased.

But be careful, Roger's an escaped murderer! And you know what? He could easily kill again. The bastard could turn at any second, at any provocation. You gotta be careful. You might say the wrong thing; you might end up fighting for your own life. Who knows what might happen then. There's always self-defence, Chris. Always self-defence.

Come on, Roger.

— Two —

Paul stood aside and let the cupboard door swing open. They both stared inside, expecting some great revelation to announce itself. Then they looked at each other in despair.

"No blood," Roger said. "Would have been nice to have a little blood, just a bit. A fingerprint in blood would be perfect…"

"How about if I try LMG or a KM protein test on the cupboard door handle?"

Roger sank to his knees. "Nah," he said at last. "You're bound to find traces of protein here, it's a kitchen. Not all protein means blood, does it. So not all positive reactions mean blood. And anyway, unless we were lucky enough to find a *fingerprint* in blood, what have we got? Nicky Bridgestock's blood in her own kitchen: proves nothing. Good idea though, keep trying."

"I'm sorry," said Paul. "I was just—"

"Hey, don't you be sorry; it's good that— Wait a minute!"

"What? What?"

"What's the first rule of scene examination?"

"Phot— No, no; look. The first rule is observation."

"Don't use posh words; *look* will do," he smiled at Paul. "Go on then, *observe*."

The cupboard was nothing special, and that's why nothing remarkable stood out at first. There were two shelves, both covered with flowery lining paper; the lower one had glasses in it, tumblers, wine glasses and even flutes. The top shelf was reserved for cups and for mugs. All sorts, a mixture of comic faces, mugs twisted into incredible shapes, *Purple Ronnie* mugs, *Pooh Bear* mugs, and then at the front were a row of plain utilitarian, sandy-coloured mugs. Six of them. All standing on their bases.

Except one.

"Shit," said Paul.

"That's what I thought." Roger came closer, "See anything else?"

After a while, Paul replied. "Nope, can't say I do."

"Look at the lining paper, see how it's darkened and rippled slightly?"

"Yeah. So?"

"So, whoever put it away, not only put it away the wrong way up, but he also put it away without drying it first."

"The tea-towel," Paul said. "It's neatly folded by the sink."

Roger nodded. "So, what's it all mean, Sherlock?"

"He rinsed his mug, eventually found the right cupboard and just put it away, wet and upside down."

Roger clapped Paul on the shoulder. "You'll make a shit-hot SOCO. I can tell. But why do you say 'eventually'?"

"It'll have been dark if they've both just got back from a night out; the curtains are open, so he wouldn't dare put the light on. He'll have found this cupboard by streetlight, I suppose."

Roger stood, stretched his legs and looked at the dirt on the white knees of his suit. He could still see Weston's blood there too. "What next, then?"

"What next..." Paul considered. "Masks?"

"Then what?"

"I was hoping you'd know that one; I've got them all right up till now."

"Okay, we photograph the cupboard, first with the door closed, then with it open. Then close up on the mug. When we have the mug out, re-photograph to show the damp patch."

"Gotcha."

"Then we swab for DNA. He might have taken a drink from the mug. Then, you can do a little fingerprinting, see what shows up."

Paul stood, came face to face with Roger. "Listen," he said, "I'll do the swabbing, okay, but this time I'm standing firm – I want you to do the fingerprinting. I couldn't live with myself if I smudged one or messed up lifting it, or creased it while mounting it," he shook his head, "I..."

"You wouldn't have to live with yourself," Roger said, "I'd shoot you."

"Cheers."

"Pleasure. Okay, fair enough. Now get the forensic kit, eh."

After the initial part of the photography, they both wore fresh gloves and facemasks. Removing the mug was going to be like a surgical operation. They discussed the best way of getting it out without losing any potential fingerprints and without damaging any potential DNA from around the rim.

"You know," Roger said, "if I were to put a mug in a cupboard upside down, I'd either use the handle, or grip the body."

"No shit? How else you going to do it?"

"I'm thinking out loud here, give me some slack," he smiled. "What I'm getting at is this: he's not likely to have touched the underside, is he?"

"No. So?"

"So, we tilt the mug over, slip a swab up inside and pick it out of the cupboard on the swab, then tip it all the way over onto the worktop." That's exactly the way it worked. Smooth. The mug stared at them from its new home. "Go ahead with the swabs, Paul."

"Wait," Paul said, "look here." He pointed with a gloved finger.

Roger closed up, feeling his split lip with his tongue. There was something on the mug. Red. Blood. Patterned. "It's only a fingerprint in blood!" Roger exclaimed, a wild grin on his face. "You know, I could cry, I'm so happy."

"Any detail in it?"

"Some. Enough."

"Okay. Now what?"

Roger smiled, "Your favourite bit."

"Oh no, not the fingerprint camera." Paul filled out a blue label, wrote B/W in the corner, and lightly stuck it to the mug near the mark, while Roger loaded the film and wound on to frame 1.

"You okay with this?" Roger asked.

"I've had plenty of practice." Paul took the camera and located the mark. The flash popped. "May as well use all ten frames on it."

"No," Roger said, "just five, then we need to swab and re-photo it."

"Why?"

"A new policy. It's supposed to prove you've swabbed the mark and that the blood on the swab has come from that mark."

"Ha, it doesn't *prove* that."

"No, I know, but it's how the CPS barristers want it done these days."

"I would have thought a photo of a fingerprint in blood would be incontrovertible."

Paul swabbed a tiny area of the fingerprint that Roger declared as no value, collecting a stain no larger than the nib of a fountain pen. He packaged the swab and took a gulp of water from a bottle in his kit. "Rim swabs now?"

"Yup."

Taking another plain sterile swab, the same type they used in hospitals, Paul twisted and broke its seal. He withdrew the swab, nothing more than a glorified cotton wool bud, and then moistened it with two drops of sterile water from the same phial he used on the fingerprint swab. Lightly he rubbed the swab around the outer edge of rim before re-sheathing it into its plastic tube and sealing over the torn seal with biohazard tape. He did the same with another swab, this time stroking it around the inside of the rim. He took a third swab from his supply and did nothing with it other than write his CID6 number and the date on it, before slipping it and its two companions into a plastic evidence bag. The third swab was the batch control swab; should any unusual results fall out of the laboratory computer, the scientist could test this batch swab to check for background contamination. In too went the phial of water, and Paul sealed the bag. Gratefully, he took off his mask and stood aside. "Thank God that's over."

"You did well," Roger said. "Now it's my turn." He picked the best squirrel-haired brush from Paul's meagre collection, spun the lid off the pot of aluminium powder and lowered the brush inside. Then he flicked off the excess and gently brushed around the mug's handle, inside and out. He saw something there, came closer and inspected the mark. "It's good," he said. "Right thumb on the handle. Pity there's nothing but smears on the inside."

"Great. What about the body then?"

"Let's see, eh." He charged the brush, flicked again and used small circular motions to spread the powder on the mug, avoiding the fingerprint in blood. Soon a dull silvery sheen, like polished lead, covered its entire surface. Only smears of index, middle and the ring fingers of a right hand developed on the body of the mug. That and the ghostly shadow of a matching thumb around the far side, opposite the fingers.

"You taking them?"

"Damned right I am. There's not much detail there, but it might be enough to get me off the hook."

"Okay, I'll get some acetates and a roll of lifting tape."

Roger pressed the clear rubber lifting tape onto the handle of the mug, pressed down, rolling his gloved thumb over the fingerprint, being careful not to rub the tape onto the mark for fear of scratches. Using an acetate pen, he marked a gravity arrow on the lift so the bureau could orient it correctly. He lifted the tape, stared at it, saw the fingerprint and closed his eyes with gratitude. "Gotcha now, Weston. You bastard. Always said I'd get you on forensic evidence."

Roger placed the lift onto an acetate sheet and let Paul endorse it with his name, Nicky's address and the location of the mark. He repeated this on all the marks before putting them into a fingerprint envelope. "I pray to God they're his marks. Have you seen the scene log, Paul; was Weston's name on it?"

Paul shook his head, "Don't remember seeing it."

"Good. How's he going to explain this one."

"What next?"

"We seize the mug. It's still in the old Disclosure policy. Anyway," Roger said, "we take it as insurance. It's photographed, but you can't beat having the real thing to show to a jury."

"Okay, what's my next exhibit number?"

"Let's see; photos are PB1, ESLA foil is PB2, footwear gels are PB3 to PB8, red stain swab is PB9, rim swabs are PB10, so the mug is PB11."

"What time you got?"

"1930 hours." Roger watched him writing out the CJA label, watched him stick it to a box, place the cup inside the box and seal it away.

Finally, Paul signed over his seals.

"Are you comfortable with this?" Roger asked.

"With what?"

"You know, doing this exam."

"I believe you didn't kill that girl, Roger. I also believe that someone has seriously fucked up on a grand scale – I can't help wondering why he'd want to frame you; I mean, killing a stranger 'cause he dislikes you seems seriously extreme to me. But no," he stepped back, "I'm not really comfy doing this. I haven't asked permission, I'm still on probation, and I'm in a murder scene with a man who should be behind bars." He laughed, "Not good credentials for a long career are they."

"Suppose not."

"It's down to trust," Paul said. "I trust you. You didn't kill Nicky Bridgestock. It just needs pointing out to Shelby."

— Three —

"You know something, boss?"

"Lenny, I know lots of things; you want me start alphabetically?"

"Oh, naff off, if you're in one of your moods."

Shelby stopped the car violently, sliding its front tyre into the kerb. "What the hell did you say to me!" Then Firth shocked him further by getting out.

"Forget it, Inspector Shelby. You've taken the piss out of me long enough and I'm sick and tired of being sick and tired."

"Now just you—"

"Shut up!" Amazingly, Shelby did, and Firth appeared shocked this time. "I'm putting in for a transfer." He closed the door, stuck his hands in his pockets and began walking.

Shelby leapt out, slammed his door in a temper and shouted, "Lenny Firth, you get the hell back here now."

Firth waved. Walked on through the rain.

"Lenny!" Shelby was hoarse, veins stood proud on his forehead. But it worked. Lenny stood still long enough for Shelby to walk to him. Shelby gathered his breath, then quietly said, "Lenny, I just… I'm tetchy, that's all. I got Chamberpot chewing my nuts, I got to find an escaped murderer; I can't find this new SOCO, I can't find the old one… I'm thoroughly pissed off. And I'm taking it out on you."

"And?"

"Huh? Oh yes," he cleared his throat. "I'm sorry."

Firth turned. "I forgive you."

"How noble. I'm still going to take the piss out of you, Lenny; you know that, don't you?"

"I know where they'll be."

"Go on, spit it out."

— Four —

Chris was alone. He bit his nails. He sat in an old fabric recliner in the corner of his back bedroom; the one he used as a junk room, the one with an old school desk under the window. Fifty yards away a streetlight glowed. It disturbed his thoughts, so he drew the curtains and sat back down in the darkness. He began thinking of his situation, and ten more minutes dropped out of Chris's life. He spent it with Conniston; he wondered where Roger was, and he wondered when he would call around and accept the much-needed help he asked for. After all, Chris was his friend; Chris was here to help wherever he could.

His feet were clenched tightly into fists again, burrowing into the carpet. They hurt but it didn't matter.

Chapter 28

— One —

THEY HAD EMPLOYED THE same technique for getting out as they had for getting in. And minutes after leaving Nicky's house, Roger was trotting back up the mud path to Weston's patrol car. To his left, and through the gaps between the houses, he heard Paul's van drive away up the street.

Paul agreed to go straight back to the office and lodge the swabs in the Scenes of Crime freezer before heading over to the bureau and beg if necessary for them to search the fingerprints from the mug. While they searched, Paul would visit the Footwear Bureau and the Photographic Studio to deposit his evidence. Then he'd go back to the Fingerprint Bureau hoping for a result.

Roger took out the phone and from the depths of his memory, summoned up Chris's home phone number. He dialled it and listened as a recorded voice told him the number was unavailable. "Shit." He found the patrol car keys, and drove out of town, watching for other patrol cars, and praying he made it to the safety of Chris's house without some sharp-eyed copper pulling him over. The radio was still dead. The day had been a long one, and only neat adrenaline kept him going. He was tired beyond measure, and hunger fell marginally into second place. His heart beat fast and he held the steering wheel extra tight so as not to feel his hands trembling. He tongued his split lip.

He had to get to Chris's house; had to. Chris would keep him safe. Chris would stand up for him. But Roger stopped thinking about Chris. He was half way there when his earlier intention resurfaced and screamed *go to Weston's house!*

Roger pulled over and sat in the gloom. The more he thought about it, the more urgent it became. If he could get into Weston's house and find conclusive evidence linking Weston to Nicky, such as a pair of shoes with the same pattern as those on Nicky's kitchen floor, it would add to the evidence he and Paul already had, and it would blow this murder charge to hell.

Going to Chris's could wait until later.

"No, it's not a mistake," Roger convinced himself, and he turned the car around, driving through the evening traffic towards Sandal, hands trembling more than ever.

As he passed the open gates to Weston's house, he saw a patrol car on the driveway, a single officer inside. A hundred yards further along, Roger turned into an exclusive estate where the houses just got bigger, the size of small hotels, with top-end cars parked on cobbled driveways. He kept turning right until, between the houses, he could see the street lamps on the main road. Then he parked the car and walked boldly through someone's garden until he came to the rear wall.

Roger peered over the top, and could see Weston's house two or three houses away to his right. It was in darkness, only a string of glowing garden lamps illuminating what looked from here like an ornamental pond and a gazebo. Time squeezed him; urged him over the wall and onto a mud path that ran along the backs of the grand houses.

Minutes later, Roger nestled beneath the dripping gazebo. His hands and arms were freezing, his nose running and his ears were numb. Only then, did he realise he had nothing with him to break into the house. "And what if it's alarmed?" he whispered; the absence of an alarm bell box on the wall meant nothing.

The collective glow from the rough circle of garden lamps barely grazed the house, but it was enough for him to see the way in. The bathroom window was ajar. It would mean climbing up a drainpipe, and negotiating a two or three-yard shimmy along a sloping tiled roof that was probably growing its own moss carpet, but it was his only chance.

Blowing into his hands, he scampered across a stretch of spongy grass, shadows dancing around his feet.

— Two —

Paul approached Bishopgarth, a six-acre West Yorkshire police site that once housed the Bishop of Wakefield and his staff over a century before. The old Bishop's Palace was a CID training block now. The footwear and fingerprints bureaux, and the Fingerprint Development Laboratory, were secreted in a recent addition to the complex on a lower level than the rest of the buildings; it looked like a fugitive from an industrial estate.

Out of breath, Paul descended the stairs and jogged along a corridor, rushing towards its end where a sign stuck onto the double doors proclaimed 'The Fingerprint Bureau'. Smirking to himself, he opened the door marked 'The Finger', and stepped into a large office he hadn't seen since his training days.

Even though night had fallen, it was bright in here; reflective windows stretching down one side of the office bounced light from diffused fluorescent tubes overhead. There were at least thirty desks, and at most of them sat the fingerprint examiners, hunched over their work areas, quietly doing their jobs while immersed in music from a radio or cassette player. Above the desks were divisional identifiers hanging from the ceiling: AA, AC, BA, BB, CA, CB, and the like. No one sat at the desk below Paul's divisional identifier, DA.

Across the back wall was the police file, a huge metal cabinet with locked roller shutter doors. It contained all the fingerprints of serving police officers and civilian staff, over six thousand employees, and it was there to aid elimination from inadvertent contamination at crime scenes. Paul knew that his fingerprints had been picked out of there for comparison twice since he became operational. Once he lifted his own marks at a burglary, and again at a rape.

"They used to send out fingerprint brushes sprayed gold and mounted on a plinth if you lifted your own marks."

Paul turned. It was Barry Goodwyn struggling through the door with a tray of hot drinks. "Here, let me help."

Barry put the tray on a table and shouted, "Tea up!" and then to Paul he said, "Back in the old days, when we had time for a bit of fun, *you'd* have received a couple of golden brushes by now, young Mr Bryant."

Paul blushed. "Barry," he said, moving to one side. "I could really use your help if you can spare half an hour."

"What's up?"

Paul followed him to the desk below 'DA' and pulled up a spare chair. *Radio 2* played to the furry animals paper-clipped around the back of Barry's workstation.

"What's it to do with?"

Paul opened his CID6 book.

The word 'Murder' stood out, and Barry read the address. "Aw, not more Bridgestock stuff. I've just got back from telling Inspector Shelby about the Bridgestock marks."

"What about them?"

"Hasn't he seen you?"

"No. Why would he?"

"I think I'll let him explain it."

"Now I'm seriously worried."

"Okay," Barry said, "but if he asks how you know, I didn't tell you."

"Fine. Shoot."

"One of the marks that you submitted has a speck of blue paint sandwiched between the lift and the acetate."

"Shit," Paul whispered.

"He'd like a word, I think."

"I bet he would," his thoughts steered away to Shelby, an anger management candidate if ever there was one.

"Anyway, what you got there?" Barry asked.

They can only sack you once, he thought, handing over the envelope. "Marks from the kitchen area, this time; a mug actually."

"How come you went back? I thought they'd about wrapped that scene up and put it to bed."

"Just tying up loose ends, I guess," he shrugged.

"Let's have a look then." Barry pulled out the fingerprint lifts and asked, "Why haven't they been photographed?"

"Ah, yes. They're a rush job."

"Chris behind all this, is he?"

"Well, you know—"

"Supervisors are the worst offenders of all."

"They are?"

"They can't abide others breaking the rules, but when it suits them, they're all for it, and they always get someone else to do the dirty work for them. Do as I say, not as I do; a favourite saying among that lot, I'm afraid."

"So you always have them photo'd first."

"Supposed to. But if they're a special rush job, we can usually oblige." Barry sipped his tea and then pulled his magnifying glass over a small easel mounted on top of his desk, raked back at such an angle as to provide comfort and prevent casting his own shadow across his work. "Let's see them."

— Three —

Roger scurried towards the drainpipe and gripped the cold steel with numb hands. He climbed, feet scrabbling for purchase, and eventually was high enough to haul himself up onto the slick roof using the gutter. Cautiously, he shuffled along to the open transom. It was a simple reach away. He paused there, looked into the garden below, and listened. Traffic drone from the front of the house permeated around to the back.

Roger gripped the window frame and heaved himself up. Only then did the question occur to him: Is there anyone still inside? Will someone see me? But the most important question came last: how the fuck do I get back out without breaking my neck?

That's when he fell headfirst into Weston's bathroom. The back of his legs clattered against the open window, and his shins grated against the frame. He landed in a heap on the tiled floor, and the window clattered loud enough, Roger thought, to flush out anyone still left inside the house. Seething at the pain in his shins, and hands planted flat against a warm radiator, he waited for the footsteps. None came.

At the doorway, he peered across the landing. An orange light bleeding through a window glistened on a chandelier high above him. Leaning out, he saw the landing disappear into the shadows thirty feet away; there were no PIRs.

Prowling along the landing, he could see three doors to his right, three to the left. The first on the left was a walk-in airing cupboard, the second a guest's bedroom, and the third was a games room, furnished with a full-sized snooker table, dartboard and its own bar. Nothing in any room to incriminate Weston. "The wealth of an Inspector," Roger whispered. Dejectedly, he crossed the landing, opened the first door into a palatial bedroom with a carved four-poster and lace-edged canopy. This room was at the front of the house, and the same orange hue that lit up the landing, shone through two large windows onto an army of Lladro and Royal Doulton figurines.

Barbara Taylor Bradford novels splashed the oak bedside tables, but with nothing of interest lying in the drawers beneath them. Where does Weston sleep? he wondered.

"Well?"

"Well what, woman?"

"How do you feel, Colin?" Geraldine Weston fidgeted with her handbag.

"How the bloody hell do you think I feel?" He raised his voice, "I've been slammed around the fuck—" he saw DC Clements observe him through the door's window. He waved her away, lowered his voice. "I'm leaving," he said. "Now."

The uniformed officer accompanying Clements looked in too.

"But you can't," Geraldine said, "you've suffered a concussion."

"And every minute I spend in this god-forsaken shit hole is making me suffer even more!"

"But—"

"Oh stop your damned whining, woman, and get out the bleeding way."

Geraldine stepped aside as Weston threw back the covers and staggered to his closet. He took out his uniform trousers and pulled them on.

"Why must you go home anyway? What's the urgency?"

"Don't question my decisions," he snatched his shirt from a hanger. "I'm expecting a phone call."

"But your health—"

"Shit." Drips of blood across the collar, and more smeared down the back. "You didn't bring me any clothes, did you?"

"They said you were staying overnight."

"Come on, we're leaving." Weston dressed and barged through the door, glaring at Clements as she approached him. "And you stay the hell away from me, as well." He gave the same look to the uniformed officer. Geraldine slipped out behind him, her coat over her arm, car keys clutched in her hand.

"Inspector Weston," Clements began, "You can't leave. You're—"

"Pissed off? Damned right I am. Now go away, little girl."

"Sir," said the officer, "we're under instruction—"

"Fuck your instructions, boy. I am free to go whenever I please."

Weston marched up the corridor, past the nurses' station, and Geraldine scurried along behind, glancing back.

"Who was he calling *boy*?" the officer said.

Clements took a deep breath and rang Shelby.

Roger tiptoed along the landing and entered the next bedroom. Old cigar smoke poked him in the eyes. No Lladro in here; only a couple of photos showing Weston with considerably darker hair, his nose bloody, hand curled into the red knot of a fist held aloft in victory. Roger looked away from the picture and swallowed.

A double bed with the covers awry sat between the windows. Underwear was piled on top of a bureau, and a wicker basket by its side dripped clothes onto the floor. In this room, there were no bedside cabinets. Weston used the windowsills to hold overflowing ashtrays, and the net curtains were smeared with burns. A copy of *Bravo Two Zero* and a stack of girlie magazines lay on the floor among a scattering of empty cigar boxes.

After finding nothing of interest in the first of Weston's wall of wardrobes, Roger opened the second, and that's where he found the shoes.

"Are you finished yet?" Micky asked.

Helen didn't even raise her head, just continued writing and said, "I have paperwork to do. And interruptions don't help. I've already had Shelby in here beating Jon up, and then Paul nattering for directions to the bureau or something; the last thing I need is—"

"Can't it wait? I'm off duty in half an hour; I thought maybe we could..."

She put down her pen, slid her hair back behind her ears and folded her arms.

Micky fidgeted. "I know I've been a bit distant lately."

"Distant? I need a telescope to see you these days."

"Will this make up for it?" He took out a small navy blue box. Helen looked hopefully at his smile before news from his radio spoiled their privacy.

"XW to Delta Alpha Three."

Micky's eyes rolled. He was one half of the double-crewed unit known as Delta Alpha Three. "I don't believe this," he said, keying his mike. "2894 receiving."

"2894, can you and your partner expedite to one-zero-three Sandal Road?"

"From 2894, yeah, I think you must have my duties mixed up," he said, "I'm due off soon, over."

"2894, 10-20 your last; instructions passed from DI Shelby though, we have no other units to attend, over."

"10-20 that. Pass details again please." He shook his head at Helen.

"Yes, 2894, address is one-zero-three Sandal Road, Sandal. You are to place Inspector Weston into protective custody; he's due there shortly after discharging himself from Pinderfields, over."

Micky gasped. "XW, er, 10-7 please."

"2894, you heard me right, no need to repeat, over."

"I thought that address was already under guard, over."

"It is, 2894, and it has to stay guarded. Chief Inspector Regan is authorising Inspector Weston's arrest for his own protection."

"XW from 2894, 10-20, en route."

"XW further," said the operator. "A room on the secure ward at Pinderfields has been made available. And 2894, you're to remain on his door until we receive further instructions."

"Think I'll save the paperwork for tomorrow." Helen looked at the box. "Shall we save that for later too?" at last she smiled at him.

Micky nodded, put the box away, and was about to lean forward and collect a kiss, when he suddenly thought of something. "Shit!" he bolted for the door, stopped and turned, "Helen, ring my phone, tell him to get away from Weston's house."

"What? Tell who?"

Micky whispered, arms flapping, "Roger. He borrowed my phone. He went to Weston's house. He might still be there."

"Micky, I don't think that's very funny. Roger's in serious—"

"It's true!"

She laughed, "I know he's dumb enough to break out of a cell, but... You *knew* about Roger and said nothing? Micky, I didn't think *you* could be that dumb."

"Do it now before Weston finds him there. He'll kill him."

Chapter 29

— One —

Quickly, he grabbed one from each pair and hurried to the window. "Fuck," he whispered, "no *Hush Puppies*." Roger sighed. They're downstairs, he thought. Have to be; it's where I'd take my shoes off. He put them back, closed the doors and exited.

The last door on the landing was to neither a closet nor a bedroom, but to another staircase. The steps wound tightly up to an attic room, the same room he saw on one of his recces, he guessed, where the light was on at some ridiculous hour. A tingle ran up Roger's back and he gripped the banister.

The higher he climbed, the more it smelled of stale smoke. He emerged into an attic so black he could have been wearing a blindfold, and swept his arms before him until he collided with the cold smooth surface of a leather office chair. Nearby was a desk.

Micky's mobile phone rang. "Shit!" Panicking, he tore at it and whispered, "Hello?"

"Roger, Roger, it's me, Helen."

"Helen? What—"

"Get out of there!"

"What?"

"If you're in Weston's house, get out now; he's on his way home."

Goose pimples flashed across his body. All he could think of was Weston exploding into the room and ripping his heart out.

— Two —

"What's so urgent about this phone call anyhow?"

"Geraldine, it's business, now stop it with the questions while I'm driving."

"You'd better be careful, Colin, all this 'business' is liable to see you inside one day."

"Mind your tongue! It's business that keeps you in foreign holidays and expensive jewellery; so treat me with some bleeding respect for a change." He turned onto the drive and was not the least surprised to see the patrol car, or to find it blocking his favourite parking position. "Arsehole," he said.

"What's he doing—"

"Leave this to me, Geraldine. I mean it, keep your trap shut."

— Three —

Roger closed the door and moved swiftly along the landing. He could hear voices outside, and crept to the window. On the driveway, Weston stood in front of the patrol car, arguing with the officer. Roger's heart kicked. And then he heard a warble of sirens growing louder.

Ignoring visions of Weston's victorious fists, he shuffled back across the landing, and into the bathroom. He climbed on the edge of the bath and then the sink, opened the window and hoisted himself up before he heard the sirens stop. Doors banged. More voices.

He was shaking.

He heard a key in the front door. Weston's voice boomed; several others responded and then, as Roger pulled himself through, the front door opened and Weston shouted, "You have no fucking authority to arrest me!"

The house phone rang.

Roger lowered his legs out into the cold and then his feet touched icy roof tiles.

The phone stopped. Footsteps thudded up the stairs. Weston. The landing light came on. More shouting. More footsteps on the stairs.

Roger's feet took his weight. Until they slipped. He hit the roof on his side and then rolled off the edge and landed on the spongy grass. He couldn't breathe, just squirmed, arms and legs moving feebly, feeling the rain on his bare face. In the glow of the garden lamps, he could see his glasses only a few feet away. Roger scooped them up and limped across to the gazebo.

"I should've started downstairs!" Still shaking, and slapping the steering wheel in a rage, Roger sped around Wakefield's ring road, following a stream of red lights past Sainsbury's, past Thornes Park and along towards Denby Dale. "Wasted chance." Regardless of the fury, he tried to rationalise the defeat, knowing that once Paul processed all the evidence from the Bridgestock scene, Shelby would finally understand, and would have to search Weston's house for evidence anyway. And, he reasoned, it would negate any worries he had about illegality or cross-contamination.

All this theorising didn't prevent him feeling robbed again.

It was quiet when he turned onto the narrow road leading to Chris's house. He drove straight past, staring at it and its surroundings, and keeping a watchful eye out for police. He saw no one; turned around and parked fifty yards from Chris's house: a compromise between not having far to run dressed as he was, and not parking the car on the drive and scaring Chris away, or attracting the police unnecessarily.

Not forgetting the car's torch this time, he walked towards Chris's house at a fast pace, breath clouding, fingers cold again, and bare arms numb and tender.

The driveway was empty. There were no lights on inside the house. The white arms which he had torn from his suit earlier, still protruded from beneath the fallen fence, and the smell of dog shit wafted over from next door. He peered through the kitchen window, hands cupped to the glass. It was all quiet in there. "Where the fuck are you, Chris?" he whispered. "Should have been back hours ago."

He tried the handle. Locked. All the windows around here, around the back of the house, were shut tight. Even the bathroom window around the side of the house was shut. How the hell...

Roger considered the dilemma of breaking and entering again. The back door was white UPVC with a window in the top half and a plastic panel in the bottom half. Strips of plastic beading held this panel in place. And if he wanted the beading out, he needed tools.

He searched through Weston's boot; moved aside the large WYP canvas bag containing foul weather gear, moved aside Weston's assault boots, and lifted the carpet to access the spare wheel. Next to the spare was the jack, the wheel brace, a small selection of spanners. And a screwdriver.

Quietly, he closed the boot.

"Everything alright, officer?"

Roger dropped the screwdriver.

An old man walking his dog stood on the footpath. The dog pulled at its leash, eager to resume its walk.

"Fine, fine," Roger retrieved the screwdriver. "Hush though; I'm on a job, okay."

"What kind of job?"

"Ah, sorry, I can't tell you."

"You've got blood on your lip, officer, did yer know."

"Ah, yeah—"

"Drugs isn't it? There's loads o' drugs round these parts, you know. You don't have to tell me," the old man nudged the side of his nose, "I know what's goin' on." He looked down at the dog, "C'mon, Tappy," he said. "Don't worry," he whispered to Roger, "I won't say nothing."

"Thanks, appreciate it."

Tappy walked obediently by his master's side, as his master took out a mobile phone and began talking, something about police around here again, and drugs.

He set the torch down so that it shone towards the back door, and used the screwdriver to bend the beading away. It pinged and sprang out onto the path. The other three pieces surrendered and fell out without opposition. And that left only the panel, which, after a slight tap, dropped into his hands.

A black hole stared at him. He crawled through and into the claustrophobic silence of Chris's house. He'd been in this house only once; it was the Christmas before last, just after Chris split from his wife and they sold their old house; this being the place he bought with his half of the cash. Back then, it was tidy, well kept; the original a-place-for-everything-and-everything-in-its-place kind of home.

He pressed the light switch. Nothing happened. He shone the torch around the kitchen, and blinked at what he saw. The kitchen worktop was invisible. A small mountain of chicken bones and pizza boxes covered it, empty KFC boxes. Dead cans of Pepsi and Coke lapped at the rim in the sink. The smell was not dissimilar to Sally Delaney's house. He shuddered, "Jesus."

Part-burned candles and a scattering of dead matches lay on the windowsill, soot marks on the glass. In the corner, near the cooker was a small plastic bin. It was on its side, spilling rubbish and candle stubs, a pile of shoes nearby, one upside down. In the opposite corner, a blue Calor gas bottle hooked up to a portable stove.

Roger edged into the lounge. There were no lights of any description; no standby lights on electrical equipment, no LED clocks, only a mild orange glow from the streetlamps fell into the room through the dirty window. He searched for the light switch, found it and turned it on. Again, nothing happened.

He waved the torch, more part-burned candles. But what snatched his attention was a sagging green velour armchair with high wings and tasselled valances. A transistor radio, aerial extended, lay next to it on the carpet like a dead dog next to its dead master. And beside it, on a tiny round table was a phone, a pad and a disposable pen.

Roger took off his glasses, tried to warm them up to stop them fogging with condensation. He replaced them, then, torch swivelling from side to side, inched deeper into Chris's lounge.

There wasn't a single picture or photograph on any wall. A real bachelor pad, Roger thought.

On the floor, by the armchair, were heaps of newspapers, copies of *The Racing Post*, form guides and magazines the summit of which would give a small child altitude sickness. In front of the chair was a pile of empty noodle pots, plastic forks inside, noodle juice stains on the cream carpet, more pieces of dead chicken and dozens of empty *Lucozade* bottles, and more soda cans. There was dust everywhere, and webs hanging from the corners of the room.

"Shit, Chris, what do you do on an evening?"

Below one of the larger cobwebs, was a mahogany shelf. It was a big shelf. The wood strong enough to hold a TV and VCR maybe. It supported nothing except a loose pyramid of paper, not newspaper or writing paper, but slips of paper all with the same red border and all with tick boxes, and each bore scribblings in black pen. In Chris's hand writing. The slips were headed 'Tony Paxman, Bookmaker'. And there were others from William Hill, and Ladbrokes. Hundreds of them. Thousands of them.

Shaking his head, amazed by what he saw, Roger turned around. Nothing else but shadows of varying degrees of intensity.

He reached across the empty chair and picked up the phone. It was greasy. He held near to his ear. No dial tone. On the pad was a red bill from British Telecom. Dated October 12th 1998.

He took out Micky's mobile phone and dialled the SOCO office number, hoping from some news from Paul.

No answer. "Shit."

— Four —

As Shelby and Firth climbed out of the car, the officer guarding Nicky Bridgestock's house hastily flicked away a half-smoked cigarette and fumbled with his tie. "Can we see the scene log, please?" Firth asked.

"Sure, yeah, no problem." The officer leaned into his car and pulled a clipboard off the dash, passed it to Firth with gloved hands.

Firth scanned through it. Shelby stared at the officer.

"Christ," said Firth. "The last entry on here was Paul Bryant signing out twenty minutes ago."

"No, that can't be right." Shelby snatched the clipboard. He read the entry and asked the officer, "Describe him to me."

"He was young with a big purple tie—"

"Bastard! Come on, Lenny. That's why we couldn't find him back at the nick."

"Was he alone?" Firth shouted back.

"Yeah," said the officer. "What's all this about?"

— Five —

Paul looked on as Barry slid the lifts this way and that, peering through a lens, marking intersections and bifurcations with a long pin. "Right hand," he said without looking up. "You've got the thumb there. And opposite, on this lift, you've got index and middle fingers." He now took the third lift, scrutinised it, "Again, a right hand. Thumb's useless this time though, but ah… my God, these are good. Look," he said to Paul, "see there, his name and address."

"That good?"

He laughed. "If only it were true."

"So they're good marks?"

"Yep, very good. You've got a right thumb with a left-hand loop, a right index with a tented arch, and right middle with another tented arch." And then Barry offered a weak laugh.

"What?"

"It's strange how things can stick in your mind."

"Such as?"

"Well, I mean these marks. They look familiar."

"A set of fingerprints can look familiar?"

"I mean the classification is nothing unusual, but the points... well, they seem familiar. See the delta below the loop on the thumb?"

Paul looked through the glass and Barry slid his pointer from the centre of the loop down, across the ridge detail towards a triangular section of convergence just below it. "I see it, yeah."

"Five points between loop and delta. I just have the feeling I've seen it before very recently. Maybe it'll come to me later."

"There's a small problem that I forgot to mention, Barry."

He sat upright, clicked his back, and said, "I hate it when people say that. Means snaggy."

"Chris thinks they might belong to Weston."

"Who?"

"Inspector Weston. Colin Weston."

"Right, let's eliminate Inspector Weston then. Good," he said, "it saves hours of work if we can eliminate an attending officer before we start ploughing through the categories." He walked to the big cabinet by the far wall.

"How come all this isn't done by computer these days?" asked Paul.

"Some of it is." Barry unlocked the shutter door and slid it up. He knelt by 'W'. "But with jobs like this, it's easier and quicker to do it manually. Besides, who wants to be in front of a computer screen all days plotting minutiae when you can stab 'em with a pin?"

"What a choice."

"Here we go. Weston, Colin."

"Paul Bryant!"

He froze.

Barry said, "I think Inspector Shelby would like that word now."

"We have several things we'd like to speak with you about," Shelby said in his best calm and controlled voice. He breathed though flared nostrils.

Paul hadn't messed up. The mark itself, labelled 9, did indeed have blue gloss paint sandwiched between the adhesive lift and the acetate. Shelby quizzed Paul; flapped the fingerprint lift constantly in his face, almost had him in tears, but it was Paul who remarked how much like 'police station blue' it was. And from there, it didn't take him long to lead Shelby and Firth to the doorframe in the Scenes of Crime office – the only natural conclusion.

Though the doorframe had been cleaned of its black powder, the physical fit of the paint was unmistakable. "But it's your handwriting on the acetate," Firth said, "with Nicky Bridgestock's address."

"We both did the fingerprinting in the house, we both lifted and mounted marks, but I wrote them all up as mine to save time and inconvenience. This was an exercise," he pointed to the doorframe, "a test, so I knew how to handle the fingerprint camera when the time came." His eyes flicked from Firth to Shelby and back again. "I remember seeing Inspector Weston having a good look at them, the marks on the frame, I mean. He asked me what I was doing." Paul bit his bottom lip, afraid he'd done some real damage. "And I remember him smiling, seriously weird."

"Seriously weird?" Shelby asked. "Can't you use proper words? What the fuck does *seriously weird* mean?"

His fingertips tapped the side of his leg. "I don't know; he was smiling…"

"And that's why your details are on the identity label on the photo of the mark? Because you were asked to put them there by Chris?"

"It was an exercise," he shrugged. "Chris asked me to fill in the label as though it were a real scene, he said let's make it the bedroom doorframe, but then he told me to leave the date blank." He paused, "Have I done something wrong? Am I in trouble? I'm still on probation and—"

Shelby said to Firth. "Who owns a late model Ford apart from Roger?"

"Weston has a motive, boss."

Shaking his head, Shelby said, "No, Weston's drives a flash BMW."

"Maybe. But his wife owns a late model Ford."

"I'm aware of that. But I'm sure Weston didn't have access to Nicky's scene."

"Yes, he did. He had access to the scene after everyone left for the night."

"That scene was guarded all night. His name wasn't on the log."

"No, it wasn't," Firth said. "But you know how persuasive he can be."

Shelby was about to ask why Weston would do something like this, but he already knew the answer. Hatred. Simple. Hate is hell inside your head. "Send Clements back up to the secure ward. I want some answers from him. I want to know if he went in Nicky's house at all, I want to know why he took an interest in this black powder exercise. And I want to know why he went into Roger's cell." And he remembered Weston taking an unhealthy interest in what evidence they found at Delaney's scene.

"Okay, boss."

"But, Lenny, most of all I want to know why he went in there *twice*."

"Okay, boss. Oh, shouldn't we contact D & C about—"

"Lenny!"

"Sorry, boss."

Firth backed away up the corridor, nodding at each new aspect on Shelby's list of requests. Shelby sighed. He knew what Firth meant, and he knew he had precisely four hours left in which to contact Chief Inspector Cuthbertson at Discipline and Complaints – soon to be renamed the Professional Standards Unit – and hand over all the information he had concerning Weston and his... transgression of duty and the resultant effect his actions had on 'the status of a prisoner'. But that was for later.

Shelby turned to Paul, even had his finger pointing ready to lay into him, when down the corridor at a dangerously fast pace bounded Barry Goodwyn.

Paul's face melted with relief.

"Oh, what now?" Shelby asked.

"I've found a match."

"Didn't know you smoked, Barry."

"Pardon?"

"Never mind. Go on."

"I've found a match for the marks on the mug."

"What mug?" Shelby asked.

"The mug from the kitchen." Barry looked between Paul Bryant and Inspector Shelby.

"Did you go there alone, Paul?"

"I can explain, Inspector Shelby," Paul said awkwardly. "But listen to Barry first."

"There are two phrases I hate, Paul, and 'I can explain' is one of them."

"What's the other?" Barry asked.

"Who went with you?" Shelby's temper was getting thinner.

"Who is it?" Paul asked Barry. "Who?"

"It's strange," Barry began, "they belong to—"

"What mug?" Shelby looked at Paul.

"I can explain, Inspector Shelby," Paul said.

"They match the fifty pound note from the Delaney murder," added Barry.

Shelby stopped dead, finger still poised. He turned to Barry. "Are they identical?"

"I'm having an expert verify them now. But I think they're good enough for court, yes."

Shelby started walking. "Barry, my office now. Paul, bring coffee, lots and lots of coffee to my office in ten minutes. Right?"

"Right, Inspector Shelby."

Barry set off down the corridor, trying to catch up with Shelby. He turned around to Paul and apologised, "Sorry;

dead end," he said, "the marks from your mug belong to an attending officer."

"Who!"

"They belong to—"

"Come on, Barry!" Shelby roared.

— Six —

Tappy and his owner ambled back past the front window. The old man peered in as he walked, didn't bother to conceal the fact; he craned his neck, saw Roger's silhouette and even waved.

It was freezing in here. He shivered and rubbed his bare arms. Rain hit the window with the tic-tic sound that a cheap pen makes as it writes. Roger saw the old man disappear, and then followed his torchlight up the stairs, eager to be away from the lounge, and needing to relieve himself anyway.

The bathroom looked like a bizarre altar. There were candles everywhere. On each corner of the bath, another two on the windowsill, and next to a filthy shaving brush and a pack of Bic razors, was a pile of dead matches, three cans of deodorant and a bottle of strong aftershave. Roger laid the torch down, took off the t-shirt, unzipped the suit and sat on the toilet, phone in his hand. He tried the office number again, not expecting it to pick up now, at this time of night, whatever this time of night was. But it did.

"Paul Bryant, Scenes of—"

"Paul, Paul," he said, "it's me, Roger."

"Oh, Roger. We've seriously blown out on the fingerprints."

"Fuck." Roger closed his eyes. "Go on, give it to me."

"You're not going to like it."

"What, Paul! Just fucking tell me!"

"They're a no go. They belong to an attending officer. We'll have to hope the footwear brings us more luck."

He stopped dead. A noise came from down the landing. A creaking.

"You still there, Roger?"

He listened. Heart racing.

"Roger?"

"Noises in here."

"Is Chris there?" Paul asked.

"Hurry up, Paul," he swallowed. "The marks, who do they belong to?"

"When you see Chris, tell him he's in line for a Golden Brush."

Chapter 30

— One —

IT WAS ONLY A short landing, but walking along it took an age. Every floorboard creaked. His suit crackled as he put one foot in front of the other. Even his hand, guiding him along the wall, seemed to scrape loudly like someone dragging a shovel over a concrete floor. He ran his tongue over his swollen lip.

The door at the end of the landing stood slightly ajar, only endless grey beyond it. Roger pushed and it swung silently open. A smell of alcohol and sweat wafted out from the shadows. It was colder in here than in any other room, and as he stepped inside, not bothering this time to search the wall for a light switch, he wondered why Chris hadn't yet returned home. He wasn't back at the office either, Paul had said so.

Roger's nerves pulled tighter. He crept forward and the yellowing torchlight fell upon an old school desk. On the desk was a large angle-poise magnifying glass with a lamp around the lens's periphery. A strange item for a junk room, surely? Also on the desk was an open ream of A4 paper, and next to it a glass beaker with a clear liquid inside. Surgical spirit. Why would Chris want a beaker of surgical spirit, and why would Chris keep a pair of stainless steel tweezers in it? Roger's concern grew. There was a scalpel, more tweezers and a black cotton bag. At the back of the desk, a box of latex gloves and a box of 3M masks.

"Roger."

"Fuck!" Roger leapt backwards into the desk, knocking the beaker onto the floor. The beaker shattered and surgical spirit splashed across the carpet. The lamp rocked and then steadied. "Fuck," he shouted again. "Chris, you bastard—"

"Sorry, Roger," Chris said, getting to his feet from a chair in the darkest corner of the room. He removed a large overcoat and slung it over the chair. Its silk lining shimmered in the torchlight. "Didn't mean to scare you." He grunted; his feet cracked as he stood, and like an old man disturbed from a long sleep, he lurched forward, hands behind his back. "The lamp works, it's battery powered. Go ahead, turn it on."

Roger kept the torchlight in Chris's face as he fumbled behind him for the lamp and its switch. The light came on.

"Would you mind turning your torch off, or at least taking it out of my face? It's very uncomfortable."

"What's going on here?" Roger asked. "Why no mains?"

"Someone made a mess of your face, Roger."

He looked at Chris's cardigan, at the stain there, and at the new blood-shiny beard that had grown on his chin. "Could say the same," Roger said, an edge of caution in his voice.

"Yvonne said you needed me."

"I did, but it's sorted now."

"Really?" Chris's eyes narrowed.

"Oh yes. I got it covered."

"She also said that Bell gave you the promotion."

Surprised, Roger asked, "You didn't see him? I thought you were having a meeting with him."

Chris shrugged as he inched closer. "One of those things, I suppose; he forgot to send for me."

"I'm sorry about that. It's—"

"Never mind. I wonder if he's had to re-schedule our meeting anyway, since you're not now eligible for the post." He smiled gently, "Looks like I got the job after all." Chris's shadow loomed on the far wall.

"I examined her scene, Chris."

"Whose scene?" he whispered.

"Your victim's scene. Nicky Bridgestock."

Chris stopped walking. "Aw, shit. Roger, you just said the wrong thing." He looked away. "I've been waiting for you a long time. Hours. I've had time to think; had a sneaking suspicion you might do that."

"And I just had some really interesting news from Paul." He tried to see into Chris's eyes, but they gave nothing away, his face blank. "There was me thinking it was Weston all along. You going to tell me why you did it?"

Chris eventually smiled and resumed his steady advancement. Glass crunched and pierced his feet. He didn't flinch. "How did you know?"

"You were always the Professor. All of us in the office looked up to you when it came to tricky scene examinations. You always had the answer, regardless of what the question was. You deserved the title we gave you—"

"How?"

"You made an error, Chris. Fingerprints. On the cup inside the kitchen cupboard."

Chris closed his eyes and an ironic smile touched his lips.

"I've known you all these years," Roger said. "I can't believe you would kill someone. Why!"

"And I can't believe I made such an elementary mistake."

"Why make it look as though *I* killed her!"

"I thought I'd done a thorough job. I considered every detail—"

"Except your habit of keeping cups open-end down."

"I should never—"

"Why blame *me*, Chris? What did I ever do to you?"

Chris considered the question. "Take a look around. Does my standard of living impress you? I've had no electricity for a month, and no phone for three months; I've got no food other than tins, which I can't cook properly. I can't even have a cup of bastard *tea*." A strand of grey hair fell across his damp forehead. With deftness, he pulled it aside and continued. "I siphon petrol from the vans. Did you know that? I'm trying to sell the house too. Going cheap if you're interested. And all because I owe seventeen grand to people who snap legs for fun."

"What? Why didn't you say something? Christ, I would've helped!"

"You condescending prick. You don't have the faintest idea how hard it was asking people for money to bail me out of a mess I got myself into. Would you have lent me seventeen fucking grand?"

Roger said nothing.

"No. You wouldn't."

"The promotion—"

"The promotion was my way *out*." He jabbed a finger towards Roger, and his face flooded with colour. "I'm the Professor, remember." He waved his arms around. "The Supervisor's job was mine, had my name all over it. But he gave it to you. He was always going to give it to you."

"No. I don't think so. Someone once told me that this job'll find out your lies, and when it does, it'll spit you out like gristle. If you want something, my friend, you have to want it for the right reasons." Roger shook his head, "Money ain't the right reason."

"I'm not your fucking friend, Roger. And I don't go for sanctimonious bollocks like that. If you want something, you go out there and you get it any way you can." Chris smiled again in the weak light. "I taught you well. Congratulations on spotting my little ruse."

Roger's free hand curled into a fist. "You can't call murder a little ruse, Chris. It's like saying the Titanic was a fucking trawler. It's like saying Mars is a short walk away."

"Don't preach to me—"

"I can't believe you killed a girl for promotion. We're talking a girl's *life*. You're fucking *sick*!" Roger swung a fist towards Chris's face but he moved aside with remarkable speed.

"Hunger makes a man quick, Roger. It makes him do all kinds of stuff."

"You wasted a life! Why didn't you just kill *me* if you needed the job so bad?"

Chris almost laughed, "You would have volunteered?"

"Why were you so hostile towards me?"

"Because it was easier to hate you. Easier to kill Nicky if I didn't like you." Chris's face looked ruined, old and weathered; his voice a croaking whisper. "Killing a stranger's easy, Roger. Easier than I thought it'd be. After years of seeing victims, I think I became immune to a stranger's death anyway. But I think if I'd known my victim," he shrugged, "I wouldn't have been able to do it. I thought it would do wicked things to my head."

"And?"

Chris took a slow step forward. "And now... My priority is staying out of prison. I don't think I could survive in prison. I think *it* would do wicked things to my head. Anyway, killing you..." He stared at Roger sideways on, a curious look in his eyes. "It won't be so difficult."

Roger felt his legs shaking. "It can all be over, Chris."

"Really? Stand aside then, and let me walk out of here."

"I despise you. I know people who have literally nothing, *nothing*, but they don't—"

"Hobnail hasn't got the fucking wits—"

"He's got pride though."

"Are you going to let me pass, Roger?"

Roger shook his head. "I've never let a killer walk free yet."

Chris lunged. They hit the floor, the torch crashed through the doorway and died. The desk toppled, the lamp fell, but stayed lit. Silence exploded with screams.

Roger felt a weight heavy on top of him and then a scalpel was at his face. It slashed.

He felt hot blood down his cheek. "Get off meeee!"

Chris slashed again.

Roger turned and the blade sliced across the bridge of his nose and tore the glasses off his face. They rattled against the door. Now his attacker was ill-defined, a fast moving blur. Blood ran into his eye.

Roger caught Chris's wrist and smacked his hand into the desk leg. He threw a punch at Chris's chin. He missed, struck Chris's throat.

The scalpel fell and so did Chris, rolling onto his back and holding his neck, struggling for breath. His fingers searched the carpet in a frenzy.

Roger began to panic, hands flapping around, scrambling to where he thought the door was.

Chris grabbed his arm.

Downstairs a door banged. Glass smashed.

"Quick!" Roger called. "I'm up here." And then to Chris, "They're coming, you twisted fuck."

Chris's fingers found the scalpel.

"Hurry up!" Roger screamed.

The footfalls were on the landing.

Chris brought the scalpel up.

Though blurred, Roger saw it glint in the lamplight for a fraction of a second. But by then it was too late.

"Noooo!"

Torchlight blinded him; incoherent voices like mini thunderclaps attacked him. Confusion. Everything was a hazy blur. But he saw the scalpel plunge into Chris's neck. Flowing redness swamped the blade and the handle, engulfed Chris's fist. His eyes blinked rapidly.

"You bastard!" Roger yelled, "Don't you dare die!" He looked at the torches, "Do something, for fuck's sake, don't let him die." Roger reached for the scalpel handle.

"Stop!" Shelby grabbed Roger's arm. "Leave it. It's done."

"I have to stop him; I can't let him die—"

"Too late, Roger. I saw what happened. Just leave it."

"It was..." Chris looked up at Roger.

"What?" Roger bent lower.

The room stood in silence.

Chris's eyelids flickered. "You'll never be as good as..." His eyelids stopped moving. The blood from his neck slowed to a rhythmic trickle that spattered into a growing puddle. A final exhale sounded like bubbles in thick liquid. The shakes stopped and Chris's bloody hand fell to his side.

Roger slumped, body spent, hands shaking.

"Fuck," said Firth, "he likes neck wounds, doesn't he?"

"Get downstairs, Lenny. Now."

Firth offered no argument, he turned and something crunched. "Are these your glasses, Roger?"

"Lenny!"

"I'm going, I'm going."

From the landing, a timid voice asked, "Is he... dead?" Then there was a loud thud and more voices as officers tried to revive the fainted colleague.

Trying to scrape blood from his eye with a knuckle, Roger made it to his knees. "I need to—" He stood, tilted and fell again.

"You need to do nothing," Shelby said. "Stay there a minute."

"Graham, I... we fought and he was mad he was crazy and he—"

"Leave it, Roger."

"He tried to kill me, and then—"

"Shut up, Roger." Graham Shelby stepped around the body and revealed a doorway full of peering faces. Radio traffic belched. He crouched at Roger's side and tried to help him stand. "Save it all for later. Come on, eh?" He called to the officers who remained on the landing, "You lot, clear a path. And get me a blanket or a spare coat or something." He said to Roger, "You're shaking, mate. We need to have you looked at."

With Shelby's help, Roger stood and then stumbled into the overturned desk. That's when the desk lamp illuminated it.

"Wait," Shelby said, "what's that?" He shone his torch, leaned closer and inspected the desk's contents. He smiled up at Roger. "Need a change of underwear?"

— Two —

The peering faces stepped smartly aside for Roger and Shelby who left Chris's body to the inevitability of a forensic examination. Roger stopped, cocked his head. He heard running water.

Shelby turned into the bathroom, "Never use the facilities at a bloody scene!"

Firth waited for them at the foot of the stairs. "You okay, Roger?"

Roger pulled his twisted glasses back on, and swung a fist. Firth landed in the heap of noodle pots.

"Hey, hey, come on, Roger, that's enough! We don't need any more fucking paperwork." Shelby grabbed Roger by the shoulders, and then to Firth, said, "You okay?"

"Yeah, I think so."

"Shame. Now call a fucking ambulance."

"I said I'm okay."

"Not for you, tit. For him."

"I don't want an ambulance," Roger said. "I'm okay."

"I don't care, I'm having you looked at."

Roger faced Shelby. "When are you going to start listening for a change? I don't want a bastard ambulance!"

"Okay, okay, have it your own way."

"Hallelujah."

"But I'm having the police surgeon look you over back at the nick."

"Wrong. I'm not going back—"

Their eyes locked. "You want a tenner on that?"

"I'm not a gambling man."

"Maybe not, but you're still under arrest until I say otherwise. We have procedures to follow."

"But *he* did it. Chris killed Nicky Bridgestock."

Shelby said, "He also killed Sally Delaney."

Roger froze.

"Found his prints on a fifty pound note in her diary," said a voice by the back door.

"Paul?"

"Did I do well, or did I do well?"

"What're *you* doing here?" Shelby shouted.

"I think I've earned the right." And then to Roger, "Fuck! Your face..."

"Don't worry, couple of cuts and bruises, that's all."

Blue lights stabbed the lounge window. Police running, shouting into their radios, curtains twitching.

"You wanna do a scene while you're here?" Firth rubbed his chin. He saw Shelby glare at him and stayed back.

"Why? What do you mean?" No one answered. "Roger, what's he—"

"Chris's dead."

"Roger, you didn't—"

"No, he didn't," Shelby said. "Though who could've blamed him."

Roger looked stunned, didn't feel Shelby's grip tighten until it stopped him falling over. He leaned against the kitchen doorframe until the dizziness left him, and after a moment, began laughing.

Shelby looked at him, curiosity in his eyes, and concern too.

"Look over there," Roger laughed louder. Paul leaned in, peered towards the bin where Shelby's torchlight settled.

"What are we looking at?" Shelby asked.

"The shoes," Paul said. "They're Hush Puppies."

— Three —

As they walked out to the car, Roger stopped and faced Shelby. "I have to ask you something."

"I should warn you, I am not in a good mood. I have a feeling Chambermaid will want to do something horrible to me when we get back."

"Yvonne. I want to go see her."

Shelby was shaking his head before the request left Roger's mouth.

"Why?"

"We could bring her to the nick," Firth offered.

"She ain't well; you're not taking her anywhere."

"Okay, listen to me," Shelby said, still holding Roger's arm. "You are still formally under arrest for murder, and listen closer, I don't mind slapping cuffs on you just to get you back; I will if I have to, Roger. You are, *were*, an escaped prisoner—"

"My turn, dammit. My wife thinks I killed someone, and if I get out by teatime tomorrow, I'll be lucky. Please, I'm begging you, Graham, let me see Yvonne. Just for a couple of minutes, to reassure her, to tell her I'm innocent—"

"Alright, alright, I give in. Just a minute or two, mind, that's all."

"That's all I need."

"I'll get a patrol car to follow us," Firth said.

"No need," Shelby said. "I don't think you'll do a runner again, will you Roger?"

"I won't. It's sorted now, isn't it, Graham? I'm in the clear, aren't I?"

Shelby stared. "We won't need the cuffs."

"See you back at the nick, Roger." Wearily, Paul waved and walked through the small gathering of people to his van.

"Paul?"

"Yeah."

"Hey, thanks, mate. You did *seriously* good."

— Four —

On the journey home, Roger said, "Have you any idea how pissed I am at you?"

"I can imagine," Shelby said. "But we did nothing wrong, Roger. We followed every lead and we acted on evidence found by a SOCO at a murder scene. That is what we do, that is how we solve crime; the enquiries lead us to the suspect. You follow the evidence and you get what it gives you."

"And now the evidence points to Chris Hutchinson."

"Yup, it does. And you know what," Shelby turned in the passenger seat so he could see Roger. "The Professor made mistakes. For someone with his capability, he made some serious errors."

"There's no need to sound so disappointed."

A noise similar to a laugh fell out of Shelby's mouth. "Lucky for you he wasn't as perfect as he thought he was."

"Lucky for me I had a chance to dig deeper."

"You took a risk with Paul; could've got him into some serious shit."

"It still could. Depends how Bell's feeling when he hears."

"Depends how CPS sees it all in the light of day," Firth said. "They could sack you for beating Weston up. And you can expect a disciplinary hearing at the very least for breaking out of custody."

"If I hadn't broken out of custody, Lenny, you'd still think I was a murderer!"

"Still broke out."

"I could have you for false imprisonment—"

"No you couldn't—"

"Alright! Shut up, you two," Shelby said.

Roger took the t-shirt off, found a clean part of it and dabbed at the blood, which had curtained the right side of his face. Firth stopped at a petrol station, and bought a packet of wet wipes to help clear the worst of the crud off Roger's face and from his hair.

Shelby checked him over, tutted at the gash in his cheek and the slice across his nose. "You'll live," he said. "Hold that wipe over it though, 'cause it's pissing blood out everywhere. You need stitches, Roger; it's a fucking mess."

A pile of red-stained wet wipes was on the seat beside him. "How's Weston doing?"

"You're worried about that tosser?" Shelby said. "He's earned an over-nighter in Pinderfields. Concussion, that's all." And then, "Don't see what he achieved by letting you go though."

"He didn't let me go," Roger said. "We had a fight and I legged it. He was out cold when I left."

"No, he told Clements he was conscious the whole time."

"I hope he gets the sack for this."

"Don't think so," Shelby said. "He's already mentioned how he relieved Ellis Coldworth, and when he checked on you, you smacked him and escaped."

"But that's not true!"

"What goes around comes around," Firth said.

Roger stared at him, cold. "I'm out to get him. I'm going to catch him red-handed; I'm going to prove that he's dealing in weapons—"

"I'd steer clear of him," Firth said. "He's fucking mad."

"Steer clear of him because he'll have you for harassment if you don't. Understand, Roger?" Shelby warned.

Roger chose not to answer, there was no sense arguing. He'd sort Weston out once everything returned to normal.

Firth pulled up outside Roger's house on Wedgwood Grove. Roger and Shelby got out. Yvonne was at the lounge window, staring out at him; her hand over her mouth and mascara streaks down her face.

"Hope you're going to back me up, here."

"I will, don't worry."

"Hmph, don't worry." They walked through the darkness up the drive, and Roger said, "Sally Delaney and then Nicky Bridgestock. I remember him saying that he was motivated, but..."

Shelby tucked his hands into his pockets, and changed the subject. "This promotion, I think it'll suit you—"

Shelby didn't get a chance to finish before the shot came. Following it was a flash like lightning and then a fierce crack like a whip. They both turned and ducked at the same time. The bullet whizzed off the brickwork. Roger threw himself to the ground. And then another shot rang out. Shelby tripped and fell against a wooden bench.

A scruffy youth with a skinhead ran across the street aiming a gun at them.

There was a screech of tyres.

Another two shots flashed as Firth ran the CID car into the youth.

Thanks...

Many thanks to my superb editors Kath Middleton and Alison Birch, without whom this book would not have turned out so well.

About the Author

Andrew Barrett has enjoyed variety in his professional life, from engine-builder to farmer, from oilfield service technician in Kuwait, to his current role of senior CSI in Yorkshire. He's been a CSI since 1996, and has worked on all scene types from terrorism to murder, suicide to rape, drugs manufacture to bomb scenes. One way or another, Andrew's life revolves around crime.

In 1997 he finished his first crime thriller, *A Long Time Dead*, and it's still a readers' favourite today, some 200,000 copies later, topping the Amazon charts several times. Two more books featuring SOCO Roger Conniston completed the trilogy, *Stealing Elgar* and *No More Tears*.

Today, Andrew is still producing high-quality, authentic crime thrillers with a forensic flavour that attract attention from readers worldwide. He's also attracted attention from the Yorkshire media, having been featured in the *Yorkshire Post*, and twice interviewed on BBC Radio Leeds.

He's best known for his lead character, CSI Eddie Collins, and the acerbic way in which he roots out criminals and administers justice. Eddie's series of novels and collection of first-person novellas continue to grow, and there's still more to come.

Andrew is a proud Yorkshireman and sets all of his novels there, using his home city of Leeds as another major, and complementary, character in each of the stories.

You can find out more about him and his writing at www.andrewbarrett.co.uk, where you can sign up for his Reader's

Club, and claim your free starter library. He'd be delighted to hear your comments on Facebook (and so would Eddie Collins) and Twitter. Email him and say hello at andrew@andrewbarrett.co.uk

Also by Andrew Barrett

Did you enjoy **A Long Time Dead**? Please click on the image below and you'll be taken to a special landing page where you can choose your next Andrew Barrett book from your favourite store. Next in the trilogy is **Stealing Elgar**. Or visit your local Amazon store and search **Andrew Barrett**. Or take out your mobile phone and your camera app should take you there via this QR code:

Try a CSI Eddie Collins short story or a novella. Read them from behind the couch! Also available as a box set entitled

Short and Curlies, and includes a special extra novella, *Eye Contact*. **Please click here.**

Please come along and visit the website:

Readers Club

Sign up and Read

As a thank you for joining the Reader's Club, I want you to enjoy a couple of free books, a starter library - I call this **Sign up and Read**.

I'll make sure you get a brilliant thriller and a stunning CSI Eddie Collins novella written in first person.

The Reader's Club features a monthly newsletter with details of new releases, special offers, and other goodies, together with news and snippets of interesting items. How do you join the thousands of other crime-thriller fans there? Simply click this link to my website (or type it into your browser), www.andrewbarrett.co.uk, and sign up today.

Printed in Great Britain
by Amazon